I0639371

YARK

The Published Works Of
Mark E. Rogers

Samurai Cat Series
The Adventures of Samurai Cat *
More Adventures of Samurai Cat *
Samurai Cat in the Real World *
The Sword of Samurai Cat
Samurai Cat Goes to The Movies
Samurai Cat Goes to Hell (St. Martin's Press:Tor)

Yark
The Dead
Nothing But a Smile (Zenophile Books)
The Art of Fantasy (SQP, Inc.)

Zancharthus Series
Blood + Pearls
Jagutai + Lilitu
The Night of Long Knives
Zorachus
The Nightmare of God

Blood Of The Lamb Series
The Expected One *
The Devouring Void *
The Riddled Man *

YARK

Written and Illustrated by
Mark E. Rogers

Dedication:
This one's to Brian, for getting it done.

Curled up in a pit in a giant fruit was a yark named Snash. He didn't *know* he was a yark or that he was named Snash, although he would once he needed to; he didn't know he was curled up in a pit either, although he'd have to figure that out for himself, later. To the extent he knew anything at all, it was that he wanted to snooze some more---he was perfectly happy in the warm wet darkness, at least when he wasn't being disturbed by the tremors, although he forgot those as soon as they stopped.

Even after the bangings and the thumpings and the liquid sucking noises started up, he managed to drowse on, though the noises made him twitch. But once he began to hear the voices---one guttural, the other higher-pitched and snotty in tone---he got progressively more awake. Having just enough room to slide his clawed hands up, he pressed his ears---they were long and rather like a dog's---down over his ear-holes, but the voices still penetrated, and he found himself paying more and more attention to what they were saying.

"Garn!" one snarled. "You're like a boil someplace I can't reach...you ask too many filthy questions, Snurgit."

"I'm a *brain*, Mogrog," Snurgit replied. "Brains ask questions."

"And you should all go straight to Hell," Mogrog said. "Your heads are too big for your breeks."

Snurgit asked: "Haven't *you* ever wondered why we can just *do* things?"

"Do things?"

"Like talk? Right from the first, I mean, just as soon as we're pried out?"

"Everybody can talk," Mogrog shot back.

"No."

"If they're the kind what talk at all."

"*No*," Snurgit said. "You take men now..."

"You take 'em."

"The young ones don't know a thing. They're...blank slates."

"Blank slate my bum. I'm sick of listening to you..."

Snash could see how Mogrog might be, given Snurgit's awful tone; on the other hand, Snurgit's questions were genuinely interesting. Snash wondered: was *he* able to speak even now, or would he have to be pried out first? Certainly, he understood what was being said. He wondered what Snurgit and Mogrog looked like; for that matter, what *anything* looked like...

"You're just mad because you don't have a great big brain," Snurgit was saying.

"Well maybe I don't," Mogrog replied. "But why don't *you* save all your stupid questions for someone *else* with a great big brain?"

"I asked my chief," Snurgit said. "But he had me copying parchments, and said I didn't need to know, and when I kept asking, they sent me down here---"

Mogrog laughed. "And you *still* can't figure it out."

"I have a theory, though," said Snurgit. "There must be something---magic maybe---in the pellets, the ones that get things going in the pits."

"Pits?" Mogrog asked. "You mean these?"

At *these*, Snash heard a wrenching sound, and suddenly whatever he was curled up in tilted, then settled back down with a muffled gurgling noise.

"No, that's not a pit," said Snurgit.

"Came out of a big fruit, didn't it?"

"But it's not what I mean when *I* say pit---"

"Whatever," Mogrog growled. "Come on, you pansy, lend a claw---"

More wrenching; Snash's comfortable little envelope rolled up and out of wherever it had been, and he found himself turning over a couple of times before it came to a halt against something---dim yellowish light was seeping through the sides now. Snash blinked. He'd never seen any light before, and he didn't think he liked it...dark things were moving around out there, blocking out the light in places. The word *shadows* leaped to mind...

"There, look," said Mogrog. "A *pit*, see? Just like all the other ones we've pried out."

"The pit," Snurgit said, "is the thing the fruit grows in."

9

"You're both wrong, you maggot-heads," came a third voice, more distant, from someone who'd apparently been listening in. "The pit's this whole place. The big cave, see? Those holes in the ground, they're the *shafts,* and those things we dig out of the fruits, they're the *seeds.*"

"What festering dung!" broke in a fourth voice. "You should keep your mouth tucked under your hairy armpit, Kruzhnagh, if you're going to come out with shit like that. The big cave is the big cave. The *pits* are the holes in the floor, and nobody calls those things we dig out of the fruits *anything.*"

"Nar," Kruzhnagh answered, "I told you, I call 'em seeds."

"And I call 'em pits," said Mogrog.

Snurgit said: "It's almost as if---"

"*What?*" asked the other three, all at once, sounding very irritated.

Snurgit went on: "Whoever put the words into our heads really hadn't thought it all through---"

"That's cursed rebel talk!" cried the fellow who wasn't Mogrog, Kruzhnagh, or Snurgit.

"I was simply speculating---"

"Want me to report you?"

A sullen silence followed. But presently Mogrog said: "You know, you brains aren't very smart."

Snurgit didn't respond.

Mogrog laughed. Then a jolt went through Snash's seed, or pit, or whatever it was, and Mogrog said: "Not sure I want to bother with this one. We've already made our quota for the day, and this is the damn runt, and the runts are the hardest to get out."

Snash knew that a runt was something small, pathetic and not very worthwhile. Snurgit asked: "What then?"

"I'm tired," Mogrog said. "Let's just mark him stillborn---" Snash felt another jolt through the shell, "with the old grease-rod, and the next shift'll just haul him away and toss him in the fire."

Fire? Snash thought desperately. He had, of course, never seen fire, or anything else except the light through the wall of his pit (or seed), but he knew they were talking about something that would eat him.

"What if he's *not* stillborn?" Snurgit asked.

Mogrog answered: "Who cares?"

Snash registered his concern with a squeak.

"He's alive," said Snurgit.

"Won't be after *this*." Snash heard a rasping sound; one of the shadows moved; suddenly something hard came through the wall and went right between his thigh and his body (he was curled up, remember) then jerked back out again.

"There!" said Mogrog.

"They'll see the hole!" answered Snurgit.

"We'll plug it with trash and paint over it...here, use this bit of stuff..." Snash saw the shadows moving again. "And mark it, now, if you know what's good for you..."

"Hola there, vermin!" came a new voice, very ugly and loud. "What're you up to?"

"This fellow's stillborn, captain!" Mogrog cried. "We were just marking---"

Snash squeaked again.

"What was that rat-noise?" the captain cried.

"I didn't hear anything," said Mogrog.

But the captain was having none of that. "Get him out of there, and no more nonsense! There's a runt shortage upstairs!"

There was a pause after that. Then, as if the captain had gone away, Mogrog said disgustedly:

"Runt shortage. What good are the little lice anyway?"

"They're fast," said Snurgit. "Carry dispatches."

"Who do you think you're talking to? You think I didn't know that? My question is, what do we need dispatches for? If you have someone to *carry* the damn orders, why can't he just tell you what the order is, and skip all that writing shit? Reading makes my head hurt."

This was enough to fetch the snot back into Snurgit's tone. "Get a lot of dispatches, do you?"

"Bite...my...bum," said Mogrog. "But in the meantime, let's get this damn runt's...*pit*---"

"Seed?"

"Open."

It took them a while; Snash heard much huffing and puffing, and all kinds of scraping and knocking, and his pit was jerked and jostled something awful. Then, finally, nasty hard points broke through on one side, and a line of light opened up beside him, and widened....Mogrog and Snurgit's grunts and curses suddenly sounded a whole lot clearer. Snash coughed out two lungfuls of fluid, blew his nose and took his first breath, wincing at an influx of horrible smells.

"Now!" cried Mogrog. "Come on, you---"

There was a loud *crack!*, and all at once the whole top of the pit lifted up; two blurry figures leaned into view. Purely by reflex, Snash swiped gunk from his eyes and blinked.

Yarks, he thought...the term hadn't crossed his mind until then. Holding pry-bars and wearing harnesses studded with metal, they had black skin...looking at his arm, he saw it was the same shade. Bald, with shiny scalps, they had long ears that hung down (just like his), and slitty glinty eyes that were black all the way across. Both yarks towered over him from about the same height (he guessed it was because he was a runt and they weren't), but they were very different in build. Downright skinny, one had a swollen head which looked too heavy for his scrawny neck, and since he seemed *just* like a brain, Snash guessed he must be Snurgit, which meant the other, who was a great big mass of bulgy muscles, his harness creaking, was Mogrog.

A...bull, Snash thought. *Bulls, brains, runts...*

Mogrog gave Snash a closer look.

"Not a mark on him," he said. "How did I manage not to stick him?"

Snash noticed a tool stuffed into Mogrog's belt...he believed that items like that were called mallets. Without warning, Mogrog took it out, leaned farther down, and bopped Snash on the forehead, asking:

"Feel that?"

Snash rubbed his head and nodded.

"Understand what I'm saying?" Mogrog asked.

Snash nodded once more.

"How many fingers am I holding up?"

"Two," said Snash.

Mogrog squatted down next to the pod. "Now listen up, you wretched little gob of phlegm…I know you were listening in there, but… you didn't hear anything, right? I didn't try to stick you, and you have no complaints at all, see?"

"But…" Snash squeaked.

Mogrog bopped him on the head again.

"Oww!" Snash cried.

"I've got some mates upstairs," Mogrog said. "You make trouble for me, and they'll make trouble for you. You'll be going about your business, and one of them'll come up behind you, and you'll have your throat cut to the spine….How does that sound?"

"Bad," said Snash.

"Then mind your own shitty breeks," Mogrog said, and bopped the runt a third time. "Or we'll mind 'em for you."

Snash wrinkled his nose, wondering why Mogrog and his mates would want to mind his shitty breeks (if he ever acquired any breeks at all).

"Get up!" Mogrog snarled.

Snash uncurled himself and stood, dripping slime.

"Look at 'im," said Mogrog. "Garn, I hate runts…and he's an even bigger runt than most."

"What do you mean by that?" Snurgit asked, and this exchange went on for a while, but Snash was too busy looking at his surroundings to pay any attention.

The big cave, Kruzhnagh had said…Snash knew what *big* meant, but this cave was bigger than anything he'd imagined. It just went on for, well, a very long distance, and its ceiling, upheld in spots by pillars of rock, was quite some way above the floor. The light, pale yellow, was coming from luminous creatures, themselves very big, hanging from the ceiling on long strands…the word *spiders* came to mind. Every once in a while they dropped down, grabbed yarks from the floor and climbed back up with them.

As for the floor itself, it was full of holes, the openings arranged in very orderly fashion, separated by broad lanes. A few of the holes seemed to have what Snash guessed were fires burning in them; black against the red light, figures were feeding the flames with pit-halves and bodies.

But most of the shafts seemed to be filled up with great yellow fruits, bulging up one to a hole, blotched with black--- many were in the process of being hacked up by two-and-three-yark teams wielding long-bladed implements that were midway between cleavers and swords. Snurgit and Mogrog had blades of the same sort slung across their backs, and were standing, still arguing, ankle-deep in the insides of one of those giant fruits. Off to the side of them, Snash was squishing from foot to foot in the guck. Lengths of peel were stretched out in five directions, like the arms of a starfish, although he was kind of fuzzy about what a starfish was...Bits of pulp were scattered all around.

He began to watch a team working on a fruit two shafts over...after spreading the peels out, they thrust their bars deep into the pulp until they found something, then went back to work with their cleavers, removing material until they could pry the pits out. Once those came free, the teams opened them up with the bars, freeing gooey yarks who looked mostly like Mogrog, although there were some big-headed ones like Snurgit as well.

As the teams started in, the fruits were well down in the shafts, but once a bunch of their insides were pulled out, the fruits rose higher and higher, as though something were pushing them up, now that they were getting lighter...Snash saw a fruit, cleaver-team and all, rise suddenly out of one shaft on a burst of greenish vapor; it didn't quite rise as high as a gigantic glowing spider hanging right above it, but the spider remedied that by dropping down and snatching two of the workers before the fruit fell back to the floor...

Snash heard a rumble, and a tremor passed through the chamber, coming up through his legs out of the fruit below him...he had to fight a bit to keep his balance, the spiders above all began to swing rather crazily on their lines....off to his right, a crack broke open in the stone, and a long thin stream of bright orange lava began to squirt up---

"What do you have for me?" a voice bellowed.

Snash looked round to see that a bull even bigger than Mogrog had come up, carrying a whip...a deep scar curled his upper lip.

"Slagbag," said Mogrog.

"Mogrog," said Slagbag. "What do you have?"

Mogrog pointed to Snash.

Slagbag cracked his whip. "Get over here, runt!"

Snash began to muck his way across the pulp...once he stepped out of it, shaking the stuff off his feet, Slagbag got behind him, gave him a hard shove, cried, "Get moving!" then flicked a bit of hide from the runt's naked behind with the whip. Snash yelped and started running, along between the shafts...having been curled up in a pod for his whole existence, with the exception of the last few minutes, he felt pretty stiff.

"Faster, you stinking bloodclot!" Slagbag bellowed.

Arms churning, Snash obliged, working his protesting muscles and ligaments as hard as he could. Still, he wasn't going fast enough for Slagbag, if the next flick was any indication. The whip bit Snash right where it'd bitten him before, seemed to hurt him twice as much as last time, and got him working even harder, so much so that he swiftly pulled way out ahead of Slagbag---the thud of Slagbag's boots faded quite a bit, at any rate. Finally Slagbag cried:

"Hola there! Slow down, you grub you!"

Snash didn't think he knew much about grubs, although he had a definite impression that speed was rarely an issue with them; even so, he slowed, and as Slagbag toiled up, began:

"I thought you wanted me to---"

"How can I whip you if I can't keep up? Garn, you runts are a bad idea! What's the point of a yark who's too fast to whip?"

He snapped the lash at Snash once more, catching him on the chest---Snash winced, turned, and sped off, although not *too* speedily.

They stopped after a bit though, long enough for Slagbag to pick up another couple of newborn bulls along the way; Snash was glad to have them, because they were bigger and slower than him, and he could easily stay out in front, keeping them between him and Slagbag, who didn't seem to care who he was whipping....as he ran along, Snash noticed other teams of newborns being driven along other lanes by lash-wielding drivers.

It took quite some time before he neared the curving wall of the cavern; there was a huge opening in it, into another vast chamber, apparently, and the lanes converged to pass through. On either side of the yawning mouth, crowds of naked newborns were penned in thorny enclosures....off on the right, a party of yarks in head-to-toe leather suits were stringing fresh thorns even as Snash's party approached. Even though the stringers were wearing hide gloves, they were constantly recoiling and flinching, as though they had stuck themselves--- Snash heard them crying: "Ow!" "Ah!" "Garn!" "Nar!" "Shit!" "You filthy---!" and other things along similar lines.

A long gate stood open in the pen on the left; guards with halberds motioned Slagbag's charges inside.

"All yours!" Slagbag snarled; halting inside the enclosure, looking back between black sweaty bow-legs, Snash got a glimpse of him loping off, and wasn't sorry at all to see him go.

Several more troops of newborns came in shortly afterwards; then, somewhere, a horn sounded, its harsh notes echoing through the cave. New guards replaced the bulls at the gate, who departed, crying: "Out of here!"

Looking back out towards the shafts, Snash saw dozens of new teams replacing the ones on duty. The shift-change seemed to excite the spiders, who started picking off yarks with greater frequency. They appeared to occasion a certain amount of upset in the immediate area of their descent, but for the most part, everyone seemed to be taking it in stride, resuming work right after the spiders went back up with their wiggling prey....Snash heard a lot of whips cracking.

The other newborns fell to talking among themselves; it wasn't long before a quarrel started up, right behind Snash:

"And I say you *do* stink worse than the rest of us!"

"And I say you're smelling your own stink!"

Certainly someone was unusually ripe, which was really saying something; they snarled the same witless exchange over and over again...Snash turned to see two muscular brutes practically snout to snout, bodies tensed, muscles quivering...not surprisingly, it was hard to tell just from eyeballing them which one smelled worse...Snash thought maybe the one on the left looked stinkier.

Finally one of the bulls from the gate thrust his way up beside Snash and bellowed: "Shut your gobs, you carrion!"

"Or *what?*" sneered the debater on the left.

"Or *this!*" answered the guard, thrusting his halberd into that yark's shiny black forehead, then pulling it out...yanked forward as the blade jerked loose, the victim rocked off his feet, the guard stepping aside to let the corpse drop right at Snash's toes.

The guard sniffed, then squatted next to the corpse and sniffed again. "*Was* him. Phew!" He stood back up, fanning his face...after wiping both sides of his halberd-blade on Snash, he roared: "All right then! No...*QUARRELING!*" and went back by the gate.

The newborns were pretty silent after that, although there was some whispering, much of which was so soft that it couldn't be understood, and had to be repeated. This state of affairs lasted for some while, until three yarks came over from the other enclosure, a bull with a round-headed spikeless mace backing up a pair of brains...one of them was extremely skinny and veiny, a strange cup-like tube with a glass at the end of it affixed over one eye with a strap.The other brain had a bit more meat on him; his cheekbones were higher, and his nostrils had a pronounced arch, giving him a haughty, sniffy look; he was wearing sandals, and leather robes with a badge clipped on...There were letters on the badge, red against black, an I and an E---for the first time, Snash realized he could read.

"Line 'em up!" cried the brain in the robes.

The gatewards banged the butts of their halberds on the stone and shouted: "Four ranks! *Now!*"

The newborns scrambled to comply....Snash wound up in the front line. Once everyone was formed up, the brain with the eyepiece began side-stepping from yark to yark, giving each an examination, looking in their ears, eyes, noses, and mouths, then sniffing them all over....leaning forward a bit, Snash saw him ten newborns down, standing in front of a bull who looked a bit malformed, even by yark standards...Eyepiece nodded, apparently to someone behind the yark being scrutinized. There was a loud *bok!* and the bull grunted, and fell face forward, twitching on the stone. "Compost," Eyepiece said, and produced a little white stick, and drew a letter on the dead bull's back---Snash guessed it was c for compost, wondered briefly how he knew that.

Same way you know how to speak, he decided. At any rate, the white greasy *c* stood out very clearly on the black corpse.

The examiner had already resumed his slow sidestep along the line. Snash leaned back, looking between the first and second ranks...the mace-bearing guard who'd accompanied the two brains was moving along with the inspector, stopping behind every yark the inspector stopped in front of....each time he halted, the guard stood grinning and nodding, hefting his weapon, as though he simply couldn't wait to crack another skull. Suddenly the mace-bearer noticed Snash looking at him, and growled:

"What do you think you're looking at?"

Snash just gulped and leaned forward, waiting in awful suspense as Eyepiece proceeded down the line towards him, stopping at last before the big muscular brute on Snash's left, a specimen so impressive that Snash thought he'd surely pass muster; but the inspector didn't seem to be very far into his inspection before he nodded to the guard, and Snash heard that *bok!* again, and down the big fellow went. Eyepiece drew a B on the corpse, said, "Burn," apparently to himself---

And then stepped in front of Snash. Trembling, sure he was about to die, since he was so pathetic, even if there *was* a runt shortage, Snash just stared down at the inspector's black-taloned toes sticking out through the front of his sandals.

"Lift your chin, damn you!" the examiner snarled. Snash lifted his face, but closed his eyes.

"Open your eyes," the brain said, and Snash did so. The examiner looked into his facial orifices, lifted his arms and sniffed, then prodded him in various places in the belly and throat, something which he hadn't done to any of the other yarks...Snash was more certain than ever that Eyepiece was going to nod, and that the last thing that he---Snash, that is--- was going to hear would be the sound of the mace striking his own skull. But then the inspector simply stepped one yark down, and Snash was still alive, feeling a certain amount of relief, even as he remained desperately unhappy with his situation.

It took a while for Eyepiece to look everyone over...Snash heard the mace strike several more times, off to the side, and behind him. Then the inspector reappeared in front, and told the brain in the leather robes:

"Done, sir."

Sir grunted deep in his throat and nodded approval, then turned to the freshly-examined newborns and said:

"My name is Captain Spigrat, and I'm from I and E, as you can see---" Laughing at his little rhyme, he pointed to his badge with a talon-tip. "That's Inspiration and Exhortation. It's my job to welcome you into the system now that you're hatched out. Fire you up, and tell you what you already know, which is...you are minions of Serpentar, the Yark Lord, King of Tenebria and Master of Mount Adamant. You were *created* to further His aims, to give Him, if need be, your final breath and the last drop of your blood. Think of it! Every single one of you, even the lowliest runt, can be coals in His furnace. You have but to trust in His design---your every detail reflects His will. Immolation is not an idle word for you. As surely as you are yarks, it is within your grasp.

"So then! Do not vex yourselves! When your muscles crack and snap, and your joints pop with strain as you turn a capstan...when you feel the skin flying off at the flick of the lash...when you face ten thousand blazing blond fays with only a wooden spoon clutched in your claw, *rejoice!* You are not sacrificing, and being sacrificed, in vain. Each of you has a part to play in the Five-Thousand Year Plan. Consider those who have no purpose in life, and weep for them! You are cogs in a machine that never stops, that grinds the grist of the Future; turning and turning until you can turn no more, you will pulverize the foes of the Inevitable, our King on High!" Spigrat lifted both claws towards the ceiling, then flung one arm down, pointing a talon at the floor, and cried: "On your *knees*, you crushing gears, you instruments of annihilation! Abase yourselves to Lord Serpentar!"

While Spigrat stood nodding, the ranks knelt...Snash's

knees were quite knobby and bony, and going down on one was painful, although he tried not to show it....He wished desperately that he was back in his pit, or seed, or whatever it had been, and that he could just go back to sleep and never wake up...

I hate being a yark, he thought.

Chapter 2: Glolob's Lair

Afterwards, the newborns were allowed to rise; the two brains withdrew and fell to whispering with each other. Snash didn't catch any of that, but he did hear some back-and-forth between the brains' bull and the gatewards. The Inevitable had just snagged one last enemy bigwig, who had a name that seemed to end in "button" or "bottom," or something like that...not very scary-sounding. But his capture had cleared the way for a "final push" into Merriador, (wherever that was) and preparations had begun.

After the brains left, a squad of whipwielders arrived, and all the newborns were herded out of the enclosure onto the road, where they joined the newborns from the other enclosure, who were being herded by their own troop of motivators; once the newborns were organized into a column five files across, the drivers started in with their lashes, going up and down between the lines, and the company started forward, into the next chamber.

Snash had tried to place himself at the head of the column, but had only succeeded in landing himself ten ranks back in the leftmost file. Being all the way over on the side, he was able to get a good look at the chamber they'd just entered...it seemed pretty similar to the last one, although all of the shafts seemed to be empty, and nothing seemed to be going on. There was also much less light, since there were far fewer spiders, as though most had gone elsewhere since there was no food, or the powers that be were economizing on spiders since there was no work that needed lighting, or some combination of both...Snash wondered why he was considering such matters, then wondered if any of the other newborns were theorizing about the lighting, or indeed anything else; listening to them grunting, he decided it was unlikely and told himself he didn't really have much in common with them, a thought which comforted him.

About two-thirds of the way across the chamber, the column reached the brink of a great crack in the floor, with redlit smoke rising up out of it; a work-crew was in the process of making (or repairing?) a wooden bridge over the fissure, and the newborns had to pass over it single-file. Looking over the railing, Snash couldn't see much of anything except the smoke, which was very hot, and stank. Something below was *chugging*...he would learn later on that lava chugged like that.

He was still out in the middle of the bridge when there was another tremor; the bridge began to creak and sway, and the line started to move much faster. Even after the rumbling stopped, the bridge kept swaying, from all the frantic movements of the yarks upon it; the workers shouted at them to slow down, but no one listened. Certain the bridge was going to collapse, Snash managed to slip ahead through the line, shooting between yarks and the railing (and yark-legs when he had to), swiftly reaching the far side before any of the others even seemed to realize he was line-jumping...Once over, the newborns simply collected in a crowd, although the whipwielders were soon forming them back into a column...Amazingly, almost everyone got across, although the bridge finally did give while the last thirty or so yarks were on it, along with a bunch of the workers....Snash heard them all screaming as they plunged into the redlit depths, and he was terrified to think of what was going to happen to them at the bottom. But all the others who had made it across didn't seem to be bothered in the slightest; indeed, some of them immediately began laughing about it, shouting: "Better you than me!", "Flap *harder*, damn you!", "Make a wish!", "What's that chugging down there?", and, "Happy landings!"

Shortly the motivators put a stop to all this frivolity, and got the column moving again, into the next chamber, where there was a great deal of activity and a lot more light...wagons filled with compost that was a mixture of trash and dead yarks were being pulled up alongside empty shafts, and tipped sideways by fifteen-foot tall ogres in aprons and hoods of hide, the compost dropping down into the holes and filling them up...Farther along, all the shafts were filled to the brim.

The column pressed on into a third chamber, where the pits were leaking green vapor and stinking most horrid, some of them belching up burps that knocked pieces of offal high into the air; there were more wagons pulled up alongside the shafts, but instead of being loaded with compost, they had gigantic crossbows mounted upon their beds; ogres spanned the crossbows with cranks, whereupon yarks lifted shiny black balls, about the size of a brain-yark's head, out of steel boxes and placed them in slings attached to the strings. Snash remembered Mogrog saying something about pellets getting things going in the pits, and indeed, once the weapons were loaded, the ogres pushed them out through a gap in the side of the wagon, on a rolling arm, tilted them straight down over the offal-filled shafts, and pulled the trigger, firing the black pellets deep into the compost.

At the far end of this third chamber, there was a great ramp that spiralled up through the black stone, its floor worn concave by the passage of countless pounding feet and rather hard to pound on as a result; at the top, the troop was driven along a torchlit hallway, very wide, its walls hung with black banners blazoned in scarlet with slogans like: "Love Your Destiny," "That Which Whips Us Makes us Faster" and "The Inevitable is Inexorable."

At length the motivators steered the column off into a place which seemed basically like an even wider version of the corridor outside. It was full of yarks, arranged in about twenty files, although there was still room enough for Snash and all his companions, who took up at the back...The files weren't perfectly straight, and he couldn't see very far along the lanes. There was a long wait as his line crept forward; he wasn't sure exactly how long an hour was, but he thought that several must've passed before he got close enough to the front to see and hear what was going on. Everyone was getting another inspection; brains were working their way in from right and left, marking black hides with grease-rods and barking, "mountain," "motivator," "pits," "desert," "mines," "smith," "security," "political," "clerical," "runner," "mail room," and so on, with brains getting jobs that seemed to call for, well, brains, while the bulls were being classified as fighters and laborers, and the few runts were all becoming runners. But aside from those basic divisions, it was hard to see how the inspectors were making their judgements, distinguishing a motivator from a miner, for example, when all the bulls looked pretty much the same, at least to Snash. At any rate, once someone was classified, they were hustled off to the sides by guards.

Finally Snash reached the front, where he thought he'd be pronounced a runner like all the other runts, but a brain looked him over, marked him, said: "mail room," and passed on, even as a guard shoved Snash in the opposite direction.

Along with a crowd of other yarks, Snash found himself in a smaller chamber off to the side, where there was a great deal of shouting and confusion as everyone was sorted out and taken charge of; but Snash was the only runt in the whole place, and there was no one from the mail room to lead him away. Since there was a steady outflow from the bigger chamber, a few runts showed up from time to time, but the officers who claimed them weren't interested in Snash at all, and no one would answer his questions...finally, though, after what seemed like a very long time, during which he was getting more and more frantic, a brain came over to him and asked:

"How did *you* get through inspection?"

"The inspector inspected me..."

"Well, if you're *not* defective, then why are you doing your damnedst to stand there like a halfwit?"

"I was assigned to the mail room——"

The brain looked at Snash's grease-mark. "Think I can't see that, flyspeck?"

"But no one will take me, sir."

"Can't you do anything yourself, you mote of dried pus?" the brain snarled.

"I don't know the way."

"Ask," said the brain.

"Where's the mail-room, sir?"

"Never been there," answered the brain. "Ask someone else."

"Why don't we know where everything is?"

"What?" asked the brain. "So that anyone could go anywhere and do anything, whenever he pleased? What kind of an idea is *that*?"

It sounded to Snash like a good one, although he didn't say so...

"Get out of here, you bleeding bowel-worm!" the brain

25

cried.

It was some while before Snash managed to thread his way through all the activity, but at last he found an exit and headed off along a passage. When he asked some passing soldiers where the mail room was, they guffawed, and told him to keep going the way he was going, so he stayed that course for a time. He went up some steps and down some more, and the passage kept getting narrower...when he asked for some more directions, he got a very complicated answer, much of which he managed to forget after the first few lefts and rights...still more directions only left him farther along but with even less hope of getting where was supposed to go.

Eventually though, he came out of a stairwell to find himself in a vaulted, high-ceilinged hallway, and all that space was a relief, but the passage was lined with tall iron doors covered with rivets, and all the bars and padlocks were disquieting touches. To the left, the hall receded into what seemed a limitless distance; to the right, after fifty feet or so, was one end of the passage, another of those great doors, with a tremendously fat bull standing in front of it. Snash headed to the right.

But as he padded along, something roared behind one of the doors right next to him, the sound barely muffled by the iron, or so it seemed; he halted in fright, knees knocking, as other things, each sounding very different but equally as menacing, answered from their own cells, some of them hurling themselves against the doors, knocking rivets to the floor and making the padlocks jump. Once Snash began to get his wits back, he considered turning around and dashing right back into the stairwell; but the fat bull beckoned, and Snash continued up the hall, heart in his throat. As he approached, the bull lifted a pendulous arm, raised a metal tube he had hanging from his neck, and blew into one end of it...Snash felt a piercing sensation in his ears, and all at once the roaring and the banging halted.

"Can't stand the whistle, they can't," said the bull, then told Snash: "If you aren't completely lacking in breeks, my name's not Sluglik."

"Yes, well..." said Snash.

"What are you doing in my corridor, you barenaked nit, waking up my monsters?"

"That first one woke the rest up."

"But who woke *him* up, you extra-salty fleck of snot you?" Sluglik asked. "You did, with your nasty flappy feet."

"I wasn't making very much noise."

"As if you'd have to, if Number Seventeen was listening. He listens all the time, as nearly as I can tell, with his big sweaty ear right up against the iron...He can't stand the whistle though. None of 'em can---"

"Please," Snash said. "Can you tell me how to get to the mail room?"

"*Mail* room?" Sluglik broke in mockingly, and looked as though he were just about to tell Snash to get lost when he got a peculiar expression on his face---Snash didn't know how to read it, although he chalked that up to being about a half a day old---and nodded.

Sluglik pointed a clawed thumb over his warty shoulder. "As it just so happens, this is the mail room right here."

Snash tried to step past him, but Sluglik pushed him back, saying: "Hold on there! Let me get my keys."

Sluglik reached behind his back and pulled out a ring with lots of them, big ones with complex jagged teeth; they jingled as he looked through them.

"Why's the mail room locked?" Snash asked.

"What do you care?" Sluglik replied. "Do you think anyone gives a shit if barenaked nits are puzzled?"

"No, but..."

"Do you want to get in there, or not?"

"I do," said Snash.

Sluglik picked out a key, fitted it into a lock in a smaller door within the door, twisted it...the lock snicked. "There you are."

Snash hesitated.

"Go on," said Sluglik.

Snash put his claw out and pushed the door, which

27

creaked inwards a few inches...the glow coming through reminded him of the light down in the breeding-caves. Snash stepped back.

"What's the matter?" Sluglik asked.

"Spider-light," said Snash.

"What else?" asked Sluglik. "It's a big damn room, and torches just wouldn't do."

Supposing it made sense, Snash decided he'd simply have to be wary...after all, the yarks down in the breeding-cave seemed to have come to terms with the constant threat...

"What are you waiting for?" Sluglik asked.

Snash took a deep breath and shoved the door open further, but hardly had he stepped through when it slammed behind him, and he heard the lock click, and Sluglik bellowing laughter on the other side.

Ahead was a chamber that was obviously very large, although he couldn't tell just *how* large it was, since there were strands of spider-silk trailing down from the ceiling everywhere; from some of them hung huge globes with things moving and thrusting around inside them...the captives, or whatever they were, were glowing, their light muted by the sacs...even as Snash watched, one of the bags was breached from within, and a luminous spider, not as large as the ones down in the breeding-caves, but still pretty big, came crawling out, and lowered itself to the floor on a thread, others soon following. Quite sure by this point that this wasn't the mail room---he certainly detected no hint whatsoever of postal activity---Snash turned and began to pound on the door, squeaking:

"Let me out! Let me out!"

Sluglik's only response was a fresh spate of laughter.

Given this, Snash really had no good reason for pounding and begging any more, although he kept on with it until he heard the tapping sounds behind him...turning, he saw four of the baby spiders advancing upon him, rubbing their pedipalps together hungrily, and whispering, "Succulent, succulent, succulent," apparently referring to him, much to his dismay.

Suddenly something dropped down from behind a

curtain of strands; there was a loud thudding crackle, and the babies scattered away to the sides and dived into holes in the floor, revealing what looked like the withered husk, still glowing, of a spider five times their size…even as its body continued to fold and crack after that impact on the stone, the legs twitched, just a bit, in a way that suggested the thing was not quite dead.

"Still alive, hubby?" came a voice from above…much larger than any of the other spiders, even the one that had just dropped, a bloated arachnid, plainly the chamber's main source of light, descended into view, filling all the dangling silk with her illumination…all at once she plummetted, landing athwart the husk, swollen body sinking down in the midst of her legs, belly striking her mate and crushing him cracklingly a bit more before she rebounded, almost as though she were on springs…Lifting up her behind a bit, she tilted her head forward, caressed his with her pedipalps, said: "Can't get enough of you, honey," and sucked whatever was left to suck out of him. Then, wiping a palp over her mouth, she tilted her head back up, and…

Looked right at Snash with her manifold eyes, obsidian domes that were the only dark things on her.

"What's this?" she hissed.

"Could you tell me the way to the mail room?" he replied.

"Afraid not," she said. "I don't think they even *had* a mail room when I got here…it's been about two thousand years since they locked me up."

"That's a long time, isn't it?" Snash asked.

"Some might say," she replied. "Don't you know who I am?"

He thought a bit. "Mrs. Spider?"

"Glolob the Great," she said. "And who are you?"

"I believe my name's Sna---"

"Have you marked my luminosity, Sna?"

"Yes…hurts my eyes, actually."

"I sucked the light from the Larch of Effulgence, in the West That Went Elsewhere, back in the First Eon."

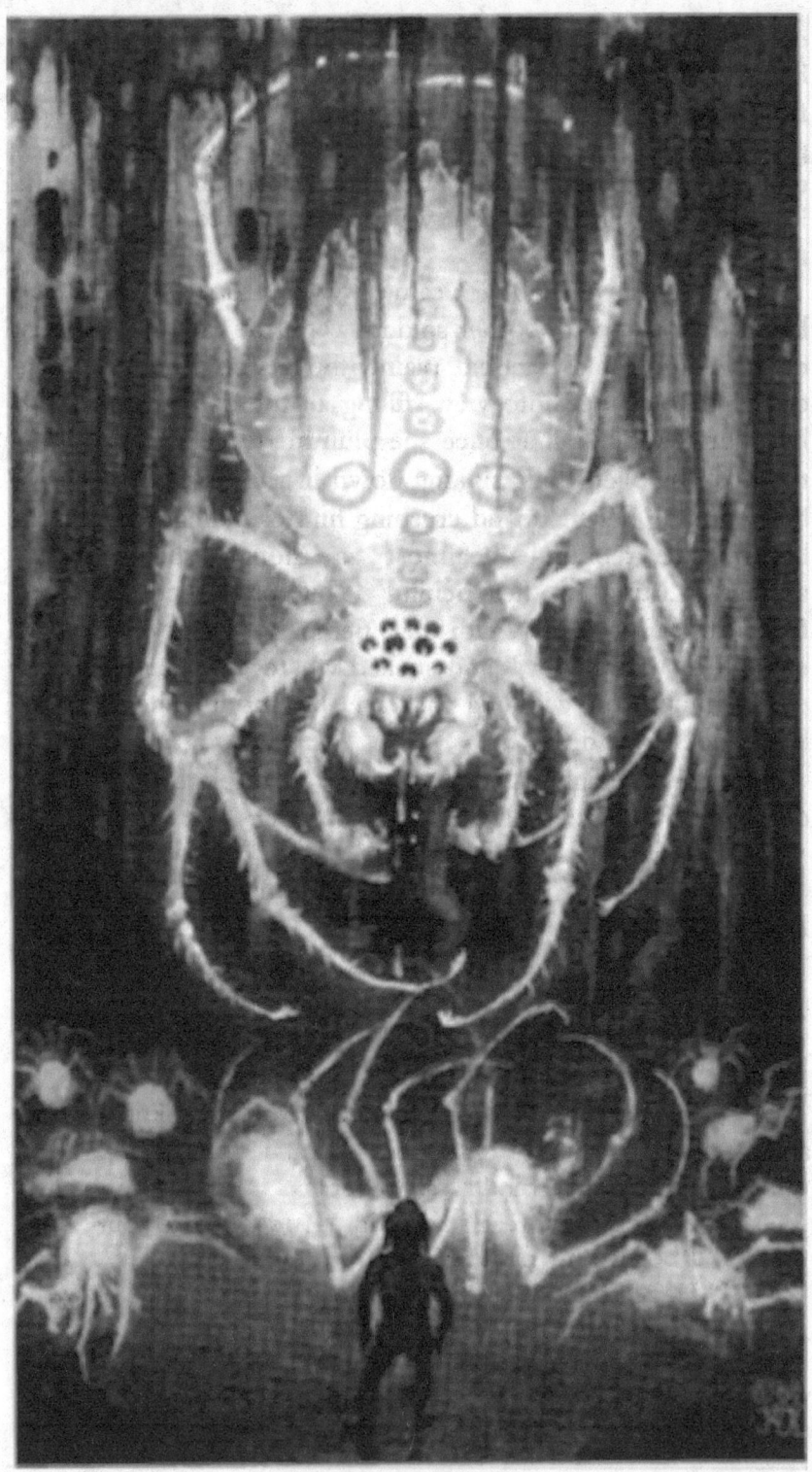

Having not been vouchsafed any of these terms, Snash didn't understand, although, perhaps for that reason, he didn't doubt her. It certainly *sounded* like quite an exploit.

"I've never done much of anything myself," he said. "Of course, I'm only a few hours old." He paused. "Is there someone else I can ask about the mail room?"

"Sluglik, through the door, I suppose," she answered.

"He sent me in here. Might you be willing…"

"To?"

"Ask him to let me out."

"He wouldn't, even if I did, and---I won't. I'm still hungry."

Snash gulped. "You just ate your husband---"

"*Drank* him, more like. I always save a little room for dessert, though…usually have to make do with one of the kids, but…."

Leg-tips clacking against the floor, she began to haul her great bulk forward. Snash ran back to the door and began banging on it again.

"As *if*," she said behind him.

He kept pounding….he heard the other monsters beginning to act up on the other side, but that piercing sensation went through his head again, as though Sluglik had just used his whistle once more, and the roarings and screechings subsided.

"What do you think of her Highness?" Sluglik cried.

"She hurts my eyes, and wants to eat me!"

"That's her, all right!" Sluglik laughed.

Snash heard the leg-tips clacking near…he whirled.

Glolob was bearing right down on him now, looking as though she planned to bite him, or at least seize him with her palps and thrust him into her mandibles. But her forelegs, after the fashion of such limbs, were out in front of the rest of her, and struck the wall, and even with them fully folded---Snash was in between---she couldn't bring her mouthparts to bear, and had to back up, and try to stand off and spear him with her legs.

That, however, wasn't an easy matter; he was very quick, and dodged and ducked, and she kept missing him, and ramming her leg-points into the door, and the littler door within it, bang, bang, bang....suddenly he heard a loud squeal, as though a metallic something had spindled and torn. Diving---just barely---beneath a thrust that put a friction-burn across the top of his shoulder, he looked under his arm...the door-within-a-door had been smashed clean off its hinges, and was lying outside in the hall, on Sluglik, apparently---at the very least, the door was heaving as though someone was underneath it and trying to push it off. Without another look at Glolob, Snash spun and went out the opening like a quarrel from a crossbow, only to be tipped over as Sluglik thrust the door off himself at last.

But Snash was too quick to let himself be pinned; even as the door slammed against the floor, he was up and backing away down the passage. Outlined by the spider-light from the postern, Sluglik was rising, shaking his head...leaning sideways to look past the corpulent bull, Snash saw that Glolob had gone motionless, but he had the distinct impression that that state of affairs wasn't about to last. He thought of warning Sluglik but decided he had no obligation, given their short but awful history. Sluglik reached for a falchion at his belt, snarling:

"Get back here, you---"

This demand was cut sharply short; he arched back even as an impact thrust him forward with a thud...right under his ribcage, where his gut started to bulge, a glowing spider-leg, hairs pushed back but popping back up, lunged out of his insides. He opened his mouth, but the only thing that came out was spider-light, welling up his throat. Then he was jerked backwards into Glolob's prison, prompting Snash, who had really lingered far too long, to run away just as fast as he could, feet slapping; cell by cell, on either side of him, the monsters behind the other doors started roaring again as he dashed by, almost as if they were devices he was tripping. Absolutely terrified, he saw the arch to that stairwell coming up fast on his right, slowed, almost fell, turned on one foot, then leaped inside...as he raced up the steps, he could still hear the roars progressing down the hallway below, as if the ongoing reaction no longer required him, if it ever had at all. He didn't halt till he reached the top, a good twenty landings above.

Chapter 3: Postal

Snash wandered some and got more directions that he didn't trust but followed anyway, for lack of a better plan, but as luck would have it, he'd gotten them from a bull who wasn't trying to trick him, and they weren't bad...he passed several runts all running the same way, carrying either scrolls or packages, with motivators laboring to keep up with them; guessing they must've come from the mail room, he went the way they'd come, and presently he was eyeing a pointed arch with an inscription above it that spelled out Mail Room in runes. Two lofty iron-shod doors stood open; a guard with a pike was leaning against the one on the left. The activities that Snash could see inside appeared to be perfectly consistent with the notions of postality implanted in his head...but when he tried to go in, the guard lowered his weapon, squinting at him.

Snash pointed to the grease mark on his chest. "I was assigned here."

"What's the password, you quarter cup of piss?" the bull demanded.

Snash bit his lip...had they given him one?

"They didn't say anything about a password," he replied.

"Then you'll just have to go back and ask 'em---"

Wearing a long hide apron and elbow-length gloves, looking very tired and stressed, a brain with huge bags under his eyes stepped up behind the guard. "Stop that shit, Grutnug."

"Just having a little fun, Nizhnikh," Grutnug said, and raised the polearm... but when Snash started to go by, Grutnug suddenly bared his long yellowish fangs and barked, and Snash flung himself back against one of the doors.

"Let him through," Nizhnikh told the guard wearily.

Grutnug just laughed, and turned. Snash slid sideways along the door, into the room.

"Report to Postmaster Khuttarh," said Nizhnikh.

"Where can I find him?" Snash asked.

Nizhnikh pointed, said: "Up those stairs," and started to head off.

"But," cried Snash after him, "I don't have any breeks!"

33

Nizhnikh kept going---undoubtedly he didn't give a damn about Snash, or his breeklessness...in all likelihood, and if he and Grutnug hadn't already been at odds, he'd never have intervened on Snash's behalf. Even so, Snash called:

"Won't I make a bad impression if my ass is hanging out?"

But even this argument failed to get a response from the brain.

Feeling very naked, Snash headed towards the stairs, which led up to a shelf far up along the lefthand wall. Everywhere he saw yarks looking about as hectored and harried as Nizhnikh...scrolls, parcels, packets, and packages of all sizes were tumbling out of openings in the walls and landing in large bins attended by bulls with big flat shovels; driven by brains, carts drawn by creatures rather like giant horned toads pulled alongside the bins, whereupon the bulls shovelled mail into the vehicles...once the carts were full, the brains drove them away...as Snash mounted the steps, he saw that they were all converging on an area in the center of the room, where, he guessed, the mail was being sorted...he glimpsed all kinds of other arrangements for doing other postal things, and many comings and goings, but before he could make much sense of them, he was at the top.

In the wall at the back of the shelf was a deep torchlit recess, the brands set in a wheel that depended from the ceiling on a chain; along the sides of the cave were tall racks filled with piled scrolls. Towards the rear was a black stone writing desk, carved with intricate motifs of grotesque horned demonic scribes drafting and sending missives, and other demons, having received these communications, grinning as they gleaned undoubtedly sinister information from them. Behind the desk, a black-hooded swarthy man with a long hooked nose was scribbling away furiously with a four-foot long quill pen whose black plume swooshed through the air...it was some moments before he became aware of Snash, and gave him a glare that was worse than anything Snash had ever seen on a yark...still, even though the man was no longer looking at the page, he continued scratching at it, and didn't stop for a while.

"Come closer," he said at last, and beckoned with a

long bony sharp-nailed finger.

Snash stepped nearer...depositing his quill in an inkwell shaped like a fat little yark who was getting something thrust into its head, the man asked:

"You realize I'm the Postmaster?"

Snash nodded.

"Why then have you come to see me with no breeks?" Khuttarh asked.

"I'm sorry, sir---"

"As well you should be. It makes a very poor impression, let me tell you."

"Nizhnikh sent me up here---"

"Like *that*? With your yark-crotch clearly visible, and most offensive to my delicate eyes?" Khuttarh leaned forward, pointing emphatically with inch-long fingernails to the dark-rimmed offended orbs.

"Yes, sir," said Snash, wondering if he'd been the victim of yet another joke.

"Well, perhaps it's true...Nizhnikh gives every sign of being thoroughly burnt out. It is very stressful, working down here. Still..."

"Still, sir?"

"I am the Postmaster of Mount Adamant, the Lord of the *Mail*, and will not be mocked. No one shows Khuttarh their crotch and lives. Stunkrog! Smazhgug!"

All at once, two cunningly-concealed trapdoors opened in the floor, on either side of Snash, and two huge bulls in lamellar armor leaped out...Snash started to backpedal out from between them, but they were very quick, and reached out with their long, long arms, snatching him before he got too far.

"Stunkrog!" Khuttarh said. "Fetch Nizhnikh."

One of them grunted and left, whereupon Khuttarh, acting exactly as though there was no one else in the cave with him, started a new letter...shortly Stunkrog returned with Nizhnikh, whom Khuttarh immediately asked:

"Did you send that runt---" he pointed at Snash, "---in here starkers?"

"Never seen him before," said Nizhnikh.

"How did he know your name?" Khuttarh asked.

"How should I know?" Nizhnikh replied.

"He's lying!" Snash squeaked.

"Why would I send a naked runt up here?" Nizhnikh asked.

"Because you're burnt out, and you don't care any more," answered Khuttarh.

"If I don't care any more, why would I lie?" Nizhnikh asked.

"Because you're too burnt out to think things through."

Nizhnikh shrugged. "I need a vacation."

"As your superior, I take your vacations for you."

"That's why I *need* one," said Nizhnikh. "At full pay."

"As you know full well, your pay is held in perpetual trust, to make sure that you invest in the future."

"I think," said Nizhnikh, "that I'd rather get paid in the present. But---" He reached suddenly behind his apron and yanked out a miniature crossbow, "I *could* just start killing everyone, and settle for that!"

He aimed the weapon at Khuttarh, but Stunkrog tried to grab it; Nizhnikh ducked, there was a moment of struggle, the crossbow *thapped!* and Stunkrog fell with a bolt in his knee. Even as Smazhgug let go of Snash and drew his scimitar, Nizhnikh pulled a knife from somewhere and slipped round the desk, getting behind Khuttarh and putting the blade to his throat....Smazhgug halted.

"All right," Khuttarh said. "Now what?"

"Catch!" cried Nizhnikh to Snash, and tossed him his miniature crossbow. Snash plucked it from the air. "Pull the cord back!"

Snash pulled it back till the mechanism clicked. Then Nizhnikh threw him a quarrel. "Load it!"

Snash laid the missile in the groove.

"Maggot!" cried Stunkrog from the floor, gripping his knee.

Snash lifted the weapon, and pointed it at Khuttarh.

"You wouldn't dare!" cried the Lord of the Mail.

Wouldn't I? Snash thought, then decided: *No,* and shifted his aim a bit to the side, towards Nizhnikh's face. He had, of course, no experience with crossbows, (although he did have some ideas about them) and he fired a bit before he should've…the bow jumped in his claw and rather startled him. But the quarrel went right through Nizhnikh's ear, and that was good enough as it turned out; Nizhnikh yowled and dropped his knife, Khuttarh slid away, and Smazhgug got behind the desk and put Nizhnikh down with a slash to the jaw, giving him several more blows after he hit the floor.

Rubbing his throat, Khuttarh looked at Snash.

"You still going to kill me, sir?" Snash asked.

Khuttarh shook his head. "Since you saved me just now, I'll forget about seeing your crotch…you'll be snuffed out soon enough. Find someone to tell you your duties. And get some *clothes*."

Snash started off, but Khuttarh said, "*wait*," and scribbled something on a small parchment, then handed it to Snash. "Show that to the outfitters."

Snash went back downstairs, but no one wanted to help him, even after he brandished Khuttarh's name at them; eventually, though, while he was making his fourth circuit of the mail room, one of the brains, saying he was "sick of seeing his bum," directed Snash to the chamber where the post-yarks (including the runners and their motivators) were outfitted.

There he was issued mail room runt-gear---a tunic, light shoes with treads on the soles, a belt with several scabbards with knives of different shapes tucked into them, and a leather helmet with a moveable visor. In addition, he was given a sack of small wooden blocks with parchment along one side, which could be peeled away to reveal some kind of very sticky stuff. However, when he asked what those, and various other items, were for, he got answers that were obviously false. Moreover, some of his gear was defective; when he tried to fasten the belt, the buckle fell apart, and the helmet's visor came off one of its hinges when he tried to flip it down. The brain behind the counter didn't want to hand out any replacements, either, so Snash just had to settle for a visor that hung down on the left, and a belt that he had to knot---luckily, he was so thin that there was enough slack.

Back in the main chamber, he finally attached himself to another runt, who, as it turned out, was also named Snash, although he was somewhat older and had a vile temper, having been, apparently, considerably soured by his experiences...even after Snash explained that he was simply trying to learn what a mail room runt did, the other Snash simply went about his business in a surly fashion and tried to be unhelpful, frequently in some very dangerous ways.

Even so, Snash learned quite a bit. The primary function of a mail room runt was to climb (chimney, actually) up inside the mail chutes----there were scores---and rectify the frequent blockages. Thanks to small pockets of luminous material embedded at intervals in the walls, there was just enough light for yarks---who didn't require much---to see; during his first shift, Snash followed the other Snash up five separate chutes, and the other Snash, prying parcels and packages loose, made every attempt to send them straight down at Snash and dislodge him at the very least.

But Snash kept at it, and made some close observations---it was very important to remove the bottommost parcels with the utmost care, so as to keep the whole blockage, which was sometimes quite large, from falling down all at once. To this end, the other Snash made use of those sticky blocks, which he attached to the walls, to hold certain items in place until he was ready to remove them. Even so, in the fifth chute, everything came loose too suddenly; thrust downwards by a great mass of mail, the other Snash landed on Snash, and the two of them slid down hundreds of yards before they finally spilled out into the bin at the bottom...having had a good deal of time to think about what he was going to do when he *reached* bottom, Snash rolled out from under his alter ego before the other Snash could really settle, and the packages could really settle on him...Snash was over the rim of the bin before he knew it, looking back at the stuff coming down, the other Snash already completely buried...the whole bin, which had been mostly empty when the avalanche started, just about filled up.

Snash looked to a shoveller who was standing beside

the bin.

"The other Snash is under there!" Snash said. "Dig him out!"

"No hurry," said the shoveller. "That was a lot of mail....Might as well wait till the next wagon comes up..." He grinned. "That was a neat trick, you getting out of there like that...never seen one of you runts survive a mailslide *that* big."

Snash looked past him, saw another shoveller beckoning. "Hey you, runt!" said the bull. "Blockage!"

Fortunately for Snash, it wasn't too high or too much, and when he came back down, it was shift-change...the day crew (Snash knew what day was, abstractly, although he never expected to live long enough to be blinded by one) was coming in, smaller than the night crew---even though Lord Serpentar did his level best to keep things shadowy in Tenebria, things simply slowed down when the sun was abroad, and less mail arrived.

Tagging along with the other members of his crew, Snash, simply famished, was delighted when their motivators whipped them directly into the mail yark's mess hall. Even though he was barely tall enough to slide his pig-iron tray along the railing, he managed, and stayed well back with the other runts...having tucked their whips into their belts, the motivators were up front, pushing trays themselves.

There were two main courses---fell beast-flesh, and the clawed scaly feet of some kind of great bird. Word was that there was man-flesh from time to time, but that was rather a delicacy, and today, at any rate, was not the day. There was also fell-beast cheese, and *extremely* hard tack, which came with small hammers and chisels. As for drink, there was, in addition to filthy brackish water with oily aftertaste, fell-beast milk and blood; Snash had the flesh, the fell-beast cheese, some tack, and fell-beast blood, and went to sit at one of the runt trestles, which, like all the other tables, was made of rusty rivetted iron.

But even though he was among his own kind, dinner was fairly nerve-wracking; if his tablemates weren't trying to play practical jokes on him, the other, bulls and brains were trying to play jokes on them, or each other, and there were several eruptions which were quelled only by mace-bearing guards. Snash ate as quickly as he could, although chiselling the hard tack into bite-sized chunks was quite a project...

Upon finishing their meals, the yarks headed off for the mail room barracks. The chamber was very long; five walls ran down the middle of it, looking as though the room had been carved out around them. Two hundred feet tall, they went floor to ceiling, honeycombed with tubelike excavations, sleeping-slips, into which yarks were climbing.

At the front, a couple of brains behind a stone counter assigned spaces and lockers; even though they switched numbers on Snash, he figured out that his locker-number was a tube-number in short order, and after stowing his gear, climbed up to his tube, using handholds that had been gouged into the stone---his berth was the next to last before the ceiling.

He paused before going in; there was a sour smell, but that wasn't why. Just below the number (which was graven next to the entrance) a chisel had been applied to some other inscription, which was only partially obliterated. Snash thought he could make out the words *Hrag-Urshathur*, or, roughly translated, *He Who Is Much Better.*

"Than what?" he muttered.

Than Serpentar, he told himself. *Of course...*

But he was far too tired to go further with this train of thought, and he climbed into the tube. The smell was, unsurprisingly, much thicker inside; little biting things were all over him in a matter of moments. There was no blanket, although that hardly mattered since it was so hot. All of his neighbors seemed to be snoring, each of them doing it differently, some even barking or hooting. Still, none of this was enough to keep him from falling off, which he did in a matter of moments.

When a horn began to bray, rousing him from his (insufficient) slumber, he realized that he'd been so tired that he'd forgotten to stow his belt, and had fallen asleep on two of his knives, whose scabbards had dug cruelly into his hip; sitting up, he banged his head on the top of the tube. When he took his belt off the scabbards seemed a bit reluctant to leave the dents they had impressed into his flesh. His eyelids felt swollen, and his mouth was vile---he could still taste the fell-beast blood, which seemed to have clotted on his tongue; bits of meat were wedged rather painfully between his fangs. He scratched at his bites, dislodging critters---lice? fleas?---that were still at him.

Outside, the horn stopped braying, but a grating voice started up from beneath:

"Get up, you tapeworms, you dungbats, you earwax pies! Rise and shine! Mail never sleeps!"

It occurred to Snash that mail actually *did* sleep, sort of, at least during the day, but since there was no one in the tube with him, he didn't say anything, and forgot all about it as he hung his belt around his neck and climbed down the handholds to the bottom, where the motivators were warming up, doing knee-bends and cracking their whips, some flicking each other just for sport.He was hoping for breakfast, but the whipwielders drove everyone right past the cafeteria and straight to the mail room, where he began another long, dangerous shift. Very much like the night before, the worst blockage saved itself till next to last, and he had to climb very far to find it.

The cause was a large leathery egg-case that someone had simply slapped an address and postage on; how this thing had gotten so far through the system, Snash hadn't the foggiest, but it had hung up on a couple of sticky-blocks that some other runt had left on the sides of the chute...Snash couldn't see very far past it, but there appeared to be all sorts of things piled up above it, some of them leaking.

Worse yet, even as he approached, whatever was in the egg started to wake up, and snarl, and push the sides of its flexible prison, bulging them out in one spot after another. A rip opened; a long continuous string of goo streamed out, much thicker and smellier than the other stuff that was leaking down; suddenly the tear got wider, and something long, dark and glistening that Snash never got a very clear impression of came slithering out, blurring past him down the chute.

Looking up, he saw the egg-case yielding to the pressure from above, slipping from the sticky-blocks now that it was emptied; he heard things sliding and shifting…the egg-case came sliding down, followed by two small packages. Flattening himself against the side of the chute, he helped them on their way.

After that, things seemed to have stabilized themselves up there; he had just begun to chimney back up when he realized that something was biting his left shoe. Looking down, he saw it was that long glistening thing. He whipped it back and forth at the end of his leg, smacking it against the wall…it let go, slid down a few yards, then came back up at him. He climbed a bit farther, halting right under the sticky-blocks, the other packages jammed right over his head…wedged against the walls, he pulled a knife and stabbed at the creature…it refused to die and got up past the knife, sliding all over him wherever he wasn't pressed flush against the chute, pausing only to take little bites. All the while he was trying to stab it, although he got himself half the time; ultimately, he jabbed one of the sticky-blocks by mistake, and between that thrust, and all the weight pressing on it from above, the block came loose, and the mail just started to fall. A long rectangular box, sliding past Snash's head, swept the creature away; then something came directly and painfully down on his helmet, hurting him even through the lacquered leather, dislodging him…he blacked out for what seemed a few moments.

When he came to, he was jammed sideways in the chute, the mail having coagulated above him; wincing at the pain in his head, he shifted a bit, found that the blockage was pretty solid, and didn't require him to support it. He went down the chute a bit, waited for his head to stop throbbing, then chimneyed back up, planted some stickys, and worked his way carefully up through the jam, which was not all that big. Then he removed his blocks, went farther and removed the ones the other fellow had left, and headed back down, feeling an odd sense of accomplishment.

During the nights that followed, he struck up

conversations with his fellow runts, and even some of the brains, and between that and his own observations, he got a clearer sense of how the mail room (and indeed the whole mail system of Mount Adamant) operated. Urgent messages were passed by runner-motivator teams; less urgent posts were moved in huge lots, on slowly moving service lifts powered by fell beasts. Much of the mail originated inside the fortress, and passed between floors and departments; but the majority of it came from outside Mount Adamant. Serpentar had many vast armies in the field, and pretty much lorded it over the whole world, with the pesky exception of Merriador; all manner of tribute, dispatches, and strange goods and specimens were constantly being received.

Snash proved good at his job, and when he survived thirty shifts, there was much comment on it, since few of the blockage-rectifiers had ever lasted that long before. He managed to get a belt with a functioning buckle and a helmet with a visor hinged on both sides, came to know each and every one of the chutes, and was well aware of their individual peculiarities and particular dangers; judging by the kind of material that came down, he even could even tell which department was using a tube. After a time, he began to develop ideas on how the system could be improved, and tried to share them with anyone who'd listen to him.

But the runts and bulls had no interest whatsoever in making the system work better, and the brains thought runts were too stupid to have any good ideas, and the upshot was that he decided to speak to a higher-up, one of Serpentar's human servants, and that meant, of course, Khuttarh. It took Snash some time to work up his nerve, but one night while Khuttarh was making his rounds with Stunkrog and Smazhgug, Snash raised his helmet-visor and presented himself to the Lord of the Mail.

"Back to work, you!" snarled Smazhgug.

But the Postmaster raised his hand; Smazhgug subsided, and Khuttarh asked Snash:

"Aren't you the runt who reported to me naked as a drunken slug?"

Snash nodded. "I also saved you from Nizhnikh, My

43

Lord."

It was a few moments before Khuttarh answered, almost as if he had forgotten *that*. But then he said: "Ah, yes...Do you have something to report?"

"I have some suggestions, sir," Snash replied.

"Suggestions?"

"Meaning no disrespect, sir...things run very smoothly as it is. But anything can be improved, and---"

"What makes you think I'd be interested in your...advice?"

Snash answered: "I've survived a hundred and twenty shifts, three times more than any chute-runt that anyone's ever heard of."

"I've never heard of one lasting that long," Khuttarh conceded. "Well, then...what *is* your name, by the way?"

"Snash."

"You and half the yarks in here."

"About a third, sir."

Khuttarh's dark-rimmed eyes narrowed at this impertinence; but he seemed to be in a good mood, and let it pass. "So then, Snash. How could we do better?"

"The chutes are too narrow," Snash replied. "That's why there are so many blockages."

"But if we enlarged them, it would be harder for you runts to get up inside."

"Meaning no disrespect, sir, but that's not quite true. They could be reamed out a good deal, and we'd still be able to chimney on up. Might even be easier---it's kind of awkward as it is."

"Is that so?"

"Also, the chutes seem to have been carved out at different times by different hands, and some of them aren't well-carved. There are narrow places, and bends, and even places like corkscrews. It's the worst towards the bottom, where everything feeds in...the main chutes aren't much bigger than the feeders."

"Widening the mains would be very expensive," Khuttarh said. "Have you given any thought to that, little Snash?"

"I have," Snash replied. "The fact is, a lot of treasure comes in through the ducts. But the ducts are stopped up a lot of the time. Slows the whole fortress down."

"Does it?"

"Stands to reason, sir. Sand in the works. Orders don't pass, departments don't pay each other, blokes don't get their gear..."

"Very true."

"Also, I've given some thought to those lifts, the ones that carry most of the mail upstairs...why not make smaller, faster ones, and reserve them for the runners, the way those stairways are reserved for them now?"

"What do you know about those stairways?"

"I've only heard about them, My lord. But it got me to thinking---"

"Just bursting with ideas, aren't you?"

"If you say so, sir."

"Odd for a runt...maybe there were more brains than usual in your compost."

"Maybe, sir."

Khuttarh puts his hands on his knees. "Tell you what...why don't you come with me, and you can tell me every clever idea you've ever had?"

Khuttarh brought Snash up to his office, and listened to him attentively for about an hour, even taking notes. At the end, the Postmaster said, "Care for a bit of manflesh?" and opened a steel box graven with etchings of men being roasted on spits; taking out a strip of dried meat that might well have been human-jerky, he waved it in Snash's direction---it was a few moments before Snash realized he was expected to catch it with his mouth, but then he opened up, and Khuttarh flung it to him. Snash snapped it out of the air, seized an end with his claw, and wrenched off a bite. It was very salty, and tasted little different from Fell Beast...he wasn't quite sure what the fuss was.

"Now off with you," said Khuttarh.

"My Lord," said Snash, bowing, and left.

There was still about an hour left to the night-shift; one of the shafts that brought outside mail was clogged---"unproductive" was the term, and Snash promptly went up to see what he could do. The blockage wasn't very far up, but it was pretty big---it took him quite a while to get through it, and during that time, he heard the shift-change down below. By the time he got back down, there was practically no one nearby; most day-mail was internal, and most of the internal chutes were some distance away.

He looked around for a motivator to whip him to the cafeteria; spotting one far off who didn't seem to have anyone to lash at the moment, he was just heading in his direction when a largish box came thumping down onto some mail in a bin off on his left....Snash thought he heard a soft voice inside it say something like: "*Ach! Scheisssss!*"

He moved closer, listening, and stopped by the rim. The box was motionless, and quite silent now.

His stomach, however, was anything but quiet, and he needed to get to the cafeteria before it closed. Still, he decided to wait a bit longer, and crouched down, just peering over the rim, even as he told himself he really didn't need to bother with this---

Thud.

He picked up a packet and threw it edgewise...as it struck, there was a strange, strangled-sounding cry from inside the box, which tilted up as if something had hurled itself against the far wall of it; then the box slid partway down the far side of the small mound of mail.

Snash went round to the other side of the bin and crouched down again, saying:

"I know you're in there."

The box was wrapped in twine, and had a lid, which raised about a half-inch before a white bladelike thing, a piece of sharpened bone perhaps, came out and proceeded to saw through the cords. Once the strands were all snapped, the bone retracted, and a brace of long skeletal yellow-green fingers came out and hooked the underside of the lid, pushing up.

"Glargle, glargle," said the voice from inside.

"Come on out," said Snash, drawing his favorite knife, the one with the longest blade.

Up rose a noseless round green face with big bulging slimy-looking eyes and a very wide mouth…on the upper lip was a small, square, bristly moustache. A single grey hair tilted up and forward from the front of the scalp, several inches long.

"Glargle," said the thing again, "*Vas ist, mein liebchen?*"

None of this meant anything whatsoever to Snash.

"Who are you?" he asked.

"Glargle," the thing replied.

"Is that your name?"

The thing nodded, turning its face, showing a large flat circular area on the side of its head, some kind of strange ear perhaps, a slightly darker green than the rest of the creature's skin.

"Who mailed you here?" Snash asked.

Glargle just shrugged again, and kind of laughed, in a glotty, mucousy kind of way.

Snash squinted at the return address---it was smudged.

"Who mailed you?" he asked once more.

"Meinself, meinself, I did, I did," the creature answered. "No uzzer vay in, I've tried, I've tried---" Suddenly it clapped both hands over its mouth, as though it had said too much.

"Get out of that box," Snash said. "You're coming with me."

"*Ach,* sss, don't sink so."

Snash looked around for reinforcements, but they were as far away as ever---when he glanced back at Glargle, one of those green hands had balled into a fist (which looked rather like a dead spider, all curled up) and was shooting right at Snash's face, which it connected with an instant later. Snash rocked back and landed on his bum, whereupon Glargle sprang high into the air on long unfolded skinny green legs, and landed on the bin-rim, saying: "Vhere *bist du, mein liebchen?*"

He rubbed his hands together and glanced about, the bones in his skinny neck crackling, then galloped off on all fours---Snash, holding a bloodied nose and very dizzy, turned to see him heading in the direction of the internal mail-chutes.

But just then a motivator, pulling his breeks up, came out of a garderobe on the left; Glargle swerved round him, went on a ways with the motivator running after him and shouting, then bounded into a bin and vanished up inside a chute...Snash was stumbling towards the motivator as the bull turned and asked:

"What was *that*?"

"I don't know," said Snash.

"Well go up there and get him!" the motivator answered.

Snash remained where he was, shaking his head...the bull cracked his whip.

"All right, all right," Snash said, and went up the chute. He could hear Glargle glargling and "ach, sss-sing," some distance above, but even though Snash did his level best (which was not very much at the moment) to catch up, the sounds faded steadily as the creature widened his lead...Finally Snash went back down. The motivator was squatting next to the bin at the bottom.

"Got away, eh?" he asked.

Snash nodded.

"Well, you'll have to file a report, and I don't want to be you."

"You didn't catch him either."

"I was in the crapper."

"As if anyone would buy *that* excuse---what say neither of us saw anything?"

The motivator considered this, then laughed. "I'm going back in the can," and returned to the garderobe.

Chapter 4: Runner

Not long after, Snash was switched over to the day-crew; arriving in the mail-room, he discovered that part of it had been shut down so that the chutes could be widened out; great rotary stone-reamers with extendable shafts had been brought in, and two were already in operation, their long cranks manned by teams of extremely burly ogres, overseen by men from Engineering. The air was cloudy with rock-dust and everyone was coughing, but even though that was so annoying, Snash felt a distinct pride, and congratulated himself on having one of his recommendations adopted; he thought perhaps he'd been put on the day-shift as a reward.

One of the chutes that hadn't been shut down had a blockage; he spent a good long time taking care of it, way up out of sight. When he came back down, he saw Khuttarh, rather to his surprise because it was the day-shift, and went right over.

Looking back, Snash would wonder why he'd been stupid enough to approach him again, but that was the future, and this was now; Khuttarh *had* listened to him before, and had given him a strip of manflesh; Snash thought he had good reason to expect a pat on the head, and thought further that Khuttarh might even be inclined to listen to a few more ideas, which Snash had come up with in the meanwhile.

The Lord of the Mail, a large packet under one black-sleeved arm, was speaking with a motivator...Snash noticed a scar on the bull's upper lip and recognized him as the very first driver who'd driven him, down in the pits, Slagbag...he was much less heavily armored now.

But, as though he were seeing someone whom he didn't want to be reminded of, Khuttarh gave him one brief glance, then told Slagbag:

"Take *him*."

"Take me where, My Lord?" Snash asked.

"Slagbag's just been transferred from the breeding-pits," Khuttarh said. "Needs a runner to motivate, and that would seem to be you....You'll need new gear." Eyes still averted, he handed Snash a blank requisition slip.

The runt bowed. "My Lord."

Khuttarh started to head off, robes rustling, then seemed to realize he was carrying an envelope, and held it out beside him, never stopping. "Take this over to Engineering," he said, and Snash ran after him to get it....Slagbag came up, glowering down at the runt.

"Don't you remember me?" Snash asked.

"Why should I?"

"You whipped me after I was pried out of my pit."

"I'd wager there are about four thousand runts who could say the same, you not especially choice morsel of toejam...why did you remember *me*? The scar?"

"First one I ever saw," said Snash. "And it's a good one. Deep and mean-looking."

Slagbag seemed flattered...but cracked his whip. "Get moving!"

Keeping ahead of the lash rather effortlessly, Snash raced off and exchanged his blockage-rectifier gear for a runner's kit, while Slagbag waited outside. After turning in his tunic, shoes, helmet, knife-belt and stickies, Snash got a belt *without* knives (nowhere near as good), a skin bottle, a map, a pouch for carrying dispatches, and a tunic without a back, for greater ease of whipping. Standing on a runt-block, which lifted him high enough for the brains behind the counter to deal with him, he donned the new tunic and tried to put on the belt---the buckle worked just fine, but the strap snapped. Rather to his surprise, he was given a replacement immediately, although he leaped straight to the conclusion that he was being set up for something...when one of the brains glanced at the skin bottle, and showed the barest hint of a smile, Snash shook the bottle, sloshed the contents, and asked:

"What's in here?"

"Juice," said the brain.

"From?"

"Those fruits they grow us in. Has everything a yark needs to keep him going..."

But Snash was barely listening by then...he was looking at the map, and he didn't like it. Supposedly, it showed the level he was on, with the main routes marked in red...they all ended up at the central shaft of the Spike, the vast chimney-like tower that had been raised on the rim of Mount Adamant...there was a cross-section of the Spike on the other side of the sheet. But the paper was poor ratty stuff, and much of the printing was blotted...moreover, a lot of details were very much at variance with what Snash knew already.

"Give me a real map," he told the brain.

The brain smirked. "That *is* a real map. Get out of here---"

Suddenly he glanced over Snash's shoulder, and the smirk dropped from his thin lips...Slagbag stepped up to the counter, saying:

"What's all this then?"

"He gave me a fake map," said Snash.

One of Slagbag's long muscly arms shot out, and he grabbed the brain by the throat, jerking him partway up on the counter.

"Stop wasting our time, you twenty-gallon jar of fell-beast diarhhea," he said, then flung him back. The brain barely kept himself from falling, staggered off and got a real map, which Snash immediately perused...it appeared to be the genuine article. He almost got down from the runt-block, but then, all at once, found himself wondering about what might be in the bottle...opening it, he took a sniff, then recoiled.

"What is it?" Slagbag asked.

"Not sure," Snash replied, closed the bottle back up, then laid it back on the counter. "But whatever leaked it had very bad kidneys."

Slagbag grinned, and shook two fingers at the brain. Then he brought his fist down on the bottle, which was pointed right at the trickster...out flew the cork on a blast of stinking whizz, dousing the malefactor.

"You, lacewing!" cried Slagbag to the other brain. "Bring my runt here another bottle, with something better in it!"

The brain rushed to comply, and momentarily Snash had a bottle whose contents smelled exactly like yark-fruit.

"Let's go," said Slagbag.

Snash stepped down from the block and headed for the door.

Engineering wasn't far from the mail room, and all the way there and back, Slagbag didn't succeed in whipping Snash once; he was grumbling as they reached the sorting-station in the mail room.

"You know, it makes me look bad, you staying so far out in front," he said.

"I don't need motivating," Snash replied.

"That's what you say now," Slagbag answered. "Wait till they send us up into the Spike. I did some pounding around up there, before they had me driving newborns. Running on stairs is *way* worse than runnin' on the flat...once you slow down, I'm really going to take it out of you."

"No you won't," said Snash. "It'll be just the same. I'm faster than you, and I'll still be faster on the stairs....if they're going to have someone whip us, it should be other runts."

"But who'll whip *them*?" Slagbag snarled.

"Who whips *you*?" Snash asked, just as one of the sorters handed him a scroll and said:

"Slogans, Fifteen Hundred and Sixty Two."

"The *fifteen hundredth* floor?" Snash asked.

"They had to put it somewhere," the sorter replied, whereupon Slagbag, who had apparently been contemplating Snash's back all along, gave him a good hard snap right between the shoulderblades.

"*Got* you!" Slagbag cried, even as Snash squealed and took off, circling wide round Slagbag, determined not to let him tag him again.

Up till now, Snash's only ventures into the Spike had been up inside the chutes; this time, however, his route was the Great Spiral---finding his way with the map as he outpaced Slagbag, he came at last to the mighty stairway that wound its way along the interior of the chimney. Knowing he'd better not lose Slagbag entirely---regulations stipulated that messengers had to be accompanied by their motivators---Snash halted on the landing to give him a chance to catch up, and while he was waiting, looked over the edge, down the shaft. A hot sulphurous wind swept his face…it was hard to lean out over it, and it gave him a precarious, off-balance feeling, even though he was in no danger from it, since it only would've tipped him backwards.

The view itself was dizzying, an awesome plunge into a distant glowing lake of lava, with the spiral staircase descending some distance below the chimney and along the wall of the crater the Spike had been built upon…there were hundreds of landings with archways opening upon them, and thousands of figures, some of them in columns, were coming and going through the doors, and up or down the steps, or across the many bridges, some narrower, some wider, that had been thrown across the gulf. Great banners with slogans like, "If It Hurts, You're Doing It Right," "The Whip Is Your Mate," and "Abasement *IS* The Answer" were fastened to the curving wall.

Snash straightened and looked up. There was much less light, and it was more sullen red than orange---the farther things were from the lava-lake the less illumination they received. Still, there were torches, and enough red from beneath for him to see the underside of the bridges above, well up into the shaft…he thought he could just make out the mouth of the chimney, a black circle above the bridges. He had never seen the sky before; he'd been told that little lights shone in it sometimes, when rents opened in the dark clouds that covered Lord Serpentar's realm. But there was only murk tonight.

"What are you waiting for?" came Slagbag's voice.

Snash turned to see him charge out onto the landing.

"You," said Snash, and headed up the steps.

During the early part of the ascent, he got so far out in front of Slagbag that an officer from Burning Curiosity stopped him, and asked what he was doing without a motivator---when Slagbag came toiling up, the officer let them both go, but after that, Snash decided it would be best if he didn't press his advantage so much, lest Slagbag be replaced with someone faster. Besides, he really couldn't see the harm in allowing Slagbag the dignity of an occasional near-miss.

But after a while, Slagbag ceased to be a concern--- the climb itself got to be the only thing on Snash's mind, sheer torture after a couple hundred floors or so, even for a fit little fellow like himself. The hot air rising from the lava far below really took it out of him, drying his thin lips till they cracked, his nostrils till they started to bleed, his tongue till it felt like a piece of leather in the bottom of his mouth---he drained the juice in his bottle before he got halfway up, and his ankles, calves and knees grew terribly sore.

Yet bad as it was for him, it was obviously much worse for Slagbag; Snash had to stop constantly just to stay in his vicinity, and by the time they were closing in on the Fifteen Hundredth floor, Slagbag could barely stay on his feet, and was weaving back and forth from one side of the steps to the other, banging into the wall on the left, and teetering near the edge on the right.

Reaching 1500 at last, Snash sat down on the edge of the landing, panting, watching Slagbag, his tongue hanging out, slog towards him...coming up over the top, the motivator simply collapsed beside the runt, and there he lay until Snash noticed a couple of I and E boys approaching along the hallway. Standing up immediately, Snash nudged Slagbag with his foot until the motivator rose as well.

Snash was expecting the Inspirational Exhorters to say something, but they were too busy chewing the rag with each other, jawing about "victory," "Merriador," and how "the whole lot" were "in the bag now," although one did direct a quick sneer Snash's way. But Snash knew that he and Slagbag would not, in all probability, continue to be so lucky, and he tugged on Slagbag's wrist, leading him towards 1562, the motivator stumbling behind him.

There was a great deal of scribbling going on at Slogans, and brains mumbling lines under their breath, or testing them out on each other, with variations...everyone looked very tense and jumpy, and it seemed that no one's efforts were being well-received...Ritragh, the Sloganeer-in-Chief, looked at the scroll in Snash's outstretched claw as though it were going to bite him, and after reading it, said:

"Bad enough that I've got the whole weight of the world on my shoulders...Now this!"

He waved the missive and shook his head.

"What is it, sir?" an underling asked.

But the motto-honcho just shook his head.

"Excuse me, sir," said Snash.

"*What?*" Ritragh asked.

"Might we have some water?"

"Water? This is Slogans. We deal in *spiritual* refreshment up here."

"Can't do without that, sir. But---"

"Here's my latest: 'Serpentar---Bow to the Inevitable.'"

Is that new? Snash thought.

"What do you think?" Something about the question left Snash with the impression that the slogan had already gotten a lukewarm response from Ritragh's flunkies.

"Sir," the runt said, "I bow to the inevitable every day--"

"But does it make you want to bow even *lower?*"

"Yes, now that you mention it, sir," said Snash, and bowed very low indeed. "But could you give us some water?"

"Why do you need water when you have a new slogan?"

Slagbag tapped Snash on the shoulder. "Let's go."

Ritragh's voice suddenly sharpened: "Stay *right* where you are."

They froze.

He said: "I detect... a lack of enthusiasm."

"I'm sorry, sir," said Snash. "But we just ran up fifteen hundred floors, and---"

"*We* just spent the night coming up with a new slogan," the officer replied. "And you act as though it's nothing!"

"I never meant to---"

"Don't you realize what you're part of here?" the brain broke in. "What we're *all* part of? We are *arrows* in the *quiver* of *history!* Hobnails on the *boot* of the future! *We* wear the road down! *We* make what happens happen! What is replenishing one's bodily fluids compared to fulfilling Lord Serpentar's Five

Thousand-Year plan?"

When Snash and Slagbag continued silent, the brain, quivering with indignation, continued:

"I'll tell you what! It's only a tiny little thing!"

To illustrate this point, he held his taloned thumb and forefinger right in front of Snash's nose, the miniscule gap between them representing, with great clarity, the relative size of replenished fluids in proportion to the Five Thousand-Year Plan.

"You're quite right, sir," Snash replied.

"Don't give me that," said the brain. "You're not inspired---I can see it in your whiteless slitty black eyes."

"Sorry sir."

"Why do I even bother?" The brain's shoulders slumped.

But seeing that, Snash suddenly realized how to handle him, and said: "Well sir...if *you* fellows were to give up, how could the rest of us get on?"

The officer shot him a glance.

"Did Lord Serpentar ever give up?" Snash asked.

The brain shook his head.

"Well, you mustn't either, sir," Snash went on. "And really, I think you came up with quite an excellent slogan. It'll be running through my head the whole way back down, all fifteen hundred floors, I'm sure of it. I also was very moved by, '*We* make what happens happen.' Did you come up with that just now, on the spur of the moment?"

The officer's look brightened. "I did."

"Excellent work, sir," Snash replied. "'There is no I in Tenebria,' wasn't one of yours, was it?"

"It was indeed," said the officer, although one of his assistants got a look on his face that suggested otherwise...reminded of the situation between himself and Khuttarh (and well aware that there *was*, in actuality, an 'I' in Tenebria), Snash said:

"That slogan has quashed my self-regard on any number of occasions, sir."

The officer turned to the actual originator of "There is no I" and said: "Get them some water."

Once Snash and Slagbag were heading back down the steps, side by side, their fluids replenished and their bottles filled, Slagbag said:

"I really hate those I and E bastards."

"Same here," Snash replied.

"Tarting everything up," Slagbag said. "All that shit about 'History' and the 'Inevitable.' 'We make what happens happen.' What the Hell is that? I mean, there's those that whip and those that get whipped…"

And those that those that whip can't catch, Snash thought, although he knew just what Slagbag was talking about.

"Nice and simple," Slagbag went on. "Everybody knows where they stand." He poked Slash with an elbow. "Thought you played him nicely, though."

"I did at that."

"Let's go find ourselves some spot where we can hide for a bit."

"Sounds good."

Going down below the I and E floors, they came to a level that was vacant due to construction, although there was no work going on at the moment; working their way well back through the corridors, they'd just found a likely spot in a dark empty chamber when Snash asked Slagbag:

"Ever seen the outside?"

"Outside of what?"

"The fortress. Mount Adamant."

"No," said Slagbag.

"I'd wager, if we keep going, we'll come to a window or something. Let's find some place where we can look out."

"Why would we want to do that?"

"I don't suppose we'll know until we give it a try."

"What if we're spotted? You know who's out there, don't you? The bleedin' Black Thirteen, flying around on their nasty great fish?"

Snash nodded, thinking: *Gage Ghouls*. Princes once, of Humanor, they'd accepted magical gauntlets from Serpentar, only to fall under the power of the master gage, the Gauntlet of Dominion, and their mounts were giant winged sharks; after mountains had risen beneath the ancient oceans of their ancestors, the fish, adapting over long eons, had taken to the air...Snash didn't know why that particular fact had been imparted to him, although he thought it was intriguing...

"I saw a sharkrider once," Slagbag went on. "This was before my stint as a baby-driver...I was way down in the main shaft, motivating some hod-carriers...sometimes the ghouls fly down there, just to spook everyone. Down comes this bastard on his fish and just hovers in the chimney, staring at us...we all just about wilted, but once he left, everyone worked like mad...Have to admit, it was just what was required. No slogans, just good old honest fright."

"I could do without the fright too," said Snash.

"Who wouldn't? Fright's *clean*, that's all. Compared to slogans. More honest...Of course, if I could get away from the whole lot, I'd do it in an instant. Go off and set up on my own. But there's no chance of that, is there?"

"Isn't that the same as saying you *do* have to bow to the inevitable?"

"Maybe. Just between you and me. But I don't need some pus-sucking fatskull to tell me. Or to tell me I've got to like it. Or that it's better than water. Got it?"

"Got it," Snash said. "I'm still going to try and take a look outside, though."

Leaving Slagbag behind, he headed farther in the direction that they'd been going...he began to hear great cracking and rumbling sounds, and saw a hanging hide sheet, a gap in the middle of it with red light (and intermittent white flashes) coming through...Snash went and looked out.

Up till then, his only glimpse of sky had been that dark circle at the top of the Spike's central shaft, but there was a lot more to see now, a solid ceiling of red-lit cloud. The glow was coming from below, lava, he guessed, although his view was blocked by the semi-circular court extending before him, the top of a large bartizan. Smallish black creatures---the name *grawks* came to mind--- on two legs were moving about or sitting, but as Snash thrust his way through the gap in the hide, they all grawked, bounded into the air, unfolded pinions and flapped away.

Flinching at the thunder, grimacing at the lighting-flashes, he went some distance out onto the bartizan, then turned and looked back towards the tower, which, looming up against the red-lit sky, seemed to lean over him, thousands of tiny red openings showing in it sides, like eyes. Every time the lighting flashed, the red lights seemed to go out, turned into little black holes in blanched stone. Clinging to the Spike's sides, or rising beside it, were many lesser spikes, some rising to a point, others with rounded tops...as for the top of the main tower, it was lost in the clouds, which were going round in a slow swirl.

He turned once more...a rim enclosed the court, and he went out to that. It came up about chest-high on him, and he rested his arms on it and his chin on them. Even though there were truly some vast expanses inside the fortress, he had never seen anything that could approach the vista he saw now, a tremendous flat area studded with small volcanoes, outcroppings and huge boulders, and crawling with huge glowing streams of lava, which were flowing down Adamant's slopes, tingeing masses of drifting vapor. Bounding the plain were serrate dark mountains, fringed by bluish-grey light.

He heard movement behind him...rather to his surprise, Slagbag came up alongside him and rested his palms on the rim.

"I wouldn't have thought it," he said.

"What?" asked Snash.

"That the outside could be bigger than the inside," Slagbag replied.

"Outsides *have* to be bigger than insides."

"I suppose. It's just that it's so *big* inside, you know....but this...it's really amazing. I'm not sure I like it, but I'm not sure it matters. Look at that color off there!"

"What color?"

"There, behind those, what do you call 'em, mountains!"

"That's called *blue*."

"Yeah, I know, it was just on the tip of my tongue…Don't see it too much inside."

"No," said Snash. "Not much of it out here, either. Although, I've heard that the sky's that color."

"*That's* the sky," said Slagbag, pointing.

"Those are *fumes*," said Snash. "And they're *between* us and the sky. Lord Serpentar makes them. To keep everything shadowy. They come up from the lava, but they've been treated---"

"Treated?"

"So they don't darken till they hit the air up there. And most of the poison's drawn off below, by big wheels."

"Big wheels?"

Snash nodded. "They're connected to machines, which turn them. There are shafts that run out from the chimney, and the poison's drawn sideways by the wheels. Serpentar lays spells on them…the poison's full of gold, and it forms a crust on the wheels…When the machines are stopped, teams go and scrape the gold off. Sometimes, Serpentar lays different spells on the wheels, and then he gets diamonds instead of gold. That's why the mountain's called Adamant. *Adamant's* another word for diamond."

"Diamonds are jools, right?" Slagbag asked.

"Right."

"How come you know so much?"

"I listen to the brains, down in the mailroom."

"They talk to you?"

"Not much. But they talk to each other…"

"I've never met a runt like you."

Snash replied: "Lord Khuttarh said there must've been more brains than usual in my compost."

"Want some flesh?" Slagbag said, taking out his flesh-wallet.

"What's it from?" Snash asked, accepting a strip.

"Who knows? At least it's got a lot of salt on it."

They ate a while in silence.

"Glad you wanted to come out here," Slagbag declared, and proffered his wallet again. "Want some more---"

He broke off as a loud screech tore the air.

Looking up, Snash saw a tremendous flying shape swooping round the outside of the main tower, a black shark with fins so big they amounted to wings; steel gleamed on the appendages, out near the tips---blades had been fastened to the edges. Mounted on the monster was a black-hooded figure whose cloak was whipping well back over the dorsal fin, almost to the tall, rudder-like tail.

"Down, down!" Slagbag said.

He and Snash cowered behind the rim…Snash was sure the sharkrider must've spotted them, but whether he hadn't, or had some more pressing errand than punishing a couple of slackers, he didn't come after them…they heard the cry again, but much more distant this time, and when they got up and looked over the rim once more, the rider was nowhere in sight.

"We'd better get inside," said Slagbag.

They headed back across the bartizan, but as Snash neared the arch with the hide hanging from it, he paused, noticing some scratchings on the wall beside.

"'*He Who Is Much Better,*'" he read aloud. "I've seen this several times."

"And a lot of gouges where it's been chiselled out?" Slagbag asked.

"I think. What do you know about this?"

"That I'm not going to work myself up over scratchings on a wall. You can get yourself a one-way trip to the torture chamber for even talking about it."

"Who's he supposed to be?"

"A yark. Someone like us. Obviously, it's complete shit. Serpentar's *real.* Hrag Urshathur isn't."

And with that, Slagbag stepped through the gap in the hide.

"Coming?" he asked.

Snash eyed the scratchings for a few more moments, then followed.

They never did get *used* to running messages up the central shaft, although it got to be less of a torment for them, eventually; they brought more juice and water, and extra salt, and figured out ways to go more slowly without drawing any sanction, such as placing themselves behind columns of heavily armored yarks, men, or ogres. Not that they were always running the Spike; a lot of their deliveries were on the flat, or mostly, down inside the volcano. But one result of all this was that they were acquiring a good working knowledge of the entire fortress, and it was getting harder and harder for anyone to give them bad directions any more.

When Snash was handed a scroll marked "Extremely Urgent," and "For Your Glowing Eyes Only," addressed to the "Lord of the Gage Ghouls, Two Thousandth Floor," he knew that was the very pinnacle of the Spike, even though he'd never been up there---even Serpentar's chambers (which Snash had never been to either) were a level down, but due to the take-off and landing requirements of their flying sharks, the gage-ghouls were stationed right at the top.

Since Snash had never been the whole way before, the ascent proved a very sore trial, even though he and Slagbag had a very slow column of ogres to follow for much of the distance---ogres were always smelly, but these were so awful that Snash had trouble breathing. Moreover, once the beasts turned aside, a column of eastron men came pounding up, not very heavily armored ones, either, and those fellows set a brutal pace. As soon as the eastrons got where *they* were going, Snash and Slagbag simply stopped and sat down on the steps, and it was some time before they could even contemplate starting on up again...Barely forcing their legs to bend and straighten, they managed to get up ten more floors, and *still* weren't at the top.

They were, however, on One Thousand Nine-Hundred and Ninety-Nine...a huge brazen plate on the wall said so.

Serpentar's floor, Snash thought.

A tall pointed arch was set well back in a semi-circular recess, but he couldn't see a door, try as he might---if there was an entrance, it was blocked by what appeared to be a gigantic tangle of steel thorns, interwoven with great bronze snakes. Before the barrier a troop of ogres stood at attention; Snash had never seen ogres, who were generally slouchy, standing erect that way before; armed with huge two-headed axes which they were clutching across their chests with both mitts, the beasts were most intimidating. Blazoned on their armored chests was Serpentar's device, The Prying Eye, a round red orb looking through a magnifying glass.

As Snash and Slagbag stood swaying and panting, a pale tall very thin man with a shaved head stepped out from behind the ogres, blue eyes glinting under his lowering brows...he was clad in a long curious assemblage of studded straps. Attached to his shoulder was a lacquered red-and-black Prying Eye Pin.

"What's your business?" he asked.

"Message for the Shark Lord," Snash said, using one of the ghoul chieftain's many honorifics.

"Then why have you stopped *here*?" asked the man.

"Tired," said Slagbag.

"The Inevitable," the man replied, "does not *believe* in tired...Don't you know where you are?"

Slagbag just blinked and wobbled, but Snash nodded.

"Would you like to see what's on the other side of those thorns and snakes?" the man inquired.

Snash shook his head.

"Then I suggest you keep going," the man said.

Snash plucked at Slagbag's arm, and they resumed the climb. Even though it wasn't very far, that last stretch was murder, after all they'd endured, but finally they came stumbling up onto the broad flat ring that bordered the mouth of the shaft. Strictly speaking, it wasn't the *very* top of the tower---thirteen smaller towers (one for each sharkrider, Snash guessed) were set at intervals around the circumference of the ring like tynes on a crown. Serpentar had been laying off on the smoke a bit---the cloud ceiling wasn't swirling so low, and only swept the points of those smaller spires.

There were yark-sentries at the stairhead, but they were content to let Snash gulp water and suck air for a bit...capping the bottle once he got his spit back, he took the scroll from its pouch, saying:

"For the Shark Lord."

"That's his tower," the guard said, indicating a spire which stabbed so high into the clouds that the top disappeared...Slagbag waited outside as Snash announced his errand and was admitted through a postern.

Floating on the other side was a mass of black fabric...Snash wasn't quite sure he was looking at a figure at first, until he made out a dim sad hooded face, grey behind a veil...on the apparition's chest, if chest it could be rightly said to have, was the sign of a black fin against a red circle....recalling that the Shark Lord's mansion, like those of the other gage-ghouls, was said to be staffed by the spirits of dead men, Snash felt a sensation like a cold rill down his spine.

Beckoning, the phantom led him across the cavernous first floor (whose furnishings and arrangements Snash couldn't quite get a handle on in the gloom, although they struck him as extremely unnerving), through a chamber centered on an immense circular pool filled with green-scummed water, and then onto a stone runway projecting from the side of the tower....out near the end, the Lord of the Gage Ghouls was stroking his gigantic mount (who was standing on four stumpy legs) and seemed to be having a rather animated conversation with another sharkrider. Both wore long black-leather robes; the ghoul chief had a spiny crowned helmet thrust down onto his hood.

"Thy new fish, as swift as that?" he was hissing to his lieutenant as Snash came up.

"Aye, My Lord," said the other.

"Thou art saying thou canst return to your tower, mount, swoop down---"

"I do say it, liege."

At that, the Lord of the Gage Ghouls turned towards Snash, and the runt's knees began to quiver as he got a look at the sharkrider's glowing red eyes, which seemed to be hovering inside his hood, almost as though they really weren't fastened to anything. Indeed, the one on the right began to *rise*, much as if the ghoul were lifting his eye rather than an eyebrow.

"Dispatch, sir," said Snash.

The Shark Lord took it, then said to the other ghoul: "Thou wouldst wager thy *dacha* on the Sea of Hot Mud?"

66

valley; it sure looked as though the sleigh had had made that

Snash had no idea of what a *dacha* was.

"Against the Iron Saddle of Moggoth," the subordinate answered.

The chief nodded. "So be it...let us, then, proceed."

And even before he finished saying *proceed*, he seized Snash and tossed him over the side.

At first Snash was so startled that he didn't even realize what had happened to him.

Then, with the air beating into his face and blowing his lips open, making his eyes tear up and his ears thutter, and the side of the Spike blurring past him on his left, and the spires beneath still distant but getting less so every instant, he began to appreciate the gravity of his situation.

A bartizan whooshed by to the side, and he wondered if it was the one he and Slagbag had gone out onto...approaching from the right, a flight of grawks appeared in his field of vision, as though they were making for the balcony, and he waved his arms to fend them off, but he struck several, and one of them wound up stuck to his face, grawking madly before he peeled it off and flung it over his shoulder.

Passing through a drifting plume of bitter-tasting smoke from a chimney, he saw a tower rushing up, a slender bridge connecting it to the Spike, tiny figures going to and fro upon the span. For a few moments he was certain he was going to strike the bridge, right on the edge; the yarks below lifted their faces, and he thought he heard them taking bets as to whether or not he was going to hit. He recognized a fellow messenger by the name of Rakhrik (a nasty little git), who cried: "Hullo Snash!" even as Snash dropped past, grazing his scalp on a projecting bit of stone. To increase his leeway, he pressed his head against his shoulder, but another projection clipped his ear, and even after he plummetted below the bridge, something struck him on the back of the skull, as if one of the boys up there had pegged something down at him; he clapped palms to the crown and back of his head.

Soon he was well down among the lesser towers, and below there was a horrible thicket of still *lesser* ones, bristling with every kind of point, some *stacked* with impaled dead yarks....it sure looked as though the Shark Lord had made that bet scores of times. There were just plain old points, but also grotesque vanes, and lighting-rods, and sculptures of beaky birds and beasts, and *actual* birds and beasts squatting with their beaks turned up.... he was just about to land face first on a truly awful needle-nosed critter which had just shut its trap and lifted its snout to impale him when...

He heard a tremendous rush---

Even as he felt the first faint tickle of beak-tip on eyelid, a shark, flipped up on its side so it could slip between towers, swept alongside, seized him with one foreclaw, and zipped out between more spires, which looked so close together that Snash couldn't imagine the fish negotiating a passage until it actually did so and started to climb...the Shark Lord's lieutenant had made good on his boast, although Snash didn't feel the least bit grateful to him.

Up and up the monstrous fish soared, alongside the Spike...just before it touched down on the ringlike summit, it dropped Snash to the stone, and as it settled he rolled aside, remaining prostrate until it folded its fins.

As the winner dismounted, up came the Shark Lord, and the two of them paid poor Snash no attention whatsoever as he stood there trembling. He listened to them discussing the finer points of shark-breeding for a few moments before he turned and headed off...Slagbag was, of course, waiting for him outside the Shark Lord's gate, although Snash didn't tell him the whole story until they were safely hidden in a hiding-spot well down inside the Spike.

"And it was all just on a *bet*?" Slagbag demanded.

Snash nodded.

"Someone should toss *them* over the side," Slagbag said. "See how they like it."

"That's cursed rebel talk," Snash laughed.

Slagbag grunted and nodded. "Yeah."

They killed enough time at that spot to ensure that they'd get back to the sorting-station just at the end of their shift. The cafeteria was serving man-flesh with sump-scum and beetles, and Snash, feeling better after he ate, went to bed hoping for a good night's sleep. But he kept dreaming about falling from great heights, and woke dejected and in no mood to be running dispatches, not that he was ever very *much* in the mood.

When the sorters gave him his first parcel, he was pleased to see that it wasn't going up in the Spike, but to one of the few areas downstairs he was still unfamiliar with---he'd need a new map, no *two*. The name above the address was Arachnia Effulgencia, which meant nothing to him, though he was pretty apprehensive about "For Your Multiple Eyes Only." When he asked Slagbag about it, over his shoulder, the motivator didn't have a clue either, not that Snash had expected him to.

"I don't know anyone with multiple eyes," Slagbag said. "Who has multiple eyes?"

"Spiders," Snash answered.

"Who'd send a dispatch to a spider?" Slagbag asked.

Snash checked the return address. "This is from Power and Luminance..."

He knew that *luminance* and *light* were the same thing; spiders were used to light caves; maybe P and L *would* be dispatching dispatches to a spider after all. He seemed to recall that Glolob *had* said something about effulgence....he didn't know what the word meant but he'd never heard it anywhere else. Might Arachnia Effulgencia be one of her titles? If she could talk, might she also be able to read? And wouldn't her cell be in one of the areas he didn't know too well, since he'd only found his way in and out of it once, some time ago, when he was just hours old?

He didn't *want* to believe it, although that never kept things from being true...

There are lots of spiders in Mount Adamant, he reminded himself. Maybe it wasn't going to *her*. Then again, if he was taking it to some *other* giant spider, he might as *well* be taking it to Glolob...but he told himself he just wasn't going to find out until...

He actually did.

Still, as they closed in on the address, he found the surroundings disturbingly familiar---they seemed to be heading in the direction of the monster cellblock....a flight of dank stone steps *exactly* like the one he remembered cinched it for him...as he and Slagbag came out in that corridor lined by those big padlocked steel doors, he was already steeling himself to the thought that he was going to have to deliver mail to Glolob.

"Be very quiet as you go past Seventeen," he whispered to Slagbag, as they snuck along. "He listens."

"You've been here before?" Slagbag asked.

Snash nodded.

"Who's that dispatch going to?"

"A *very* big spider. Behind that door, right at the end---"

They were just in the process of passing Number Seventeen, and not whispering softly enough, evidently; whatever was inside began roaring and tripped every other monster in the place.

But the guard down by Glolob's door, Sluglik's replacement, didn't voice any complaints, having something else entirely on his mind; leaning against the barrier, he was dripping wet and trembling badly, one arm a good deal darker even than yark black and so swollen Snash thought it might pop from a bad look.

"What happened to you?" Slagbag asked.

"Her Ladyship," the guard replied, sweat dripping from his chin. "She bit me."

"What were you doing in there?" Snash asked.

"She said she'd knitted me something...Serves me right."

"I have a message for her," Snash said. "I don't suppose you'd be willing to---"

"Take it in for you? Are you mad?"

Even as Snash looked, the swollen area crept up into the guard's shoulder and over towards his neck.

"I say we slide it under the door," said Slagbag.

"No, you can't," said the guard. "She really hates that. Thinks it's terribly rude."

"Rude?" Slagbag laughed.

"She reported the last fellow who tried it," the guard said, slinging sweat from his brow. "They yanked his eyes and tongue out before they tossed him in with her."

"So our choices are---?"

"Being eaten...or being eaten without your eyes and tongue..." The side of the guard's neck had started to swell; he tilted his head.

"I got in and got out," Snash said.

The guard's eyelids drooped. "Is that so?"

"A while ago...there was another fellow here then...will you leave the little door open---?"

But the guard was sliding down beside that, having just passed out.

Snash took his keys and fitted them until he found the right one. Pushing the door-within-a door open, he asked Slagbag:

"Will you back me up?"

Slagbag eyed him steadily...he was giving it some serious thought. Snash didn't want to endanger him, but...he didn't want to die, either.

"If it wasn't for me," he said, "you'd never have seen the color blue."

Slagbag nodded. "That's a fact...On the other hand, if I ever want to see it *again*..." He shook his head, dismissing the possibility. "Hell, it's not like I have a life to be attached to...I will let you go first, though."

"Can't back me up otherwise," Snash said, and went through into the spiderlight....given the glow, he assumed that Her Ladyship was some distance ahead and above, where a large mass of web near the ceiling was positively ablaze...he and Slagbag got well out onto the floor before he noticed that there seemed to be many different lights, all moving about, and when a couple of baby spiders descended into view below the strands, he realized his mistake. But suddenly a gigantic light flared behind him; he and the motivator turned to see Glolob lower herself swiftly between them and the door. It had never occurred to Snash that she might be able to turn her light on and off.

"Why, if it isn't little Sna," she said.

He bowed tremblingly.

"Who's this with you?" she asked.

"My name's Slagbag," the bull said.

"Charming," said the Spider. "I must say, Sna, I never expected to see you again."

"I have a dispatch for you." Snash said.

"From who?"

"Power and Luminance."

She beckoned with a pedipalp. "Give it here..."

Snash stayed right where he was.

"Come on," she said. "I've got you trapped already. You might as well."

Ready to backpedal at top speed if she betrayed the slightest hint of aggression, he brought her the missive, which she took between the points of two of her forelegs and opened...Snash retreated hastily, and planting himself beside Slagbag, watched as the spider produced a set of wire-rims with multiple lenses and put them on.

"Dear Arachnida Effulgencia, blah blah," she began, reading aloud, "It has come to our attention that your offspring are in short supply...Spider-Rot combined with overall attrition...informed that you haven't been mating lately, and have been eating the males we send...blah blah...in order to ease the shortage, request that you mate with each male at least once...non-compliance will force us to refer this matter to You Know Who Himself ....Yours truly...blah."

After tucking her glasses back from wherever she'd gotten them from, she flung the dispatch at Snash, who ducked it.

"*Mate with each male at least once,*" she said. "*Mate* with them!"

Snash tried to look sympathetic.

"They're barely fit to *eat*" she went on. "If Power and Luminance want my co-operation, they could at least send me some real males, not these little sissies that barely have the nerve to approach me!"

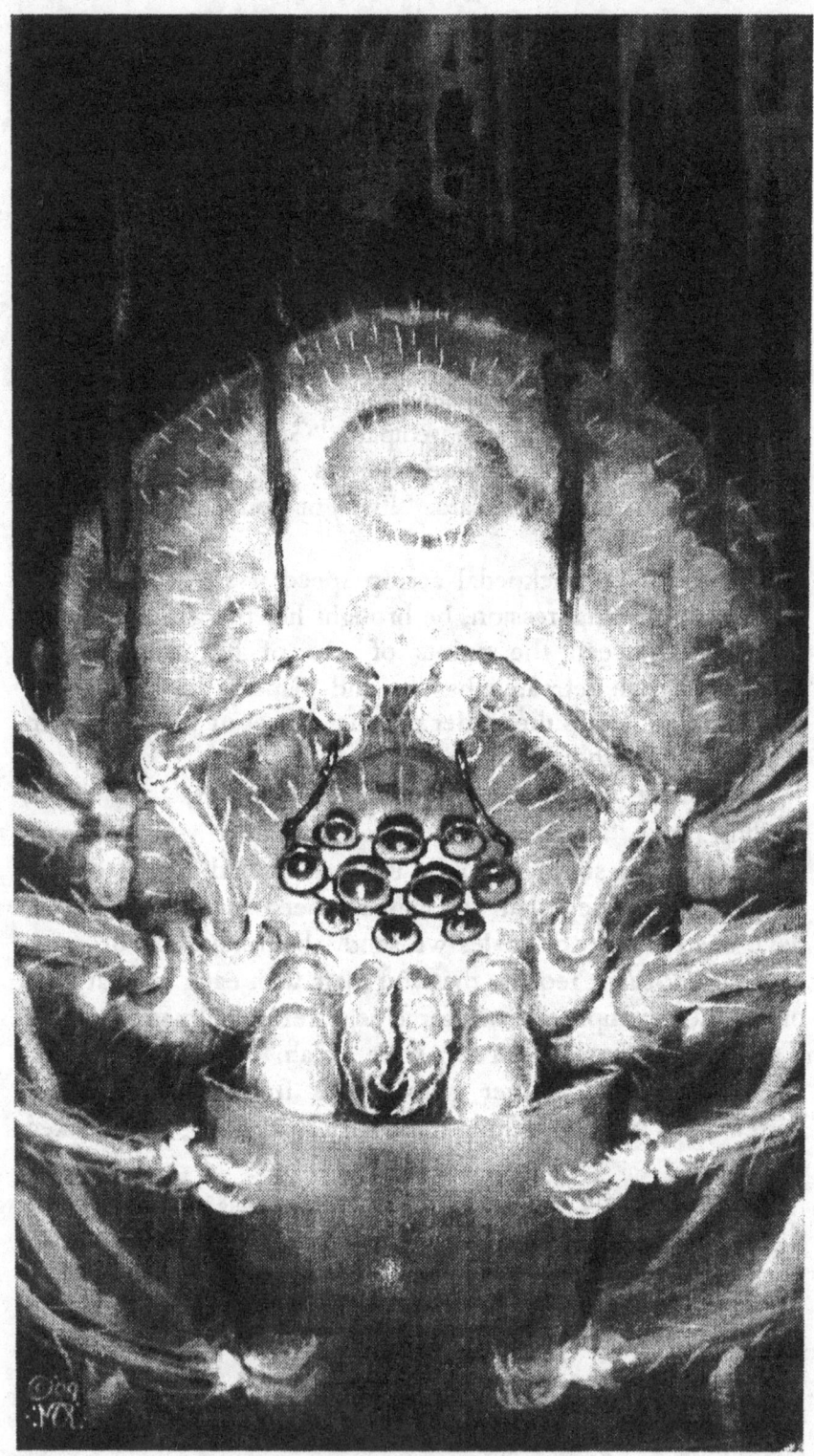

She began to pace back and forth before the door. "Infuriating! Insulting! Simply disgusting! They lock me up, feed me fell beasts on their last legs, then send me mates who'd rather mate with each other, and they expect me not to slake my hunger! I ask you! I *ask* you!"

She stopped, turning towards the yarks.

"You ask us...what?" Snash replied.

"It was a rhetorical question," she answered.

"What if..."

"What if *what*?"

"We conveyed your concerns to P and L?" Snash replied.

"Conveyed my concerns?" she sneered, no small trick for a monster without an upper lip or nose. "You put that oh so nicely, for a yark."

"Thank you," said Snash.

"And, I suppose, in order to have my concerns conveyed, I'd have to let you out of here."

"You would."

She thought a bit. "You don't have anything to write with, do you?"

"Sorry," he said. "Although...I've got a good memory, and I'm quite sure I could relay the gist."

"To think that I'd be reduced to this," she said. "Entrusting a runt with my gist."

"However did you find yourself in such a situation, My Lady?" he asked.

"I was tricked," she replied. "By Serpentar. He put out the word that there was a second Larch of Effulgence. But it turned out to be a phony. I started sucking, and before I realized I wasn't getting any sap, down came the net."

"I'm so sorry," said Snash.

"Save it," she answered. "Just deliver my message."

She drew her huge bulk aside.

Trying not to hurry *too* blatantly, Snash and Slagbag went by her and out the door, which they closed and locked.

"Where's the guard?" Snash asked. "Didn't think he would've gotten much of anywhere..."

"Didn't," said Slagbag, jerking a thumb farther up the

hall, where the torchlight was glistening on a lot of dark stuff...yark blood was a tarry-black, and in spite of the fact that the guard had burst and splattered walls, floor and ceiling, the mess wasn't particularly easy to see.

"Aah," said Snash. It was a while before they worked up the stomach to thread a path between the puddles, and the bits and straps of poisoned meat.

Given that a report from Glolob had doomed that "rude" messenger--- the one who'd slid the missive under the door---Snash assumed that her discomfiture must count for something with the higher-ups, and decided he'd *better* relay her concerns to Power and Luminance; Slagbag found his arguments convincing enough, and so they went. P and L was up in the Spike, but not very far, not much more than a short jog. But when Snash and Slagbag got there, they had a hard time finding a brain who'd speak to them (let alone the right brain to speak to) and the one they did find had a good laugh at them.

"Nobody cares if she's discomfitted or not," he said. "If they cared, they wouldn't be sending her those little sissies, would they? It's someone's idea of a joke, if you ask me. There's no spider shortage. Not for the next hundred years. She's just mad about something, and someone's pulling her chain."

Snash said: "The guard at her door---"

"Said what?" the brain demanded.

"That she reported messengers if they were rude."

"*Rude?*"

"That didn't go right in and deliver the message."

"As opposed to?"

"Sliding it under the door."

"Is that how he talked you into going in there?"

Feeling like an idiot, Snash looked down at his feet.

"Get out of here," said the brain.

But just at that moment, Snash heard a lot of bumping and slithering from a ventilation-port in the side of the wall, followed by a runtish voice crying: "There he goes!" and a good deal of "*scheissing*" and "*ach* sss-sing," getting louder by the moment; suddenly a pale greenish body came rolling out of the port and dropped to the floor, unfolding into Glargle the instant it struck. Gasping, he looked about, saw Snash, Slagbag, and the brain, and cried "*Nein! Nein! Raus, mein liebchen! Raus! Schnell! Ach!*" And with that, he scrambled on all fours through the door, just before two runts dropped out of the vent and asked the brain:

"Where'd he go?"

The brain pointed to the door, and they sprinted out in hot pursuit.

"What in Hell was all that about?" Slagbag asked.

"That," said the brain wearily, "Was Glargle."

"But what is he?"

"No one seems to know. But whatever he is, he's crazier than a garderobe rat. Word is he got one of his skeletal long-fingered hands into Lord Serpentar's gauntlet, two thousand years ago...His Lordship got it back about fifteen minutes later, but it drove Glargle completely mad in the meantime...Glargle's been trying to steal it ever since. Actually snuck in here a couple of times when security was more lax, although he was chased out soon enough...no one had seen him for about a hundred years. But now he's gotten back in, and he's sneaking all over the place. He's been haunting our vents for a while now...some say it's an omen of the End."

"The End?" Slagbag asked.

"Yes, it's the opposite of the Beginning," the brain said. "Didn't I tell you to get out?"

Later that shift, they got a dispatch for the Warden of The Nail, which was the tallest of the lesser towers; set upon a crag rising from the shoulder of the volcano, connected to the Spike by a bridge, it served as Serpentar's maximum security prison, and word was that it was full of all sorts of very dangerous customers, although no one knew exactly who or what they were.

"Know what?" said Snash to Slagbag, "I got this scrape---" He indicated the one on his scalp,"---on the side of this bridge, when the Shark Lord tossed me off the top of the Spike. One inch to the side, and I'd have clipped the edge...I bet the top of my head would've flipped right off, like a lid."

"Yeah, you're a lucky little bastard, you are," Slagbag said.

They were almost across the span; ahead, the portcullis was going up, and out on some errand came Rakhrikh, the runt who'd said, "Hullo, Snash," as Snash dropped past the bridge.

"Hullo, Snash," he said again.

"Did you throw something at me?" asked Snash. "While I was falling?"

Rakhrikh laughed. "Did it hurt?"

"What was it?" asked Snash, turning as Rakhrikh passed him.

"Bit 'o pave," said Rakhrikh, pointing downward---

Just before Slagbag brought the butt-end of his whip down on the runt's pate.

"Oww!" cried Rakhrikh, clutching his head.

Snash turned back around. The portcullis was still up; he and Slagbag went through.

"Parcel for the Warden," Snash said, showing it to the sentries, a pair of eastrons wearing armor made of small square plates laced together.

"There's a big round room up the hall," one said. "Take the stair...checkpoint at the top. The boys there will tell you where to find him."

Since Serpentar's human henchmen were nowhere near as given to malicious jokes as yarks, Snash didn't see any reason to mistrust the directions; leaving Slagbag with the sentries, Snash proceeded along a shadowy passageway with a vaulted ceiling, from which decorative stone stalactites depended like black fangs. At the end the runt came to the circular chamber that the easterner had described---a stairway wound round its wall, and Snash headed up.

He was about halfway to the top when he heard voices---human and yark--- crying: "'Ere now!" "What's this?" "Who let 'er out?" "Mind 'er damn flute!"

But all that stopped as a swift sweet dextrous tootling, quite unlike anything that had ever gotten into Snash's ears, started up; there were sounds like armored bodies falling, and weapons clanging on a floor, and Snash began to feel lightheaded, and stopped where he was, somehow sure that if he went any closer to the tootling, he'd black out completely.

Before long, though, the music stopped; sitting on the steps, still lightheaded, he heard a bunch of rummaging...getting to his feet, he staggered further up, the effects of the flute-playing wearing off rapidly once he got his legs moving. Almost to the stairhead, he saw a faint golden light playing above it, and caught, along with the rummagings, a swishing as of long soft garments. He halted, wondering if he really wanted to see what was happening; but then a high-pitched, silvery voice, once again quite out of his experience, said: "Oh, for goodness sake, where is it?" and he simply had to look.

But when he peeked over the top, all he saw was unconscious men and yarks lying on the floor; close to the edge, one of the men was a very thin bald hawk-nosed fellow, in the crimson robes of one of Serpentar's human wizards. The light, which was moving back and forth, seemed to be coming up from behind the counter of the checkpoint that the eastron had mentioned. Snash crawled over the top of the steps, went through a gap in the counter, and...

Was stunned by the loveliest vision he'd ever seen...indeed, since he'd never seen *anything* lovely before, (aside from that little patch of blue sky beyond the mountains, maybe) he was stunned even more than he would've been otherwise.

Clad in a long white lacy flowing garment that was vaguely translucent but not in the least indecent, a blonde fay-woman (he knew she wasn't human by her pointed ears and the feelers on her forehead) stood up tall and straight even as he looked at her, shaking her golden locks in frustration, having rummaged unsuccessfully beneath the counter, or so he guessed. Tucked into her girdle was a flute, fashioned perhaps out of bone and inscribed with flowing letters....Heart racing with a longing he didn't understand, Snash loosed a sigh.

Immediately she was aware of him, and reached for the flute at her belt as though it were a weapon. but when she saw the expression on his face, she seemed to realize that she had nothing whatsoever to fear from him, and asked, in her wonderful voice:

"You wouldn't know where the spell-book is, would you?"

"Spell-book?" he replied, not having any idea of what she was talking about, but hoping desperately to hear a few more lovely words from her.

"The one for the cells," she said. "I managed to break the spells on *mine*, but I need to let everyone else out, in a hurry."

"And there's a book that tells you how?" he asked.

"Don't you know anything about it?" she asked.

"I'm just a messenger---"

Hearing that, she fell to searching again, going through various volumes stacked up below the counter.

"Did you search the guards?" he asked, hoping *so* to be helpful.

"None of *them* would have it," she answered.

"What about the redrobe?"

"He *should've*," she said. "But he didn't..."

She continued looking beneath the counter.

Snash looked at the wizard, thought he detected a rectangular bulge in one of the man's wide red sleeves.

"Did you search his *sleeves?*" Snash asked.

She seemed not to hear him, so he looked for himself...there *was* a book, in a kind of pocket.

"Is it small?" he called.

"Eh?" she asked.

He showed it to her. "This it?"

"Yes!" she cried, coming out through the gap in the counter. Crouching down on the other side of the wizard, she reached for the book, but just then the man growled and started to get up...taking the flute from her belt with a swift but very ladylike movement, she rapped him smartly, and the instrument was evidently much heftier than it looked, because he slumped right down, even though the flute broke in two.

Then she reached for the book once more.

But before Snash could turn it over, a troop of yarks appeared out of an archway, and yelled when they saw all the men and yarks on the floor, and the Fay-woman free; she whirled and tried to put them all to sleep, but of course her flute was broken, and she didn't even have the end with the mouthpiece...as the guards closed in on her, she backed up, managed to get over the wizard, but tangled up on Snash, and the two of them went rolling down the stairs. Half-wrapped in white fabric, which was swishing the whole while, he took a number of dreadful knocks, particularly on the knees, elbows, and head, and squeaked in pain at each impact; the Fay-lady, on the other hand seemed barely put out by her unceremonious descent, and only came out with an occasional "Ooo," and "Ah." Still, when it was all over, and they banged to the bottom, she was out cold, though he wasn't quite.

His hand was underneath him, and there was something in it...he still had the spell-book.

He could hear the guards clattering down the steps...without thinking, he raised himself up a bit, thrust the book inside the neck-hole of his tunic, then lay back down as the other yarks collected about the escapee, squatting and leering.

"Garn!" one cried.

"You said it, Gorlub!" another replied.

"All that white *flesh*," said Gorlub.

"Yeah!" said the second.

"Makes me want to...want to..."

"*Eat* her?"

"Well, of course, Batghash, goes without saying---"

"Eat her *alive*?"

"Yes, but---"

"What?"

"I want to *do* something...*else*."

Batghash and the others laughed filthily, as if they knew just what Gorlub was talking about; Snash was skeptical, however, since he had been filled (by her) with a yearning that was almost agonizing, even as it left him without a clue about how it might be satisfied.

"We could drool on her!" one of the other yarks suggested.

"Goes without saying as well," said Gorlub. "But---"

"What then? Pinch her? *Tweak* her?"

One after another, getting very worked up, they began to shout suggestions:

"Hang her in chains."

"Scream at her!"

"Make faces!"

"Eat her food right in front of her!"

"Scrawl nasty sentiments on her walls!"

"Hit her with a dead toad!"

"Hit her with a live toad!"

"Blow our noses on her!"

"Put on her clothes and jump around like idiots!"

"Fart in her cell!"

"Show her our butts!"

"Show her our butts and *then* fart in her cell!"

"No, no," said Gorlub, shaking his head. "There's something else."

"What?"

"You do it with females," Gorlub said.

"What's a female?" Batghash asked, whereupon Gorlub slapped him and nodded towards the lady, snarling:

"*That's* a female, you splat of Grawkshit!"

"And what are we?" Batghash asked.

"We're *yarks!*" said another, hopping.

"Yeah," said Gorlub. "But we're all male, see?"

"And there's something males do to females?" Batghash asked.

"Besides showing them our butts?" asked that other yark.

"Yeah," said Gorlub. "But...it's making my head hurt, trying to think of it."

"Well, while you're working on that," said Batghash, "let's show her our butts."

"No point till she's awake," said Gorlub.

"Oh, right," said Batghash sourly.

Gorlub seemed to become aware that Snash was

looking at him, and turned. "*You* don't know what males do with females, do you, runt?"

Snash shook his head.

"Is she dead?" came a voice from up the stairs. Snash saw a red-robed man---not the same fellow that the lady had cold-cocked---coming down the steps.

"No sir, Warden," said Gorlub, he and all his comrades rising...Snash got up as well, the book sliding down inside his tunic, as far as his belt...he moved his parcel-bag over to cover the bulge.

"And how exactly did Princess Luvliel get out of her cell?" the Warden asked.

"Don't know, sir," said Gorlub. "But when we came to the guard-station, everyone was down, and there she was, loose...we charged her, and---"

"I tripped her," Snash broke in.

Gorlub glared at him, then told the Warden: "She was already backing towards the stairs---"

"But I made sure she backed over *me*," said Snash.

The Warden glanced at Gorlub. "Is that what happened?"

"More or less," Gorlub said.

"What's your name?" the warden asked Snash.

Snash told him.

"Messenger, eh?" the Warden said...his glance lingered a moment too long on the parcel-bag...because of the book, there was a space between the bag and Snash, and of course the Warden had noticed...Snash cursed himself...how could he have been so stupid?

But the Warden only said: "You one of Khuttarh's boys?"

It was a moment before Snash realized that he hadn't been found out...then he opened the bag, said, "Brought a parcel for you," and handed it over.

The Warden gave it a cursory glance. "You like working for Khuttarh?"

Snash said nothing.

"Sick of running the Spike?" the Warden asked.

The question raised a whole series of possibilities...

If you worked in the Nail, Snash thought, *You'd be near Her...Maybe you could figure out how to use the book, let her back out...*

"Do you need any runts, sir?" he asked.

The Warden shook his head. "Not really. But you deserve some reward, I think...In the meanwhile, though, I have underlings to chastise...Be off."

Off Snash went.

Chapter 6: Yarks of Interest

Later, while Snash and Slagbag were off shirking in the Needle, an abandoned tower that had served as the maximum security prison until the Nail was built, Snash told the motivator what had happened, and even showed him the book. But, after listening to the whole story without a single interruption, Slagbag, unable to control himself any longer, finally burst out:

"Has your brain gone wormy? Is *that* it?"

"Maybe," Snash conceded.

"What are you going to do with that book?"

"Keep it in my locker."

"But what do you *want* with it?"

"Maybe I can use it to help *her*, somehow."

"What's she to you?"

"She's just..."

"Just?"

"So lovely."

Snash got such a perfectly idiotic look on his face that Slagbag just wanted to smack him, and barely kept himself from doing it, saying instead: "You are daft, daft, daft."

"You don't understand," said Snash.

Being told this didn't make Slagbag understand any better. "You're damn right I don't."

But Snash went on: "She'd make you feel...the way you feel when you're looking at the color blue. She's like that."

"Blue?"

"No, no...She's all pink and golden and white."

"Striped?"

"No, she has pink skin, and golden hair, and a white garment that you can kind of see through, but it isn't at all indecent."

"What's *indecent*?"

"I'm not sure..." Snash paused. "Also, she has this *light* about her. I could see it even when she was down behind the counter."

"What counter?"

"It's not important."

Slagbag eyed him narrowly, then shook his head. "You

are *begging* for the axe, you know that?"

"Maybe."

"For one thing, you shouldn't have told me. How do you know I won't go straight to the higher-ups?"

"You wouldn't," Snash said.

"I could get *myself* a promotion."

"Nah," said Snash.

"Why wouldn't I?"

"We're mates."

"Are we?" Slagbag asked.

"Well, since we don't have a word for *friends, mates* will have to do."

Slagbag weighed this point. "I suppose. But...even if we are mates, *you're* going away."

"What do you mean?"

"You're going to leave me. Get a transfer."

"Oh, right," said Snash.

Slagbag asked: "What am I going to do?"

Looking as though he felt very sorry for him, Snash shrugged. "You know, I hadn't even thought about that."

"I don't *want* another runt," said Slagbag.

"Ah, cheer up," Snash said.

"Why should I? I'm a slave. My master's Evil Incarnate. I have to run up and down inside a two-mile high *smokestack*, and the best runt a motivator could ask for is about to be taken away from me and replaced---no doubt---by a shitty runt that's no good at all."

"Well, how about this?" Snash asked. "The Warden said he didn't need any runts...what do you bet he'll forget all about me?"

"Think he might?"

"The Higher-Ups don't care about us."

"But yarks *do* get promoted, sometimes."

Snash nodded. "But I've got a hunch that nothing will come of it."

"Of course," Slagbag said, "maybe the Warden will figure it all out, and you'll get a transfer to the back of a compost-wagon." He paused. "Me too."

"There's that."

"Tell you what, though. You might do better hiding that book someplace other than your locker. Somewhere in here, maybe."

"Good idea," said Snash. Looking about for a likely spot, they found a crack in the wall of an old armory; all the weapons were gone, but the racks were still there, and after Snash put the book in the crack, he and Slagbag moved one of the racks in front of the fissure. Then they went back down to the mail room.

Snash soon had cause to be glad he'd hidden the book up in the old prison; the following night, as he awoke for his shift, he came down to find two brains with Burning Curiosity badges, (which showed the Eye of Serpentar glaring through a doorway at a tiny cringing figure) searching his locker.

"You Snash?" one asked.

Snash nodded. "What's wrong?"

"Where is it?"

"Where's what?"

"The book."

"What book?"

"All right, have it your way...Where's your motivator?"

"I meet him at the mail room."

"Let's go."

They headed off with him.

"Snash?" Slagbag asked as the three of them came up.

"You're coming with us," the brains said.

"Where?"

"Burning Curiosity. Lose the whip."

They went to the Spike, where, listening to the brains complain to each other, Snash learned that they'd just been transferred to the Main BC Office from a lesser branch lower down, and weren't used to the stairs; as soon as they were reduced to a truly laughable plod, they requisitioned a whip from a passing motivator, and ordered Slagbag to lash them with it. Snash stayed well out in front, listening to the cracking of the whip, and their yelps of pain; staggering to the door of the Main Office, they took the whip away once they recovered (it was a while), and without a word of gratitude to Slagbag for his services, got behind the motivator and Snash and followed them inside. A clerical brain looked up wearily from a writing-desk, while a couple of ogres glowered nearby, arms crossed on their massive scaly chests.

"What have we here?" the scribe asked.

"Yarks of interest," said one of the brains who'd brought Snash and Slagbag.

"What investigation?"

"Five Hundred and Three."

The scribe looked at Snash. "Name, class, rank, number."

Snash gave them, and the Scribe scribbled them down. After Slagbag gave his, the ogres came forward, and Slagbag was tucked up under an armpit as though he didn't weigh anything at all; even as Snash marvelled at Slagbag being thrust there so effortlessly, the other ogre locked a thickly callused, all-but bone-crushing grip around Snash's arm, and he was slung face-down over a massive shoulder, which was none too comfortable, particularly once the ogre got going, since the creature's scales were like great warts or studs....the brute's every movement made Snash's chin scrape against the lumps, which seemed to have even smaller lumps upon them, apparently the better to abrade him.

On both sides of the hall were wooden doors, banded with iron...already very low and squat, they got much squattier farther along, and Snash guessed they were the doors of cells for runts, a surmise soon confirmed when he found himself inside one of the little smelly holes, where there was barely enough headspace for him to sit up. Holding his knees, chin upon chest, he waited in the darkness, simply assuming that he was doomed, and that someone at the Nail must've seen something, or simply must've figured it all out. He wasn't much worried for himself; he was much more concerned about Slagbag, and he wished he'd never revealed anything to him.

But as for Luvliel, he couldn't quite convince himself that he should've acted differently...thoughts of her overwhelmed all his arguments...every detail of her appearance kept running through his mind, the pointed ears, the feelers, those bright blue eyes, the silky blonde ringlets, that wonderful translucent fabric, and above all the *glow*...he fondled every word she'd ever said to him, especially, "You wouldn't know where the spell-book is, would you?"

Repeating her name was also very soothing.

Luvliel, Luvliel, Luvliel, he thought, and lulled himself to sleep in that stifling cramped space.

He had no idea how much time had passed when the door swung open, and a great vambraced ogre-arm reached in, seizing him with a blunt-clawed four-fingered hand; moments later, he was slung over a shoulder again, and the beast was carrying him along the hallway, muttering to itself about "stinky soup" in a low, muzzy voice. Since there were about twelve different sorts of Stinky Soup---Snash preferred the kind with chunks of leech--- Snash wondered which variety the ogre was going on about, although he felt a bit too drowsy to ask him.

When he got to the interrogation room, though, Snash's head cleared pretty quick---it was the barking more than anything else. About the width of a breeding-pit, there was a hole in the floor in the middle of the room, and the barking was coming from that---a brain wearing elbow-length leather gloves and a leather apron told the ogre: "Show him," and the lumbering monster unslung Snash from his shoulder and dangled him out over the pit. It was full of small but extremely muscular canines with hairless white skin and oversized pointy-snouted heads that looked fully a third the size of their bodies...seeing Snash dangling above them, the creatures began to leap straight upwards, snapping at him with frothing jaws lined with double rows of long sharp fangs.

"Ever heard of pit-wolves?" the brain asked.

Swinging by the arm, Snash shook his head desperately.

"Well, *that's* what they look like," said the brain, pointing. "This is our first go with them...thought we'd give them a try. They're supposed to be better than pit-hogs---"

Snash *had* heard of those.

"---Superior leaping characteristics. Don't know if it'll make that much difference, though…" The brain signalled the ogre, who promptly set Snash down on the edge…then a bull extended a gaffing pole over the pit. Suspended from chains that hung from pulleys on the ceiling were two harnesses, one runt-sized…the bull snagged the smaller rig and pulled it over, then cinched Snash into it and gave him a shove. As Snash swung back and forth over the pit, staring down at the little naked wolves with their gaping, snapping oversized jaws, the brain said:

"My name is Ripsnag, and I'll be your interrogator tonight."

He nodded towards the bull, who went over to the wall, unhooked Snash's chain, and payed out about a yard of slack…as Snash jerked to a halt, something on the back of the harness popped, and he tipped forward, as though whatever fastened the chain to the harness was now less securely fastened itself.

"Don't make 'em like they used to," Ripsnag laughed. "Is there anything you'd like to tell us?"

"Like what?" Snash cried.

"What happened with Princess Luvliel?"

"How she escaped, you mean?"

"Yes. How *did* you arrange it?"

"I didn't have anything to do with that!"

"Really?"

"I came to deliver a message."

"To the Warden?"

"To the Warden."

"Had you ever been to the Nail before?" Ripsnag asked.

"No---"

Ripsnag nodded to the bull again, who lowered Snash another yard, whereupon something else behind him popped, and he tipped forward even further, although his feet *did* swing up, and so were not as close to the pitwolves as they might've been otherwise…

"Are you *sure*?" the interrogator asked.

"They keep a log, down in the mail room," Snash

answered. "Check it. That was the first time I ever delivered anything to the Nail."

"Do you know a runt named Rakhrikh?"

"Yes."

"Did you speak to him on your way into the Nail?"

"Yes."

"About what?"

"Him hitting me with a rock."

"When?"

"I was tossed off the top of the Spike by the Shark Lord."

Ripsnag laughed. "*You* were tossed off the top of the Spike by the Shark Lord?"

"Yes."

"Why would he bother with that?"

"Haven't you ever seen all the yarks impaled on the tower-tops below the Nail?"

"Actually, I don't get out much."

"The Sharkriders make bets with each other," Snash continued. "They toss yarks down, and see if they can catch them."

"What a vivid imagination you have, little fellow," said Ripsnag, and nodded to the bull a third time.

But before Snash could be lowered any further, a voice from the shadows on the right said, "Hold," and the bull paused....Eyes straining into the gloom, Snash made out a seated black figure, eyes burning red in the darkness of a hood. Ripsnag went over and bowed...Snash heard whispering. Then Ripsnag said, "Very good, My Lord," and returned.

"So Rakhrikh hit you with a rock?" he asked Snash.

"As I dropped past the bridge."

"But you and Rakhrikh go back a bit, don't you?"

"I knew him down in the mail room. But I hadn't seen him since he was transferred...Until I dropped past him, that is."

"When you worked in the mail room with him, were you...*mates*?"

"I hated him," said Snash. "He was always playing jokes on me."

"Didn't you meet him when you ran the Spike?"

"No."

"Come on...the two of you discussed Princess Luvliel."

"I told you, I hadn't seen him since---"

Ripsnag broke in: "He never mentioned a...*book*?"

"I have no idea what you're talking about---"

"Broggduf," said Ripsnag to the bull, who lowered Snash yet again...nothing else popped in the harness, but the pit-wolves were in a snarling, snapping frenzy, drops of their slabber striking the runt's feet.

"We've already questioned your motivator," said Ripsnag. "He says you met with Rakhrikh more than once, in the Spike, and that you discussed a book."

"I don't believe it," Snash said.

"Oh," said Ripsnag, "I assure you, he did."

"You're trying to trick me."

"How do you know that?"

"Because I never met with Rakh---"

"Broggduf," said Ripsnag, and down went Snash still further, until the pitwolves were nipping at the tips of his toes.

"I'll ask you one more time," said Ripsnag. "What is the nature of your association with Rakhrikh?"

"We weren't mates!" Snash cried. "He treated me badly! When I was falling from the Spike, and about to be impaled, he hit me with a *rock!* I never did any plotting with him, and I don't know anything about a book...Doesn't it *matter* that I tripped that princess or whatever she is when she was trying to escape---"

"Enough," said the darker shadow amid the shadows.

"My Lord," said Ripsnag. "Do not trouble yourself. This is a matter for an underling, of humble abilities, such as my own."

"Too humble," said the shadow. "Draw him up."

Broggduff complied, grunting. Chains clinking, Snash ascended in a series of jerks...since nothing else had popped the last time he was lowered he was sure something was going to now, but it didn't. Not having really thought things through, he was relieved, but only until it occurred to him that the sharkrider was about to take a hand.

Rising at last, the ghoul emerged from the darkness, tall and terrible, his swift silent gait the most sinister Snash had ever seen, hands down. Between the fact that the sharkrider had confirmed Snash's story about being chucked off the Spike, and the fact that Burning Curiosity was headed by the Shark Lord himself, Snash guessed that the awful approaching apparition could be no one else...The Right Hand of Serpentar came up to the edge, then stopped, eyes burning in the shadow of his hood.

Enduring that glowing gaze was bad enough; squirming, Snash wished the harness would just drop off the chain so the wolves could get him. But awful as the eyes were at a distance, they got still moreso as the distance *closed*...with a shock, he realized that they had begun to drift forward, out from under the sinister snood. Slowly they floated towards him, until, after a seeming eternity, they were hovering a few inches before his face, one cocked a bit higher than the other.

"Snash," said the eyeless void inside the hood.

"My...My Lord?" the runt replied, heart racing madly.

"Dost thou know where the book is?"

It seemed at first that Snash really needed to answer the question, truthfully at that...the eyes were very compelling...his heart would surely burst if he didn't tell.

But---

Before he could betray himself, he summoned up, without even realizing what he was doing, a blessedly clear memory of Luvliel, interposing the image between himself and the eyes. His heart steadied; terror faded; he was no longer quite sure where he was.

"Snash?" a voice asked. Snash thought, vaguely, that it belonged to the Lord of the Gage Ghouls, although, it seemed strangely un-threatening, indeed, almost uninteresting, as though he didn't quite have to pay attention to it...still, just to be prudent, he decided he'd better make some sort of response.

"What was the question again?" he asked.

"Dost thou know where the book is?"

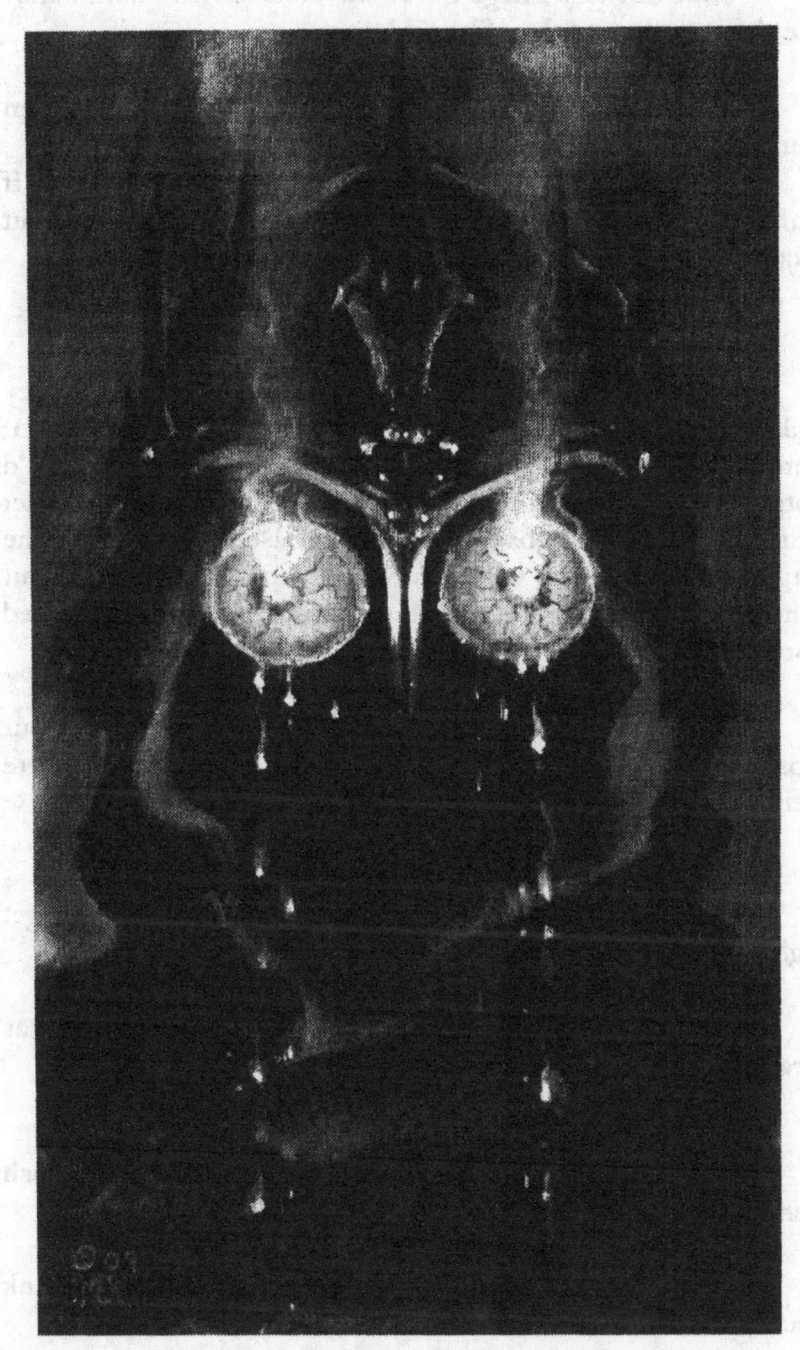

But Luvliel's image never wavered...Snash could barely see the eyes through her. She said:

"What book?"

"What book?" Snash said aloud, lipreading, then remembered nothing after that---

Until he came to on the edge of the pit, with Broggduff unfastening him from the harness...the runt looked about dazedly...he didn't see the Sharkrider anywhere.

"Take him back to his cell," said Ripsnag to the ogre.

Snash was held a good while longer, and although they didn't question him any more, they didn't feed him either; getting very hungry, he was beginning to worry that they'd forgotten about him altogether when a jailer came by and let him out, even as Slagbag was being released from one of the larger cells down the corridor. When they were brought out where the scribe was and told to get back to work, Snash asked for a note.

"A note?" the scribe asked. "What do you mean?"

"A slip," said Snash. "Something we can show our bosses. 'Snash and Slagbag missed work because they were being interrogated,' something like that.'"

The scribe just laughed. "We don't do that."

"Well you should," said Snash. "We'll get in trouble."

"You know, puke-stain," answered the scribe, "I'd get right out of here, if I were you, and count myself lucky."

"Is that so?" asked Slagbag.

"You know how many yarks of interest wind up as dead yarks that no one's interested in at all?"

"How many?"

"A very high percentage."

"Please," said Snash. "Couldn't you just dash something off?"

"Where *did* you get this idea from?"

"Perhaps it's innate," said Snash. "We're not blank slates, you know."

"Then why doesn't everyone ask for notes?"

"Because you kill so many of us off?"

"Get these comedians out of here," said the scribe to an ogre.

"Leaving, leaving," said Snash, and he and Slagbag rushed out the door before the ogre could toss them.

They had another hideout nearby, a rather dangerous one, at the bottom of an old crumbling airshaft, and after making sure that they weren't being followed, they went there. It turned out that Slagbag had gotten off far easier than Snash, who asked:

"They didn't hang you out over pit-wolves?"

"What's a pit-wolf?"

"A wolf---"

"In a pit?"

Snash nodded. "You get hung out over them."

"Nope, nothing like that," Slagbag said. "There were two brains questioning me, and only one of them seemed to think I knew anything. They started quarrelling, and just let me go after a bit."

"You never told them I spoke to Rakhrikh a couple of times?"

"About?"

"The book."

"Never came up."

Snash had expected to hear as much.

Slagbag said: "Now they *did* want to hear about you and Rakhrikh, though. I just told 'em the truth...."

"They think it was an inside job," Snash said.

"What do you mean?"

"That the Princess had help."

"Besides you?"

Snash nodded. "But I'm pretty sure she didn't."

They were silent for a while. Then Slagbag asked:

"So what did they do to you, besides hang you out over pit-wolves?"

Snash told him about the grilling, and the intervention by the Shark Lord.

"His eyes floated *all* the way out of his hood?" Slagbag

asked.

"They did. They were *this* far from me." Snash showed him.

"That's an unsettling detail," said Slagbag. "Although…what do you think would happened if you just grabbed his eyes?"

"I bet it would *hurt*…they look like live coals."

"What if you grabbed 'em and real quick, dashed 'em on the floor?"

"I don't know," said Snash.

"*And* stepped on 'em?"

Snash shrugged.

"Well," said Slagbag, "maybe I just better hope I never have to."

Snash thought this was sound thinking.

Chapter 7: The Yark Lord

Expecting to be taken for questioning again, Snash was pretty jumpy for a while. He suspected he was being followed, and whenever he saw a couple of BC brains, he assumed the worst, and tried to resign himself.

Yet nothing happened. To *him*, at least; word was that the Warden lost his head, but that seemed to have settled matters, as far as the higher-ups were concerned. Snash kept on being worried about the book, though, and had to fight the temptation to go and get it, and hide it somewhere else---coldly considered, the fissure in the old prison was as good a place as any (probably better than most) and if he *was* being followed, he'd simply lead his footpads to the prize.

But despite all the apprehension, he was bolstered by the knowledge that he was capable of extreme nerviness; between helping the Princess, and taking the book, he'd committed his first, definite acts of rebellion, although he had no idea of what to do next.

That was probably just as well, since a crackdown had started---Serpentar himself had declared war on practical jokes, and the whole yark population of Mount Adamant was being terrorized even more than usual. Although Snash felt no inclination to trick his fellow slaves, that didn't ease the pressure on him at all, since there were so many other Snashes he could be mistaken for, *and* it was simply assumed that yarks were tricksters by nature. Even the BC brains and Inspirational Exhorters, who generally suppressed their own tendencies, were under intense scrutiny. Banners with an especially furious-looking Prying Eye and the Slogan, "*He* Is Not Amused!" hung everywhere, and before long, there were lots of dead yarks---with placards around their necks proclaiming, "The Joke's on Me!"--- hanging up too, from hooks projecting from the walls of the great chimney, and over the sides of the bridges that spanned the shaft, and the corpses didn't improve the smell one bit.

For all that, the yarks never really let up on each other---their malice simply manifested itself through informing, rather than tricks. Blokes who would've been knocked over other blokes who'd gotten on all fours behind them were denounced now, as practical jokers; Snash and Slagbag somehow managed to keep out of trouble, but several fellows that Snash knew were taken away and hung up….all in all, it was a bad time, even by Tenebrian standards.

And that was *before* Snash was handed a parcel addressed to Nognomen the Nameless, Serpentar's Chief of Staff.

"Where we off to this time?" Slagbag asked.

Snash showed him the label.

"Doesn't *Nognomen* mean No-name?" Slagbag asked.

"I believe it does," said Snash.

"So, he's No-name the Nameless?"

"Yes."

"But…wouldn't that be his name?"

"I don't know…Not his real one, at any rate. I've heard he forgot that."

"Deliberately?"

"I guess…but ever since he forgot it, he won't let anyone else use it."

"Why?"

"Because then he'd remember."

"But…if he *really* forgot it…How would he *know* if they used it?"

"Maybe you should ask him when we get up there," Snash suggested.

"I'll just wait outside, like I always do," Slagbag answered, and cracked his whip. "Get moving, runt!"

And so they set off….as they reached the Spike, Snash looked up to see a couple of sharkriders spiralling slowly about inside the shaft, one ascending, one descending, obviously with the intent of dissuading any potential practical joker from even *thinking* about it. As Snash and Slagbag were about halfway up, one of the Gage Ghouls took an interest, and reined his fish over to the side. With the sharkrider so close, Snash slowed down so that Slagbag could actually whip him…Wings flapping languidly with a boneless-looking motion, the shark, without any more prompting from its rider, rose alongside the two yarks, turning to follow them, polishing its already-white teeth with a tongue several times longer than Slagbag...it seemed to be laughing under its breath, and its tall tail was swishing through the air. Snash tried to avoid looking at the sharkrider's eyes; he more than half expected them to come floating out of the hood and drift on over, although that never happened...the ghoul was content to keep his eyes inside his invisible head.

This situation continued for some while; Snash could tell that Slagbag wasn't whipping him as hard as he could, but even so, the runt's back was feeling pretty raw by the time the sharkrider decided to go watch someone else.

"See ya," said the shark, and wheeled about as the rider tugged him down and to starboard.

Snash and Slagbag passed the other rider farther up, although he paid them no apparent mind; with both ghouls below, and no one else very close, they halted and took a drink...then Slagbag inspected Snash's back.

"Tried not to hit you too hard," he said.

"I know," said Snash.

"You're not sore?"

"Well, I am," said Snash. "But not at *you*, if you take my meaning."

Slagbag laughed. "You know, all the while that shark was watching us, I was wondering what it would be like to whip 'im, right in the boggly oglers."

"What is it with you and eyes?" Snash asked, thinking the shark's had been more beady than boggly.

"I don't know. But if I thought I could've gotten away with it, I would've flicked that bastard's right out of their sockets."

"Would you have stepped on them?"

"If they'd flown all the way over here? Sure. Like as not they would've dropped down the shaft, though."

"Ah," said Snash. Even though he wasn't all that thrilled with the thought of violence to eyes, the idea of Slagbag stomping on shark-eyeballs (or burning Gage Ghoul orbs) did have a distinct appeal.

From below came the throb of huge wings.

"Time to go," Slagbag said.

They resumed the ascent, and as they neared Serpentar's abode, a terrible oppression began to weigh on Snash; he had felt much the same thing when he passed the Yark Lord's door on the way to the Gage Ghouls' aerie. But now he was further afflicted by the knowledge that he'd actually have to go *inside*; he'd spoken to other messengers that had done so, and though none had gone into detail, they'd plainly been frightened half out of their wits. One had died in his sleep shortly afterwards, while another had simply refused to carry a second dispatch up there, and had been summarily executed; the third had become twitchy, drooly, and incontinent.

Snash was thinking about that third fellow and getting more and more dejected when someone rattled up on his right in a shirt of scale-mail, feet flapping....the mail hung down very low, and the fellow's helmet was bobbling all around. Where it showed, his skin was kind of strange looking; most yark-hide was a shiny brownish-black, but his was a flat blue-black and uneven in tone, as though he'd rubbed himself down with soot. His fangs were all wrong too, sticking clear out of his mouth, and there were bulges under his upper lip, as though he had tucked little sharpened bones up there.

"*Ich bin yark,*" he said, and tapped himself on his armored chest. "*Sehen? Sehen? Ja?*"

Glargle, Snash thought.

Glargle, evidently, read something on his face, and slowed, running alongside him, as though he were trying to decide what to do...finally he simply pressed on ahead.

"Something very strange about that boy," said Slagbag.

Snash said nothing. Since they were getting very close to Serpentar's chambers, he guessed Glargle was harboring some fantasy of getting inside, undoubtedly with an eye towards stealing the Yark Lord's gauntlet. Snash knew he'd benefit tremendously if he raised the alarm---also that he'd suffer all the torments of Hell if it were discovered he'd recognized Glargle and done nothing. But the chance of anyone finding *that* out seemed remote...after all, he'd managed to keep the Shark Lord himself out of his head. Ultimately he chose to let Glargle keep going.

Hasn't done you any harm, he told himself. *And, who knows? Maybe, just maybe, he'll cause some trouble up there…They might not let anyone in, tell you to leave the parcel and get lost…*

Indeed, once Glargle got to the landing and disappeared, off to the side, things seemed to break Snash's way---if the commotion that started up was any indication, Glargle's ludicrous disguise was seen through immediately, and came scrambling down shortly afterwards, shooting past Snash and Slagbag, *"verdammting,"* and *"scheissing,"* his way-too-loose armor flapping madly about him.

But hard on his heels, feet pounding the stairs like great hammers, came a squad of ogres who barrelled down towards Snash and Slagbag as if they didn't care a bit about smashing them to paste in pursuit of their prey, or shoving them over the side…Slagbag darted to the left, flattening himself against the wall, while Snash had no choice but to slip to the right and cower on the brink as that grunting avalanche of armor, muscle and bone rumbled by. One of the thick two-toed feet brushed him below the knees, knocking his legs out from under him, and he toppled onto his hip.

Another ogre was hammering his way; Snash swung his body out and down, hanging on by his claws, his long pointed nose hooked over the edge, the tip of it very nearly getting stamped off before he jerked his head back. He hung for a few moments, swearing, toes knocking against the side of the shaft.

Hang on, he thought. *Hang on, hang on, hang on….*

But the ogres had already passed.

Slagbag came rushing over---Snash saw him looking down with an expression of terrible fright---and then the motivator was reaching with his long black arms, seizing Snash below the wrists and pulling him up panting with terror onto the steps.

"You know," said Slagbag, "I think that was that Glargle bastard, got up as a yark."

"You don't say," said Snash.

As soon as Snash felt up to it, they resumed their ascent, coming to Serpentar's floor. Even though it had seemed to Snash that all the ogres in Tenebria had come thundering down the steps, there were still some standing in front of the thorn-and-snake gate. As the two yarks approached, the ogres didn't appear to pay them any attention at all, but then that pale thin man in the leather stepped out, much as before, except....

For the fact that he had a dark handprint, fingers trailing down over his forehead, impressed into his bald scalp, patches of what appeared to be bone showing through in spots.

"Stop looking at my head," he said venemously.

Snash fixed his gaze on the man's Prying Eye pin.

"What's your business?" Handprint asked.

"Parcel, sir," Snash replied, removing it from his pouch.

"For?"

"Chief of Staff."

Brusquely the man motioned Snash to give it to him, and all the while he was examining it, Snash hoped desperately to be told that Serpentar's quarters were completely locked down, and that he could simply leave the parcel and go. But at length the man said:

"That little sneak who just came up here---"

Without thinking, Snash looked up, his eyes going immediately to the impression in the man's scalp, or rather, to a particular patch of bone visible partway down the middle finger....

"Stop looking at my head!" Handprint snarled.

Snash's eyes went back to the pin.

"Now then," said Handprint. "The sneak!"

"What sneak?"

"The one my ogres chased back down---"

"What of him, sir?"

"Did he speak to you?"

"No," said Snash.

"We heard his voice..."

"He was speaking to himself, sir. In a language I didn't

104

understand."

Straps creaking, the man put his hands on his knees, his light blue eyes drilling into Snash's black ones. "Why didn't you raise an alarm?"

"Sir, it's murder coming up those steps...It was all I could do just to keep my legs moving...I wasn't paying much attention..."

"You noticed he was speaking a foreign tongue."

"And I didn't know what to make of it. So I just kept my mind on doing my duty, being a hobnail on the boot of the future, sir, one cog among many, in a great grinding mass of cogs."

"What about *you*?" Handprint asked Slagbag.

Slagbag snapped to attention. "There is no I in Tenebria, *sir*!"

"And that's why you paid no attention to the sneak?"

"Sir, I was just trying to whip my runt. And be a hobnail on the cog."

"Very good," said Handprint. "You stay here." He gave the parcel back to Snash. "Come on."

"Where am I going, sir?" Snash squeaked.

"Inside. Like a good little cog."

"Aren't you locked down?"

"What, because of that *sneak*? The Machine doesn't stop for the likes of him. The Inevitable is Inexorable."

"There's no way in---"

But Handprint just led Snash between ogres to the wall of thorns and snakes, then said something under his breath, and clapped. There came a weird metallic rustling, or slithering, and the bronze serpents began to crawl sideways through the vines, sliding in and out between the steel barbs and each other...as they disappeared to right and left, apparently into holes in the sides of the arch, openings appeared in the spiny wall, through which Snash could see a pulsating red glow, like firelight. Once the snakes had withdrawn, the thorns, as though they had been unlocked by the passage of the serpents, began to shrink upwards themselves. At first Snash thought they were withering, then realized they were merely *tightening*, with frightful squeals of metal on metal, every gap between points was filled, by other points, all this shifting and compression lifting the hem of the barrier up off the floor.

"In you go," said Handprint, and shoved Snash over the threshold. Hardly had the runt stumbled through when he heard the thorns squealing again, and turned to see the spiny vines loosening, the larger openings closing as smaller gaps appeared. Last of all the snakes slithered back out again, threading the gaps and sealing off the light from outside.

He turned once more. Ahead stretched a wide, low passageway with a shiny floor like black glass, squat braziers with high-mounting flames arranged at intervals along the sides; like the barrier behind him, the walls and ceiling seemed to be made up of densely tangled steel thorns. The mere sight of all that twisted complexity made his head spin…tens of thousands of sharp slightly curved spines, overlapping each other, were silhouetted against the red light at the far end.

Heart in his throat, he started along the hallway…his soles were sticking slightly to the shiny floor, making his feet seem even more leaden, perhaps, than they would've otherwise…his mouth, which was usually terribly dry when he was up in the Spike, felt even more cursedly saliva-free than it had ever felt before. His throat was tight, and each heavy beat of his heart pained him slightly.

As he walked along, he became aware of things moving in the vines on either side. Pausing and peering into the shadows on the left, he thought he made out more snakes, crawling with slow contractions of their muscles through the tangled spiky web. He started walking again and went faster and faster without ever quite breaking into a run.

But as he went in deeper, he noticed that the vines had all changed; indeed, there were *only* snakes now, bronze or whatever, he couldn't tell, huge thick ones with smaller ones coiling around them and branching off, straight out with their tongues protruding, as though the bigger serpents were the creepers, and the littler ones their thorns…worse still, unless his eyes were deceiving him---and he dearly wished they were--- the end of the hall seemed to be….

Receding.

Can't take this, he thought. *Have to lie down and curl up and die.*

He didn't quite know how to handle the dying part, however, and that kept him going; so did the fact that the hall, even as it stretched---indeed, as a *consequence* of its stretching---was also *tightening*, the serpents drawing inwards. Even if he wasn't going to get to the end, he wasn't going to sit still and wait to be multitudinously snaked.

He also reminded himself that couriers *had* to come and go through this horrible passageway, and there wasn't any reason to kill them, at least until they'd delivered their messages, although plainly Serpentar saw some point in scaring them half to death...Snash clutched the parcel to his chest as though it were a talisman.

There has to be an end, he told himself. *The snakes won't get you. You have a* PARCEL, *and you're going to make it...*

He kept repeating all this in his mind, and almost as if his arguments had some sort of power over the hall, it seemed to stop constricting, and its end stopped receding, and he was just thinking he was going to make it out when a great snake, wrapped all around with smaller ones, peeled away from the ceiling, and curled its head back to look at him, stopping him dead.

"Business?" it hissed---even as the word was passing from its fanged mouth, all the smaller snakes took it up too; an instant later, it seemed as though every single snake behind the runt was following suit....a plethora of tubular breezes, exactly the sort of air-currents that might've originated in a host of elongated bronze throats, washed over him...he smelled a strong coppery smell.

"Parcel for the Chief of Staff," he said, and held it up. The snake snaked its head towards it, cocked eyes at it from right and left, licked it, then went back up to the ceiling.

"Come," said a sepulchral voice from the chamber beyond.

Snash crept out of the hallway.

The room was a dark oval, surrounded by a colonnade of low thick pillars, bulging in the middle, that looked as though they were being crushed into the floor. In the middle of the chamber was a writing desk, shaped rather like Khuttarh's but larger and made of steel instead of stone, and more ornate; sitting behind it was a bald figure in black, his back to Snash. On either side of the desk, facing the runt, were two brains, one of whom, looking most impatient, was signalling Snash to come quicker. But the thing that really caught Snash's attention, indeed, dominated the whole room, was the ceiling, or rather, a black point that came down right from the middle of it, directly above the man's head---if for some mad reason the blackrobe had jumped straight upwards, he'd have killed himself outright. Snash had no idea what the point's point was, although it certainly did give one the feeling that the man in the chair had a great deal to be concerned about.

In response to that one brain's gesticulations, Snash sped up, and got almost to the desk before anyone said anything to him.

"For me?" It was that deep voice again...Snash assumed it was the blackrobe's, although the man was still facing the other way.

"Lord Nognomen?" Snash asked, halting.

"I do not answer to that," said the man. Snash blinked---he thought he'd seen something subtle playing across the back of the bald head, almost a suggestion of---

He shook his head, trying to keep his mind on the conversation.

"I meant no disrespect, My Lord," he said. "But I have a parcel here, adressed to Nognomen the Nameless."

"That is a name. And I have none."

It was a moment before Snash responded...again he'd seen those faint shadows, the hint of a face on the naked skin, complete with a moving mouth...

"Yes...well...I see," he fumbled, laboring to keep his voice from drying up altogether. "Will you accept the parcel, though? Sir?"

"Who is it from?"

Snash looked at the return address, and tried not to look at the Nameless anymore afterwards. "The Commander of the Lefthand Tower of the Mouth."

"He of all people should know I have no name," the Chief of Staff replied. "We renounced our names together. It was his idea, as a matter of fact. We were out in the desert, and we made a little makeshift altar to Lord Serpentar..." His voice trailed off, and he seemed to slip into a reverie.

"That's very interesting, My Lord---"

But before he could finish, the Nameless burst right back in: "It's hard enough being nameless without people trying to trip you up!"

"I can see how it might be, sir," said Snash.

"He's always twitting me. Thinks he's more nameless than I am. Wouldn't be a bit surprised if that parcel's empty, just a snare, to trick me into answering to my non-name, *although*... since I've forgotten the *real* one, I suppose my non-name mightn't *be* my non-name after all..."

"Sir, these are very deep waters," said Snash. "But...how *should* your mail be addressed?"

"To the Chief of Staff. I am what I do. I have effaced myself, in the service of My Lord."

Sensing that Nognomen was expecting some sort of flattery, Snash said: "I can barely restrain my adulation."

"Don't bother."

"But...what should I do with the parcel, sir?"

"Oh, bring it here," said the Nameless wearily.

Snash stepped forward and proffered it, assuming that one of the brains would take it, or that the Chief of Staff would turn around. But then, to Snash's astonishment, the C of S extended a hand, across the desk, and the runt realized that Nognomen had been facing him, if it could be called that, all along---evidently, in the course of forgetting his own name, he'd forgotten his own countenance, *literally* effacing himself...via whatever unfathomable vocal arrangement he employed, he told Snash, "You should close your mouth."

Snash shut his gob.

"If I wanted runts to know which way I'm turned," said Nognomen, taking the parcel, those barely perceptable ghosts of his former features playing across his skin, "I would've kept my face."

"Well, *this* runt was most confused, My Lord," said Snash. "Extremely confused, yes indeed. But if you don't mind, I think I'll just be---" He pointed over his shoulder.

"Sendeth me a yark," came a rumbling, sullen, hot voice, washing over Snash as though a furnace door had just been opened. He looked about, trying to see who'd spoken; but there was no one besides him, Nognomen, and the brains...Noname had gone bolt upright in his seat, and his assistants had stiffened too; all three adjusted their garments, the brains looking apprehensively towards their master, as if they thought that he might send one of them. But Nognomen had another idea. Nodding towards Snash, he said:

"You."

In a voice even higher than his squeaky usual, Snash asked: "*Me?*"

As if to answer his question, a gigantic bronze snake-head opened on the other side of the room, jaws blossoming, two long fangs swinging down into place, a forked tongue unrolling out onto the floor.

"He's waiting," said Nognomen.

"That snake?" Snash asked.

"No," said the Nameless.

"Oh," said Snash, cringing with realization.

"Get moving."

"But...What could *He* possibly want with me?"

"Who cares?"

"Actually, My Lord, I care quite a bit---"

"Go," said Nognomen.

Gulping, Snash skirted the desk and crossed the floor, the upper jaw of the yawning serpent-head looming higher and higher above him, metal scales gleaming. Coming to the tongue, he hesitated before going up into the mouth...there didn't seem to be any sort of opening at the back.

"In, in," called the Chief of Staff.

Snash looked round to see the brains making shooing motions at him. He considered flight, but had no illusions whatsoever about getting back through that corridor with the thorns and the snakes...there were other ways out of Serpentar's abode, he knew, but he didn't know how to find them, and even if he stumbled across them, he couldn't hope to get out of the Spike, let alone Mount Adamant....

Might as well go in, he told himself, shrugged, and went

up the tongue. *Maybe it won't be so bad...*

That hope evaporated almost instantly as the mouth started to close; he was already crouching as the roof of the mouth came down on him. He had time for one short, sharp scream before the metal beneath his feet suddenly seemed to soften, and tilted him forward; he rolled towards the back of the mouth, where a great mass of flexible stuff closed around him, tightened, and squeezed him farther in...

Swallowed, he thought, certain he was dead. But then the throat expanded, letting him go, and light opened over him....he was in another snake-mouth, this one facing the opposite direction, and swinging wide.

He was on his feet in an instant; hopping out over the teeth that rimmed the lower jaw, he found himself in another corridor, lined with tall demonic figures up to their bellies in shooting, roaring flames...wings folded on their backs, they stood with their arms crossed over their chests, and their heads bristled with horns. The giants were completely motionless, and Snash thought they might be statues, but by now he knew better than to assume anything about them.

He heard a creaking sound behind him, sensed motion; even without looking, he knew that the snake-head was closing, and a gust of wind thrust against his back, impelling him forward....even though he wasn't sure why he shouldn't get his wretched little life over with, and simply run to meet his fate, he slowed himself down....

Yes, he thought, *your life* is *wretched and it is indeed little, but it's yours....*

He hadn't yet gotten between the statues or whatever they were...since he was heading into Serpentar's sanctum, he wondered if they might be the dreaded Hellrogs, rebel angels who'd fought on Serpentar's side during the war in heaven, and had joined him in exile...he had a bodyguard of twenty.

Snash counted the giants.

Yep, there were ten to a side.

But if indeed they were something more than facsimiles, they weren't revealing it at the moment. Of course, given the snakes, they might *still* be metal, *and* capable of movement...Snash wondered if the real hellrogs were

somewhere else, then wondered why he was bothering with such a thought.

Once he'd gone by the first few, it occurred to him, very forcefully, that the ones behind might be *doing* something back there...the more he passed, the more agonizing the suspicion became...once he got beyond them all, he imagined the whole infernal crew sneaking silently after him on tiptoe, still smoking after having stepped out of their flames.

Then again, he didn't hear anything...surely he would've...they were so big, and there were twenty of them, and it was hard to believe that forty great big feet wouldn't have made some kind of noise...

Then again, the very unpleasantness of the possibility made it seem more likely...his life was simply bursting with horrible facts that didn't deserve to be true. He paused, almost turned, changed his mind, walked on a few paces, stopped again, and actually pulled his one-eighty this time.

Every one of the winged smoking demons was tippy-toeing his way, rubbing their hands and nodding in demonic glee...

"*WAH!*" he shrieked, and shot clear to the end of the hall before any of the ones in front of him could reach out and grab him, or trip him, or do anything else...not caring what awaited him in the next room, so long as it wasn't hellrogs, he got well out into the chamber before he stopped, shivering violently.

Pushed by two bulls, a long iron couch, all sinister swirling motifs upholding black cushions, was rolling towards him on casters, which were squealing like rats. Lounging back languidly into a corner of it, one leg crossed over the other, was an old white-bearded man in white robes about as diaphanous as Princess Luvliel's, although on him the effect was very different, and Snash didn't care for it. The whitebeard was puffing on a shiny black tube that had a shorter smoking white tube thrust into the end of it...smoke was coming out of his nostrils.

"The yark," he said drily, "has arrived, My Lord."

Snash looked about the room. It was domed and very large, and aside from the couch, there was no furniture. There

was, however, a single gigantic round window, set with what appeared to be a great thick lens, against which a dark manlike form, streaked with glowing red, was leaning, as though its face was pressed to the glass...a slowly-writhing reddish reflection moved upon the curving surface.

That's Him, Snash told himself, and would've swallowed if his throat hadn't been so dry.

At first Serpentar seemed to take no notice of the old man's pronouncement, but presently he turned; Snash saw what looked like a single fiery round eye. Hands behind his back, the Inevitable started across the floor at a smooth, unhurried pace.

But he wasn't walking.

He was *floating.*

"I'd kneel, if I were you," the old man told Snash, but with the light of the Prying Eye approaching, Snash was already sinking down. Below Serpentar's soles, two orange reflections were moving over the floor; his legs were red at the feet, and there was a kind of current in them, an ascending flow, that drew Snash's gaze upwards...cooling, apparently, as they climbed the limbs, squiggly vertical lines went from red to black, delineated by glowing fissures, as though whatever was behind them remained ferociously hot. It was a few moments before Snash realized he was looking at something very much like snakes, made of what he couldn't imagine, that had just emerged from a furnace. Rising along the body, they crawled up over the chest, along the neck and up onto the head, sliding at last into the hot gaping eye and vanishing inside ...snakes were crawling into the aperture from the sides and over the crown as well...standing on end in front of the hole was a teeny snake, balancing on the tip of its tail, giving the impression of a slit pupil, only wiggly

The Yark Lord halted a few yards from Snash but leaned forward; blinking in the glare from the eye, feeling very bad indeed, as though his brain were boiling inside his skull, Snash wished he could simply melt, and slip down between the cracks of the paving-stones.

"Riseth," said the hot voice he'd heard---disembodied---in Nognomen's chamber...Snash noticed the fissures on Serpentar's head widening and closing in the same rhythm as the syllables, as if those were escaping though the fiery cracks.

Serpentar began to drift round him, hands still clasped behind his back. On one was a gauntlet, heated a deep sullen red; but the naked hand was glowing more brightly than the gage, about the same shade as his feet. The hot snakes seemed to be emerging from his knuckles and folding over to form his fingers before crawling up along his arms and cooling on the way to his shoulders....

"Ah," said the man on the couch. "If only you could demonstrate on Greydolf. I should love to see that."

"Transform'd twice he cannot be," said Serpentar.

"Pity," said the old man.

"The runt will have to do, Slippriman," Serpentar replied.

"But," Slippriman said, "he isn't wearing a gauntlet."

"No need. The counterfeits, which so convinc'd thy brethren, did draw their strength from *my* gage. Gratify thine eyes with *this*."

Reaching out, Serpentar flicked Snash's cheek with a red-hot armored fingertip. Snash recoiled...but forgot the pain almost immediately. Everything around him seemed to be getting bigger; Serpentar was looming taller, the ceiling rising higher, the walls moving farther back; but then Snash realized he was getting smaller, because the floor was coming closer. And as if that wasn't bad enough, he was also *sagging*, caving in; all the bones in his body seemed to be withdrawing from his extremities and migrating towards his back, forming a great heavy mass there. The fingers in the hand he'd put up to clap against his burn suddenly drooped, and then his whole hand did to, and then his arm....his shoulders were slumping, his legs bowing...his head seemed to be softening and flattening, his eyesockets shallowing. Without any recesses to hold them in, his eyes bulged out onto his cheeks, and he had a sickening, horrifying view of the floor swinging back and forth as his eyes swung on their cords...His legs collapsed, and he collapsed on top of *them*, splaying out, even as his bones kept on forming that thing on his back. His stomach was being pressed against the floor, and he could feel himself growing all slimy beneath it; at the same time, his legs and rear were being sucked up into that mass of bone or whatever it was, which was, apparently, hollow...Snash realized he was forming a shell.

Serpentar asked: "What sayest thou, Slippriman?"

"What *fun*," said the old man. "I should've asked to see it sooner. But...why *snails*?"

"Lacking swiftness, they may be caught without effort."

"I see," said Slippriman. "How *were* my colleagues found, by the way? Once they were changed, that is?"

"The false gage would cry unto me."

"And how long did they remain mucousy molluscs?"

"Longer than the runt shall," Serpentar replied. "Enow for ease of carriage. Strangely, all had snails of different kinds become."

"And who was the biggest, My Lord?"

"Greydolf, as thou might expect...a great fat whelk became he...the Lord of the Gage Ghouls found him in a puddle in the Mountains of Trepidation, appearing most crestfallen..."

As this exchange progressed, Snash felt himself regaining a bit of internal rigidity, even if all his bones were part of his shell now...his head rose up, and the cords his eyes were hanging from stiffened into stalks, lifting...he looked about slowly. Serpentar and Slippriman were looming far above him, Slippriman rather less so, since he was seated, of course...after taking a long drag on his white burning stick, the old man rose and stepped closer to Snash.

"Can he understand us, do you think?" he asked.

"Difference it maketh not," said Serpentar, "as I purpose to crack and cook him 'neath the fiery sole of my foot."

When Snash heard that, his eye-stalks contracted a good half of their length.

"Hast thou seen a sufficiency of him?" Serpentar asked Slippriman.

"Oh," said the latter, and took another drag on his little white fag, "I have indeed."

Serpentar drifted forward. Snash's eye-stalks contracted the rest of the way...wishing he had lids to sheathe his orbs with, he stared in horror as a demonic foot positioned itself overhead, its heat beating down...there was a glowing especially hot spot right in the middle of the sole, out of which snakes were emerging from their latest cycle through the Yark Lord's body. Snash tried to console himself with the thought that, between the blazing heat, and all that weight, it would all be over pretty quickly; but as the foot began to descend, he switched to soothing himself, rather more successfully, with the thought of Luvliel...

"My Lord! My Lord!" someone was crying, off in the distance....the foot halted. Snash cocked his tiny rapidly drying eyes around. Out from the corridor Nognomen came running.

"Master Nameless," the Yark Lord said, "thy reason for this intrusion had *best* be good."

As Nognomen rushed up panting---it struck Snash that he might not be able to breathe too well without a mouth--- Snash tried desperately to crawl out from under the foot, but he was, of course, a snail, and over and above that, he was getting drier and drier in the terrible heat. Nognomen was going on about *Bimbottom*...Snash thought he'd heard the name before, somewhere...not that it mattered. He needed to concentrate entirely on moving.

But his mucous was just about gone; when at last he began to stick, he drew his head in, whereupon his shell fell over on its side...realizing he had a hatch (the word *operculum* didn't leap to mind) he closed it, but the heat got even worse, downright choking, in fact, Serpentar's red light through his shell making everything seem even more hellish.

Suddenly, though, the red vanished, as if Serpentar had gone somewhere else, and Snash opened his hatch a crack, sucking air through his little puckered snail-mouth....things had definitely cooled down out there. Once he felt his mucous starting to return, he opened his hatch wider, stuck his head and a bit of his muscular snail-foot out, pulled his shell upright again, and twiddled his eyes about. Serpentar and Nognomen were nowhere to be seen. But---

Slippriman was still standing next to Snash, smoking,

eyeing him with a slight smile.

"Ah, if only you *were* Greydolf," he said.

Snash started to crawl away as fast as he could.

"Where are you going?" Slippriman asked.

Snash ignored the question, not that he could've answered anyway, with his mouth the way it was...he did his damnedst to increase his speed, but even though *some* of his mucous was back, it wasn't enough, and he couldn't glide as smoothly as necessary. Truly, the lack of legs was a considerable drawback.

"There, there," said Slippriman. "You really don't have a chance..."

(as if Snash didn't know)

"---and it grieves me, it really does, to see you struggling so...Why don't I *just*---"

Snash felt the old man's foot upon his calcareous back.

"Slippriman!" cried Serpentar from somewhere.

"Coming!" answered Slippriman, very much like someone who wasn't about to come just *yet*.

But, between Serpentar's shout and Slippriman's answer, Snash had started to change back; he was already a good deal bigger by the time Slippriman tried to crush him, yet still sturdy enough for the old man to do no damage at all. Indeed, the sole of Slippriman's sandal was apparently so soft that he hurt *himself* when he put his weight on Snash's shell, and he yowled and almost fell.

Serves you right, Snash thought---just before Slippriman recovered his balance and kicked him a good way across the floor, well into the Hellrog Hall.

"Coming, coming," Snash heard him saying. The runt was back on his side, spinning around on his shrinking shell as he deccelerated...almost the instant his shell disappeared, he started to roll in a completely different way, bumping his newly-returned elbows and knees...without waiting to stop, he scrambled to his feet and raced on the way he'd been going, the hellrogs blurring by to right and left, before it occurred to him that he didn't know how to get through the snake-mouth at the passage's end if it was closed, and---

Damn if it wasn't.

Even though he didn't hear anything, that was just like the last time the hellrogs had snuck up after him...he wasn't exactly sure what they would do with him, but even if they merely turned him back over to Serpentar, that would be bad enough. He guessed the demons must be right close when the snake-mouth suddenly yawned, and out came not one, but two, dispatch-runners. Snash slipped between them and went up the tongue, the mouth closing over him. There he stayed for a short while, until the mouth opened again, and the runners came back in with him; this time the mouth swallowed, and he found himself in the opposite mouth, which promptly yawned, whereupon he stuck with his fellow runts, one of whom he knew quite well and was also named Snash, as a matter of fact.

Chapter 8: Overflowing Fist

When Snash came back out, he looked more rattled than Slagbag had ever seen him. Without a word, the runt headed straight down, Slagbag following, terribly curious but hesitant to ask him anything. But when Snash veered off into that area-under-construction that they'd used as their first hiding-place, and seemed to be making for the bartizan, Slagbag said:

"Might be spotted."

"I don't care," Snash insisted, and went outside. Slagbag remained behind the leather curtain at first, then thrust it aside and went after him....Snash was standing at the rim-wall, looking out over the volcanic desert.

"Couldn't stay inside a moment longer," he said, breathing in through his nostrils.

Slagbag eyed the little fringe of blue above the mountains in the distance. "So what happened?" he asked.

Snash told him.

"Turned you into a *snail?*" Slagbag said.

Snash nodded. "My eyes fell out of their sockets."

"What?"

"My eyesockets went away, because I didn't have any bones anymore, and my eyeballs just fell out and hung for a few seconds, before they turned into stalks..."

"Uggh," said Slagbag. "Did it hurt?"

"Not exactly. But I really hated it anyway. And Serpentar was hot, and he made me dry up...I had to pull back into my shell, but it was so hot in there I just about choked. The only reason He didn't step on me is that Nognomen burst in..."

Slagbag growled, shaking his head.

"He treats us very badly," Snash said.

Slagbag laughed. "You don't say?"

"Hard to believe his enemies get worse."

"*Everyone's* his enemy," Slagbag said.

Snash nodded. "I hate him. I don't worship him. I don't know if he can die, but I wish I could kill him."

Slagbag laughed. "Now *that* is cursed rebel-talk."

"And I've done enough of it," Snash said.

Slagbag misunderstood. "What, you're just going to shut up from now on?"

"No, I have to *do* something."

"Like what?"

"Use the book. Free Luvliel. Maybe everybody else they've got over there." He waved towards the Nail, which was way off to the right, lights burning in its slit casements.

"Haven't heard that kind of stuff from you in a bit," said Slagbag.

"I was biding my time."

"Because of the crackdown?"

"Right."

"It's still on," said Slagbag. "Or hadn't you noticed?"

"I don't care any more," said Snash.

"But how *far* will you get on that? Who do you think you are? Hrag Urshathur? You're just a little *runt!* What good'll it do if you just get yourself killed?"

"You don't know how I feel. You've never been turned into a snail."

Slagbag had no answer for this.

"Someone has to pull this whole filthy thing *down*," said Snash.

"Well, garn, I wish they would," said Slagbag. "But I don't think you can do it, even if you *do* have the damn book. For one thing, they've probably changed all the locks."

"Hmm."

"And they'd catch you a long time before you got near any locks anyhow."

"Maybe."

"Really," said Slagbag. "I don't mind listening to rebel-talk. I like it. Would rather listen to it than any other kind of talk, I think. But when you start going on like you might actually *do* something, it's hard to take."

Snash subsided. "Sorry," he said.

"Don't worry about it," said Slagbag.

They stared out at the desolation in silence.

"How far away is that blue stuff, do you think?" Slagbag asked.

"Farther than ever," said Snash.

At the beginning of the next shift, when they went to the sorting-station, a brain handed Snash a dispatch addressed to--- Snash.

"For me?" Snash asked.

"Duh," said the brain.

Snash eyed it suspiciously---despite the crackdown, a few incorrigibles were still playing pranks. The return address was Minion Resources, 1000th Floor. Snash broke the seal on the shaved ratskin envelope, which he unfolded---the letter was written on the inside of the skin, with ink that was flaking off in spots; the ratskin itself was rather too thin, and falling apart at the edges. The letter read:

Attention Runt 223,456, Runner First Class, Snash. You are hereby transferred to Overflowing Fist, 750th Floor. Report immediately to Internal Dispatch Chief, Smeggit, rm. 7520, for assignment.

"What is it?" Slagbag asked.

"I'm being transferred," said Snash.

"To where?"

"O.F.---"

Suddenly the missive was snatched from Snash's claw---he turned to see that Khuttarh had come up.

"What's this?" asked the Lord of the Mail, glancing at the letter, which had developed a large rip. "No more running the Spike for Snash?"

Snash said nothing.

"Really," said Khuttarh, "I would've thought you'd be quite worn out by now...Spike Runners usually don't last nearly so long...You're really something special."

Snash continued silent.

"And you think so, too, don't you?" asked Khuttarh.

"No, My Lord," said Snash.

"Oh, *please*...You're just a cog, is that it?"

"A little one."

Khuttarh laughed. "You know, it's come to my attention that you told several of your fellow runts that all my innovations down here were actually *your* idea."

"It's a lie," said Snash.

"What is? That you told them that? Or that I stole your ideas?"

"I've never said you stole my ideas," said Snash, although he had, once, to a runt named Bitblikh in an unguarded moment; he'd also said a great deal to Slagbag, although he couldn't imagine that Slagbag had ever said anything to anyone else.

"I tried to block your transfer, you know," said Khuttarh. "But it seems that someone's taken an interest in you."

"At Minion Resources, My Lord?" Snash asked.

"Higher, I think," said Khuttarh. "But you'd better not relax. I'm not going to *stay* in the Mail Room forever...I'm being groomed myself, for greater things. I have a friend too, in a *very* high place. And I'd be looking over my shoulder if I were you."

"Thank you for the advice, My Lord," said Snash.

Khuttarh tossed the transfer back to him, saying, "Get out of here."

Once they were outside the mailroom, Slagbag said: "Overflowing Fist?"

"I had no idea," Snash said. "They sure took their time...."

"My life is already bad," said Slagbag. "And now it's going to get worse."

"Look, you don't know what's going to happen. Your next runt might be even better than me."

"Don't you *dare* try to cheer me up," Slagbag sulked. "I've never been mates with anyone before, and it'll never happen again."

"Why?"

"Because I'm going to be too damned surly, that's why. Next runt they give me, I'm going to whip 'im half to pieces, I will."

"That's if you can catch him."

"I'll catch him all right. And I'll give 'im what for, for taking your place."

"It won't be his fault."

"Won't be mine either. I'm a yark. Bred to be stupid and mean."

"You have a point," Snash said.

"Yeah."

"Although…"

"What?"

"If you can *make* a point, you can't be too stupid."

Slagbag eyed him narrowly. "So?"

"Maybe you're not that mean, either."

"I am too!" Slagbag snarled.

"You've stopped being mean to me."

"I've been saving it for your replacement," said Slagbag.

"You didn't know I was being transferred."

"I've been worried about it all along. Just didn't say anything."

"Well, until you get your new runt…want to lash me on up to Overflowing Fist?"

"Yeah," said Slagbag, and cracked his whip. "Get moving."

They didn't take a breather till they were well up into the Spike, but then one of Slagbag's (new) boots went bad on him, the sole separating in such a way that it nearly tripped him a couple of times; he took the boot off, inspected it, then dropped it alongside the wall, saying: "Half the stuff we're issued is just plain crap, and that's a fact."

Snash wasn't sure if fully half was crap---he thought it was more like a third. But that was bad enough.

"Someone's head should roll," said Slagbag.

"What do you bet it's being looked into?" Snash asked.

"Ah, who knows," said Slagbag. "But I hope you're right---you can get by without a lot of things, but you need trustworthy boots. And belts that don't break. Last thing you want to see is someone's breeks dropping off, right in front of you…and believe me, I know. Was going up to my tube, after my shift yesterday morning, and the bloke above me lost his belt...down came his drawers. He reached to pull them back up, but the damage was done...I had some very *bad* dreams..."

"Come to think of it," Snash said, "remember that story, a while back? A whole platoon of ogres on drill, and their cuirasses all dropped off at once, right in front of the Shark Lord, while they were doing their squat-thrusts?"

"Yeah, and the whole lot were executed---"

"You two!" bellowed a voice from somewhere. "Having a nice chat, are you?"

Without even a look round, runt and motivator resumed their ascent; as they began to close in on the 750th floor, Slagbag began making peculiar wracking noises...Snash had never heard anything like them from a yark before.

"You all right?" he asked over his shoulder.

"I'm fine," said Slagbag---his voice sounded a bit clenched. "My nose is running a bit, though."

Snash considered all this...his throat was feeling a bit tight too, and his nose was running also, even though the chimney was so dry...he wondered if it all had something to do with knowing that he wasn't going to be seeing Slagbag any more. He'd been trying to keep his mind off it, but he hadn't been very successful, and whenever he was especially unsuccessful, his throat got tighter and his nose got drippier.

What's happening to us? he thought. By the time they reached the landing, Slagbag was sniffling and making those peculiar sounds worse than ever, and Snash was sobbing...by now he was *certain* it all had to do with missing Slagbag, even though they were still together at the moment. But Snash really didn't know what to make of any of it...it didn't seem very yark-like to him. The two of them stared at each other; Slagbag seemed to have something he wanted to say, but he didn't say it; he wiped his nose one last time, snarled, shook his head, and went back down. Quite tongue-tied as well, Snash followed as far as the stairhead, and called after him, "I'll try to get you a job up here!" even though he didn't think there was much chance of that.

Evidently, Slagbag thought pretty much the same; he didn't stop or even slow, but kept his head down and flapped one long arm dismissively.

Snash watched him for a while, then turned, drew a deep breath, and went over to the guards at the door...there were two, and they looked extremely well-fed. O.F. was all about getting the stuff necessary for running Mount Adamant, and their livery bore the device of a knuckly fist barely clenched around a whole lot of not-yet distributed abundance. Snash presented one of the guards with his crumbly paperwork, and the bull handed most of it back to him after a quick glance.

"How do I find Smeggit?" Snash asked.

The guard looked as though he was struggling with himself, absolutely desperate to send Snash anywhere but where he wanted to go....after a lot of squinting, and tilting his head, and breathing out through his nostrils, he finally said:

"Go straight on, past the front desk, past the cubicles, into the corridor, and take the first left. His room's right at the end. Although...he might not be in."

"Very good," said Snash, and started to go between the guards, then paused."Where would you have sent me if there wasn't a crackdown on?"

"Broom closet," the guard replied.

"Doesn't sound too bad."

"With no floor," the guard went on.

"Yawning shaft?"

"Five hundred feet deep. Into a soup vat."

"Ah."

"Nothing personal, of course."

"Did you pull that one a lot?" Snash asked. "Before the crackdown?"

"Tried to," the guard said. "Sometimes it worked, sometimes it didn't. Made for meatier soup, though, let me tell you...Welcome to Overflowing Fist."

Snash went through.

His orders got him right past the front desk, and he was very interested to see that there were a number of motivators in between the rows of cubicles, one to each aisle, apparently; clerical brains were coming and going, and he guessed the cubicles were full of them...he really liked the idea of them being motivated.

Maybe you can get Slagbag a job up here after all, he thought.

The air was full of unfamiliar but pleasant smells...they made him salivate and feel hungry, even though they weren't very much like any food-smells he'd encountered. He saw a couple of brains walking about, eating strange things, and just about everyone he saw, brains, runts, and bulls, had a belly--- normally, you only saw that on older yarks in positions of some authority....things were different up here in O.F., obviously.

He went up the corridor. There were a number of chambers on either side, doors open for the most part...things were being moved in and out, and many of them---plainly--- hadn't been made in Mount Adamant. There were big jars in metal and ceramic, and cloths, and baskets of fruit, and open boxes filled with bottles...most of the offices had crates stacked up along the walls. Snash knew that a lot of the stuff was brought from very far afield, the most distant corners of Serpentar's empire...undoubtedly, there was a great deal of sampling that had to be done. As a matter of fact, when Snash came to Smeggit's chamber, the brain was sampling something red from a long-stemmed crystal vessel. Snash had never seen a cup like that. He'd spent his whole life drinking from bags, or leaky rusty iron cups held together with nails.

"Who're you?" Smeggit asked, not looking as though he minded the interruption too much.

"Snash," Snash replied. "Runt 223,456, reporting for duty."

"Caught me in the office," Smeggit said. "No mean trick...You're my new runner, I take it?"

"Yes sir."

"You know what we do here?"

"You get all the things we need to---"

"No. Here. This office."

"You run messages inside O.F.?"

"Right. Or rather, my runts do. Not a bad job, really. You've been running the Spike, I take it? Up from the mail room?"

Snash nodded.

"Well, from now on, you'll be working our floors up here. For the most part. There's some other stuff downstairs, where everything comes in, but when we have to send something down there, it goes through the mail-room, as doubtless you're already aware."

"Yes, sir," Snash said, although something puzzled him.

"You look like a runt with a question."

"Why are we up here on these floors?"

"Instead of downstairs, with everything else, so we could keep better track of things? There was a Different Chief of Staff, way before my time. There are Chiefs of Staff, and Chiefs of Staff, and Chiefs of Staff, if you know what I mean. Some of them get their noses out of joint---if they have noses, that is---and think they need to keep better track of *us*...how *did* you get this job, by the way?"

"Did you hear about the fay princess in the Nail?"

"The one who tried to escape?"

"I'm the one who tripped her."

"And you're going to be glad you did....Ever see one of *these* before?"

Smeggit held up a shiny red fruit.

Snash shook his head. Smeggit tossed it to him.

"Go ahead, take a bite," he said.

Snash sniffed it, then took a chunk out of it. The flesh was crunchy, not so hard to chew as bone, and he liked that...as for the flavor, it was as agreeable as it was completely outside his experience. He had never tasted *sweet* before.

"That," said Smeggit, "is an *apple*."

Snash knew the word, although he knew no word for the taste.

"Not bad, eh?" asked Smeggit. "And there's more where that came from. Serpentar owns half the world....Be a good boy, do what I tell you, and you'll get your share."

Snash took another juicy bite.

"I'm off," said Smeggit.

Once the preliminaries---which included him being

assigned a sleeping tube on the 745th floor, much nicer than his old one---were done, Snash went right to work, although there really wasn't much of that, at least compared to what he was used to. There were drops for internal mail throughout the Overflowing Fist floors, and runners brought that up to a couple of brains who had a chamber next to Smeggit's; Snash took the mail and delivered it. Most of it simply got shuffled around the main floor, so that he almost never had to use the stairs; and the motivator---named Globduk---who was assigned to him was so fat that he couldn't even make a pretense of driving him. Most of the motivators in O.F. were about as lazy and out of shape, as a matter of fact. Everybody had food, frequently of a very tasty exotic sort brought from far away, and a lot of the brains and men dressed rather eccentrically for Mount Adamant; the workmanship of their duds was better than average as well. Observing all this, and listening to his co-workers, Snash realized fairly quickly that something most untoward was going on in the department. The personnel weren't just sampling things to make better decisions. They were keeping them, hoarding them, trading them, making deals throughout the fortress and the rest of Tenebria, indeed, the whole Empire. Worse yet, they seemed to be cutting corners, on a whole host of things---given gold or credit to obtain material, they bought substandard stuff whenever possible and kept the difference, which was, no doubt, one of the reasons why there was so much bum equipment. All of the brains and even some of the runts had something going on...Snash was amazed at how open it all was. The general opinion was that nothing much was going to happen, because the head of the department, a man named Nastimir, was under the wing of someone higher up; it was also the consensus that if anything *was* going to happen, it would've happened a while back, before the big rush (now over) to outfit the army that was going into Merriador. Down below with the troops and the smiths and the engineers, things were still pretty crazy as everything was ramping up; but since the raw materials had largely been supplied, things in O.F. were getting more and more relaxed, and stuff that had been skimmed during the rush was changing hands.

Snash, however, quite sure that the situation wasn't going to last, tried to keep his nose clean. When there was food making the rounds, he took some, particularly if it was foreign and interesting. But he never traded, and made a point of keeping his eyes open and listening. Internal Communications was certainly the place for that. Smeggit was in pretty tight with Nastimir, so much so that he was devoting very little time to his actual job; in a very short period of time, primarily to make things easier for himself, Snash took over a number of Smeggit's responsibilities, and Smeggit was happy to let him—IC ran better, and he got the credit. In return, Snash was allowed to handle things pretty much as he pleased—he was even permitted to spend some time running the Spike, to maintain his conditioning. He wasn't about to let himself go to pot.

One night, when the ostensible head of the office was nowhere to be found and, in all likelihood, would not soon be back, Snash had a visitor, a brain named Snidrag. Snidrag wasn't well-liked, and it was thought he was a spy; the fact that he didn't seem to be much of a threat (as long as Nastimir had a wing to shelter beneath) didn't make anyone like him any better.

"So what have you noticed?" Snidrag asked.

"Noticed?" Snash replied.

"Observed, heard. *Learned.*"

"About what?"

"What do you think?" Snidrag asked. "Here you are, working for Smeggit, and you don't expect to be *pressed?*"

"For?"

"Tidbits? Details? Haven't you ever wondered why you were transferred here?"

"As a reward—"

"In part," Snidrag said. "But you have a *patron* now. And you need to keep him happy."

Snash was puzzled. "Why haven't you approached me before?"

"No orders. But when you didn't get in touch with

Burning Curiosity---"

"They never got in touch with me."

"They don't regard that as an excuse," said Snidrag. "They were pretty unhappy with me, as a matter of fact, when I didn't approach *you*...but now I'm here, and we need to talk."

"Very well," said Snash.

A long silence followed....evidently getting quite irritated, Snidrag demanded at last:

"Nothing to report?"

Not at all comfortable with the idea of informing, Snash said: "You've been here longer than I have....surely you've seen everything for yourself."

"Truly."

"How would *you* describe things?"

"Everyone's dealing but you," said Snidrag.

"And what do you think about Smeggit?"

"Where to begin?" asked Snidrag. "Almost as bad as Nastimir...Hell, he's got stuff going that *Nastimir* doesn't even know about."

"Is that so?"

"He must steal a third of Nastimir's goods...undercuts him on the prices...brings in black-poppy paste from Zhond, sells it to the Eastrons...He's also passing off dried vugg as fell beast flesh..."

Snidrag went on in this vein for a good long time, and when he ran out of things to say about Smeggit, Snash asked him about Nastimir, then just about everyone else...when at last the list of malefactions petered out, Snash asked:

"Why hasn't Burning Curiosity moved against the whole lot?"

"Chief of Staff," said Snidrag. "At least, that's the rumor. Nognomen's watching out for Nastimir."

"Nognomen the Nameless?" Snash asked. "He gave up his own name, forgot his own face to serve Serpentar...*he's* stealing?"

"Don't be such an idealist," said Snidrag. "They're all bad and we're bad too...if you don't want things to get even worse, you have to make them worse yourself, or someone else will. Got it?"

Snash didn't think he did.

"Anyway," said Snidrag, "If you hear anything, come to me."

He started for the door.

"Wait," said Snash.

"What?" asked Snidrag.

"I worked with someone, back when I was running the Spike."

"Motivator?"

"Named Slagbag."

"What about him?"

"I feel sort of half-blind without him…"

"What, you want him transferred in here?"

"Four eyes are better than two," said Snash.

"I'll see what I can do," said Snidrag.

Nevertheless, Snash didn't expect Snidrag to do much of anything for him; since the powers-that-be had let the runt go on for so long without any report from him, it seemed to him that he really couldn't matter that much to them. But Snidrag contacted him several more times, and Snash handled him exactly the way he had before, and the higher ups must've thought they were getting something out of it, because Snash came in one night to find Slagbag waiting outside his door.

"Bull 1,000,601, reporting for duty," the big motivator said.

Snash couldn't quite believe his eyes. "They *actually* transferred you!"

Slagbag thrust his paperwork Snash's way.

"That should go to my boss, Smeggit," Snash said. "Although he's out at the moment."

"Lads at the door said he's usually out."

Snash didn't comment.

"They also said you're pretty much running his office," Slagbag went on.

Snash looked about to see if anyone was listening. "Come inside," he said.

Once they were safely behind the closed door, the runt

said:

"I'm the one who handles the mail, if that's what you mean."

"Pretty much...damn, I'm glad to see you."

"Sit down," Snash said, motioning towards an empty crate that doubled as a seat. Snash himself sat on a thick fayish volume set upon another crate behind his modest writing-desk---without the book, he'd never have been able to look over the top. It was full of botanical lore that no one in Tenebria was interested in, since the only plants in Serpentar's domain were a few species of nettles and thorns.

"I thought you'd be living in higher style, I must say," said Slagbag.

"Oh?" Snash asked.

"After you left, I listened close when anyone mentioned Overflowing Fist....kind of my way of keeping tabs on you, I suppose. Sounds like there's a heap of fun and games up here, all the time. That, and loads of swag from just about everywhere."

"Just between you and me," said Snash. "It's true."

"Yeah, and I'll tell you what. It makes for all that bad gear we get, and just about everyone's caught on."

"Well, it's just as I said, back when I came up here...it's being looked into."

Slagbag eyed him slyly. "Know this for a fact, do you?"

Snash nodded. "There's a fellow named Snidrag. Questioned me a couple of times....seems I was sent in here as a spy, although no one told me, at least at first...Anyway, he's the one who does all the talking..."

"You don't tell him *anything*?"

"Would you care?"

"I don't know...on the one hand, I definitely want every bloke out there to have reliable trousers. Good armor and good swords, too. On the other hand, a rat is a rat."

"True."

"And I hate the higher ups so much..." Slagbag shook his head. "Ah, you could go either way on this, and I wouldn't blame you."

"Well," said Snash, "the Higher-ups haven't been

getting what they want from me."

"They *think* they have, though?"

"Thanks to Snidrag. And since I've been keeping my nose pretty clean and doing a good job, I'm safe here, even though Burning Curiosity's going to come down on this place any time now."

"And I'll be safe too?"

"I expect. And things are much better up here, let me tell you. The sleeping-tubes are roomier, there's some bedding, less lice...you don't have to run around nearly so much, and there's lots of food. Best of all, I'm your boss, or might as well be. You'll be motivating one of my runts."

"I'd rather whip some of those brains," said Slagbag.

"Not my department. But I might be able to arrange it. Honestly, things are so slack around here, I think you could just go out right now and start whipping, and no one would say a thing. The brains would just sit still for it."

Slagbag got a big grin on his face. "You know, I'd like to give that a try."

"See you in a bit," said Snash.

Slagbag came back after he'd worked up a sweat....Snash had never much cared for Slagbag's stink, although it brought back all sort of good memories now. He was very happy to be reunited with his mate.

"Oh, I liked *that*," said Slagbag. "Snotty bastards. I could tell they'd never been whipped *proper*...those other motivators are pretty feeble, if you ask me. They've been eating too well..."

"There's a lot of food up here," said Snash.

"*You* don't look like you've been stuffing yourself."

"I eat pretty well, but I run it off...Tell you what. I've got a bit of a stash. Not enough to draw any attention, but enough for you and me. Instead of going to mess this morning, let's have ourselves a bit of a party. Do you know what wine is?"

"Yeah," Slagbag said. "Never had any, but---"

"I've got some fay-wine from out west...."

"*Fay* wine?" Slagbag asked.

"Yes."

"Won't it kill us?"

"No."

"Have you had some?"

Snash nodded.

"And you were *fine?*"

"Very."

Slagbag thought a bit. "Good enough for me."

Later on, Snash opened a chest he had against the rear wall, and spread everything out on his writing desk.

"What's this?" Slagbag asked, picking up a big round load of dark-crusted bread and sniffing it.

"What's it look like?" Snash asked.

"Bread," Slagbag said, and knocked on it. "Is it hard all the way through?"

"No," said Snash. "Tear off a chunk."

Slagbag ripped a big piece off, sniffed that, then tore a mouthful of it away. "Not bad. Doesn't have any sand in it."

"No," said Snash. "That's how men like it, apparently."

"Where'd it come from?"

"Nastimir's got a deal with some men in Prison Number 20. He gives them the makings, and they bake the bread fresh daily...they get to keep some."

"No weevils," said Slagbag.

"I know."

"I like it with weevils."

"Same here," said Snash. "But the bread itself is very tasty."

Slagbag nodded, and unwrapped a wedge of yellow cheese. He sniffed it. "Smells nice and strong...is it salty?"

"Fairly," said Snash.

With his mouth still partly full of bread, Slagbag took a bite out of the cheese.

"Maybe you'd better use the knife from now on," Snash said, handing him a wickedly-curved dagger with a roaring ogre-face on the pommel.

Slagbag sliced a slice off. "You want some?"

"Believe I do," said Snash.

"You said something about wine?"

Snash nodded towards the bottle, then got a pair of crystal goblets from a drawer.

"Are those good for anything?" Slagbag asked.

"We can drink out of them."

Slagbag examined one. "Won't the wine leak out?"

"Why should it?"

"You can see right through 'em."

"So?"

"How can you trust a cup you can see through?"

Snash got him a good heavy opaque one, streaked with rust.

"Better," said Slagbag, and Snash poured him some wine. Slagbag downed it all in one go. "Strange taste."

"It's called *sweet*."

"I'm not sure I like it."

"The taste's not the main thing. Wait a moment," said Snash, knowing for a fact that his Fay wine was much stronger than the standard swill that yarks got…it took a little longer than Snash expected, but Slagbag's legs got unsteady, and he had to sit down.

"Oh," he said. "I see now….give me some more."

"Take your time this time," said Snash, and gave him half a goblet.

Slagbag took just one gulp. "Have to say…it's winning me over." Picking up an egg, he declared: "This is…an *egg*."

"From a bird called a chicken," said Snash.

"Watch this," said Slagbag, put it into his mouth, and closed his jaws…out from between his fangs came several bright yellow streams of yolk, one of which caught Snash's cheek.

"Got you," said Slagbag.

Snash wiped his face.

"Got any meat?" Slagbag asked.

Snash unwrapped a big piece of marinated salt beef, still fairly tender....Slagbag tore off a long strip, Snash a smaller one. They sat in silence for a while, chewing happily. But presently Snash brought out some garlic and onions and said:

"These go pretty well with meat....might want to peel 'em first---"

But Slagbag had already taken a considerable chunk out of the onion.

"Oh, that is nice," he said."What kind of flesh was that again?"

"Beef."

"From...*cows?*"

"Right."

Slagbag nodded. "Even better than giant slug."

"Better than fell beast," said Snash.

"I don't know about that," said Slagbag. "Not as much character, I think..." He indicated some white grapes. "I want to say those are...*berries.*"

"They're called grapes," said Snash.

"Right, right."

"They grow them way down south, beyond the sea of Boiling Mud."

Slagbag ate one. "Sweet again."

"Right. Wine's made out of grapes."

"Will they get me drunk?"

"I think you're there already."

Slagbag had another grape. "Could be," he said, then took another gulp of wine.

Just then, there came a knock at the door.

"Who is it?" Snash called.

"Snidrag," came the reply.

Slagbag glanced at Snash.

"Quick," Snash whispered. "Everything back in the chest."

They hid the food as quickly as they could. Then Snash opened the door.

"Everything back in the chest?" Snidrag asked, very like one who had very sharp ears.

Realizing immediately that he had to change tack, Snash said: "Have you eaten?"

"No," said Snidrag. "But---"

"Would you care for some dinner?" Snash asked.

"Trying to tempt me, eh?" Snidrag asked.

"Yes."

"What do you have?"

Snash opened the chests and showed him.

"And wherever did you come by all that?" Snidrag asked.

"I'm always having things thrust my way. If I turned them down, I'd rouse suspicion."

"No one ever thrusts things *my* way," said Snidrag.

"That's because no one likes you."

Snidrag nodded.

"You're not going to report me, are you?" asked Snash.

"Not if you feed me really well," said Snidrag.

"I will indeed," said Snash, and broke everything out again...some time later, after they'd made considerable inroads, Snidrag pointed to Slagbag and said:

"Who's that, by the way?"

"The fellow I spoke to you about," Snash said.

"The one I helped you with?"

"Yes. His name's Slagbag."

"Slagbag," said Snidrag, and sipped at his goblet.

"What did you want, by the way?" Snash asked.

"Just thought I'd warn you," said Snidrag. "BC's paying us a visit, tomorrow night....You might want to dispose of some things..." He swept an arm towards the food.

"Who's being arrested?" Snash asked.

"Half the department, starting with Nastimir....but you're safe as safe, like a tick that's dug all the way in, and you can't even see his body anymore..."

"That safe?" asked Snash.

"That safe," said Snidrag. Rising, he staggered for the door. Once he was gone, Slagbag asked Snash:

"Still want to pull everything down?"

Snash wasn't quite sure what he meant. "What?"

"Play Hrag Urshathur, now that you've landed here,

141

and you're safer than a tick that's dug all the way in?"

Realizing that he hadn't had any rebellious thoughts for some time, Snash said nothing.

"Thought so," said Slagbag.

"Help me throw the food away," said Snash.

They took the chest to a chute outside and tossed the contents.

"Pity," said Slagbag.

"Won't be eating so well, for a while at least," said Snash. "Whoever takes over is going to be pretty tough at first...until he turns into Nastimir all over again."

"Well, maybe you'll get yourself sent to someplace even cushier," said Slagbag.

"Wouldn't be surprised," said Snash.

"Just remember to bring me along."

"Goes without saying."

Chapter 9: Backstabbing

To Snash's surprise, nothing much happened the next night, or the next, and the third was well along before Burning Curiosity descended on the 750th Floor; Nastimir and fully half the brains were dragged off by BC troops, bulls wearing black-lacquered armor that seemed unusually nicely designed to Snash. Even though Snash wasn't on the list, his office was searched; afterwards, he and Slagbag spent some time discussing things with some of the BC boys...a few were ex-motivators, and had actually come out of the same fruit as Slagbag. Anyway, word was that the invasion of Merriador was being postponed, due to bum equipment, particularly sunglasses---for yarks who had to go out and fight under the sun, shades were pretty vital. The situation was being rectified, though, starting with Overflowing Fist, as was clearly apparent. When the black-lacquer lads finally cleared out with their prisoners, the floor looked just about completely empty, even though it was still at about fifty percent...the brains were all cowering down in their cubicles, a few peeking up from time to time. But even though the BC troops were all gone, the motivators made a particular show of going about their duties, plying their whips with much more energy than usual. Two of the porkier ones collapsed and died.

Snash didn't know what had happened to Smeggit...the brain hadn't shown all night, and Snash guessed he must've been arrested elsewhere. But when Snash came in the following night, Smeggit was in his chamber, which had been meticulously emptied of all its contraband, and he actually began to take some part in the running of his office. Snash could only think that he'd helped the investigation in some way, had, perhaps, been spying on Nastimir himself; for a while it looked as though he might be getting Nastimir's job. A lot of things remained up in the air; no one was replaced for a while, and since O.F. was at half-strength, the arrests had actually worsened things down below. But none of those empty cubicles were filled until the dearth of materiel got really acute. As to the matter of Nastimir's successor, there seemed to be a dispute about that, although finally the matter was resolved, very much to Snash's dismay.

The new head of Overflowing Fist was Khuttarh.

"You look like you've heard the news," said Slagbag.

"I feel like a tick that's about to be dug out," said Snash.

"With a red-hot knife?"

"I don't know if I feel *that* bad, but…"

"What are you going to do?" Slagbag asked.

"Not sure, but I'm not going to let him transfer me somewhere bad… Higher-ups might not let him either…they think I've been giving them good information, so…maybe I'll have time---before he figures out how to handle me---to come up with something on him…"

"Like what?"

"Stealing. There were rumors, down in the mailroom…what do you bet he's going to strike something up with Smeggit? I might be able to find out when they're meeting, hide myself…"

"You know," Slagbag said, "for such a little fellow, you're a very big sneak."

"Does it trouble you?"

"No. I wish I was sneakier. I mean, I'd still want to be big and strong, and not a runt---being a runt looks pretty crappy to me, no offense---but I wouldn't mind at all if I could skulk about and be cunning and backstab."

"Well, just keep an eye on me," said Snash. "I'm going to backstab Khuttarh just as bad as I can."

"Can't wait," said Slagbag.

Even after Khuttarh moved in, it was several nights before Snash clapped eyes on him---Khuttarh arrived early and left late. But finally the runt was summoned to the new chief's chamber, in which things were ordered very much as they had been down in Khuttarh's old office in the mail room. There were already hundreds of scrolls in the racks along the walls, and Khuttarh, who was scribbling away furiously with a long black plume, just as he had been when Snash first saw him, was seated at the same stone desk--- or so Snash thought before he noticed it wasn't carven with motifs involving the transmission and reception of malefic mail, but graven instead with images illustrating sinister aspects of procurement. Snash wondered if Khuttarh had obtained the desk himself, or whether it had been Nastimir's. Snash had never been in Nastimir's office.

Khuttarh went on scribbling as though Snash wasn't there...Snash used the time to glance around the office, looking for places to hide---he noted that there was about a six-inch gap between the bottom shelves of the scroll-racks and the floor.

More than enough leeway for a runt, he told himself.

"So," said Khuttarh, finishing his letter at last, and dropping his quill into the ink-bottle, "here we are again, you and I."

"Welcome to O.F., My Lord," said Snash.

"You know why I called you in here, slave?"

"To try and frighten me," said Snash.

The incautiousness of this reply seemed to take Khuttarh aback, and it was a moment before he sneered:

"And I suppose you're *not* frightened?"

Snash considered the question. There was a time when he would've been, but it had long passed. Actually, now that he thought about it, he'd never had any excuse to be frightened of Khuttarh, seeing as how he'd had his run-in with Glolob before he even met the Lord of the Mail...of course, *since* meeting him, Snash had encountered so many terrifying things that Khuttarh seemed more of a nuisance than anything else, one that might be cowed by a show of bravado.

"What's to be afraid of?" Snash asked. "I've been tossed off the Spike by the Shark Lord, leered at by Hellrogs, and turned into a snail by Serpentar himself...who are you? The boss of *O.F.?* The ex-*Postmaster?* The one-time Lord of the *Mail?*" Snash laughed.

"I've got sharper teeth than you know," said Khuttarh, unconvincingly.

"Maybe," said Snash. "Haven't seen them yet. But my...*patron* has *much* sharper ones than you."

"And who's he?"

"You mean you don't *know?*"

Khuttarh was silent...not knowing himself who his

patron was, Snash found the southerling's reaction, or lack of it, pretty hilarious, although he didn't show anything more than a smirk.

"I think," he said, "that you can't do much of *anything* to me."

"You are *not* an insoluble problem, little Snash," Khuttarh replied.

"You haven't solved me so far," said Snash, and started for the door.

"I haven't dismissed you!" cried Khuttarh.

But Snash just kept going.

"You actually talked to him like that?" Slagbag asked.

"Put him off balance, let me tell you," said Snash. They were in his chamber, having some brandy from Merriador---- Snash had forgotten that he had a bottle of it tucked away in a particular spot, and luckily the black-lacquer boys hadn't found it. He and Slagbag were already a bit crocked.

"He's going to come right after you," said Slagbag.

"He'll have to figure out how."

"You're going to have an accident. He could make it look like a practical joke, pin it on someone..."

"Nah," said Snash. "BC would see through that....If I were him, I'd try to make it look like I was thieving. Like I'd gone over to Nastimir, but didn't get caught, and was still at it."

"That would be a good way to do it," Slagbag allowed. "Always thinking, aren't you?"

"I *like* thinking," said Snash.

"Give me that brandy."

When at last they went off to their sleeping-tubes, Snash found that his was already occupied, by a snoring runt who, to judge by the smell, seemed to have been drinking quite a bit himself; finding an empty tube, perhaps belonging to the fellow that had taken his, Snash crawled in and went straight to sleep.

147

He woke with a splitting headache---licking his chops, which tasted truly vile, he climbed down and leaned against the wall, massaging his scalp with his fingertips. Even as he stood there, two bully-boys from Proofs and Papers showed up…climbing to Snash's tube, one rousted the runt sleeping within it, dragged him out, and flung him ten feet to the floor…then the two bulls searched the runt, and found several papers.

"Identity proofs!" one of the P&P fellows cried.

"They're not mine!" answered the runt.

"Ah, we'll see about that, you little bit of dung still stuck in a cloven hoof after several days, you!"

And with that, they hustled him off.

Snash headed for his office, pondering all this…..clearly Khuttarh had figured things out much quicker than expected…perhaps he wasn't to be taken so lightly after all. But that merely meant that Snash had to move more quickly himself.

Luckily, though, an opening soon presented itself---Slagbag had been told to keep his eyes open, and he reported:

"Smeggit went in to see Khuttarh three times today."

"Did you hear anything?"

"No. But I saw Snidrag skulking about…you might ask him."

Snash went to see him.

"Was coming to see *you*," said Snidrag. "Smeggit's meeting with Khuttarh, after everyone leaves…You should go hide in Khuttarh's office. You could fit right under one of those bookshelves, and---"

"Way ahead of you," Snash said---just as a commotion broke out way across the floor. Yarks were barking and yelling, and someone threw a stack of parchment into the air; suddenly, around a corner, running on all fours, Glargle came tearing….he got almost all the way to Snash and Snidrag before he looked up, saw them, screamed, and went scrambling into a cubicle on the right. Just as the two motivators following him rushed into the cube themselves, Snash saw the creature scramble up over the far partition, and vanish on the other side. There was a loud thump.

"*Ach, mein popo!*" came Glargle's voice.

Snash saw the motivators vault the partition, but by the sound of it, Glargle was already well out of the cubicle beyond...motivators, Slagbag included, were converging from all over the floor, and their dark hulking forms moved up and back. There was all sorts of cursing, and they bent from sight from time to time, as though they were grabbing at something, then straightened as if they had missed...Snash saw Slagbag dip down, then reappear with Glargle climbing all over him, around his chest and back and under his armpits, round and round his head, as Slagbag tried to catch him, other yarks getting in the act, reaching with their long arms. Before long, Snash could see nothing but churning yarks, and assumed that Glargle must be somewhere in that tangle, and grabbed...but then they were all turning about and scratching their heads, as though he had somehow gotten away. Snash saw him slip over the top of a cubicle in the distance and disappear.

"Can't believe that thing hasn't been caught yet," said Snidrag.

Snash found it quite remarkable himself.

A contingent from BC came in soon afterwards, searched the whole floor, with the exception of Khuttarh's chamber; the Southerling had been there the whole while, and when the BC boys tried to get inside, he started shouting at their commander, who backed down, and Khuttarh harangued them right out to the stairs...No one paying him the slightest attention, Snash went to Khuttarh's sanctum, chose a scroll-rack in the back behind Khuttarh's desk, and crawled under it sideways, lying on his belly, face turned so he could look out the front. Gradually, he began to get rather uncomfortable, and straightened one of his legs...his foot touched something which jerked away. He looked down along his side...there was a shadowy mass under the next rack.

"Glargle?" Snash whispered.

"*Nein, nein,*" said the wretch...gesturing in the cramped

space, his great glistening eyes opening. *"Schfartblag."*

"Schfartblag?" Snash asked, then realized this was Glargle's idea of a yark-name.

"Ja, ja, ich bin yark, nice yark, chust like *du---"*

Glargle shut up as someone entered the room....the door closed, and Snash saw black robes and sandals.

Khuttarh, he thought...the new O.F. chief puttered about for a bit, then sat at the desk. Parchments riffled; Snash heard the brief clatter of a quill in a well, followed by the jittery scraping of the pen---he could practically see Khuttarh's tall black plume nodding absurdly.

This seemed to go on forever, and lengthening it out considerably was a tickle that developed in Snash's nose, bringing him to a verge of a great big sneeze a couple of times. He wasn't sure what would happen if Khuttarh caught him; it seemed entirely possible that he might be able to threaten his way out by invoking his "patron."

Then again, it was entirely possible that Khuttarh would simply kill him on the spot...

A brain named Rhizblit---Snash recognized the voice--- came in, reported on ore shipments from the Iron Crags, got snarled at, and hurried out. Another named Hratrap arrived with vague concerns about spiked lampshades; Snash couldn't tell what was worrying him, and Khuttarh couldn't either, apparently---it sounded as though he threw something at the blithering brain, whereupon Hratrap gave a high-pitched yell and fled. Khuttarh started talking to himself after that---Snash couldn't understand too much of it, because a lot was in Khuttarh's native language, apparently, although some was in Tenebrian, and the runt did catch "those stinks," "those stains," "stinks and stains in the trews," and "clean stainy-wainies right out."

All the while, Glargle was quiescent, although he did brush up against Snash's foot; sometimes he and Snash just lay there staring at each other, and the runt wondered what Glargle was, exactly, and where he'd come from, and if indeed he'd ever been in possession---however briefly---of the Yark Lord's gage. Had Glargle actually worn the thing? Had it given him any powers? Was it *possible* to get webbed fingers into a gauntlet?

But pondering such questions began to pale, and Snash's eyelids grew heavy, and he drifted away, into a dream about Luvliel.

It wasn't all comforting, though.

She and Snash were standing at a hole in the wall, looking down at a precipitous drop that seemed to fall away for miles, into a sheaf of distant spiny tower-tops....someone was coming, very loudly, and Luvliel was undoing her hair, and there sure was a lot of it, braided like a rope....just as a tremendous pounding started up at the door, she tied the rope to a small tree that had sprung up out of the floor, then snatched Snash up with one hand, tucked him under her arm, and lowered herself out the window on her hair, paying it out with her free hand.

There was a great crash above....Snash saw a yark leaning out, aiming an arrow.

"Oh, don't worry about him," said Luvliel, a moment before the archer cut loose, his shaft sped down, a dark blur, and Snash felt a big blow right where his brow met his crown...

"Don't worry about that either," said Luvliel, and, never halting her descent, snatched the missile from his head, and gave him a kiss where he'd been shot...he saw a golden light inside his skull, and his brain stopped hurting so much.

But way up above, a yark was sawing away madly at the hair-rope, and others were leaning out of other casements farther up, and to the sides, and the air was getting thick with darts.

There was a jolt...he saw the hair-rope part up above. Luvliel began to heel backwards.

"Oh damn," she said, sounding mildly distressed...

There came a knock.

Snash opened his eyes with a start.

A voice---Smeggit's---said: "Fifteen percent."

Snash could see all the way under Khuttarh's desk...someone in brain-sandals---the straps were much more delicate than in everyone else's---was standing in front.

"Seven," said Khuttarh.

"I got fifteen with Nastimir," said Smeggit.

"Nastimir? I understand he's been eating a lot of rump-steak lately---"

"I like rump-steak," Smeggit broke in.

"---cut from his own boily bottom," Khuttarh continued. "And the only reason you're not eating your own ass at this moment, you stinking trew-stain you, is because one of my friends at BC spared you, at considerable risk to himself, at my request....Now, there are two ways that these negotiations can turn out, and I'm fine with either...you can either accept my terms, or I can see to it that you and your boys are arrested."

"You're bluffing."

"Am I?" Khuttarh asked.

Smeggit asked: "Didn't you hear what happened after the last house-cleaning?"

"I could always wait," Khuttarh said. "Till the army has everything it needs. Of course, it's not as though I'd cause too much trouble in any case. There aren't that many of your lot left."

"This is pure shit, and you know it," said Smeggit.

"Don't you know about my friend on high?"Khuttarh asked.

"The one in BC?"

"Higher."

"And who would that be?"

"You mean you don't know?"

He's using my lines, Snash thought.

"Let's say I don't," said Smeggit.

"We go way back," said Khuttarh. "I handled a lot of his mail, so we struck up an arrangement, and it's all paying off with a vengeance....He dispenses advice, right at the top, though he still has time for me...You'd do well not to hinder us."

"I'm not trying to *hinder* anyone," said Smeggit.

"And I wouldn't mind benefitting from your expertise," said Khuttarh. "But it's entirely up to you..."

Smeggit made some sort of answer to this, but Snash

had ceased paying attention; the tickle in his nose was back, and it just kept getting worse. He rubbed his nostril, struggled against sneezing, thought he'd gotten past the danger---

Then let out a honk that sounded absolutely volcanic in the cramped confines under the rack. A hollow silence followed but didn't last long.

"What was that?" Khuttarh demanded.

"Sounded like a sneeze," said Smeggit. "I think it came from under one of those racks back there---"

Snash's mind raced. He glanced at Glargle, whose eyes, already very wide, seemed to take up half his face now---the creature had eight fingers in his mouth, and was in the process of shoving the rest of his hands in. Then, all at once, he was moving, trying to get between Snash and the wall. But Snash kicked him on the top of his nearly hairless head, bringing a gasp of pain from him, and Glargle went still for a moment; Snash managed to get his feet between *Glargle* and the wall, and then wedged himself in even farther, thrusting with his hands.

"Come out of there!" cried Khuttarh.

"*Nein, nein!*" said Glargle. "Not here!"

"Not *here?*"

"Eshcape already! Far avay! Shlip right out in confusion of shneeze---"

"He's lying," said Smeggit.

"Get the guards," said Khuttarh.

But even as Smeggit raced off, feet slapping, Snash stuck Glargle in the skinny behind, hard, with the sharp point of the claw of the first finger on his right hand...Glargle shrieked and flew out from under the rack as though he'd been pulled by a rope.

"There he goes, there he goes!" Khuttarh cried.

Snash heard a great deal of shouting in the distance...when Smeggit came back, Khuttarh asked:

"They get him?"

Smeggit said, "No."

Snash heard the door close.

"So what's it going to be?" Khuttarh asked.

"Ten," said Smeggit.

"Deal," said Khuttarh.

And that was that.

Khuttarh cleared out shortly after Smeggit left, but Snash waited a bit before clearing out himself, wondering how to proceed. There was no way to rat on Khuttarh without ratting on Smeggit as well...but while Snash still didn't like the idea of informing on his own kind, he reminded himself that Smeggit and his ilk had been perfectly happy to make things worse for everyone. It wasn't just a matter of pants falling off...how many yarks would've died in Merriador because of bum armor and bum shades? Snash detested the very thought of the invasion, but if his brethren *had* no choice but to fight, he wanted them to come through it alive. In the end, he decided the news wouldn't wait, and even though he'd have much rather gone to his sleeping-tube, he made the long climb up to Burning Curiosity---they were always awake up there---and asked for Ripsnag.

"Ripsnag, eh?" asked the scribe at the front. "And who might *you* be?"

Snash told him.

"Take a seat," the scribe said.

Snash tried to park himself on one of the benches along the wall, but getting comfortable, or even staying on, was impossible....the seat was made of some very slippery material, and tilted down from the back, and no matter what he did, he slid down towards the edge...unnervingly, the floor was made of some bluish-black but not quite opaque crystal, and he could see rank after rank of nails down there in the depths of it, as though they were submerged in fluid. Struggling to keep himself on the seat, he asked the scribe:

"Was this floor always like this?"

"Don't you like it?" the brain replied.

Snash quite wore himself out with his efforts, but when he stood up, the scribe told him to sit back down....just as he was sliding off the bench for perhaps the fortieth time, a BC trooper in one of those sharp-looking cuirasses and with *excellent* vambraces came out and said:

"Snash?"

The scribe pointed his quill towards the runt, the trooper signalled, and Snash followed him into the back. But instead of being taken to a cell this time, he was led directly towards the interrogation block, which he still remembered very clearly from the last time...unless he was mistaken, he even wound up in the same room with the same pit and the same chains, although he didn't hear any pit-wolves....it occurred to him that they might all be sleeping at the bottom, but he didn't want to look over the edge, and the trooper didn't give him any opportunity to.

"Snash," whispered a familiar voice from the shadows on the right; they were being cast by a peculiar structure hung with ragged black fabric, which left Snash with the distinct impression that it had been erected precisely to cast shadows...he thought he hadn't noticed it on his last visit because there was another, similar structure, much larger, shadowing *it*. Well in amid the crepuscular effects, the Shark Lord sat stygian and dreadful.

"Yes, My Lord?" Snash asked.

"Come...closer."

Snash started over at a *very* deliberate pace.

"And what is this?" asked the Lord of the Gage Ghouls. "Dost thou think thoul't never draw near if only thou movest slowly?"

Snash almost said: *Yes, that's exactly the theory*, but didn't...he wasn't dealing with Khuttarh anymore.

"Increase...thy....*speed*," said the sharkrider.

Snash complied, although he was not at all in the mood.

"I never meant to trouble *you*, My Lord," he began, "I asked to see Ripsnag..."

"Ripsnag is being ripped," said the ghoul. "And snagged."

Snash gulped. "I see."

"What didst thou want with him?"

Snash told of the conversation between Smeggit and Khuttarh.

"So," said the Shark Lord. "Nastimir's accomplices were not wholly expung'd."

"Yes, My Lord," said Snash.

"And Khuttarh would recruit them?"

"Yes."

"What wilt thou say when *he* says thou liest?"

"That I'm telling the truth."

"Verily, the right answer, but I think, mayhap, in the name of prudence, I should check," said the gage ghoul, and, much more quickly than the last time, sent his eyeballs forth. Unable to summon Luvliel to mind, Snash simply went under...

And came to in a rush of panic, sure for no particularly good reason that the sharkrider must've picked over his whole memory, and found out about his treason with Luvliel. But the ghoul only said:

"Thou art a very useful servant, Snash."

"What...what do you want me to do?"

"*Remain* useful," said the Shark Lord. "Give me more of what I want, and I shall raise thee higher."

"What about my partner?"

He expected to have to explain, but the ghoul replied: "Slagbag?"

Startled, although he told himself he shouldn't be, Snash tried to take this in stride, saying: "He helped me a great deal just now, with Khuttarh, and---"

"Thou wouldst be half-blind without him?"

"Yes, My Lord."

"We *cannot* have that," said the Sharkrider.

Chapter 10: The Fellowship of the Fin

Snash managed to get into Khuttarh's office several more times, and duly sent the dirt upstairs; during that same period he was approached several times by brains who wanted to involve him in this and that, but, sensing a snare from Khuttarh, he declined. At length, once the army was properly equipped, Snash was told that the hammer was about to fall on Overflowing Fist again, and he and Slagbag were ordered to clear out---and head on up. But even though Khuttarh was no longer an issue, the transfer was hardly a blessing. Eyeballing his orders, Slagbag swore under his breath.

"Maybe it won't be so bad," Snash said.

"Working for the *Shark Lord*?"

"Might be pretty terrible at that," Snash allowed.

"*Might?*"

"At least we'll be together."

"I'd rather we were together somewhere else," Slagbag said. "What's he going to have us doing up there, anyway? I thought his staff was all ghosts, like him."

"No, he's got a few yarks."

"Live ones?"

"I think. They work in his stable."

"Where he keeps his *shark*?"

"No doubt. But I can't imagine we'll be spying on *that*."

"We'll be spying, then?"

"I don't know."

"I don't like this."

"Nothing *to* like," said Snash.

Slagbag grunted. "Aah."

"What?"

"Like you said, we'll be able to watch each other's backs."

"Did I say that?"

"Words to that effect....let's go. Might as well get the climb over with."

Even though Snash had been making a determined effort to stay in shape, (Slagbag, upon his arrival at

157

Overflowing Fist, had followed the runt's example) he hadn't been getting as much exercise as he had when he was a runner, and he thought the ascent might be hard on him...it turned out, however, to be slightly less than middling, as torments went.

"Wasn't too bad," Slagbag panted at the top, bent over with his hands on his knees.

"Nah," said Snash. "But our worries are just beginning."

Straightening, he eyed the Shark Lord's tower on the rim of the Spike. As before, the structure's crown was lost in the swirling cloud-ceiling. Dipping down out of the fumes, two sharkriders, deep black against the burnt-umber clouds, swept by behind the tower.

"Better get over there before someone shouts at us," said Slagbag.

They crossed the pavement, entering the shadow of the gatehouse...set in sockets, torches flared sullenly on either side, their sputtering light illuminating the double doors, which were embossed with a depiction of an aerial feeding-frenzy in which flying sharks were devouring eagles, vultures, and each other.

"This is really *great*," said Slagbag. "I took a good close look at it, last time we were here, and you went inside...a *lot* of nasty details. See *that*? And that *there*?"

Not particularly interested in nasty details, Snash said, "Just knock."

Grunting with effort, Slagbag needed both hands to lift one of the knockers (which was shaped like a hammerhead shark, with one side of the head turned in), revealing a striking-plate engraved with a wincing flat face, almost obliterated, which he duly bashed, the impact loud and harsh. After a bit a little oval window slid open, and a minion peered out, long pale countenance smoky-looking behind a veil.

"What do you want?" he asked, voice faint and distant-sounding.

They showed their orders; the window closed; bolts clacked back, and Snash watched a great vertical crack open in the feeding-frenzy...fifteen feet tall, the lefthand valve creaked open.

"Enter," the doorkeeper said, garments billowing.

"Are you a ghost?" Slagbag asked.

"I am."

"What's it like, being dead?"

"Depressing."

Really *hating* that answer, Snash hoped Slagbag would leave off right there, but the motivator continued: "What do you need that window for?"

"Window?"

"That little port? Why don't you just stick your face *through* the door?"

The ghost replied: "Because the door would drive my veil back through my head, and my veil and hood would just flatten on my shoulders."

"Is it a bother getting back into them?"

"Oh yes," the ghost said sorrowfully. "The veil in particular."

Before Slagbag could pursue his inquiries any further, Snash tugged on his arm, asking:

"Do you *actually* care?" Snash asked.

But Slagbag said: "*Actually,* now that I'm up here, I'm finding it all rather more interesting than scary......how often do you get to talk to someone who's dead?"

Snash wanted to whisper that he'd already talked to the Shark Lord twice, and hadn't particularly enjoyed the experience, but Slagbag was already asking the ghost:

"Why don't you wear *ghost*-clothes, that would go right through the door along *with* your face?"

When the spirit vented an exasperated hiss, Snash broke in:

"Isn't there someone we should be reporting to---"

He felt a cold touch on the back of his neck, and a thin voice said, "Come," and he hunched his shoulders so violently that his feet just came up off the floor for a moment....looking round slowly, he glimpsed a veiled face even ghastlier than the doorkeepers', but it was even then turning away...hoping he'd never get a good long look, he followed, Slagbag's heavy tread and clinking tackle coming up behind.

"Where are you taking us?" Snash asked the ghost.

"To My Lord's chamber," said the phantom. "You are expected."

Slagbag tapped Snash on the shoulder, causing him to jump again.

"Look at that!" the bull said, pointing at a statue of a great shark which had another shark, head first, thrust into its jaws...several ghosts were (literally) hovering about the figure, dusting it with rags.

"Look at *that!*" Slagbag said again, pointing to a great long black tapestry in which the only things visible were a gauntlet (slightly lower than midway down, on the right), two red glowing spots, up near the top, and the dim metallic sheen of an efficiently rendered black crown, farther up.

"Hardly anything *to* it," Slagbag said, slowing down. "No detail at all. Couldn't be more different from that scene on the door, but...can't really argue with it."

"And what do you know about art, *yark*?" their guide asked.

"I know what I like---"

"Be quiet," said the ghost, and Slagbag shut his trap as they went up several flights of steps to several other flights of steps; Snash guessed they must be getting up near the top when the ghost led them into a chamber filled with racks and racks of apparently identical black hooded robes, each garment with a pair of black armored boots beneath it...in the middle of the chamber, the Shark Lord, heavy-sleeved arms extended on either side, was being fitted for a new robe; pins clenched in their mouths, tailor-brains equipped with tape-measures were measuring and performing various other tailorish operations on Serpentar's towering Number Two. The Gage Ghoul's hood was back, and he had no visible head, save for the two red eyes, hanging in the air...Snash wondered if it really would be possible, as per Slagbag's wish, to grab them and hurl them.

You'd have to stand on a chair, Snash told himself, then told himself he might do better to ditch all thought of stepping on the eyes, since they appeared to be turned his way, although it was hard to tell, since they were just....floating, and they were all glow and didn't seem to have any recognizable pupils...Snash looked down at the floor and tried to stop entertaining subversive notions.

At length the Shark Lord dismissed the tailors, then asked: "Thinkest thou I have a surfeit of robes identical?"

Unsure if this was addressed to him, Snash said nothing, but Slagbag asnwered:

"I don't think that at all, My Lord."

"My words to *thee* were not address'd," said the ghoul chieftain.

"My opinion is worthless," said Snash.

"I think not," said the ghoul. "Indeed, if I did, thou wouldst not be my intelligencer...True, runts rarely are my eyes...but thou hast more wit than most, and it doth make me wonder: however didst thou come about?"

"Too many brains in my compost, perhaps?" Snash asked.

"Mayhap. And mayhap thou'rt some bit of a throwback as well...Yarks from Fays were made...didst thou know that?"

Actually, that was news to Snash.

The Sharkrider continued: "Thy kind have come so far, and in such a way...I *marvel* at what My Lord hath accomplish'd in thee, and *rejoice* in the discomfiture of thy tree-dwelling, goldilock'd, pointy-eared kin. Let me tell thee, it pleaseth them not to dwell on thy ancestry...after all, they slay thee by the millions. But as I am tasked to keep thee on the side of history, *I* have pondered thee at some length, the better my job to do."

"I would've expected as much, My Lord," said Snash.

"My mind goeth constantly, pondering, pondering...Some might regard me, and think I am a mere animate costume, eyes without a head, dividing my time twixt fittings for sable raiment, the oversight of torments, and reposing upon a slab with my hands crossed over my chest. But while indeed I doeth those things for hours upon end, my life interior is rich beyond measure. Always I strive---am *compelled*--- to contemplate My Lord's will, harmonize my own with it, see Him in His works...E'en now, I remind myself that thou---to the extent thou art a yark---are His design...Knowest thou why thou wert summoned?"

Snash shook his head.

"My mount hath given me reason to doubt him."

"Your flying shark, My Lord?" Snash asked.

"Carcharias," said the Ghoul. "There is evidence---some---that he doth conspire against me, with his fellow sharks."

"Are they passing messages?"

"So we suspect."

"Do they meet in secret?"

"That suspicion we have as well, although...it boggleth this ghoul's mind to cogitate upon how it is accomplish'd. They are stabl'd separately, one in each of the other towers...I desireth thee to discover how---and what---they communicateth."

"And how can we do that, My Lord?" Snash asked.

"As stablehands."

"For your shark."

"Aye."

"What if he eats us?" Snash asked.

"Then shall I have to find someone else," said the Shark Lord. "Didst thou truly need to be told that?"

Snash shook his head.

"On the other hand," said the Ghoul, "if, by fulfilling thy task, thou justify my trust, I shall bestow another assignment upon thee."

"Thank you, My Lord," said Snash.

"Who knows how many adventures thoul't have before thou art gobbled up or whatever."

"I surely do not," said Snash.

"Now then. Go down to the stables...Seek there my Shark-Master, Hakmul. He shall instruct thee in thy new duties."

Slagbag asked: "You want me to watch the shark too, My Lord?"

"Would not Snash be half-blind without thee?"

"He would."

"Then be off, for I would ponder the Inevitable."

They went out into the corridor, the door closing behind them.

"Made from *fays*?" Slagbag asked.

162

"That's what he said," said Snash.

"Oh, that's a very odd thought."

"Yes."

"It makes me feel sort of---different."

"Like you might know something about art after all?"

"Yeah."

"We'd better get down to the stable."

"Right."

They arrived at the stable just in time to witness Carcharias's feeding...seemingly unaware of Snash and Slagbag, a big swarthy man with a fin sticking straight up on his hood was wheeling a wheel-barrow full of fish, dogs, pigs, other animals that Snash could put no name to, *and* dead runts, up to the side of the central pool...similar to the item on the man's hood, but much larger, a tall black fin protruded through a mat of scum on the surface of the water. Through cracks and openings in the scum, Snash could see a great dark shape, that looked almost flat, as though it were a marking on the bottom of the pool. But the man stamped twice on the floor, and all at once the dark thing was rising, the fin rose higher through the scum, and turned, the whole dark mass below turning as well, and rising, the scum parting as it lifted...up rose the front end of the Shark Lord's shark. The man yanked a dead dog out of the wheel-barrow. Carcharias pulled himself up onto the rim of the pool with his shark-forelegs, his mouth yawning wide...Snash had the impression of multiple rows of teeth actively *unfolding* as the maw opened.

But all at once, even as he prepared to toss the dead dog into that cavern of fangs, the man noticed Snash and Slagbag at last, and asked:

"You my new yarks?"

"Hakmul?" said Snash.

"That's *Master* Hakmul to you," the man replied.

"The Shark Lord said you'd instruct us in our duties."

"Well you'll just have to wait. Got a shark to feed, you know."

As if to illustrate his point, he threw the dog, and

Carcharias, lunging, snapped it out of the air, then sank back a bit as he bolted it down, head swelling…after that, the Shark got a pig, a huge fish, a dead runt, and several other big limp things…Snash wondered at first why Hakmul didn't simply upend the wheel-barrow into the pool, but then he realized that the Sharkmaster seemed to enjoy tossing the bodies, and that the shark seemed to enjoy catching them…Finally, the barrow emptied, Hakmul gave the monster an affectionate rub on the snout, and the giant shark subsided back into the water, the scum closing back over him.

"Come here," said Hakmul.

Snash and Slagbag went over and he got their names and led them away to the side, into a small chamber cluttered with shark memorabilia, including a number of models of sharks, complete with little riders, on stands with brass plaques.

"Trophies," said Hakmul. "I used to run a stable, back in the mountains. Before I came to work here." He sighed. "Just between you and me, the repression and the omnipresent phantoms get me rather down. What do *you* think?"

Snash almost said, *Goes way past being down,* but caught himself, Slagbag opting for discretion too…both merely shrugged.

"So then," Hakmul said. "Here to spy on Carcharias, eh?"

"What makes you say that?" Snash asked.

"Because the last two yarks that got sent in here were spies, at least until he ate them…"

"Why doesn't the Shark Lord have *you* spying?" Snash asked.

"I'm not quite trusted anymore. I *say* things. I sigh." He heaved a heavy one. "There, I just did it again." He eyed the yarks. "I know what you're thinking…why don't I just hop on Carcharias and escape?"

Snash hadn't been thinking that at all, but…

"I'll tell you why," said Hakmul. "Because Carcharias has a piece of iron in his brain, that answers to the Shark Lord's Gauntlet. All the Sharks have their little brain irons. And if they ever tried to fly off, the irons would get very hot indeed."

He was being very incautious, seeing as how he didn't know them...sensing he truly wanted out, and wasn't merely trying to trick them, Snash asked: "Isn't there some other way you could escape?"

"I doubt it...do *you* have a plan, Master Runt?"

"Sort of," Snash said, although he was thinking about Luvliel and the book, not escape. "But I don't think I've been pushed hard enough yet."

"Your new assignment strikes me as a pretty hard shove."

"Not a promotion?"

"Nooo."

"The last two spies got eaten, you say?" Snash asked.

"That's my assumption," said Hakmul. "Although...no one was quite in the mood to go through Carcharias's droppings."

"What's the best way to make friends with a shark?"

"Carcharias likes me because I give him food....you'll be doing that in any case."

"Feeding him?"

Hakmul smiled gruesomely. "One way or the other."

Besides giving the fish his chow, the new stable-hands had a number of responsibilities. They also had to lay straw down and muck the stable out....Carcharias never did his business in the pool, but the rest of the place got pretty terrible, and he seemed to enjoy watching Snash and Slagbag while they were working, which made things suspenseful, to say the least. If he was down in the water, he'd poke his head over the rim of the pool, or lift it just high enough so that his eyes came up from under the scum; if he was up on the floor, he'd follow Snash and Slagbag about, all ten tons of him, quietly sniggering. Sometimes, after they'd cleaned the whole stable out but before they'd put down some new straw, he'd make a point of depositing a fresh steaming load, then linger beside it, laughing through his nostrils and pointing with a foreclaw or a wingtip...sometimes he'd just wrap himself in one of his black shark-blankets and watch them from a corner, all hunched up, puffing on a white stick of the sort Slippriman had been smoking, only much bigger.

As for feeding him, they had to do it twice a night. Throat-slit carcasses of all sorts were being delivered fairly constantly, and Snash and Slagbag got to pile them into wheelbarrows and roll them out to the shark, who refused to play catch, at least with the bodies they tossed him; however much he enjoyed it when Hakmul threw him some carrion, Carcharias would simply spit it far far away if Snash or Slagbag threw some to him, and would only wolf (or shark) the food down if they got very close to him and allowed him to gently and slowly take the carcass from their hands, his mouth practically closing over their fingers...while this was a whole lot less violent than the other way, it was vastly more creepy, and Snash was well aware that the shark was trying to keep eye-contact with them. Pretty sure that Carcharias could talk---that other shark had spoken down in the shaft that time---Snash, hoping to butter the beast up, asked:

"What sort of meat do you prefer?"

But the shark only crinkled up his brows in an expression of obviously mock puzzlement, and shook his head.

"Come on," said Snash. "I know you can talk."

Carcharias just smiled.

"So what do you like best?" Snash asked.

Rising up from the pool a bit, the shark pointed a long curving wing-tip at a dead runt in the wheel-barrow.

"Runt, eh?" Snash asked.

Carcharias nodded---then lunged forward, mouth gaping, looking a dozen yards wide; Snash yelped and fell back on his butt. But the shark was already sliding back into the pool, grinning...there was quite a bit of bubbling as he sank.

Slagbag rushed over to Snash, hauling him to his feet.

"I wish we were back at O.F.," he said.

Despite all the harrassment from the fish, Snash *was* able to find out some things. Even though he was a most reluctant rat, he *was* genuinely curious as to how Carcharias could be communicating with his fellow sharks, and so---he watched and listened. It soon became obvious to him that something was going on between the shark and the grawks that were frequent visitors to the stable; the creatures would wander around quite close to the shark, who never made any attempt to harm or frighten them. Moreover, they were unusually noisy when they were around him, making throaty grunts, and clicking and whistling, although there didn't seem to be any response from the shark.

That was what Snash thought, at first. He never did see Carcharias moving his mouth, or gills, or breathing oddly, or doing anything that suggested that he was responding...Snash had every reason to believe that all the grawk-sounds were coming from the grawks.

But then one night Carcharias got incautious, and said something to them when Snash was close enough to tell exactly where the sounds came from. Resisting the impulse to turn, the runt kept on mucking with his rake, but he knew now that the shark spoke grawk like a grawk, at least as far as Snash could tell.

Still, Snash was hesitant to relay his discovery. He couldn't quite blame the shark for hating him, since he really was a spy. But he thought it was only a matter of time before Carcharias got around to eating him, or Slagbag, or both. Since Snash hadn't been able to make friends with the fish, he was already leaning towards ratting when the shark slapped Slagbag so hard with his tail that he knocked the big yark clear across the pool and into a pillar. Slagbag wasn't hurt too bad, but when the Shark Lord called Snash in, the runt was ready to talk.

"He uses the grawks, My Lord," said Snash.

"How dost thou know this?" the ghoul asked.

Snash related his observations.

"Clever indeed," said the Shark Lord. "T'would never have occurred to me, although, in hindsight, it should have. We ourselves useth the grawks to send messages. I even keep one to interrogate the rest...very good, Snash."

Snash said nothing for a few moments.

"What is it?" asked the Ghoul-in-Chief.

"Might I be transferred now, My Lord?"

"And why would I desire to transfer thee?"

"Carcharias is going to kill us, I'm sure of it."

"But he hath not *yet*," said the ghoul. "Which meaneth, of course, that thou canst continue thy spying…Can it be, after all this time, that thou hast not grasped the true nature of this mighty enterprise that thou art a tiny part of?"

"No, My Lord. I was merely hoping---"

"*There* is thy mistake… hope. Regard me, Snash. Consider what thou seest. Why wouldst thou feel any *hope* in my presence? Thou shouldst come to terms with thy predicament. Accept life as life is, which, for thee, means spying on a giant yark-eating shark, at the behest of the ghoul who rides him."

"Yes, My Lord," said Snash.

In truth, of course, he hadn't provided the Shark Lord with all the information he wanted; there remained the matter of whether or not the sharks were actually meeting with each other. There was some evidence of that; objects lost in one stable had turned up in another, and sharkish conversations had been overheard, during the daylight hours when Mount Adamant slept; but no one had caught any of the sharks where they shouldn't have been, and no one had the slightest idea of how they could be visiting each other---the only exits big enough to accommodate the creatures were the gates to the projecting runways, and the openings were blocked with strong portcullises, except when the ghouls took their mounts out. The two spies that had preceded Snash and Slagbag had tried to find out what was going on by hiding in Carcharias's stable during the day...and had never been seen again. But Snash thought he'd discovered a good place to watch from.

"You know those pillars?" said Snash, as Slagbag was getting ready to stretch out on his cot. They had a little room just off Hakmul's chamber.

"Which ones?" Slagbag asked.

"The ones at the corners of the pool."

"It doesn't have corners. It's round."

"You know what I mean. Those."

"The ones where there are three of them?"

"Yes. There are spaces in the middle."

"And?"

"I could get in between the columns."

"He'll see you," said Slagbag.

"Not if I get up to the top. I'll crawl in among those ornamental sharks, keep to the shadows...I'll have a pretty good view of the pool, I think."

"When are you going to try this?"

"Tomorrow. Around dawn, just as he's crawling into his pool...he'll still expect us to be hanging about. He usually faces towards the portcullis...I'll try to get up into the pillars behind him."

"What do you want me to do?"

"Do?"

"You want me to wait outside? Come rushing in if things get hairy? Stick him with a pitchfork?"

"Actually," said Snash, "that mightn't be such a bad idea."

"I half-hope he gives me a chance, the bastard...my back's still sore from hitting that wall..." Slagbag paused. "What do you think the Shark Lord would do? If I stuck his damned fish?"

"I suppose that depends on what I find out," said Snash.

The blackness was greying a bit outside the portcullis grate; Carcharias was sitting in the corner, bundled in his shark-blanket, smoking; he'd gotten a largish knife from somewhere, and a piece of wood, and was carving some sort of figure with it, his blanket and the floor about him covered with chips. Working on this project, he stayed up far later than Snash expected him to——the sky was almost pale by the time the brute laid the figure on the floor, rammed the knife down into its head, then scooted it across the floor towards Snash. As it spun to a halt, Snash saw that it was quite a good representation of a runt....he heard sniggering, and looked up. The shark was laughing, smoke rising through his gills and out of his nostrils...then he tossed off his blanket, and came crawling on his belly, huge and fluid, towards Snash, wings folded, almost *molded* against his back. Clutching his pitchfork, Snash retreated; the shark went to the figure of the runt, pulled the knife out, then backed towards the pool, going down over the edge with a great big *flep*, the algae closing above him.

Already near the side of the stable, Snash raced around by the pillars, and slipped into the assemblage on the right; putting his back against one of the columns, he pressed his feet against the other two, and chimneyed his way to the top as quickly as he could, all the while looking through the gap in front of him, down at the pool. The water subsiding, the shark's great fin sticking straight up through the scum; Carcharias seemed to be motionless beneath the green. There were some fissures and openings between rafts of scum, and through those Snash could see the shark's black body against a greyish floor.

Snash reached the top, insinuated himself into the swirling shark-sculpture...hardly had he arranged himself in a position he thought he could hold for a while when there was movement in the water below, and he saw the fin turn, the whole green surface rotating around it to the right, as though Carcharias was wheeling about beneath...all at once the shark's head, which had been facing the portcullis, rose up out of the scum, facing the stable door. He went back down for a few moments, then came back up, and drew himself all the way out of the water. For some time, Snash watched him stumping about on his short legs, or slithering around, turning his head this way and that, and up and down, as though he were looking for something. At one point he stopped, and Snash was certain the fish had spotted him; but even though the shark was staring directly at the hole that Snash was looking through, he didn't appear to have picked anything out, as he turned away shortly and continued stumping. He went out to the portcullis, made some grawk-noises; a pair of the flying creatures descended, and there seemed to be something of a conversation---Snash thought that Carcharias was posting lookouts, perhaps. Then the fish went over to a huge pile of shark-blankets, pulled one out from down near the bottom, and dragged it down into the pool, the covering revealing, for just an instant, the outline of a great black shark before it sank. There was some activity beneath the surface after that....through gaps in the scum, Snash had the sense that the blanket was being spread out, down on the bottom. There it stayed, although Snash didn't know how Carcharias kept it from floating; he guessed the shark was using weights of some sort. But however it was done, when Carcharias came out of the pool again, he left a huge dark silhouette that could easily have been him if he weren't manifestly elsewhere, and there hadn't been a glaring lack of protruding dorsal fin.

But having seen all that, Snash had no doubt that the dorsal problem had been solved, and shortly he saw how. There were all sorts of sharky motifs on either side of the portcullis, some of them about as big as Carcharias and all of them interwined with each other; going to the wall, Carcharias simply reached in between two of the sharks and pulled out something that had looked for all the world like part of the relief, but now was revealed as a long curved fake fin, complete with some sort of weight-and-chain arrangement at one end; backing back into the pool, Carcharias thrust the fake up right in the center, then folded the genuine article, which turned sideways before it settled, apparently the better to flatten against his back. Once again through gaps in the scum, Snash saw him twisting away to the right. The water heaved, the scum swayed back and forth; then the water calmed again, the scum-patches slid back together, and the bogus fin, rearing up above the scene, rapidly stabilized.

Snash, who hadn't blinked the entire while, blinked several times now...then he chimneyed back down. He thought of running right out of the stable and reporting immediately, then thought he'd better take a quick look, at least, under the water.

He glanced over at the portcullis. There were no grawks visible on the other side. He dashed to the side of the pool, bent down, inhaled deeply, and stuck his head beneath the scum, opening his eyes. Despite the stuff floating on the top, which turned everything beneath all green, the water was very clean and clear. Across from him was a rectangular opening in the wall of the pool. It was quite large---he could certainly have gotten through it. It was, however, hard to imagine that Carcharias had done so, although...

There was a distinct lack of giant shark in the pool at the moment.

Snash lifted his head out of the water, swiped algae from his pate, got up, and dashed to the door where Slagbag was waiting, pitchfork in hand.

"Did you find out how he does it" Slagbag asked.

Snash nodded. "Pity's he's such a bastard," he said. "That is one clever fish."

Snash attempted to report his findings, but was informed that the Shark Lord was lying on his slab with his hands folded on his chest, and couldn't be disturbed; later, however, the ghoul chieftain sent for Snash from his private interrogation chamber, and the runt went there to discover that one of Carcharias's grawk messengers was strapped in a grawk-sized interrogation chair and being slapped repeatedly by a member of his own species wearing black robes, boots, gloves (leather mittenish things, actually, over his wingtips), and a hood (up)...Observing from a chipped obsidian throne that didn't look at all comfortable, its surfaces gleaming with glassy edges, the Shark Lord signalled the interrogator to cease smacking, then said:

"Snash."

"My Lord," Snash said, bowing.

"That *is* one of the grawks of which thou spoke, is it not?"

The prisoner stared at Snash from his chair, eyes burning....Snash looked away immediately. He'd never meant to do anything but defend himself and Slagbag from Carcharias, and up until that moment, he'd never thought of grawks as anything more than, well, *grawks*. Of course, strictly speaking, he *still* didn't have any business thinking of them as more than grawks, but...

"He hath not told us a thing," said the Shark Lord.

"I'll beat it out of him yet!" cried the interrogator.

But before the ghoul could give him the nod, Snash said: "I know how the sharks have been getting around."

"Speak," said the Shark Lord.

Snash told him everything he'd seen, but the ghoul proved skeptical, cocking one of his glowing orbs up.

"A giant false fin?" he asked.

"Yes, My Lord."

"Of what madeth?"

"I have no idea. Wood perhaps. He has a knife. I saw him carving with it..."

"*What* didst thou see?"

"Him carving. A little effigy of me, that---"

"From where did the wood come?"

"I don't know."

"He spreads a *blanket* on the floor of the pool?"

"That's what he did."

"Then escaped, through the pipe that doth drain into the pool?"

"When I looked under the water, he was gone. And that hole *sure* seems to be the only way out."

"It would admit him not."

"He folds his fins."

"Not the top one, surely."

"Even that."

For a few moments, the Shark Lord rested elbow on thigh and invisible chin on gauntlet, then said: "The water cometh from a great cistern, to which the pools all link'd are...perchance the sharks conspire there."

"I can't speak to that, My Lord," said Snash.

"Ah," said the ghoul. "But thou wilt *have* to...When next from his pool my steed doth go, thou shalt follow him."

"Swim up that *pipe*, My Lord?"

"And listen, if thou canst. Do that for me, and I promise thee, here and now, a task yet worse than this."

"Do runts know how to swim?" Snash asked.

"All yarks have that knowledge, yea."

"Will I have to hold my breath very long?"

"I shall give thee somewhat, to grow thee gills."

Snash bowed, then felt a little tap on his leg....he

looked down. The captive grawk had spat on him; obviously itching to resume the smacking, the interrogator was cracking whatever passed for knuckles inside those leather mittens.

It was Snash's fervent hope that Carcharias, upon learning that one of his grawks was missing, would lie low, for a while at least, and cancel any meetings he'd planned; but even though Snash watched him five days running, and nothing happened, the shark was back up to his old tricks on the sixth, laying down his blanket and setting up his false fin, and sneaking out.

Even as the water was settling in the pool, Snash climbed down between the pillars and went to the rim. Inside his tunic was the gill-powder that the Shark Lord had given him---two waterproof packets, one for the return journey, since the effect was temporary. Snash took a packet out, opened it up, and shook the contents onto his tongue...the taste was very sour, and he began to salivate copiously. Even with so much spit, it was hard to swallow, although he managed.

His stomach roiled once the stuff was down, but he soon had something else to think about. The skin on both sides of his throat began to wriggle, and he felt a sharp splitting sensation as his gills opened...he ran his fingers over them, feeling three slits on the left and three on the right. They were opening and shutting, gasping in the air...he realized he was doing that himself...it was very much like gulping, and it made his ears pop.

Here goes, he thought, and lowered himself through the scum into the water beneath...just as the Shark Lord had said, he knew exactly how to swim, kicking off and breast-stroking through the green-lit water...the gills seemed to work just fine, although he did feel the need to exhale. Once he emptied his lungs, though, he felt no desire at all to refill them....the movement of the water through the gill-slits and out over his neck was cool and oddly pleasant, and the taste wasn't so bad.

Ahead, the mouth of the conduit was a black rectangular hole...even when he got up close to it, his eyes couldn't penetrate the shadow at all. He reached inside, fished around a bit, felt nothing. He floated in front of the entrance, put his head in and listened. He thought he could hear draggy and raspy sounds in the distance, but that was just what he would've expected, as there was, after all, at least one gigantic shark crawling through the conduit up ahead.

He wished he had someone to pray to. Yarks were encouraged to pray to Serpentar, and as far as he knew, some, such as the BC boys, and the Inspirational Exhorters, actually did so. Snash had, of course, never felt the slightest temptation; but all the same, he wished there was someone, somewhere, *in* authority, *on* his side. As far as he knew, there wasn't; without any definite ideas on the subject, he simply tried to remember Luvliel's face, and hope that it would help in some sort of way. Thinking of her, he lingered awhile at the threshold of the conduit, then climbed inside and began to half-crawl, half-swim his way into the blackness.

The passage curved away to the right, as he expected…the way it had been explained to him, each of the pools was connected, via the conduits, to a reservoir in a tower two towers over from the Shark Lord's; reaching up into the fumes above the spike, great pipes drew water from the swirling vapor, and the fluid flowed down through them, into the repository. No one was stationed inside the reservoir tower, which was basically a standpipe; the wheels that released the water were located on the outside. But at the base of the tower was the junction where the conduits all met, and into which the water was discharged; Snash was making for that.

On and on through the darkness he pressed; it seemed to him that he was drawing nearer to those draggings and raspings, and guessing that Carcharias, being larger, was slower in the constricted space, he stopped, so that he wouldn't come blundering up on the shark's tail in the black. All that waiting got to be pretty nerve-wracking after a while: his gills were only temporary after all, and he really didn't know how long they'd last…at length, however, the sounds faded, then stopped altogether. Had Carcharias arrived at his destination?

Most concerned about what he was going to find, and how exactly he was going to observe it unobserved, Snash pressed on, still trying to calm himself with thoughts of Luvliel.

At length a dim bluish-green tinge began to paint the left side of the tunnel ahead, welling out from behind that rightward curve…a rectangle of faint light appeared around the bend. Snash swam slowly to the opening and looked out.

It was hard for him to tell, but what he seemed to be seeing was a great circular pool, not unlike Carcharias's, but much wider, and with multiple conduits leading from it. He counted thirteen.

One for each pool…

The water was about as deep as it was in Carcharias's basin; that blue-green light seemed to be coming from overhead, but he couldn't see the source of it from under the water. There were a few rafts of scum drifting about…the water was moving, and drops were landing in it from above.

There was a mat of scum almost directly above him; he swam up beneath it and stayed there. Listening intently, he heard nothing but the knocking of the water. He put his ear against the wall of the pool, thought he heard the rumor of distant engines, but nothing that might have been giant sharks crawling about nearby. It occurred to him that he was in the release-chamber beneath the standpipe; if that were so, he didn't think the sharks could get any farther, and *must* be somewhere above him, since they sure weren't under the water…

Hardly had this train of thought passed through his head when his gills suddenly seized up on him; they just stopped, and when he reached to feel them, they were sealing back up, on both sides…desperately, he fished through his tunic, trying to locate that other packet, but it refused to be found…so long perfectly content with being empty, his lungs began to ache for some air; his brain started to reel; his vision, already dim thanks to that minimal turquoise light, darkened further. There was simply nothing to be done for it: he stuck his head up through the scum, some of the guck sliding down over his face even as some of the rest of it remained atop his bald black scalp like a little cold cap…his mouth dropped open, and he sucked in a great breath, water dripping from the pointy tip of his nose.

His sight sharpened, almost immediately. He sucked in

some more air, turning. He could just see over the rim of the pool. It was surrounded by what might have been a kind of walkway…there were glowing blue-green streaks on the wall, which was circular. He completed his three-sixty, water dripping down all about him…no sharks.

But, he told himself, *you didn't look* straight *up*…

He lifted his chin, craned his head back, the scum sliding over the back of his skull.

Clinging to the domed ceiling, tails towards the center, heads pointed outward, snouts tilted downward, were the giant mounts of the Black Thirteen, their eyes and fangs gleaming in the algal light, water dripping from their noses and teeth.

Stifling a scream, trying to think, Snash told himself that he could outswim them in the conduit, almost submerged and went back into it, but…

His gills were gone. There wasn't the slightest point in fleeing.

"Now don't you feel foolish?" said one of the sharks…Snash had no way of knowing, but suspected the voice was Carcharias's.

Shark-water dripping on his head, Snash said, "No," and despite his fear, he meant it.

"No?" the shark laughed. "Are you *not* just about to be eaten?"

"Do you think I *wanted* to come here?" Snash asked, moving out from under the drips, towards the middle of the pool.

"I think you're a lickspittle, just like all those other lickspittles I've eaten."

"Is *that* why you obey the Ghouls?" Snash asked. "Because you are what you eat?"

The other sharks all laughed, one saying:

"Oh, Carcharias, he nicked you, he did!"

"Are you going to take it from him?" asked another.

"Eat him and have done with it," said a third.

"I second the motion," said a fourth.

But in spite of the fact that all of this had been at his expense, Carcharias seemed to find it rather funny. "Yes, by all means, rules of order," he laughed. "Let's put it to a vote. How say you, brethren of the most illustrious Fellowship of the Fin? Shall I eat him right now?"

"Aye!" answered a chorus of sharky voices.

"Any nays?" asked Carcharias.

There were none.

"Ayes have it," he said, and crawled from the ceiling, down along the wall in a leisurely spiral, asking Snash: "Aren't you going to make a run for it? You might be able to beat me in that tunnel."

"My gills are gone," Snash replied.

"How sad---"

"Stop talking to the food!" one of the others cried.

But Snash asked: "Don't you want to find out what I know?"

Carcharias halted on the walk. "Actually...I think I would at that," he said, and glanced back up at his buddies. "What do you think?"

"He's stalling!" one replied.

"Yes, Carcharadon," Carcharias said. "But he probably *does* know some things."

Snash added: "Like what the Shark Lord knows."

"Might be interesting," said Carcharias to his friends.

"Eat him!" Carcharadon said. "We voted!"

"We could vote again," Carcharias replied.

"This process is awkward!" said another of the sharks.

"I quite agree, Bigmouth," said Carcharias. "I say we vote not to vote."

"I second the motion," Bigmouth said, and after it was thirded, it carried, whereupon Carcharias hung his head over the edge of the walk and asked the water-treading runt:

"Name's Snash, right?"

"Right."

"Well, Snash. Spill it."

Snash replied: "He knows about you and the grawks, and how you've been meeting, and where."

"Thanks to you?"

"Yes."

"Well aren't *you* an excellent spy? Those other yarks didn't have a clue..."

"So you ate them just to eat them? It didn't *matter* that they were spies?"

"No."

"I'm smarter," Snash said.

"Downright atypical," Carcharias acknowledged.

"Yes."

"So we can pretty much count on your replacement not being as smart?"

"Pretty much," said Snash.

"Good to know," Carcharias said. "Thank you very much."

He made as if to slide his massive self into the pool.

"*But,*'Snash said.

The great fish paused just as he was about to tip.

Snash continued: "The Shark Lord doesn't know what you're *up* to."

Carcharias laughed. "Are you expecting me to *tell* you?"

"You might want to."

"Why's that?"

"I was planning to make up a story. To tell *him*. But what if I made up a story, and it just happened to be the truth?"

"You needn't worry," Carcharias said.

"Because you're going to eat me?"

"You have it."

"You don't want to do that," Snash replied.

"No?" Carcharias laughed.

"No," Snash said. "But you *do* want to tell me what you're about, so I can be sure to make up something different."

"And why would you want to do that?"

"Because I'm on your side."

"A brave and moving declaration."

"I hate Serpentar."

"Do you think it makes you less tasty? I really like runt."

"Here, here!" cried one of the sharks on the ceiling.

But Snash was undeterred. "I'm willing to make common cause with you."

"Little you?" Carcharias asked. "I think we'd have *little* to gain."

"What if the Shark Lord turns his attention elsewhere? At least for the time being?"

"Hmm," said Carcharias.

Snash went on: "Now this is just a guess, of course, but I think you're plotting an escape."

"Haven't you heard about the iron bars embedded in our heads?"

"I have," said Snash.

"Well, they work *exactly* as intended," Carcharias said.

"And you can't figure out how to get round them?"

Carcharias just eyed him.

"But you keep pondering the problem." Snash went on, swimming closer to the shark. "Meeting here...trading ideas..." He was very close to the pointed tip of Carcharias's snout when the shark nodded, adding:

"Arguing theory."

Snash assumed he meant brain-iron theory, but the shark went on:

"Systems of government. How things might be, *should* be, for us sharks, at least. *If* we got free somehow. Myself, I incline towards constitutional monarchism---"

"With guess who as king?" Carcharadon broke in.

"---while my friends represent a broad range of opinion. All of us are, however, completely united in rejecting Serpentar's system, which seems to us a moral *and* practical disaster, completely at variance with Natural Law."

"Natural Law?" Snash asked.

"The way things actually work," Carcharias said. "Obviously, any truly just---and effective---system would have to be based on it."

"I suppose it would have to," said Snash.

"It would indeed."

"But anyway..."

"Yes?" Carcharias asked.

"You don't want *any* of this getting back to the Shark

Lord," Snash said.

"No."

"I'll lie to him."

"*If* I don't eat you."

"If."

"Do you know *how* to lie to him?" Carcharias asked. "*Our* minds are too fishy for him to see into, but…"

"I've found a way," Snash said.

"Not sure I believe you, but---"

"Please, let me go. You have nothing to lose. He's getting ready to move against you."

"You *know* this?"

"I do."

"What will you tell him?"

"That you're just a…fellowship. A club. A…giant flying shark club."

"Damn it all, Carcharias," Carcharadon called.

"What?" Carcharias asked.

"*Eat* the damn runt!"

"We should take another vote," said Carcharias.

"I second the motion!" Snash cried.

"Hey, hey, just us sharks, if you *please!*" Carcharadon replied.

The bickering went on a while longer, but presently the sharks voted to vote again, then voted on Snash's fate, and Carcharias had his way…even though Snash had to agree with Bigmouth that the process was awkward, he was impressed. Still, the sharks all seemed so *reasonable*, concerned with rights and process, that he decided he really had to chide Carcharias for all the harassment in the stable, asking:

"Why were you such a bastard at me?"

"Eh?" Carcharias replied. "Just now, when you came in?"

"No, right from the first," Snash said. "I was trying to make friends with you. We could've saved a lot of time."

But Carcharias replied: "Sharks are expected to be nasty, and in truth, we're not that nice. Also, we thought you were a spy, and you…were. Also, if it comes right down to it, it's rare for creatures to accord rights outside their own species, particularly to food. Still, I suppose a case could be made that I might've done better not to brutalize you...." He paused. "How *are* you planning to get back through the conduits without gills, by the way?"

"Not sure," said Snash, and searched through his tunic one last time...much to his relief, he found the other packet. "Ah, good. Just what I needed."

He showed the packet to the shark, who cocked his head over the side of the pool. "That'll give you gills?"

Snash said, "Watch," and took the contents.

Once the slits opened, Carcharias opined: "They don't go with your neck."

"Maybe, come the revolution, no one will need false gills."

The shark considered this, then said: "You give me hope, little Snash."

Snash nodded and submerged beneath the scum.

Chapter 12: Life At the Top

"A giant flying shark club, thou sayest?" asked the Shark Lord.

"Exactly, My Lord," Snash replied.

"And they were not aware of thee?"

"So far as I couldst tell---"

The Shark Lord's eyes glowed a bit brighter. "Art thou making sport of me?"

Snash shook his head wildly. "No, My Lord....So overwhelming is thy...I mean, *your* presence that I find myself adopting your way of speaking, which is in truth, most striking and apt."

"Ah," said the Shark Lord. "So then...let us return to the matter of this...Fellowship. They spoke no treason?"

"Not that I heardest."

"Why concealeth they these meetings?"

"They saideth nothing about that."

"Thou *art* telling me the truth, art thou not?"

"Would I dare to try and trick thee?" Snash asked. "When I wot full well that thou canst sniff out lies with thy floating eyes?"

"Mine eyes sniff *not*," said the Shark Lord, and Snash was wondering if the ghoul was about to demonstrate yet again what they *did* do when a brain arrived with a dispatch; once the Shark Lord read it, he appeared to have forgotten all about peering into Snash's head.

"I have a new task for thee," the Gage Ghoul declared.

"My Lord?"

"Hast thou heard of Yarks and Spiders?"

Snash shook his head.

"'Tis a noble game," said the ghoul. "Played on a checkered board, with living pieces...Lord Serpentar's favorite pasttime, it is much loved as well by Master Slippriman, who hath made himself quite at home in Serpentar's abode, and the two contend at whiles...many of Slippriman's servants have found their way onto the board when he ran shy of other yarks. Verily, at this moment, he lacks an orderly, having lost his last on the board. Thou shalt, therefore, enter his service in that capacity, and report whatever striketh thee as worthy of note…Once I send thee forth from here, report to Master Nathrond in Minion Resources, and he shall make pretense of assigning thee."

Taking a quill, he dipped it in ink and began to dash off a letter on parchment.

"This goeth to Nathrond," he said once he finished…after blotting the ink, he rolled up the scroll, and sealed it with wax. Snash looked at the seal---it showed a shark bursting through a circle, spreading its wings.

"My Lord," said Snash, bowed, touched the document to his forehead, and started for the door. But after a few paces he halted---did he want to ask about Slagbag? It would've been a comfort to bring him along, except for the fact that he was almost certainly better off raking shark muck; after all, Snash had no desire at all to revisit Serpentar's abode, and was quite sure he hadn't seen anything like the worst of it…

"Didst thou forget to inquire about Slagbag?" the ghoul asked.

"No, My Lord."

"Dost thou not want him with thee?"

Snash was not sure how to answer.

"Fear not, about *that* matter, at any rate…he shall join thee, and he also shall keep his eyes open, while he endures. Mayhap thou shalt even have opportunity to take counsel together."

Snash bowed once more.

"No gratitude?"

"I canst not express it," said Snash.

"Yarks and Spiders?" Slagbag asked.

He and Snash were in Carcharias's stable, the big shark listening in, resting with his snoot up over the side of his pool.

"It's a game," Snash said. "I asked around about it. Spiders on one side, yarks on the other. *Live* ones. The players push you about with magic, and when you come to a square with a spider on it, it's you or that spider…." Snash shook his head.

"Wouldn't mind watching a spot of *that*," Slagbag said.

"Sounds bloody exciting."

"Especially for the pieces."

"Can't say I'd like to be one, though."

"Well, I didn't ask for you this time," Snash said.

Slagbag looked puzzled.

"I *was* going to leave you down here," Snash continued.

"Because he'd be safer with me?" Carcharias said. "I am *truly* touched!"

But Slagbag asked Snash: "What are you saying?"

"When I didn't mention you, the Shark Lord asked me if I'd forgotten," Snash replied. "Decided to send you up, all on his own..."

"To be a *piece*?"

"I don't know. But it sounded like he didn't expect you to last too long. A lot of Slippriman's yarks wind up on the board."

"Even if the Shark Lord's looking out for them?"

"What do bet you catch it from both sides?" Snash asked. "This is all because of me. Would've been better if we'd never met."

"Don't say that," Slagbag said. "It's not your fault....just isn't." He exhaled heavily, then laughed. "Sounds like I'm never going to get the chance to tear the bastard's eyeballs out."

"Maybe not," Snash answered.

"Whatever. If worse comes to worst, might as well just buckle down and give those spiders Hell....what'll I be armed with, by the way?"

"I don't know," said Snash.

"I'd *like* an axe," said Slagbag. "Big one, though not *too* big, with a double head for the backstroke. Also, a spike on the top, in case I want to stick some spider right in the brain...How does that sound?"

"I'd rather have a bow," said Snash. "So I wouldn't have to get anywhere near 'em."

"You," said Slagbag, "are too practical."

"No," said Snash. "I'm hopelessly in love with a fay-princess I can never have, and seriously considering throwing my life away in a futile act of open rebellion. How practical

187

does that sound?"

"Not very," Slagbag conceded.

"I love it," said Carcharias from the pool.

The following night, Snash went down to Minion Resources for his papers, then back up through the Spike to Serpentar's floor. Since he'd seen before how the door opened, he wasn't surprised this time, and not nearly as unsettled; he was similarly undisturbed as he passed along the corridor, even though it was just as thorny and snaky and variable in length as ever. The serpent who confronted him at the end seemed to be just going through the motions, and Snash acted more scared than he was. Making for Nognomen's desk, he was beginning to wonder if, perhaps, things weren't going to be so bad.

Directly beneath that point that depended from the ceiling, Nognomen was sitting straight up, and Snash couldn't tell which way he was facing, but again, that was just...more of the same, at least until the Chief of Staff leaned forward and started to sign his way through a stack of documents on his desk, assisted by a brain. Spotting Snash, the fatskull gave the runt a sneer, but it was precisely the sort of look that fatskulls gave to those they considered their inferiors, and it rolled right off...even when Snash saw the great snake-mouth behind Nognomen begin to yawn, he told himself that he'd been through it and back, and was still alive.

That was, however, before he saw who came out.

Quite absorbed in what he was doing, Nognomen just kept on signing, but the brain, intensifying red light fringing his profile, was plainly well aware of the approaching threat. Looking a great deal *hotter* than Snash had remembered, eye blazing a *whole* lot brighter, Serpentar was floating slowly across the floor.

Behind the Yark Lord, at some remove, came Slippriman in his filmy white robes, hurrying at first, then slowing, as though he couldn't follow too closely, for fear of broiling. At length, even Nognomen seemed to feel the heat, and started to turn his head, then paused as if he were afraid, and laid down his pen...Serpentar halted a few yards behind him. The brain stepped back. Fifteen feet away, Snash could feel the Yark Lord's ferocious drying malice…it was like being a snail again.

"My Lord," said Nognomen. "I…"

"Where is thy face, Nameless One?" asked Serpentar.

Nognomen said nothing.

"Didst thou or didst thou *not* swear to relinquish thy face?" Serpentar demanded.

"I did," said Nognomen.

"And *yet*," Serpentar said, "thou didst *retain* it!" He motioned to Slippriman, who produced a pale sacklike thing, and tossed it onto the table in front of Nognomen, then stepped back, shielding his own face from Serpentar's glow.

"Fool!" cried Serpentar. "Worm! *Abject* wretch! Thinkest Thou the Prying Eye is blind? That if thou hide thy face under thy pillow, it shall escape my notice? Yea, I tell thee, even though thy pillow was stone and lead, it did not avail, and thy face was found and fetch'd to me."

"Mercy, My Lord," Nognomen said, trying to rise. But all at once Serpentar came up close behind him, and laid a snake-fingered hand upon his shoulder; flames spurted from under Serpentar's palm, and Nognomen, grimacing and screaming, sank back down into the chair.

"What else hast thou retained, oathbreaker?" Serpentar asked. "Thy name, perchance? Oh, I think thou knowest it still; I have it, on good authority, that when thou thoughtst no one didst see, thou didst take thy face from neath thy useless pillow, and don it before a glass, and gloat upon thy features, and chant thy own name, in contravention of thy promise to me, thy Liege and God!"

In a high whiny voice, which Snash barely caught, Nognomen merely replied: "Sorry!"

"Thinkest thou to make amends with that?" Serpentar asked. "One whined word? A million would not suffice…I *cannot* forgive a single sin, let alone thy multitude. Innocence itself will not procure my mercy, for mercy I have not."

"Sorry," Nognomen whined again.

"*Sorry* doth not soothe my snakes," said Serpentar, swelling up behind him, head blossoming, white-hot snakes retracting from his eye-cavity and rising up and spreading out into a great blazing writhing radiant hood, an eyelike fireball, brighter even than the hood, hovering under its fringe. He looked the very incandescent image of madness; Snash felt as though something were going painfully wrong with his brain, or at the very least, that it was under some sort of ferocious assault...Serpentar's arms lifted, and the fingers of his gauntletless left hand lengthened, whipping and striking, some in the direction of Nognomen, some at empty air.

"Sorry," whined Nognomen a third time.

"Join...*Nastimir,*" Serpentar replied through the gaping glowing mouths of his snakes, and stepping close to him, drove his fingers down into Nognomen's head, which they penetrated in little puffs of flame. Nognomen began to babble, his jaw working wildly even though he had no mouth. Smoke curled out of his skin, at first in fine threads but rapidly growing thicker, as his head began to glow from within. Blisters rose singly, then in masses, bulging out through the smoke, splitting open, spewing first fluid, then jets of fire...the smoke ignited, and his whole head burst alight with a thud that Snash felt like a blow to the stomach.

Behind Nognomen, Serpentar's whole body was unravelling and unwrapping, all its snakes untangling from each other and diving beneath Nognomen's flesh...jerking spasmodically, the Chief of Staff ran with fire, blazed brightly for a few moments...

Then went out with a loud *shwip!* The crown of his skull fell in almost immediately; a cindery husk, his body began to crumble into itself, the head dropping down inside his chest...black bits flew up out of the hole and drifted down side to side, looking very light, as though they were little more than dark foam. As the charred rim continued to fall in, the chair became visible, its steel glowing red.

Behind, Serpentar's snakes had reassembled themselves into...

Him.

"Methinks," he said to Slippriman, his whole body rotating in the air, "I need a new Chief of Staff."

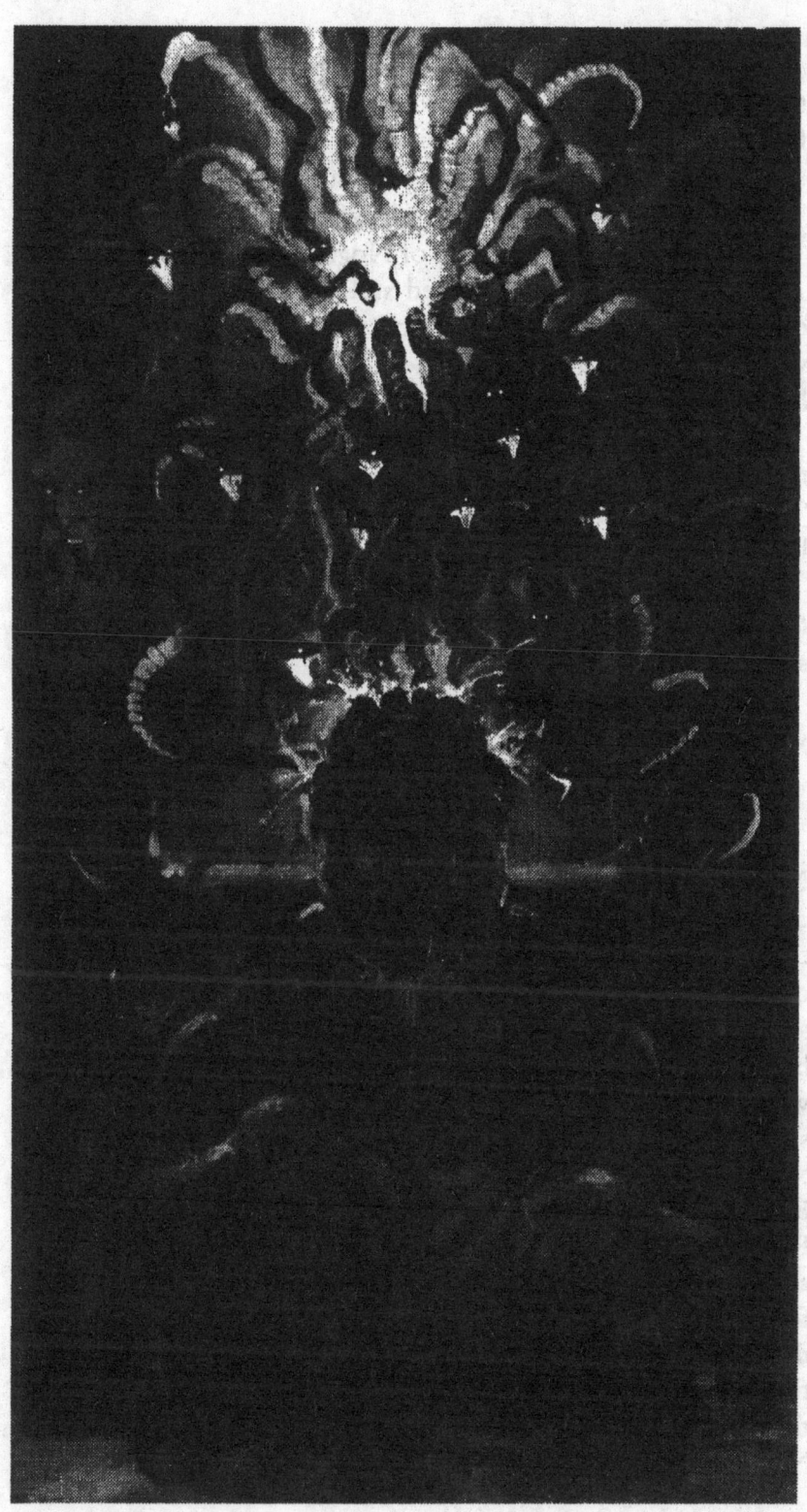

"I concur, My Lord," said Slippriman, and the two of them headed back towards the snake-mouth, Slippriman following the Yark Lord at a distance, as before, saying:

"Might I be allowed to make a suggestion..."

Snash caught no more of it after that.

He eyed what was left of Nognomen.

The husk had collapsed still further, smoke curling up out of it. Above the seat, which was still glowing, the point which had hung over Nognomen's head was incandescent too, little sputters of sparks flying out of it.

As for Nognomen's assistant, he was trembling worse than Snash... catching sight of the runt, the brain screamed: "What do *you* want?" then ran off gibbering, straight into a wall head-first, and collapsed.

Snash moved closer to the desk. Nognomen's face had turned brown from the heat, and was still curling and shrinking.

Just had to look, didn't you? Snash asked himself, wondering if he was ever going to stop shaking.

He remained just where he was long enough for Nognomen's smoke to suffuse itself through the entire chamber, turning everything grey and blurry; almost as though the ceiling-spike were made of some flammable material, it continued to smolder sullenly, an occasional shower of sparks shooting out of it with loud pops that startled Snash very badly. He walked over to see what was what with the fellow who'd run into the wall...the brain was still breathing, but seemed to be declining steadily.

Snash began to get very hungry, in spite of all the horribleness just now...he had, after all, been down to Minion Resources and back up, and all those steps would've given him an appetite no matter what. He searched the dying yark for food and didn't find any, but there was always Nognomen's desk...Snash got all the way over to it before he remembered that Nognomen hadn't had a mouth. Still, he would've rifled the desk anyway if the metal hadn't been so hot. As for Nognomen's face, it had shrunk to about one-quarter its original size, and even though there were holes in it, eyes, nostrils, mouth, they *really* didn't look like features anymore. Snash could imagine some hungry yark prying it off the metal, with a knife-tip say, and eating it, but...he wasn't that yark.

Retreating from the desk, he sat down on the floor, telling himself that someone else had to come through eventually, seeing as how Serpentar was the master of most of the world, and certainly had many allies, catspaws, slaves, etc, if no friends, that might want to consult with him, receive his orders, bring him news, especially since he was about to send forth his army. But it was either a slow night in Mount Adamant, or everyone was just afraid to venture in...finally two aproned runts with wheelbarrows and cleaning implements appeared out of an entrance to the right that had just appeared itself.

"Whew!" one laughed. "So much for the Nameless."

When they reached the desk, the second runt eyed the thing upon it. "Even *I* wouldn't eat that," he said.

"I don't know," said his partner. "I like a well-done face now and then."

"I need to report to Lord Slippriman," Snash said.

"Is *that* what you need? Never knew *anyone* who needed *that*, har-har."

"Please," Snash said.

The first cleaner said: "You see the door we just came out of? Head on down that passage. You'll smell a smell...follow that. You'll take a right, and another. His door is marked with the sign of a man, sliding down a slippery slope, and loving it."

Snash hesitated.

"Don't you trust us?" the second cleaner asked.

Snash shrugged.

"Look at it this way," the first said. "If we *do* send you off to some room full of rats, or a door that opens on the outside of the Spike, at least you won't wind up like Lord Nognomen."

"Why would Lord Serpentar burn me up?"

"You think he needs a reason? Not needing a reason is the whole *point* of being him."

Snash's stomach growled. "Do either of you have some food?" he asked.

The first runt pried Nognomen's face up with a knife-tip and wiggled it Snash's way.

Snash winced and went.

The hallway was long and mostly dark, lit only at junctions where other, narrower passages joined it, all from the left; finally he began to detect an odd smell, sweet but musty, very unpleasant; he took a right, then another, then came to the door marked with the (torchlit) sign of the Smiling Slider, who was plainly modelled on Slippriman himself, right down to his flowing robes...in addition to sliding backwards, he was leaning slightly back, although he didn't seem in the least danger of falling down, his arms crossed on his chest....As Snash approached the door, the Slider split down the middle and swung away in both directions, and Snash passed through, into a huge antechamber filled with large but elegant pots in which rather dry looking white flowers with tastefully small petals had been planted.

"Your business?" asked a brain, who came out from behind one of those swung-back valves.

"I'm Lord Slippriman's new orderly," Snash said.

Another brain came out from behind the other door, and said: "Follow me."

"I'm very hungry..."

"You'll be fed at some point. Come on."

Snash trailed him through the anteroom and into a maze of passages, many of them lined with those damn potted flowers...inadvertently, he brushed one of the blossoms, which didn't give a bit, feeling quite dry and dead to his touch, almost as though it were made of parchment.

"You'll be docked for that," said the brain wearily.

"What?"

"Brushing the flowers."

"Our pay's held in trust," Snash replied.

"Well," the brain answered, "the trust will be holding less of *yours*." He stopped before a double door where the sliding man was all the way over on the lefthand valve, as though he had slid a yard or two farther. There was a small knocker, and the brain knocked *very* lightly. The door opened from within. Snash glanced at the brain, who nodded him through...the door sighed shut.

Snash was in a large room, with rather austere but stylish black furniture. Right in the middle, in a tall seat, sat Slippriman, one leg crossed over his knee; he had a huge book in his lap, and was smoking a stick which looked about a third burned down in its long black holder.

"Come," he said.

Snash approached him. The ash at the tip of his smoking-stick beginning to droop, he almost tapped it off in a vessel on a stand that stood next to his chair, but then thought better of it, apparently, and told Snash:

"Put out your palm."

Snash extended it. Slippriman flicked the ash off into Snash's hand...Snash expected it to hurt, but it didn't very much.

"Dispose of that, after you leave, in an authorized receptacle," said Slippriman. "If I see a spot of it anywhere, you'll suffer, then die...who are you, exactly?"

"Your new orderly."

"My orderlies, up till now, have been brains."

"I don't know why I was picked," said Snash.

"Who sent you?"

"Minion Resources," said Snash.

But Slippriman didn't take his papers. "Who in MR?"

"Master Nathrond."

"And who asked him to send you?"

"I don't know."

"Who did you work for---before?"

Snash almost answered: *The Shark Lord,* then checked himself...Not knowing if Slippriman had any connections to Khuttarh, he didn't mention Overflowing Fist either. He had, of course, been working for Khuttarh in the mailroom, but more time had passed, and so...

"I ran dispatches. In the Sp---"

"Palm," said Slippriman, and Snash put it out again, Slippriman depositing more ash in it before asking: "Do you know what I think?"

"No, My Lord."

"I think you left out some things just now."

"I didn't."

"You hesitated, and you got a little shifty look on your face."

"I didn't leave anything out---"

But Slippriman was having none of that, and shook his head. "Don't waste my time."

"My Lord---"

Slippriman raised his long-fingered white hand, puffed, waited a few moments, then said, smoke oozing upwards from his mouth, "Now *if* you were to tell me who you're spying for---and help me to fool him---it would be to your advantage."

"I'm not a spy."

"So you say. But you should give the matter some thought. Things are different up here. The pace is very fast...down below, you need to be frightened all the time, but *here*...there's no word to describe what you need to feel. Remember, what happened to Nognomen---what Serpentar *did?* Seeing it was like losing your mind, wasn't it? All that hatred, burning, burning...well, you are just a little fly, and he could dry you out with a glance. But I am high in his counsels, and will be your shield, for a little while at least." He tapped some more ash into Snash's palm. "If you will be *my* fly, I might even keep you off the checkered board..." Slippriman paused. "Don't I know you, by the way?"

"We met, once," Snash said. "I'd just brought a parcel up....Lord Serpentar called for a yark...turned me into a snail..."

Smoking-stick hanging from the corner of his mouth, Slippriman clapped. "Ah, I remember now, yes! And I tried to step on you, but the sole of my sandal was too thin, and I fell over...You certainly had a close call." He signalled. Out from between two vases came yet came another brain, exceptionally sniffy-looking.

"Snitpikh," said Slippriman, "instruct---" He paused, eyeing Snash. "What *is* your name?"

"Snash," said the runt, who considered asking about food, then thought better of it.

"In his new duties," Slippriman went on. "Now get him out of here---"

Snash's stomach grumbled.

"You have an insubordinate belly," Slippriman observed, then told the brain: "Don't let him eat until you're through."

Snitpikh led Snash to an authorized receptacle, and after Snash duly disposed of the ash in his hand, he was shown, his stomach growing steadily more vehement, through a series of rooms, including Slippriman's bedchamber, laboratory, and library...there were a great number of things, all of them looking very much in their proper place, and if Snash hadn't gotten that impression already, Snitpikh, nose pertually turned up at the stomach noises, pointed to just about every single item (he seemed to overlook a few) and said: "This goes here," or, "That goes right there," or, "This is the place for this," and it got to be incredibly tedious, especially in the library. There just wasn't all that much in the bedchamber---Slippriman had far fewer identical robes than the Shark Lord, for example. And the laboratory wasn't absolutely *bursting* with arcane gear and ingredients. But Slippriman apparently set great store by books, and the library was crammed. Since Slippriman seemed to be a guest or some sort of refugee, that was kind of puzzling; Snash wondered how he could've amassed such a number of volumes, or if he'd brought them with him somehow; but there were, at any rate, thousands of them, books and scrolls, and Snitpikh, after explaining the cataloguing system, insisted on telling Snash where every single one was located, although Snash could simply see for himself...Snitpikh didn't even manage to finish the first night, although Snash's stomach had apparently given up in the meanwhile, subsiding into a silent ache...

Finally he got a small piece of bread, strangely soft with very little salt in it, or taste of any kind for that matter, along with some water, and a few moments to bolt it all down...then he was led to the chamber where Slippriman's runts bunked. Still very hungry, he tossed and turned the whole day through...when he got up, Snitpikh was right there, administered a sniff test, and decided Snash didn't pass; since Slippriman could only stand the smell of the smoke from his sticks, and the dry sweetish odor from his flowers, and could, apparently, nose out an overly stinky yark at several hundred yards, Snitpikh saw to it that Snash got cleaned up. Slippriman's yarks had much better facilities than anyone downstairs; instead of having to scrape his skin with wire brushes moistened with his own spit, the runt was actually allowed to use water from a receptacle on the wall, and pinkish soap, which had apparently been captured from Fays; it smelled very nice---rather, in fact, the way he remembered Luvliel smelling---but he wasn't very sure if it cleaned very well. He associated cleanliness with the feeling of having the first two layers of his skin sanded off.

After hygiene came breakfast, bland bread and flavorless white cheese, in very small portions....then he went back to being told where the rest of the books were. But at last Snitpikh said:

"That's that. Don't touch *anything*," and led him to a small chamber just off Slippriman's bedroom, empty but for a stool. "Now sit, facing the corner, until My Lord requires your presence."

"But what does an orderly *do*?" Snash asked.

"Nothing," said Snitpikh. "If everything's *already* in order. And Slippriman won't let anyone touch anything, or move anything, if he can help it. He likes things just *so*."

"And I just have to sit---"

"Facing the corner."

"For how long?"

"Oh, until he runs out of runts in Yarks and Spiders, I think. Which won't be very long."

"If he's so worried about messes, why does he like to see Yarks and Spiders killing each other?"

"I've never put the question to him. I've never put *any* question to him. Might be why I've survived so long, even though things go so fast up here. If I had to guess, I'd say he might be willing to abide a certain amount of mess, so long as something's getting hurt. Also, it's not as though he has any say. Serpentar just beats him. Over and over."

"I see," said Snash.

"Now go sit in your corner."

"Will someone spell me when my shift is done?"

"Oh yes, the day orderly. That's if we have a live one around...Don't fall asleep."

"I'll try not to---"

With that, Snitpikh left and took the lamp with him. Utter darkness filled the room...there wasn't even any light from under the door. Since Snash was a yark, the dark didn't bother him much, although, with nothing at all to see---even yarks required a smidgin of light----or do, he soon got rather sleepy. But staying awake didn't prove that much of a problem---whenever he conked out, which was not often because he hadn't been fed since breakfast, he simply fell off his stool and woke back up.

A day orderly did indeed come to relieve him, gave him some tasteless bread and water; Snash retired to his mean little cot among all the other mean little cots.

"When was the last game of Yarks and Spiders?" he asked Rhutzu, one of the other runts.

"Six nights ago," Rhutzu replied. "We're overdue...word is they're going to play one just before the army sets out. 'Hallowing,' is what they call it."

"Ever been in one?"

"Wouldn't be talking to you now. Serpentar always plays the spiders---so the yarks always lose."

"But..."

"What?"

"He's the *Yark* Lord---"

"Yeah," Rhutzu said. "But I suspect---strongly---that he doesn't feel any solidarity with us."

Snash wondered why he'd even raised the point. "Does Slippriman let him win?"

"Wager he would if it ever became an issue...Would *you* try to win?"

"If I was Slippriman? I'd never *be* Slippriman."

"You don't say."

"How many yarks fight how many spiders?" Snash

199

asked.

"There are sixteen on a side, I think. Not counting reinforcements, which is another---"

"Eight," called someone else.

"The players push the pieces around with magic," Rhutzu went on. "But once a spider's on the same square as a yark, or vicey-versey, they fight."

"To the death," said that other runt. "Until one side or the other's wiped out."

"Do we get weapons?" Snash asked.

"I think," said Rhutzu.

"Axes?" Snash asked, thinking of Slagbag.

"Hell, I don't know."

"You haven't run into a fellow named Slagbag, have you?"

"Pipe down!" cried someone halfway across the room, off on the left. Snash heard a sound as of someone shifting violently and peevishly in bed.

Rhutzu whispered: "Haven't met any Slagbags up here."

"Hmm," said Snash.

Next nightshift, Snitpikh was nowhere to be seen; wondering if something had happened to him (had he asked Slippriman a question at last?) Snash headed off for Slippriman's room alone, feeling pretty anxious, because he hadn't made up his mind about the whitebeard's offer. If he admitted he was a spy for the Shark Lord, he thought it was entirely possible that Slippriman would have him killed. Since Slippriman seemed a much trickier commodity than the Gage Ghoul, Snash decided that his best course would be---simply--- to keep on lying, and hope he wouldn't run into him.

But when he got to the bedroom, Slippriman was sitting at a vanity, its wooden parts painted the same shade of pink as that bar of Fayish soap. There was a big flowing capital "L" atop the mirror; Snash wondered if it had been captured along with Luvliel. Slippriman was powdering his face...once he got done with that, he tied his long white hair back, and attached a small pearl to his right ear lobe. Then he opened a big box of rings, and put two on either hand.

"Snash," he said at last, without looking around.

"My Lord?" Snash asked.

"Have you given some hard thought to that matter?"

"I have," he said.

"Then tell me who sent you."

"Master Nathrond, in---"

"MR, yes, yes." Swinging his legs to the side of the chair, Slippriman smiled at him skeptically. "You're the runt that tripped Luvliel up, yes?"

"I am."

"Worked in the mail room, did you not?"

"I did."

"Your chief was named Khuttarh, yes? Did you know that he and I are very close?"

"No, My Lord."

"And that he'll be replacing Nognomen? As Chief of Staff?"

"I hadn't heard that, My Lord."

"Are you as surprised as you look?"

Snash was pretty sure he must be, even without seeing himself---when he'd left Overflowing Fist, Khuttarh had been in heaps of trouble.

Slippriman saved him, Snash thought. *turned it all to their advantage, somehow---*

"Now," said Slippriman, "didn't you work for him at Overflowing Fist too?"

Snash nodded.

"A fact you failed to mention to me...."

"I didn't think---"

"Oh, I think you think all the time...After all, weren't you spying on Khuttarh *then*? For the Shark Lord?"

Snash said nothing.

"Would you like to know how Khuttarh slipped the noose?"

In spite of everything, Snash *was* curious; he nodded.

"On my advice, he got out in front of everything. Said he was running his own investigation. Arrested Smeggit

201

himself. What do you think of that?"

"Clever," Snash said.

Slippriman laughed. "I'll tell him you said so…He thinks you despise him."

Snash said nothing.

"He's told me some things about *you*," Slippriman said.

"He makes up lies about me."

"And why would he trifle with that?"

"Because I told him how to improve things in the mail room, and he wanted all the credit himself."

Slippriman eyed him closely, and it was quite apparent that he didn't regard the claim with the least skepticism. "That was *you*? *You're* the one who gave him all his good ideas?"

"About the mail room, yes."

"Well, that does indeed explain a few things…" Slippriman laughed. "Never did understand why he hated you so much…really, he should've coddled you. Perhaps he should be given another opportunity, yes?"

Snash wasn't sure what Slippriman was up to here. Was this punishment *and* enticement, all wrapped up in one?

"What do you say?" Slippriman asked. "*Would* you like to work for Khuttarh again?"

"No," said Snash.

"You'd do well to come to an accomodation with me. Because I'm going to turn you over to Khuttarh no matter what, and the only thing that will keep him off you is me. You should *hear* what he'd like to do to you. Oh, the *thoughts* he has fondled. One might say to oneself, he was from the mail room, now he's from O.F., how terribly humdrum, a quill-pusher, a desk-bound schemer with dreams of glory, whose biggest exploit was arresting one of his own brains. But there's a good deal more to him. That's how I sold him to Serpentar. He has *underwear* made of fellows like you. Soft little runt-skins, that's what he likes on his bottom." He shifted in his seat, as though he were more than a bit moved by the idea himself.…Snash had the queasy impression that Slippriman had taken the conversation in this direction just so he could talk about Khuttarh's underwear.

"So what do you think?" Slippriman asked.

Snash's mind raced. Obviously things were coming to the crunch...he couldn't be sure that Slippriman would kill him outright if he admitted he was spying, but he was certain that Slippriman would put a stop to him, and soon, if he didn't get some sort of commitment...

"It's impossible to lie to him," Snash said.

"To who?"

"The Shark Lord."

"You admit then that he sent you?"

Snash nodded. "But...I *won't* be able to lie to him. His eyes come out from under his hood--"

"Tacky, isn't it? I know all about it. He took a look into me, once. When I first came here. He can't see what you're actually *thinking*, but he can tell if you're telling the truth...lies are *green*, apparently. There's a way to keep him from seeing anything, though."

"And what's that, My Lord?"

"You have to think of a fay-princess. That's the standard technique, as a matter of fact. I thought of the Princess Luvliel...we were on the White Committee together. Didn't care for each other too much, but I made a determined effort to memorize her every feature, in case anyone ever tried to eyeball me for lies. I even painted a miniature portrait of her, and copied it for Khuttarh before the Shark Lord grilled him about Overflowing Fist....I've made one for you too."

With that, he gave it to Snash...the picture was in a little oval frame.

"Very good, My Lord," said Snash, putting the thong round his neck...hidden under his tunic, the miniature hung down to his belly. "But---"

Slippriman raised an eyebrow.

"I don't want to work for Khuttarh again."

Slippriman rose at last, and, white robes rustling, drew close, a hateful smile on his face. Holding his right middle finger with his thumb, he flicked it directly into the middle of Snash's forehead...Snash saw a white flash inside his head, then nothing, then woke to find himself flat on his back, twenty feet across the chamber, the back of his head hurting almost as bad as the front, his skull up against the door.

"Now go to your waiting-room and sit in your corner," said Slippriman. "Contemplate the Princess...the miniature's a very good likeness, if I do say so myself...it glows, just like its subject. You must study it four hours a night...I'll send you a clock. Now be off."

Wiping blood from his nostrils, Snash got up, and stumbled towards the door.

Snash's head was still hurting when the hated wake-up gong sounded the following sundown, but he felt better once he had a wash; even though he retained the top layers of his skin, he even felt rather clean. He put his garments back on, ate, filched a bit extra to eat later on when no one was looking, then went to sit in his room with the miniature, which was indeed a very good likeness, just as Slippriman had said....it seemed a pity that the old monster had devoted himself to treachery instead of art.

Indeed, the miniature was so much like its subject that its glow, wonderful as it was, was perhaps the least comforting thing about it...even if Snash hadn't been commanded to study it four hours a night (the clock Slippriman had sent was three feet tall and ticked loudly), he thought he still might have done so. Looking at it made him think the most interesting thoughts. He wondered how she could stand to live under the sun, and whether she wore sunglasses, and what her land was like, and if all the female fays were as lovely as she was, and why there didn't seem to be any female yarks...he felt a keen longing for female company, although he didn't dare to imagine that he'd be fit company for *her*. Female yarks would've been the solution, if not for the total lack of them, or so he thought...

About midway through the third night---the clock read 12:11---he was just about to eat the strip of meat that he'd stolen when the door opened, and in, looking very agitated, came one of Slippriman's bulls, Dufzuf.

"What's the matter?" Snash asked.

"Time to hit the board!" Dufzuf replied.

"What board?" the runt asked.

"What do you think? The one with the squares on it,

dungshovel!"

"For Yarks and Spiders?"

"Yeah, the one you're going to die on."

"I have a deal with Lord Slippriman---"

"Don't know anything about that."

They hurried away, Snash taking bites of the meat and trying to chew them just as fast as he could....Dufzuf led Snash out of Slippriman's quarters and back through the Chief of Staff's chamber. The snake-mouth yawned; when Snash hesitated, remembering the hellrogs on the other side, Dufzuf screamed, in his ear: "Go on, you little cringing turd!" and Snash went.

But the demons were conspicuously absent from the hall ahead...halfway along, a small door stood open, and Snash's companion drove him in there. A corridor led to a room with a crowd of yarks inside, some issuing gear to other yarks, Snitpikh and Rhutzu among those. Cursing and snarling the recipients climbed into scale-mail, donned helmets, and girt weapons on. Snash noted that the bulls had been given double-headed axes that looked very much to Slagbag's specifications, while the runts had gotten light curved swords, the brains spears...a scale-mail corselet thrust into his arms, Snash took a look at it before he wrestled it over his head. At first he'd thought it was made of rough leather plates, but closer inspection revealed that they were actually some sort of little dead plated animal, leathery turtles, perhaps, that looked as though they'd been squashed by mallets...he put the shirt on, fastened various buckles, then put a leather helmet on his head and cinched the strap. Then he buckled a belt around his waist, and thrust his sword into it. He wondered where Slagbag was, hoped he was still a stable-hand and that the Shark Lord had forgotten him, seeing as how there wasn't any real point in transferring him...

But hardly had all that passed through Snash's mind when Slagbag came stumbling through the door as though someone had shoved him.

"And I hope they suck the tongue right out of yer head!" cried a voice from outside.

Slagbag began: "And *I* hope that they puke *my* tongue

into *your* mouth---"

"Slagbag!" cried Snash.

Slagbag turned. "Snash! Looks like this is it, eh?"

Dufzuf pointed to Slagbag, crying: "Get your kit!"

Slagbag complied, then came back by Snash to suit up, asking:

"So who are we playing for?"

"Slippriman," said Snash. "Serpentar always plays the spiders."

"I thought he was the Yark Lord."

"That just means he kills more yarks than anyone else does."

"You there, you crusty armpit you!" cried a guard. "Shut up before I put my iron-booted foot so far up your backside they'll have to cut my leg---"

A loud clanging interrupted him before he could say *off*. Across from the entrance Snash had come through, there was another door; beside it, a bull was yanking a long string of iron bells. Looking relieved by the interruption, the guard who'd puzzled everyone cried: "All right then! Out to the board, you maggots!" and another bull swung the door open.

As the column began to move, Snash looked at Slagbag---they were back towards the back.

"Have you ever fought?" he asked.

"No. But they say we all know how to fight. And I think I feel it, in here." Slagbag slammed his chest with his fist, making a bunch of the flattened turtle-scales bounce.

"Shouldn't you feel it in your head?" Snash asked.

Slagbag just laughed...then, tackle rattling, they were jogging out through the door and down a passageway that opened on the floor of an arena, where grey stones had been inlaid into black to form a checkerboard pattern. The wall of the arena was overhung with a thickly tangled curtain of huge iron thorns...the points were bristling slowly, some lengthening, some receding, while long scaly bodies slithered through the shadows.

Above, steeply, rose rows of stands, in which hellrogs were quaffing from flaming goblets, cracking (and laughing at) demonic jokes, and eating whole roast camels and basted baby mastodons on skewers....There were also a half-dozen Gage Ghouls, including the Shark Lord, all sitting together and being rather solemn, off on the right, and a number of blackrobed men, bigwigs from various departments, or so Snash guessed...Snash recognized Khuttarh, who seemed to be staring at him as though he were quite puzzled. Again, Snash wondered: what was he doing in this situation? Undoubtedly, he wasn't BC's only spy in Slippriman's camp...had the Shark Lord been told that Slippriman was onto Snash, or even worse, decided that Snash had *actually* turned?

Maybe Dufzuf was just playing a joke, Snash thought.

No matter what, it seemed to him that Slippriman couldn't possibly want him dead, not so soon at least...should he try to attract Slippriman's attention? The wizard's gaze *was* elsewhere at the moment; he and Serpentar faced each other on---or rather, in Serpentar's case, slightly *above*--- projections that extended well out over the floor. Slippriman's white robes and hair were streaming dramatically in a breeze that seemed to be blowing nowhere else in the chamber, while Serpentar's fires were banked for the moment---seen from below, the Yark Lord was a narrow black vertical, almost a pillar, with only a few threadlike red fissures, and the sullen orange eyelike hole, to hint at the fires blazing inside him. But so painful was the mere memory of his rage, and incineration of Nognomen, that Snash averted his eyes virtually the instant he saw him. All the other monsters and grotesques in the chamber seemed almost comical in comparison.

Snash and his companions were allowed to gape a little while longer; then, at a signal from Slippriman, the guards began to arrange them on the board, bulls and brains interspersed in the back row, with Slagbag in the middle; the front rank was all runts, although Snash wound up among the eight replacements that remained off to the side of the board.

"Yarks," said Slippriman, when they were all in place.

"Spiders," said Serpentar, from across the arena, and somewhere, bells jangled. The hellrogs and Gage Ghouls and other spectators got to their feet; across from Snash the thorns lifted, revealing an arch, and out came a stream of spiders, nowhere near as large as Glolob (whose offspring they plainly were) but still plenty big to Snash's mind; effulgent and spiny and very active-looking with all their limbs churning and their leg-tips picking, they were laughing in hissy voices, and clicking a lot, and some of them got up on their hind legs and waved their forelimbs about, taunting the yarks about only having two legs and two eyes, and their inability to make silk come out of their butts. Then they'd sink back down and turn, and point at their own behinds, from which, sure enough, little streams of silk, shining whitely, would waft. Serpentar raised an arm; directed by guards, the spiders took up positions on the board, the biggest in the back, the middling in the middle, and the smallest out front.

"And now," said Serpentar, "the Invocation."

All the spectators bowed their heads, but more was evidently required from the "pieces" below, and the guards, although no one had told Snash...his fellow yarks and even the spiders were in the process of prostrating themselves, and he got down on his belly too, the last thing he saw before his face came to rest on the board being one of the smaller spiders splaying its legs out remarkably flat against the stone, except for its pedipalps, which were raised slightly, clasped at the tips.

"Here," said Serpentar, "in my own presence, in this sanctum dedicated to the pain of others and my own satisfaction, I invoke myself, and invoke myself again, and yet a third time, that all might be assured my great campaign will be truly hallowed by this sacrifice...Those things which now do come to pass have the full stamp of my will upon them; therefore witness the inevitable unfolding of my inexorable providence, and rejoice, or groan inwardly, according to that destiny which I have decreed for thee." He paused. "Slippriman?"

"My Lord?"

"Proceed."

Slippriman pointed to a runt towards the center of the front row...the runt shuddered, drew his sword, and paced two squares forward with a swift but mechanical gait that certainly looked as though it had been imposed upon him...it was bad to see, and Snash wondered how he felt with Slippriman in charge of his body, moving his own flesh and blood around like that...

Then Serpentar, with his gauntletted hand, pointed to one of the smaller spiders, directly in front of Slippriman's living pawn; the arachnid advanced two spaces as well (Snash couldn't tell if there was anything strange about its movements, because arachnids always looked rather mechanical to him), after which runt and spider closed one at a time, until a single grey square was left between them.

Snash was certain Slippriman would send the poor runt onto it, but the two "pieces" were just left to contemplate each other, while Slippriman brought up another runt, over on the right. Snash wasn't quite sure what was going on, although he guessed a battle for the center of the board was shaping up; once most of the runts and the small spiders had been moved forward, the larger yarks and spiders were brought up behind, moving four or five spaces at a time, and in the case of the brains, diagonally. Only after things got really crowded, and there was no longer room for much movement in the center, did the killing begin.

Slippriman started it, bringing up a runt and sending it one square diagonally into a small spider's square. At the instant the yark crossed the border, the weird lifeless gait left him; it was very apparent---to Snash at any rate---that the runt was acutely aware that he was fighting for his life. Certainly he moved very swiftly and fiercely, hacking away at the spider's limbs, sending pieces of them flying, only to have them bounce back at him as they struck an invisible barrier that seemed to have sealed the combatants in the square---glowing white blood was splashed on the sides. But even though things got pretty white and sloppy in there---Snash wondered how Slippriman liked the mess---the spider just didn't seem to mind its wounds very much, and finally the runt was knocked down, and the spider jumped on him...

Snash glanced away, but when he looked back, he was glad to see that the runt, who was already blackening and swelling, had gotten his revenge, having stuck his sword right up under his opponent's head. Upright between the creature and the runt's chest, the blade was the only thing keeping the spider from collapsing when it died---tilted upwards at the head, the spider quivered, then stopped moving.

When it went, so did the invisible barrier, apparently--- the splattered white hung in the air for a moment, then dropped. Bulls came rushing out of somewhere and removed the bodies....while they were at it, Snash, glancing up, noticed that Slippriman had spotted him, and looked most put out to see him in the arena. But there was, apparently, nothing the old bastard could do about the situation.

Along the diagonal that had been cleared when the bodies were removed, one of Serpentar's middling-sized spiders from his back row came shuttling, eight leg-tips pounding away; the arthropod hammered right into a square occupied by Snitpikh, and the brain proved no match for it.

But once Snitpikh was resolved, Slagbag quick-marched out of the back; crossing into the spider's square, he laid on a storm of blows, and swiftly took the spider to bits.

Using him to hold the center, Slippriman, not seeming at all as though he were trying to lose, brought up the rest of his bulls and brains...things were clearly running against Serpentar at the moment.

But after the fashion of moments, that one didn't last...Serpentar concentrated most of his spiders against Slippriman's center, then hurled two middling ones and a big mama against the runts on Slippriman's right, staving that flank in, killing Rhutzu in the process. Then the Inevitable brought out his remaining big girls, three of them, and sent them around and up behind...As Snash watched in horror, Slippriman lost two yarks for every spider...one by one, the replacements began to go in, only to be jabbed through with leg-tips and poisoned.

Things move fast around here, everyone had said. They were certainly moving fast now. It wasn't long before Slagbag was the only yark left on the board, still standing in the center, half-painted with spider-blood. Snash saw some black yark-juice streaming down through the glowing white as well.

But horrified as he was for Slagbag, Snash felt proud too...unlike just about everyone else, Slagbag was giving a good account of himself. Snash wanted frantically to run out and join him, there in the center of the board...he stepped to the edge of the square, put his hand out, felt an unseen wall——whether it had been there all along, or had risen just to stop him then, he didn't know.

Oh well, he told himself, *you'll be out there soon enough.*

Serpentar had laid off on Slagbag for the time being; right now his biggest mama was polishing off the replacements...Serpentar hadn't even begun to use his reinforcements yet. Snash counted down as Slippriman committed his reserves.

Three.

Two.

One...

The corpses were cleared. The big spider stood swaying on her skinny pointy legs, rubbing her pedipalps.

Snash looked up at Slippriman, thought he caught a slight shrug of resignation, as though Slippriman did indeed think that Snash could be put to much better use---

"Play him," said Serpentar.

Slippriman pointed to Snash...something slimy and cold spurted into Snash at the top of his spine, spread down through his body, and before he knew it, he had his sword out, and was walking very fast, stiffly, straight-legged...how he hated it. Slippriman had invaded him, shoved his filthy will into him, and he couldn't even make him move properly!

But once Slippriman deposited him next to Slagbag's square, he relinquished him for the moment, that cold sliminess slipping out the way it had gone in.

"Well," said Slagbag, "if we're both going to die..."

If Snash hadn't just been used as a meat-puppet, he would've laughed. "*If?*"

"---dying alongside you is better."

All of a sudden, Snash felt a whole lot braver, and he took a big deep breath and blew it out through his nostrils, looking at the spiders. There were still ten of them on the board, the nearest four squares away.

Out of the corner of his eye, he saw movement, up on the left, from Serpentar....one of the middle-sized spiders came straight at Snash.

"Give it to her," Slagbag said, "right in the face---"

No sooner had he dispensed his advice than Snash followed it, *crunch*. But the spider's legs still churned; with the runt's sword embedded deep in the midst of its multiple eyes, the creature pushed him back across the square, where he was jolted to a halt, his shoulders jammed against the sides of an invisible corner.

Right then, though, the spider seemed to realize it was finished, and it just collapsed; uncricking his neck, Snash put his foot beside the spider's head, at the top of one of its legs, and pushed the body off his blade. Two attendants ran over.

"Keep it up, lads," said one under his breath.

Snash glanced at Slagbag, who smiled at him over one black shoulder, just showing a hint of fang....then Slippriman's will descended into Snash once more, and moved him diagonally, one square to the left, the block still adjacent to Slagbag's.

Serpentar hurled another spider at them, a bigger one, once again on the diagonal...Slagbag chopped off two of its forelegs, struck it across the eyes with one blade of his double-headed axe, then caught the ruined face again with the other blade on the return, half-spinning the spider against the invisible wall, which stayed up just long enough for the spider to stick. Then the barrier dissolved, or went back down, or whatever, because the spider dropped with a wet thump.

But after that, Serpentar changed his tactics; move by move, his forces converged on the beleaguered yarks...Slippriman pulled Snash and Slagbag back into a corner.Finally Serpentar moved his four biggest spiders into the back row and sent them at Slagbag single-file. The big yark killed the first with a single stroke; then Slippriman advanced him one square, and the next spider came on...

Crack! Slagbag's axe descended with such power that the arachnid's head was pinned to the square and a fissure opened in the black stone; the crack swiftly overflowed with glowing blood, and the attendants splashed in it....as they lifted the dead spider, one said to Slagbag:

"I believe you might do the lot."

Then they hustled off with their drippy burden.

Slagbag asked Snash: "What do you think?"

"I think we should hand Serpentar his first defeat," Snash replied.

He glanced at the Inexorable, who was *clearly* burning hotter; then Snash eyed Slippriman, who, even at that distance, looked terribly alarmed, as though he'd realized he might actually *win.*

What'll happen to him then? Snash thought, but there was, of course, a more important question: *What'll happen to us?*

He laughed through his nostrils.

Doesn't matter.

"Thy move," said Serpentar to Slippriman.

"My Lord," said the wizard.

"What ails thee?"

"There *is* such a thing as unintended consequence..."

"Thou art a victim of *that?*"

"There is always an element of chance in this game, given the nature of the pieces---"

"Thy *move*," said Serpentar.

Snash glanced over at the Gage Ghouls...the Shark Lord was watching most intently, his hood showing just the slightest hint of motion, as though he were laughing...the hellrogs, mouths bulging with meat they were no longer chewing, were all sitting there with their camels and baby mastodons resting across their infernal thighs...the men were already leaning exitward, with the exception of Khuttarh, who looked as though he were just about to soil his stadium seating.

"Thy move," said Serpentar a third time.

"How if I... *concede?*" Slippriman asked.

"Play it out," said Serpentar.

"Really My Lord, I would prefer not---"

"Play out the game, or by my Inevitable Self, I swear that thou shalt know the full measure of my flaming wrath."

Slippriman moved Snash a square farther from Slagbag.

With a gurgle and a squeal, a middle-sized spider drove at Snash from the side. Pivotting, putting his back to an invisible wall, Snash ran his sword, with an underhand thrust, so far into the spider's mouth that the point came out between its head and its body....his hand was almost between the jaws, which were clashing against the steel from either side. But all life went out of the thing in a matter of moments, and he set his foot on the spider and pulled the blade out.

Slippriman moved him a square farther out into the board, then three squares more, then moved him back and forth, out in the middle, even as Serpentar's smaller spiders closed in from all sides....

"Slippriman," said Serpentar at last, "I needeth not thy aid."

The wizard nodded, even though he seemed to be in the midst of a rather animated whispery conversation with himself...suddenly, very like a mage who had no good options at all, he nodded again, then pointed to Slagbag, and sent him at Serpentar's second-biggest mama; *whack-whack, smash-smash* went Slagbag's axe, one last underhand blow tossing the creature up into the air, where it landed atop one of the invisible walls and hung there, pouring out luminous glop for a few moments before it died and the wall went out from under it.

Without even waiting for the attendants, Serpentar sent another spider, on the diagonal; Slagbag hacked it hard where its left legs met its body, and they came loose, and it sank down on that side, gobbling and clicking; a second blow crushed its head.

Slagbag stood breathing hard, axe dripping white. But Slippriman made no move.

"Slider, I tell thee," said Serpentar, "do not stay thy hand, for I shall not stay mine."

Slippriman screamed, his hair and beard and robes flying up...Slagbag went to a square, killed its occupant, killed another spider who charged him, marched to another square...the attendants simply couldn't keep up. At last it was just him and the really big spider...again Slippriman, staring at Serpentar with an agonized look, simply froze up.

"Send thy yark," said Serpentar.

Slippriman shrieked once more, and Slagbag shrieked too, and so did the spider...the instant Slagbag crossed over into the next square, he hurled his axe. The spider was rising up, and one blade drove deep between its mandibles; in its pain the spider heeled up even farther, whereupon Slagbag rushed across the square, pulled out the axe, and gave the spider three terrible blows in the abdomen.

But even such frightful strokes weren't enough to knock the body all the way backward, and Slagbag slipped on Spider-blood, and he fell, cracking his head on the floor, the Spider landing atop him---Snash thought he saw one of the jaws go right into his neck. The runt drew in a sharp breath, felt a pain deep in his chest, as though he'd just been stabbed in the heart.

"Slagbag!" he cried, and tried to burst out of his square, but the invisible wall held him; attendants rushed over to Slagbag, listened for breath, shook their heads.

"Slagbag?" Snash cried.

But there was no answer from that inert form.

"Slagbag?" he cried again, and as the attendants dragged his mate away, memories rushed into his mind, the big lug out on the bartizan, gawping at that distant blue sky, or up in Snash's office at Overflowing Fist, complaining that the bread didn't have weevils in it...then, all in a rush, anguish such as Snash had never imagined rolled over him, and indeed he had no word for it; any pain that he'd ever experienced seemed like nothing in comparison....he thought he'd rather have had his arm cut off, his teeth pulled out.

"Slagbag," he whispered. Snash's eyes filled with water, his nose with snot. The board seemed to be reeling beneath him, and his legs nearly gave out.

But he decided he wouldn't let them; he steadied himself, blinked and wiped his tears away with the heel of his hand.

You have work to do, he told himself, and, suddenly furious, looked round.

There were four more spiders, small ones...he wished they were bigger, so he'd have more blood to spill.

You'll just have to manage, he thought, and spat.

As they closed in, Slippriman shifted Snash back and forth between two squares. It seemed to be plain indecision; he could've delayed the outcome a bit more if he'd moved Snash back, into a corner perhaps, but he didn't seem to want to do that; if Snash had been him, he would've moved himself straight at the spiders, hoping he'd be killed. But Slippriman didn't want to do that either, perhaps because it would be so obvious he wanted to lose...

All at once, as he contemplated the dilemma that Slippriman had gotten himself into, Snash felt a great calm settle upon him. It didn't matter to him if the Inevitable *was*

Inexorable. There he was, just a runt, and he was four spiders away from beating Serpentar. Even if he died, what an ending to his life!

And maybe, he thought, *just maybe, the Evitable is Exorable.*

"Thy move," said the Yark Lord to Slippriman.

Apparently deciding to get everything over with, Slippriman moved Snash into a square with two spiders waiting at the corners.

Serpentar gave the runt a good long time to contemplate the eight-legged assassins. Undoubtedly this was meant to demoralize Snash. But they were pretty jittery, and Snash was nothing of the sort.

"I'm going to kill you both," he said, "for my mate Slagbag."

"The Hell you will!" one cried shrilly. "We've got poison, we've got eight legs, we're a *whole* lot stronger than you are, and we can wrap you up in silk."

Snash answered: "But you'd rather be somewhere else, and I wouldn't."

"You're a...*little crappy yark,* and...and...I bet you're not happy to be here at all!"

"You tell 'im, Umbrugol!" said the other spider.

"I'm going to send you straight down to Spider Hell," Snash said.

As if that were a particularly dire threat, the second spider seemed to lose whatever nerve it still had left, and nudged Umbrugol, saying: "I don't *want* to go to Spider Hell--"

"Kill 'im and you won't have to---"

Umbrogol broke off as Serpentar's will descended on his comrade...but the instant the demoralized arthropod got into Snash's square and the Yark Lord relinquished control, the spider just folded up and went still.

"Is he dead, you think?" Snash asked Umbrugol.

Umbrogol scratched his head with a leg-tip, then recoiled as Slippriman drove Snash into his square...one slash, and Spider Hell had another inmate.

Snash turned, eyeing the last spiders, both of them two squares away. Slippriman moved him a block closer, and Serpentar sent one of them in almost instantly...it was a little shit, smaller than Snash even, but fierce and swift and nimble, swaying from side to side, dodging blows, raising itself up, then thrusting itself down, then leaping high into the air...landing on top of an invisible wall, it perched there for an instant, then flung itself off. Snash ducked, and it passed over him...He whirled, and it did too, jabbed him shallowly with a leg-tip beside the stomach, and then in one shoulder, knocking him back against the wall. As he slid down, it didn't even make the mistake of scuttling forward and trying to bite his throat, when it could just as easily pump him full of poison through his leg. But just before it could jab a fang into his thigh, Snash jerked forward and sliced it clean across the face, left to right; the thing flipped up on one side, and Snash stuck it through the underside of its head, killing it instantly

He rose, turning towards the last spider. It was crouching in the center of its square as though it was about to spring; Snash hauled the dead spider up by a leg, then stood watching, waiting for Slippriman to impel him forward, sensing the murderous tension tightening above him, straining towards a climax, Slippriman's desperation, Serpentar's rage...

"Thy move," said the Yark Lord to the wizard.

Yet again Snash felt the Slippriman's cold will descend...into the next square he marched, then hurled the dead spider once Slippriman departed; the live spider dodged the flying body handily, leaping to the left.

But that was why Snash had tossed it to the right...things went exactly as he'd anticipated, except that the luminescent splatter that his stroke brought forth was huger than any he'd seen...not even Slagbag, hacking that biggest big mama, had fetched such a splendid splash.

Panting, he considered tossing his small curved sword, then decided to keep it. There came yet another shriek from Slippriman. Snash lifted his chin...robes streaming, Slippriman ran off to the left, into a cavernous doorway. Then the chamber filled with red light; the thorns began to scrape and twist, the serpents writhing in them to crawl more restlessly; feeling a tremendous heat wash over him, Snash looked up and to the right. There, still slightly above his arch, floated Serpentar, radiant with fury, head unravelled, hood extended, iron snakes wriggling and striking, his hovering eye glaring down at the runt…behind the Yark Lord, everyone, including the hellrogs, was shrinking back…

Snash bowed to Serpentar, then turned and went towards the door of the chamber where he'd suited up, fully expecting Serpentar's wrath to blaze forth and incinerate him. Yet for some reason, for the moment at least…

He was spared.

Perhaps he was just too insignificant. But he couldn't help thinking that Serpentar had just made a terrible mistake.

The Evitable is Exorable, he told himself.

Chapter 13: Gauntlet and Tongs

He had, of course, no idea of what to do. Either Slippriman or Serpentar was going to kill him, and while he thought Slippriman might be killed along *with* him, Khuttarh too, that didn't give him any more hope for himself. But he really didn't care too much. He and Slagbag had *beaten* Serpentar, if only on a gaming-board...it was hard to imagine that there would be anything to life after that.

Still, though, he meant to preserve his little black self as long as possible.

The hellrogs hadn't yet returned to their posts in the hall; he found himself at a dead stop in front of the snake-mouth, which was closed...he'd just have to wait till someone opened it. Once he slipped through, he could get his dispatch-runner's pass, and see if he couldn't flee out into the chimney. The idea seemed better and better to him as he turned it over in his mind. He couldn't imagine that anyone was really looking for him yet. Certainly not Slippriman. Undoubtedly, if the wizard was worrying about anyone, it was Serpentar—just as, undoubtedly, Slippriman was on Serpentar's mind. Snash was nothing after all. Taking comfort in his insignificance, he nodded to himself.

If you could just get to your locker...

A troop of bulls came up with an armored man in charge; he opened the snake-mouth, and Snash followed them into the Chief of Staff's chamber, which was empty for the moment. An angry voice echoed in the distance... Snash didn't recognize it.

He headed off towards Slippriman's chambers...the shouting was getting louder, and before long Snash could tell that the voice was Slippriman's. Snash went into the parlor with all the dried flowers. No one was there, but the door that led to Slippriman's bedchamber was open, and the shouting was coming from that.

Yet Snash didn't have to go through the bedchamber or even past it, to get to the servants' quarters. Given the time of night, and the fact that so many of Slippriman's yarks had been killed on the board, Snash wasn't expecting to find anyone in the sleeping hall, but there were a handful of fellows in one corner, talking to each other excitedly; spotting Snash, they all shut up. He ignored them, took off his armor; when they came over, he continued silent, putting on his old dispatch-runner gear.

"Are you *Him?*" asked a bull named Rokhrog.

"Who?" Snash replied.

Rokhrog looked both ways before answering: "Hrag Urshathur."

Snash was dumbfounded (even if he *had* beaten Serpentar on the board, he still didn't feel like a savior) and about to ask: *Me?* when Slippriman's voice rose to a shriek, then suddenly broke off.

"Who's he yelling at?" Snash asked.

A runt called Nustu answered: "Khuttarh, must be."

Snash grunted.

"Did you *really* beat Serpentar?" Nustu asked.

"Me and Slagbag," Snash answered, feeling a pang as he said his friend's name.

"Did Slippriman try to lose?"

"He couldn't figure out what to do---" Snash stopped.

"What is it?"

"No more shouting," Snash said. He put the miniature of Luvliel in a little sack, which he hung around his neck on a thong. "I'd better go."

"Are you *Him?*" Rokhrog pressed.

"I don't think so," said Snash.

"What are you going to do?" Nustu asked.

"I don't know."

"Well, when you do it, think of us." Nustu took Snash's hand. "Be Him, we beg you."

The other yarks all nodded. Snash stood speechless, then recovered his wits and raced for the door---

Only to trip in a most un-messiahlike way over a booted foot at the end of a long diaphanously-draped leg stretched out suddenly at the threshold. Hardly had Snash hit the floor when someone was upon him; a strong grip seized his ear, yanked him well off his feet; he twisted, saw that Slippriman had him. Back by the door, Khuttarh was straightening.

Snash reached for the hilt of his sword, but Slippriman got it first, pulled the blade from Snash's belt, and tossed it away.

"Back to my bedroom," he told Khuttarh.

Evidently vastly stronger than his skinny old self looked, Slippriman dangled Snash all the way by the ear, then slung the runt down hard in the chair before the vanity and whirled the seat round...Khuttarh closed the door, locked it, then joined his master, who asked Snash:

"The Shark Lord put you up to all this, didn't he?"

"No," said Snash.

"*I* didn't send you out there!"

"Well, no matter who did," Snash answered, "no one said anything to me about *winning*."

"You expect me to believe that?"

"I don't care what you believe---"

Slippriman smacked him across the face with the back of his hand....thinking he'd felt every damn ring on it, Snash fell off the chair, but Khuttarh picked him up and jammed him back onto it.

"Winning was *your* idea?" Slippriman asked.

Blood trickled down Snash's cheek. "And I'm very proud of myself, too---"

Slippriman hit him again, although Snash grabbed the chair with one claw this time, and the seat went over--- Khuttarh flung it back up, and it almost tipped the other way, then settled.

"Well," Slippriman said, "*I'm* not going to roll over and play dead. Not when I'm Serpentar's Supreme Unrecognized. Not when I've just replaced Nognomen with my man. I'm going to give you to Serpentar, and *tell* him who put you up to this. And he's going to burn the skin off you one thin layer at a time, and send his snakes down inside your bloodveins, until you tell everything you know, and then...he's *really* going to go to work, because you *beat* him! You *beat* him! Didn't you think about what would happen to you?"

"To *us*, you mean?" Snash asked.

Slippriman eyed him narrowly.

"Yes, *us*," said Snash.

"You said it was all your idea."

"But you don't believe me. And I don't think Serpentar will either. He won't blame the Shark Lord, though. I was *your* piece."

Slippriman looked as though he'd been backhanded himself, by someone with jewelry *clotted* on every finger---whatever color there was in his face drained right out. "He'll see through you," he said at last.

"Even if I think about Luvliel?"

Khuttarh said: "We should just kill him. Right now. Say he tried to escape."

"Serpentar will want him alive," said Slippriman.

"All the more reason," said Khuttarh. "Just present him with the runt's head. Who knows? It might turn out all right. You know how to lie to him---"

There came a sharp rap at the door.

"What is it?" Slippriman demanded.

"The Lord on High wants to see you," said a big bullish voice. "With the new Chief of Staff. And the runt. In the Hall of Holes."

Khuttarh glanced at Slippriman. "We could still---"

Slippriman shook his head. "Too late," he said, and went and opened the door.

Two great long-armed bulls in heavy armor waited outside.

"Where's the rat?" one asked.

Slippriman stepped aside and pointed, whereupon the bull got Snash and bore him off under an armpit, which was preferable to being toted about by the ear, in Snash's opinion...

Leaving the flowers in Slippriman's chambers for the snakes in Serpentar's, they came to a cavernous hall with a number of round black holes, about a yard wide, at the base of the walls; at the end was a single tall, pointed window, barred with rods lined with very thin and sharp-looking hooks...outside, the light was bluish-grey.

In the middle of the room, Serpentar was hovering just off the floor with his head tilted back and his arms down at his sides, a beam of orange light issuing from his great round orb. Arranged about him in a ring, rearing up, were a number of large snakes, the color of molten iron. In twos and threes, they'd slither up onto him, and slip between the snakes that comprised his body... then they'd re-emerge somewhere else on him, hotter than before, and return to the circle. Snash had no idea what the point of this was, never expected to, and in truth, never found out.

Serpentar hissed something in a language Snash didn't understand; snakes stopped nosing in, and those still inside nosed out...dropping to the floor, they all slithered away in different directions, like small streams of living lava, vanishing into those holes in the walls.

"Slippriman," said Serpentar.

The wizard bowed. "My Lord---"

"I am... *affronted*."

Slippriman dropped to one knee, trembling.

"I tell thee," said his master, "I shall not bear it."

Slippriman put both hands together and pressed them to his brow. "I didn't *mean*---"

"What shouldst thou have *done*?" Serpentar demanded.

"In truth, My Lord, I was confused---"

"Thou didst confuse *thyself*."

"I admit it---"

"Thinkest thou to save thyself by conceding?"

"No, My Lord---"

"Then why concede?"

"I'm confused---"

"*Again*?" Serpentar cried, swelling, the glowing crevices between his snakes widening so much that it looked as though he were on the verge of bursting.

"You said you didn't want my aid---"

Serpentar asked: "Didst thou expect the truth from me?"

"No, My Lord---"

"What?"

"Yes?"

225

"No? Yes?" Serpentar laughed. "This is what I mean *exactly*. Back and forth thou twist thyself, like a worm on a pin....think, Slippriman: what did I *want?*"

"I wouldn't presume---"

"What doth Serpentar *always* want? To be Serpentar is to *triumph*. And thou didst deny me. Triumph is my due, by virtue of who I *am*, and once it became plain as my manifest greatness that my rights were to be trodden upon, thou shouldst, after more agony than thou showed, have *lost*, slain the runt thyself, done whatever necessity demanded."

"But you insisted---"

"*Never* should *it*--- to *that*---have cometh."

"I never *meant* for it to come to that, and in truth, My Lord, I was deceived..."

"By the runt?"

"And the Shark Lord, who sent him."

Serpentar motioned to the yark holding Snash, and Snash was hurled straightaway to the floor. Serpentar fixed his lidless gaze upon him, and said:

"Speaketh thou."

Snash's first impulse was to say that the wizard had put him up to it. But somehow, since Slippriman was already in such terrible trouble, Snash just couldn't bring himself to give him any of his victory...

You *beat Serpentar*, the runt told himself. *You and Slagbag*...

"My friend and I were fighting for our lives," Snash replied. "That's how it started. But then when we saw how things were going, we decided to *win*."

"Thou wouldst have done better," said Serpentar, "to die *then*."

But somehow...

Snash thought not.

"He's a spy for the Shark Lord!" Slippriman cried.

"Was," came a voice, from away to the left. "Until thou turn'd him."

Sitting up, Snash saw the ghoul chieftain leaning against a wall...he had no idea when he'd arrived.

"Hence," the ghoul continued, "his presence on the

board."

"He's my orderly, nothing more!" Slippriman cried. "I had no idea you were going to send him out there..."

"If---truly---thou didst not see it coming...the more fool you. Am I not Chief of Burning Curiosity, and Spy of Spies? Am I not tasked to watch everyone in Mount Adamant, with the exception of my Lord and Master?"

Slippriman eyed Serpentar desperately "I don't question his *right*---"

"Nay, thou didst not," Serpentar replied. "But when thou accuseth him of plotting against me, thou speakest nonsense. He is a Gage Ghoul. And who doth wear the Gauntlet of Dominion?" He raised the article in question.

"I think," said Slippriman, "it doesn't work all the time."

"Thou art the expert, art thou?" asked Serpentar.

"I have given the matter much thought."

"And why would *my* gage be *thy* concern?"

Slippriman nodded towards the Shark Lord. "He gives every indication---"

"Of?" Serpentar asked.

"Volition."

"*Doth* he now?"

"He *claims* to have a rich interior life...he says it consists of contemplating your will, but that's plainly an afterthought..."

"Is it?"

"He *readily* admits to not spending as much time on his slab as one might think...."

"He quite escapes my control, is that it?" Serpentar asked.

"I *grieve* to have to point this out to you..."

"Speak not of thy grief," said Serpentar. "Telleth me but this: why doth thou lust so fiercely for the gage, when it worketh imperfectly?"

"Because, with a surer hand inside it---"

"*Thine* perhaps?" asked Serpentar.

Suddenly realizing what a length of slip he'd shown, the wizard clapped his mouth shut.

"Too late," said Serpentar. "Thou hast said it. Ever since thou camest to me, and I bestowed upon thee such reward as only the Emperor of the World can give, my Prying Eye was on thee…and thou didst have some uses, and know some secrets, and I let thy indiscretions pass, and thy new enterprises thrive. But lately, thou didst question me too long and lovingly about the Gage; and, growing warier---for wary I always am--- I kept thee closer than ever, and raised thy lackeys, that thou might let thy guard down. Little did I think that a mere yark might trip thee up, and commence thy unravelling, but…such is chance. And here thou art, wretch, arguing that my mightiest retainer, the Shark Lord himself, would betray me, when he is a thousand years in my service, and no longer a man, and lacking any will of his own, at least regards myself. Slippriman, I would not have thought thee capable of venting such stuff."

"Let me redeem myself, My Lord…"

"Who *dost* thou think thou art conversing with?" Serpentar asked, fissures expanding more emphatically than ever…Snash couldn't imagine what was holding him together. "I deal not in redemption. I wish thee *ill*, and never moreso than when thou art licking my red-hot foot!"

Slippriman cringed and seemed to shrink, but just as it seemed Serpentar was about to exterminate him, Khuttarh, showing a lot more nerve than Snash ever would've expected, broke in:

"My Lord and My God---"

And the Prying Eye turned his way.

Sweat raining from his face, Khuttarh pointed towards Slippriman. "I could tell you a few things about him,"

"About thy dealings at Overflowing Fist?" Serpentar asked, his glow fading a bit…Snash saw that as mere trickery and prelude, but Khuttarh seemed to think he'd actually improved his chances, replying:

"Yes, My Liege."

Serpentar asked: "Didst thou think I knew not of them? That I thought thou wert merely investigating on thy own? However thou contriv'd to lie to the Shark Lord, I have many ways to learn the truth."

Even *if* Serpentar's fires were banked for the moment, Snash knew his words for exactly what they were: a declaration that the cruellest mind in the cruellest realm in all the world had taken Khuttarh's offer as an insult.

Khuttarh, on the other hand, *still* seemed to think he had something to bargain with, asking: "But have you learned it *all*, My Lord?"

Snash felt a pulse of heat from Serpentar. "The Prying Eye sees all, fool," the Yark Lord said. "But...if thou wouldst betray thy friend...say on."

At that, as though he'd been *aching* to do it for a long long time, Khuttarh started right in spilling his guts.

Getting up, nobody apparently paying any attention to him at the moment, Snash slipped away to the side, and---

Completely stopped listening.

Out from one of the snake-holes in front of him crawled Glargle, dragging a squarish bag with two handles on it...seeing Snash looking at him, the creature rose to a crouch, and put a long finger to his froggy lips. When Snash obliged, Glargle opened the bag and began to take out what appeared to be dark garments made of reptilian scutes....he donned a long scaly coat, then belted it at the waist, then drew on high boots with toes, and long gloves as well...

Snash looked back at Serpentar and the others...none of them seemed to have noticed Glargle at all. Serpentar was, of course, facing the other way, towards Khuttarh...all the rest were in front of *them*, and Snash thought maybe they couldn't see through the glow.

He glanced back at Glargle...the froggy gremlin had pulled on a helmet, and was strapping it beneath his chin; after snapping a curved clear visor, of crystal perhaps, down over his face, he drew an elongated object out of his bag and unfolded it, extending it by at least three times in the process---when it proved to be a pair of tongs, Snash suddenly realized what Glargle was up to.

He's going for the Gauntlet...

Hunched over, the very image of a sneak, the creature crept towards Serpentar, who, it seemed, had finally wearied of Khuttarh's performance...

"Enough," said the Yark Lord, and floated straight at him, leaning a bit forward, hands down at his sides. Khuttarh ceased his revelations and started to crumple, but Serpentar said a word that Snash didn't recognize, and Khuttarh remained on his feet, even though he was swaying.

Jumping up, Slippriman darted towards his former flunky, spat upon him, then slipped away to the side, towards Snash.... As for Serpentar, the snakes were sliding out of his eye-hole now, his whole head coming undone, just like before, the serpents spreading out to form that horrible radiant hood before they all began stabbing into Khuttarh, pumping him full of fire.

Undoubtedly seeing in Khuttarh's punishment a prefiguration of his own, Slippriman looked away, apparently at Glargle, who, protected by his scaly garments, was *still* sneaking up on the Yark Lord, who was *still* apparently oblivious to the fact that he was being snuck up on...

Slippriman glanced at Snash almost as though he wanted confirmation of what he'd been seeing...Snash glanced at Serpentar, who was already withdrawing his snakes from what was left of Khuttarh, even as Glargle tiptoed yet nearer, and began to extend his tongs...

Snash looked back at Serpentar, whose head had re-formed, the eye gazing at his victim's crumbly yet still-upright remains. The skull had gone completely to cinders, but those were floating in the air, in a skull-shaped cloud...the arm-bones were detached from the shoulders, but hadn't drifted far. Serpentar uttered another word, and the stuff all dropped, striking the floor and going to chunks and powder.

"I left more of Nognomen!" the Yark Lord said. "A woeful post is Chief of Staff! Two in quick succession! Needst I one at all?"

"Bear in mind that I am merely an extension of thy will," said the Shark Lord, "and that thou might as well be holding converse with thyself, but...the post is barely a century old, as thou knowest, and thou hast not had much profit of it so far."

Serpentar nodded, and his heat diminished...now that the light was lessening, it seemed the Shark Lord was looking past his master, and had spotted something, as indeed there was something to spot, since Glargle's pincer-tips were just about---

There.

But before the Shark Lord could raise the alarm, Glargle tonged the gage right off the Yark Lord's snakefingered extremity. Snash blinked in amazement as Serpentar dropped to the floor, feet striking with a clang...the Yark Lord's whole body had become an expression of surprise, bristling with hot startled snakes, their heads sticking straight out, forked tongues extended ...he twisted round.

"Who dares?" he cried.

"*Zie hiessen mich Glargle!*" came the answer. But making this bold declaration right in Serpentar's face seemed to excite the gremlin so much that he took a hand off the gauntlet to lift a fist, and the tongs opened, and the gauntlet fell to the floor and bounced in a shower of sparks.

"*Scheiss!*" he cried. "*Verdammt!*"

He hesitated for a moment, did a little dance of maddened frustration, then tried to grab the gage again with the pincers.

Serpentar emitted a blast of flame...when it dissipated, Glargle was nowhere to be seen.

Nothing left at all, thought Snash.

Then he heard him *ach sssing,* and realized he'd been blown back into the hole he'd come out of.

But Serpentar made no attempt to finish the thief; the ultimate talisman of domination had been wrenched from him, and he went for that first.

Out of the corner of his eye, Snash saw Slippriman make some sort of pass, and the wizard uttered something under his breath....the gauntlet went shooting across the floor, away from its master's grasp....

Without even thinking, Snash sprinted for the snake-hole and slid inside, clambering over Glargle's smoking garments, which were a few yards inside. He heard the creature up ahead, and resolved to follow him, thinking:

Knew a way in, must know the way out...

Even after flinging the gauntlet across the floor, Slippriman waited, mind going full speed. Should he simply flee, try to catch that Glargle creature and use him as a guide? Or should he go after the Gauntlet, which had always been his goal? Without it, Serpentar was weaker, but Slippriman doubted he could defeat him even then. There was also the Shark Lord, and speaking of him...

The ghoul was even then speeding toward Slippriman.

Both cried out the Black Humanorean for *stop in thy tracks,* but---

In the event of a simultaneous utterance, the wizard with the better pronunciation wins, and despite the fact that the Shark Lord was an *actual* Black Humanorean, and Slippriman wasn't, the gage-ghoul had learned a vulgar dialect; thus it was that the ghoul stopped in *his* tracks, while Slippriman was able to turn tail and dive into the snake-hole before Serpentar could get his gauntlet back on.

But even so, Serpentar was taking steps; Slippriman hadn't gotten too far into the tunnel when he heard the Yark Lord cry: *Awake and seek!* in Burning Viperian, and all at once, two entrances up ahead, on either side of the passage that Slippriman was in, began to glow, as if fiery snakes were coming with some dispatch to pay him a nasssty visit...

Following Glargle proved no easy matter for Snash---it was one thing to hear the gremlin, quite another to tell where the sounds were coming from, as there were snake-holes branching off in every direction, right, left, up, down. Some showed red-hot reptile light, but Snash decided he could rule those out...listening very hard, he decided the clamberings and gobblings were coming from a hole in the floor, and he slid down into that, but he hadn't gone far when he heard someone scrabble down after him, then Serpentar roaring; suddenly there was a great deal of light behind him, and metallic slithery noises. Snash lunged down a corkscrewing incline, worming frantically around the bends, doing everything in his power to widen the distance between himself and the light...forgetting all about Glargle for the moment, he went into a black mouth, found another opening by touch, kept going…he could hear things wriggling somewhere behind, but they didn't seem to be following, at least not for the moment.

Stopping and listening some more, trying to sort out anything that might distinguish Glargle's sounds from the rest, he thought he heard a *verdammt* and a *ssss*, and followed those. But even though he wasn't making much noise, his own movements still made Glargle hard to hear. What light there was was the reptilian variety, coming from a passage directly above him, and although he couldn't see the snake itself, it sounded like it was pretty near. He crawled forward once more….reaching a triple fork, he thought he caught a faint *scheiss*, and went into the passage on the right, but after a short distance decided he hadn't heard anything at all and started back.

Light was growing, up at the intersection…he went out into the junction. Snakes were approaching from the sides, but their glow was dim, and they sounded as though they were still a way off; directly ahead, though, one was much closer, its light preceding it around an elbow; Snash reached for the sack containing the miniature of Luvliel, slipped it from around his neck, and opened the drawstring just as the snake appeared, tiny sparks shooting out all along its red body, its eyes yellow-white, its fiery tongue flicking…seeing Snash, it raised its head, still advancing.

Taking out the little painting, he thrust it towards the snake. Out of the miniature burst a white flare that revealed myriad hovering dust-motes and drained all the red from the snake and turned it quite black. Even though Snash wished he could've liked the light, it was pretty hard on his yarkish peepers, and he squinted and grimaced; but the snake, being obviously in complete wicked opposition to it, flinched back, turning its head from side to side, as though it were in excrutiating pain…

Snash flung himself forward, touching the thing with the miniature. Still rearing, the snake went completely rigid, then tipped sidewards, its head knocking into the wall of the passage with a clang….Snash felt its heat vanish. He looked at the miniature, eyes watering. The paint seemed to have taken no harm; he put his hand over it to feel if it was even warm---it wasn't. But as his hand obscured the image, and the junction went dark, he saw that the snake had been completely robbed of its glow. He touched the snake. It had gone cool.

He heard slithering, and a snake-head, tongue flicking, poked from the tunnel on the left; Snash just surged right at it. He didn't think he actually touched the serpent with the miniature, but as he retracted the little portrait, he saw that the snake had stiffened, its tongue still out...he wondered if the painting had just brushed the bifurcated feeler.

Suddenly, without hearing anything or getting any hint of trouble, he remembered the tunnel on the right, and turned to see a third snake rearing on the threshold...the head came shooting for his face, its jaws wide open, mouth a yellow about as fiery as its orbs; Snash only saved himself at the last instant, holding the miniature up--- the snake-strike pushed it back into his right eye.

But then the serpent's warmth went...as Snash lowered the painting, he heard a couple of strange little metallic *dinks!* as two sparks flew from the side of the snake's darkened cooling head.

Now that the snakes were taken care of, the light from the likeness dimmed, to Snash's relief, but didn't go out completely...with no choice now but to use the painting for illumination, Snash hung it around his neck without putting it back in the bag, then went to the tunnel that the second snake had come out of.

There was an upward passsage not far in, and, hearing something that he thought might've been Glargle, he went up into it, finally reaching a wall that he guessed was the boundary of the snake enclosure. But there was a big crack through it, which split the floor and ceiling for a short way as well. The maze had been made from a kind of black artificial stone, called quick basalt, which was easily melted and poured, and could even be pumped, by great engines of Serpentar's devising. Most of the upper part of the tower, for reasons of weight, was made from it, since, being full of little air-pockets, it was much lighter than regular basalt, and could be bolstered with internal supports made of steel rods. For the most part, it served very well, its rather dull and not particularly sinister appearance concealed by facades, that leant the semblence of cut stone-work. It did have a tendency to crack after cooling sometimes, and Snash had come to such a fissure now. Hot air was blowing up through the crevice....He tossed a rock down and heard it bounce off the sides, but it never did seem to strike bottom. The sides of the fissure were seamed with smaller fissures as well, and there were many little recesses and pockets, as well as a ledge of sorts, on the right side. Working his way out onto that, he drew himself along, facing the stone, pulling himself around the corner and onto the floor on the other side.

He had come out in a space between two curving partitions--the far one was quick-basalt too, just like the barrier he'd come through. The floor was the same stuff; the crack ran most of the way across, but didn't quite reach the other wall.

He heard movement, lots of it, far back in the maze---- all sorts of things were going on, but nothing seemed to be getting consistently closer.

Much nearer, something stirred softly, off to the right, and, thinking it might be Glargle, Snash headed that way, but as he continued round the curve, he saw a great funnel of web up ahead, blocking the passage, suspended between the walls, spiderlight welling through the silk, source well back.

Something scraped behind him, sounded like it might have been back by the fissure...there was more of the same, then a clatter like small rocks falling and bouncing.

He went closer to the web. The glow hadn't moved, although he assumed that the spider was merely biding its time...a bunch of dead yarks were suspended in the web, black bodies in white thread, mostly runts, grinning.

That's what you'd look like if it got you, Snash thought.

"*Kommt! Kommt!*" whispered a voice suddenly, from out of the funnel. "She's *toht!* Dead! *Kommt!*"

"Glargle?" Snash asked.

"*Ja, ja! Du* didn't tell on Glargle, Glargle helps *du! Kommt!*"

"What about the web?"

"Dried out! Not shticky anymore!"

Hearing that, Snash went forward into the funnel, sweeping web aside, trying not to brush the hanging yarks...when, despite his best efforts, he accidentally touched one, the line it depended from suddenly parted, and the bundle struck the floor feet-first and pancaked, crackling, contents still retained by the silk.

"*Shtill, shtill!*" Glargle told Snash. "Somevun else back zere, ja?"

Snash nodded.

"Hide light," Glargle said.

Snash covered the miniature with his hand. For the moment at least, with a dead spider up ahead, there was more than enough glow to get on with.

"How long has she been dead?"

"Glargle sink long. Dead when Glargle come up here. No vun vill come in here, zough."

Snash eyed the dead spider. She wasn't glowing as brightly as a non-defunct spider, he thought, but the attitude of her body was still pretty lifelike, and he could quite understand why no one would want to get too close to her...

"Shpiders, shpiders," Glargle said. "Get into places zey shouldn't," He looked back at Snash with a gruesome smile. "Chust...like...*uns.*"

They came to another crack, this one running along the floor into the lefthand wall...Glargle climbed around the corner...Snash uncovered the miniature, shining its light through the split. Glargle was leaning into view, looking back, but when the light hit him in the face, he cursed and jerked out of sight. Snash found himself peering into a very large chamber...the crevice in the floor closed after a few yards....a light was moving on the far side of the room, and he was briefly alarmed before realizing he was looking at a reflection of the miniature.

As with the last crack, there were enough hand-and-footholds for him to round the wall, and he went out into the middle of the chamber, Glargle following. The walls were made of very smooth, highly polished obsidian, in effect, black mirrors.

"Zey never come in here," said Glargle. "Doors over

zere---" he pointed, "but searchers go by. Alvays safe here."

"You've been all over the tower, haven't you?" Snash asked.

"*Ja*."

"Do you know how to get to the Nail?"

Glargle blinked his huge eyes. "Nail?"

"The second-biggest tower," Snash said.

"Ze Prison?" Glargle asked.

"Yes. Have you ever gone there?"

"Zey kept me zere. Ze first time I came..."

"I need to go there."

"Vhy?"

Snash pointed to the miniature. "They've got *her* there. She's a fay princess. And I mean to let her out."

Glargle laughed and tapped Snash on the head. "Ziss full of *scheiss*."

"I'm going to do it."

"*Vhy?* Fays and yarks enemies."

"Serpentar is everyone's enemy."

"Zo...fays should like yarks? Vhy *should* zey like yarks? Yarks vurk for Serpentar."

"I don't," said Snash.

"Did."

"Not anymore....I helped *you*, didn't I?"

"*Ja*, but---"

"I'm going to help her too. I've got a book...took it from the Nail and hid it. It's full of spells...they control the locks."

"Und zo, you're going into prison?"

"Yes."

"Ze place mit cells, *und* racks, *und* vheels, *und* torturers to use zem?"

"I'm not afraid."

"*Ja, du bist scheisskopf*, as Glargle already say...*Auf weidersehen.*" He flapped one of his froggy hands at him, as if to wave him back towards the crack in the wall.

But Snash wasn't going. "*Is* there a way to sneak down there?"

"Back vay, ja. Inside vay. Betveen valls, srough cracks.

Go places ze spiders like. But...*du* vould get lost, Glargle sink. Even if Glargle told *du* vhere to go."

"Lead me down there."

"*Nein*. Glargle *nicht scheisskopf*. Not care about fay princess. Never met fay princess. Glargle vant ze *Leibchen, ja*, glargle, glargle."

"By which you mean the Gauntlet of Dominion, correct?" came a silky voice from back behind Snash...he whirled to see Slippriman coming out of the crack, hair and beard filthy, face smudged, garments scorched.

"Sss!" Glargle hissed. "*Nein! Nein!* Glargle's room! Get out!"

"Your room?" Slippriman replied. "Oh, I think not...I believe this must be the old shrine, where Serpentar used to worship himself...he's got a much bigger one now, but...it's no wonder no one ever looked for you in here. No one but Serpentar may enter..."

"What do you want?" Snash asked.

"A place to hide," Slippriman said. "Just like you. But I couldn't help overhearing, just now....this idea of yours, freeing Luvliel...I must say, it has potential...especially if we free everyone *else* as well."

"Everyone else?" Snash asked.

"The whole White Committee. Don't you remember? I believe Serpentar and I were discussing it when you were a snail...The whole plot was laid out before you. The members of the Committee, one by one, carrying false Gauntlets of Dominion into Tenebria, and being captured...Serpentar has the lot of them. Even Tim Bimbottom."

"Who's that?"

"The wierdest and queerest of the bunch. Also the hardest to handle...right at this moment, there in the Nail, Serpentar is holding everyone needed to overthrow him. I say we let them *all* out." He looked at Snash sidelong. "You have the spell book, you say?"

"Hidden," said Snash. "But...they know it's missing."

"Yes. So?"

"Mightn't they have changed the locks?" Ever since Slagbag raised it, this possibility had been weighing on Snash,

239

but he thought Slippriman might know what was what.

"There aren't any," the wizard replied. "Patches of wall disappear, form a doorway. Each spell is based on the prisoner's true name. And there's only one of those. Trust me."

But even though Snash had every reason to believe him about the spells, he didn't like to hear him talking about *trust*...reading Snash's face, Slippriman said:

"Don't want to get in the habit, eh? Well, it's not as though I *need* your trust. If you don't co-operate, I can compel you, with the spell we use in Yarks and Spiders. But you have me all wrong, really. I've been working *against* Serpentar."

"You were his Supreme Unrecognized, whatever that is---"

"Let me explain. When I learned of his plot, I thought I might still be able to warn someone...came here and was captured. Serpentar made me an offer. But I merely *pretended* to switch sides, and was biding my time..."

"You want the Gauntlet," said Snash.

"*Mein liebchen*," said Glargle.

"No," said Slippriman. "I want to *destroy* it."

"Deshtroy *mein leibchen*?" Glargle cried.

"You didn't tell Serpentar you wanted to destroy it," Snash said. "You said it would work better if you *had* it."

"I said I'd put it to better use," Slippriman replied. "By which I meant, undoing all that was done with it, by putting it into the fire."

"You didn't say that and you didn't mean it!" Snash cried.

"Too bad we didn't have a scribe there."

"You're a traitor," Snash said.

"I understand why you think that. But appearances are deceptive. And I had good reason to appear less appetizing than I am...The world is at stake. All freedom and beauty will die if Serpentar triumphs. Such a situation calls for quick thinking and ruthless measures. If I hadn't pretended to switch sides, I'd be down in the Nail myself, with no hope of freeing anybody. As it is, Serpentar's just about to launch his attack on Merriador...the order goes out tomorrow night. But I mean to stop him."

"That's because you want to *be* him."

"Oh, how can you say that? Just look how he runs things...fire everywhere, soot, stench, sweaty yarks, spiders in the walls, a very limited dreary palette, rivets, hobnails, cogs...then look at me. I mean not at the moment, since I'm all so infernally dirty, but...you saw my apartment. The flowers, the elegance, everything in order...If I were in charge, Tenebria would be very very different...."

"You want to be Serpentar, only neater."

"*You* can't prove it. And if, when we free the others, you say anything, none of them will believe you because you're just a yark, and I'm the head of the Committee."

"And you'll get the Gauntlet?"

"It'll be hurled into the chimney and destroyed in the volcano where it was made," said Slippriman. "You have my word on it."

"Von't help," said Glargle.

"*Vill*," Slippriman said, then uttered a couple of words and drove Glargle to his knees with a downward sweep of his hand before asking:

"Just where are you from, by the way?"

"Vaterland," Glargle said.

"Never heard of it," Slippriman said. Turning to Snash, he started to repeat the spell---then snatched the miniature away from him, almost as though he thought it might interfere. But even as he spoke the spell again, Snash thought of Luvliel's face... after nosing frigidly at the back of his neck, the magic slid off, thwarted, like water from steel.

Even so, Snash went to his knees the way Glargle had, and Slippriman seemed to buy it, saying:

"There now---"

He cocked an ear. Beyond the doors, feet were clattering, the sounds muffled by the valves...yark-voices snarled, but the searchers went right on by.

"I think we'll stay in here for a bit," he said. "Wait till they're sure we're gone. They'll assume we fled downstairs. They've obviously been making that assumption about Glargle here, all along....And then, once the order passes, and the tower begins to empty, it'll be even easier to get around...if we *do* manage to free my colleagues, we'll have a lot fewer yarks and ogres to contend with."

"That just leaves the sharkriders---"

"Generally," said Slippriman, "there are only four or five at the tower, while the rest on long patrol, although---right at this moment, three of them are assigned to lead the army."

"---and the hellrogs---"

"We *will* have to cope with all of them, I'm afraid."

"---and Serpentar himself."

"He'll be a job for old Tim, I think," said Slippriman.

"Hard to believe he could be beaten by a *Bimbottom*," Snash replied.

"Shows what you know about Bimbottoms," Slippriman said, did a peculiar little step for no reason that Snash could think of, rapped Snash sharply on the scalp, and added: "Ding-dong!"

Chapter 14: Luvliel Revisited

As it turned out, Glargle had been making regular trips down to Overflowing Fist, and had brought---he said *schlepped*---a good deal of very nice food and drink up to the Shrine; Slippriman was surprised, saying:

"I would've thought you ate worms and insects."

"Glargle does," said Glargle. "But he eats the little salty fish eggs vhen he can get zem, too."

"They're called caviar," said Slippriman, opening a jar full of them and sniffing it. But he didn't seem to want to stick his fingers in.

"Come from out east," said Glargle. "Sea of Shtur...Shtur...."

"Sturgeons," said Slippriman.

Snash had heard of it...he'd acquired a taste for caviar at Overflowing Fist, although at the moment, he wasn't in the mood. Slippriman kept looking at his jar, as if he was screwing himself up to do something unfastidious...finally, he stuck his bony fingers in, then sucked the eggs off them, kind of slowly and languidly, as if this would be less sloppy, although the effect was perhaps more repulsive than it might've been otherwise.

Trying to ignore him, Snash had some salted fish and some wine.

"Don't drink too much," said Slippriman, little black eggs jiggling in his moustache.

"I'm pretty dry," said Snash.

"Be that as it may," said Slippriman, "keep your head clear."

Time and again, they heard activity beyond the doors, and back between the walls, but no one came into the shrine, and finally, after hours and hours, the searches stopped. Not long afterward, though, there came a hammering of drums and a blare of trumpets, and that just went on and on, together with a slight vibration, as if the fortress were being shaken by the pounding of heavy hobnailed boots uncountable. Slippriman said:

"Those horn-calls---they're the sort that the elite troops use, the eastern men and the shock-yarks. Their barracks are being emptied, the ones in the Spike…farther down, the order would've passed a while ago. Serpentar has quite a good plan for moving everyone out very quickly…tunnels built expressly just for this moment, never opened till now…won't be long before the whole plain surrounding Mount Adamant is black with yarks, although it is, admittedly, black already…And then, when the time comes, the whole lot will go pouring out through the Yawning Maw, which stands between the Towers of the Mouth…and the whole *rest* of the world will be black with yarks, which will be rather more of a change, since it *isn't* black already…" The wizard paused. "*If* I don't free my colleagues, of course."

"If you *do* free them," Snash said, "what will you do with *us*?"

"Us?"

"Yarks."

"Oh, as I think you could tell by my tone just now, I'm not entirely put out by the thought of yarks blackening the earth, provided they bathe every once in a while. I think, if their armor were nicely lacquered, and there was a judicious use of color, red or gold trim, the effect would actually be quite striking. Imagine five thousand perfectly straight jet ranks, easily distinguished by rows of blue plumes, and banners, maybe, worn on the back…I would *love* to have a yark-host like that."

"So we'll be *your* slaves instead of Serpentar's?"

"What do you *want*? You're just yarks. Even if some of you *are* more clever than others."

"We're descended from fays," Snash said.

"But you're not fays *now*," said Slippriman. "And no one's going to give you any rights."

"Luvliel would," said Snash.

"Think so?"

"Yes."

"What a *lot* of insight you acquired in the half-minute you spent with her."

"She *would*," Snash insisted.

"If you say so. But if I were you, I'd try to be more realistic. See things as they actually are."

Remembering the Shark Lord saying something similar--it seemed like ages ago---Snash replied: "I started off in the mail room, beat Serpentar in Yarks and Spiders---and escaped. I'm the only reason you have a hope of setting your friends free."

"And?" Slippriman asked.

Snash fell silent.

But Slippriman just smiled. "Thinking how you might rid yourself of me?"

Snash glanced at Glargle, who was making faces and rude gestures behind Slippriman's back.

"No," Snash said, although he didn't think Slippriman believed it for a second.

Slippriman waited until the marchings and the blowings and the drummings got a good deal more distant, then rose and asked Snash:

"So where did you hide the book?"

"There's a tower near the Nail," Snash said. "It's called the Needle. Abandoned---"

"Yes, yes," said Slippriman. "It was the prison for big shots before the Nail was built..." He glanced at Glargle. "Do *you* know a good way to get down there from here?"

"A shneak-route?" the gremlin replied.

"Yes."

"*Nein.*"

"Why don't you...take us anyhow?"

"Don't vant to," said Glargle.

"Shall I force you?"

"Force Glargle vhere? *Du* don't know shneak-route. *Du* can make me moof, but...*sehen* ze problem?"

Slippriman wasn't even stumped for a moment. "Very well, consider *this*. I know a way to acquire someone else's memories. It is most repulsive, but I will use it if I have to."

"Vhat are *du* goingk to do? Eat Glargle's brain?"

"That's the last step, but..."

245

Glargle looked at him sidelong. "Vhy vould *du* even sink of somesing like zat?"

"I didn't think of it. I was browsing an obscure manuscript. And I'm not going to let one brief nasty meal stand between me and the tidying of the whole world."

Snash wasn't sure about this...he thought it might just be a bluff, since there was only one way to find out. But Glargle was cowed.

"Okay, okay," he said. "Glargle vill knuckle under."

"Lead on," said Slippriman.

Out they went through the fissure and the web-funnel between the curving walls, coming to the crack that led to the snake-maze.

"Down here," Glargle said.

"What, through the floor?" Slippriman asked.

"Inside shplit in wall."

"How?" Slippriman asked.

"Plenty handholds," said Glargle. "Or do ziss---"

Flinging himself into the crevice, he wedged himself in place with his feet and hands against one side, and his back to the other; then he ooched down a couple of feet. "Or *ziss.*" Ooching back up, he suddenly changed position, holding himself in place with his hands and feet stretched out...pushing with his legs, he scrabbled up farther, then scrabbled back down, and twisted suddenly to one side, snagging hand and toeholds as he drew himself along the wall and back out beside Snash and Slippriman. Turning, pointing into the crevice, he said:

"After *du, mein herren.*"

"No," said Slippriman. "After you."

Glargle clucked and started in, head down, looking quite the frog....Slippriman went next, chimneying, and Snash went last, simply climbing down the lefthand side, using the holes and fissures.

"How far does this crack go?" Slippriman asked.

"To bottom of vall," said Glargle. "Five hundred feet, more maybe. But ve don't go zat far. Get out into passage, go to *kleine* stair. But you should shtop mit qvestions. Hussh now. Bad enough ve grasp und rasp mit fingers on valls."

"Don't tell me to be quiet," Slippriman said.

"Chust a little vurd to wise."

As they descended, they went by a number of red portals, off to the left.

Still the snake-maze, Snash thought. Apparently the labyrinth extended some distance beneath Serpentar's floor. But before long, Snash and his companions were beneath it; they passed what appeared to be a dimly torchlit storeroom filled with huge barrels; Snash thought he made out a fat yark porter sitting up against the wall, sleeping, dead drunk, perhaps. On the next floor down, an empty corridor ran alongside the crack; below that, there was a dormitory with many cots, all empty.

So it went for a while...Snash could easily imagine how Glargle, moving silently and cautiously, had been able to get up and down the fissure; it was a good thing, though, that the Spike had been largely emptied...the runt doubted that he and Slippriman, less practiced at stealth, could've gotten very far if much of anyone had been around.

At length they reached the passage Glargle had spoken of, and climbed out onto the floor; the corridor was very musty and dusty, and so was the little stairwell that opened off it...keeping as much as possible to areas under construction, or abandoned sections, Glargle led into other fissures, and gaps between walls, and down ramps, and narrow accessways---with metal rungs--- that had been left open so that Serpentar's engineers might make inspections. Huge arches and buttresses ran right through the walls; there was a great deal more open space than Snash had expected, and while he never guessed why, the reason was weight reduction, same as with the quick basalt.

Glargle followed narrow zigzagging ledges down clifflike faces, and crossed slender bridges, and descended chains, and ropes. Huge webs were stretched between walls, with blots of luminosity behind overlapping shrouds of silk, and spider-light shone from tunnel-mouths and cracks; but Glargle knew how to bypass the nets, and Snash never saw any of the spiders themselves.

They heard yark voices, occasionally; the hunt still seemed to be on. But the searchers, who were down below, at least a thousand feet, Snash guessed, always continued to descend, apparently in the belief that they were flushing the fugitives before them. Thinking there was every chance that the hunters might persist in their error, he told himself:

We're going to make it, down to the Needle at least—

But that was before a door swung open on the ledge before him. Out came a troop of yarks, led by a black-robed man holding a torch.

Glargle darted to the wall and went up it like a lizard...Snash and Slippriman just stopped.

"Who goes there?" the man demanded.

"It is I," Slippriman said.

Looking most unhappy to see him, the man halted, his yarks bunching up behind him.

"Recognize me?" Slippriman asked.

"No," said the man.

"Yes, yes, I think you do."

"Not at all."

"Oh, please. You were sent to look for me, isn't that right? But now that you've found me, you're too frightened to do anything about it."

"I don't know who you are," the blackrobe said.

Slippriman sniggered.

"We just got lost down here," the man went on.

"Doing what?"

"Looking for a way back to the central shaft..."

"You came to look for a way back?"

With that, the man just cracked, saying: "All right, all right."

"What?"

"We won't tell anyone."

"That you found us?"

"I swear," said the man.

"Oh," said Slippriman, "I think you might. And so...."

Snash already knew that Slippriman had been planning to do them in...the whole conversation had been remniscent of Serpentar grilling Slippriman, even if Slippriman wasn't anywhere near as scary.

That didn't mean that the blackrobe and his yarks were any less doomed, though.

Slippriman raised his hand, then lowered it swiftly, uttering some magic words. At first it seemed to Snash that Slippriman was driving the man and the yarks to their knees, much as he'd done to Glargle, back in the shrine...then it looked as though holes had opened under them, and they were falling in...then, at last, Snash realized that they were getting *smaller*, shrinking inside their robes (in the case of the man) or armor (in the case of the yarks)....half its original size, the man's face dropped from sight inside the neck-hole of his garment, his hood collapsing. The yarks' helmets were landing atop the plated shoulders of their corselets, the mailshirts deflating...within moments, fifteen byrnies and one black robe were lying on the stone, with things struggling and squeaking inside them.

Slippriman stepped forward to the robe, rummaged till he found the tiny naked man within, then threw him sideways at the wall, where the little fellow struck with a slapping noise, then peeled off and dropped....Slippriman straightened, and went from mailshirt to crumpled mailshirt, stomping the shrunken yarks inside.

"Do you *have* to do that?" Snash asked.

Slippriman paused, foot hanging over the last one. "What's this?" he asked. "Concern for your brethren?" Down came his sandal. "Would you rather they raised the alarm?"

"In their little squeaky voices?" Snash asked. "*If* they'd ever got out of that armor? We could've been long gone..."

"Uggh," said Slippriman. "A yark with a conscience. The worst of all possible worlds....does this mean you won't co-operate any more?"

Snash bit his tongue.

Slippriman looked round. "Where's Glargle?"

"Here," Glargle said, well above him on the wall.

"Get down here," Slippriman said. "Stay where I can

see you."

Once Glargle complied, Slippriman started unsheathing the dead yarks' daggers, found himself a very keen one, then softened his whiskers with water from a yark's bottle, and sawed off most of his beard, shaving the rest. Having thus made himself a good deal less Slippriman-like in the looks department, he put on the dead man's duds---plainly, the reason he'd chucked the fellow against the wall instead of stomping him inside the robes was that he'd planned to wear them all along. Pulling up the hood, he said:

"There now. Let's get the book."

Glargle took them into the Needle through a back way---although Snash had always used a different entrance, he knew where he was, and had no difficulty finding the door of the armory where he'd hidden the book. But Glargle paused near the threshold, snuffling.

"Schmell yark," he whispered.

"Me?" Snash asked.

"*Dead* yark."

"Smell anything alive?" Slippriman asked.

"*Nein.*"

"Then there's nothing to worry about."

"Don't like."

Slippriman looked to Snash. "Get going."

Snash went through the door. There were narrow casements in the wall to the left, and outside, feeble cloud-shrouded day had come---there was more than enough light for his yark-eyes. He looked about apprehensively...with all the empty weapons-racks, broken and otherwise, some of them tipped over each other, there were plenty of places for someone to lie in wait, if they weren't dead, that is. Farther in, he began to smell dead yark himself, and wondered where the corpse was, and if its stink might be covering the smell of something living, whatever Glargle might say...

Coming to the rack that he'd hidden the book behind, he began to pull it away from the wall...Glargle laughed and ran up, saying: "Glargle hide schtuff here too!" and helped, getting in back of it and pushing. Looking into the crack in the wall, Snash saw several jars of caviar along with the book, a couple of dried fish and what appeared to be a spare loincloth. Snash was glad Glargle had an extra, if indeed that was what it was. The idea of the skank without the loincloth was...unendurable.

Glargle laughed, tapping the book. "Oh, *ziss*," he said.

"Oh, that," said Slippriman, knocking Snash and Glargle out of the way....Snash turned to face the wizard, who had the volume and was leafing through it greedily.

All at once something came flying in from the edge of sight, struck Slippriman in the back of the noggin with a thud, and bounced off, clattering on the floor.

"Oww!" said the wizard, reached to feel his scalp, and turned, blinking. He looked down, but didn't look like he could see clearly. Snash saw a rock about the size of one of his own fists lying at Slippriman's feet.

"Who did that?" Slippriman demanded, lifting his chin, Snash raising his gaze as well...a second rock caught the wizard, *bok*! square in the forehead, which he put both hands to, then started tottering.

"Hit me with rocks, will you?" Slippriman cried. "I'll rip the skeleton right out of your body!"

Snash saw a hulking bull-silhouette come out from between two weapon racks, silhouetted by casement-light...the rock-thrower got several steps closer before Snash recognized...

Slagbag!

Slippriman started making sorcerous gestures, but one of his legs folded, and by the time he got back up again, Slagbag was on him, knocking him against the wall with a jabbing punch and following that with big swinging lefts and rights that simply *sucked* through the air and connected with great meaty *smacks*...Snash had to laugh out loud, watching Slippriman's head snap to and fro. Finally Slippriman slid down the wall, landing on his behind, sitting upright against the masonry, head slumping forward. Snash sensed he was out cold.

"Snash," said Slagbag, blowing on his fists.

"Slagbag!" Snash cried, thrilled to his marrow to see him alive, even if he did smell like yark-compost....but before he could ask Slagbag what he was doing still alive, Slagbag asked:

"That's Slippriman, isn't it? Without his beard?"

"Yes."

"I *thought* I recognized that voice."

"So you just decided to hit him with a rock?"

"What of it?"

"He might've come in handy---"

"Are you mates now? Didn't sound like it---"

Suddenly remembering he *still* didn't know why Slagbag was alive, Snash cried:

"Slagbag!"

"What?"

"I saw that spider get you!"

"Don't know what you saw," Slagbag said. "But I just banged my head on the floor. Woke up in a compost-heap, along with the blokes who'd been killed on the board, and a lot of other boys who were much farther gone...Anyway, when they came to load me on a wagon, I let 'em, then crawled out when they were taking us down in the lift...once he got over his shock, the man in charge told me to go see a surgeon, and I started to do just that, but then I heard you'd escaped...figured you'd go for the book..."He nudged Slippriman with his foot. "What *are* you doing with this double dose of dung? And the Frog, by the way?"

Leaving the question of Glargle aside for the moment, Snash said: "Slippriman followed me when I escaped, and when he found out about the book, he decided to free Luvliel and all her friends himself, so he can use them to get the Gauntlet."

Slagbag picked up one of the rocks. "Why don't I just finish him right now? He's going to be mighty angry if he comes round."

Not at all convinced that Slagbag should kill him--- there *was* that little matter of the wizard's utility---Snash gave Slippriman a good close look and said:

"He's stopped breathing."

"Glad to hear it," said Slagbag.

Snash took the book from Slippriman's hand, then pulled the miniature out of his robes and hid it in his own tunic.

"*Du* go to Nail now?" Glargle asked.

"Change your mind?" Snash replied. "Want to come?"

"Vouldn't say *vant* to..."

"I understand."

"Glargle apprehensiff..."

"We can manage without you, find our way from here."

There were a few more moments of amphibian indecision. Then Glargle said: "*Vill* come."

"Vill you? I mean, *will* you?"

"Musst get *liebchen*, or die tryingk. Iff ve vin, *du* giff me."

"No one should have anything that powerful."

"Glargle *iss* no vun. Chust *kleine* veird geek. Can't do anysing *mit liebchen*. Chust like it. Take it avay to cave and sit in mud mit it..."

"What makes you think I can just give you the Gauntlet of Dominion?"

"Snash ze...*meister*. Ze *leiter*. Ze boss. Beat Serpentar in game... No vun ever beat Serpentar in anysing. All zose people in Nail---if zere freed, Snash do it. Zey von't free zemselves. You say Glargle get *liebchen*, he get."

"You know," said Snash, "I really don't think it's up to me."

"Don't care. Meister say Glargle get Gauntlet, zat goot enough for Glargle."

Snash looked at Slagbag.

"Ah, give it to him," said Slagbag. "Once Serpentar's dead and all..."

But Snash was still deeply dubious, telling Glargle: "Those others---the ones we're going to free---they might not let me keep my promise."

"You schvear, goot enough for Glargle."

"I see," said Snash.

"Should be off now," said Glargle.

"I didn't swear to anything," said Snash.

"Goot enough for Glargle."

Slagbag was still holding that rock; eyeing Slippriman thoughtfully, he weighed it, then gave him a couple of cracks in the head...Snash cringed.

"Don't be like that," Slagbag said. "If he was already dead, so what? And if he *wasn't*..." He paused, then took that yark dagger that Slippriman had appropriated. Snash tensed, thinking that Slagbag was about to make *extra* sure of the wizard. But, looking disturbed by Snash's attitude, Slagbag didn't, asking: "How *are* we going to get into the Nail?"

"Nobody's looking for *you*," said Snash. "So..."

"I act like I arrested you?"

"Right. Me and Glargle hold our hands behind our backs, pretend they're tied. I bet no one will notice."

"And then what? Can you use the book?"

"No. That's why Slippriman would've been helpful. But...there are jailers, in red. Turnkeys, except they don't turn keys. They can open the doors. If we can just grab one---"

"Let's go," said Slagbag.

"Take food," Glargle said, handing them each a dried fish and a caviar-jar.

They went back out the back way, shnuck through shneak-routes for some of the distance, then emerged, Snash and Glargle out front, in the corridor that led to the bridge between the Nail and the Spike. A squad of bulls was approaching, and one, a brute named Ruksuk---he'd been a motivator down in the mail room---called his fellows to a halt.

"Ho there, Slagbag!" he cried. "Caught something, hey?"

"Used to be my runner," Slagbag said.

"I remember," said Ruksuk. "He's been making heaps of trouble, I hear...got the frog, too, I see---"

"Any of you fellows have a spare sword or axe?" Slagbag asked. "Lost my chopper catching these two, and all I've got is a knife..."

"Mograt," said Ruksuk.

"What?" asked one of his lads.

"Give him your spare axe."

Mograt had a single-bladed axe with a topspike thrust into his belt, and while he looked pretty sour about handing it over, he did it anyway, muttering.

Ruksuk sniffed, then asked Slagbag: "What *did* you get into?"

"Compost," said Slagbag.

"Smells like it. Be seeing you."

As Ruksuk and his lads headed off, Slagbag drove Snash and Glargle farther along the corridor. At the end was an arch, and through it Snash could see the bridge that ran from the Spike to the Nail. They were just about to the threshold when some sort of commotion started up behind them. Snash heard yarks screaming, then a great blast, then horns, and all sorts of other sounds he could put no name to.

"Slippriman," said Slagbag.

Snash was pretty sure he was right.

"Should've stuck him," said Slagbag.

"Just as well you didn't," Snash replied. "He's still going to come in handy."

"How?"

"We're going to go right on across, and he's going to distract everyone---"

He broke off as a shrill cry---Snash recognized it as a sharkrider's---reached them from outside, faint but chilling.

"Gage Ghoul," said Slagbag. "If they're flying around out there, they'll see us."

"They'll still go for Slippriman first," said Snash, and headed out onto the bridge. Ahead the span was empty...at the end, the Nail loomed dark against a grey sky, all its windows black. Snash guessed there were lights burning inside them, but the day, dim as it was, was still too bright for him to see them.

He heard another cry, far above; a distant dark speck, a sharkrider was circling around the crown of the Spike...but even as Snash looked, two more took flight from the pinnacle.

"What are they waiting for?" Slagbag asked.

"The Shark Lord, maybe?" Snash replied.

A fourth rider soon joined them, confirming that, his mount looking---to Snash's eye---quite a bit bigger than the other sharks.

Carcharias, Snash thought. Wanting desperately to break into a run, he restrained himself, although he did start to walk faster, achieving a pretty stiff clip. He kept looking up. The sharkriders circled a bit more, then broke from the ring one by one, spiralling down. So far away, they didn't look like they were moving very fast, but Snash knew better.

They'll be down here any moment...

He thrust his panic aside.

They'll go for Slippriman, you watch...Also, you're almost there.

He was coming up hard on the portcullis, amazed at how much bridge could be crossed with a fast walk. The eastron guards in their laced armor were looking out through the bars, one asking Slagbag:

"What's all the trouble over there?"

"Slippriman," Slagbag said.

"What? Has he gone bonkers?"

"Yes."

"And what do you have there?"

"Prisoners," said Slagbag.

"Is that that froggy thing everyone's looking for?"

"And the runt. Let us in."

"Shouldn't you have taken them up to BC---?"

There was a thunderous detonation...Snash glanced over his shoulder. Thick smoke billowed from the arch across the way, but suddenly, as if struck by great gusts of wind, it dispersed...down came a sharkrider.

"Let us in," said Slagbag, just before there was a third blast. The eastron signalled to someone, and the portcullis began to go up, chains clinking. As he entered, Snash heard great wings thudding, and looked over his shoulder again.

Two more sharkriders landed on the span, one facing the Nail...Snash had the impression that the ghoul was looking right at him.

But then came a weird sizzling sound, and green lights flashed in the smoke behind, and the sharkrider wheeled his mount round, and leaped from his saddle....Snash saw two more, airborne, one still descending towards the bridge, the other hovering.

"Get moving," said Slagbag.

Good advice, Snash thought.

As they made their way up the corridor with the black stalactites on the ceiling, a bunch of eastrons came clattering, but ran right by...entering the circular chamber at the hallway's end and going up the stairs, Snash et al. were likewise ignored by more easterners coming down...when they got to the top and neared the checkpoint counter, there were only a few men in evidence, including one of the wizard-turnkeys.

"What's happening outside?" the redrobe cried.

"Slippriman," said Slagbag. "He's gone...uh, *bonkers*."

A couple of the eastrons said something to each other in their own language, then came out from behind the counter and went to the edge of the stairs.

"Who's that you've got there?" the wizard asked Slagbag, coming out as well.

"Didn't you say the turnkeys wear red?" Slagbag asked Snash.

"That's what I said," said the runt.

The wizard was clearly puzzled by such an exchange between captor and captive, but even as his expression changed because he'd twigged what was going on, Slagbag swung a hard right cross into the turnkey's jaw, and the redrobe collapsed. Then Slagbag pulled his borrowed axe from his belt, whirled, and went for the men standing by the stairhead, only one of whom, turning, seemed to have heard anything...Slagbag caved his helmet in, then hacked the men on either side of him while they were still looking the wrong way. Shoulder and thigh-guards flapping, three bodies were already rolling down the steps when Slagbag rounded upon the last man and sent him to join them with a blow between shoulder and neck. Getting back to the redrobe before the man came round, Slagbag hauled him up the instant he started stirring.

"Luvliel," the bull said.

The redrobe indicated an arch blocked with a gate of iron thorns, much like the barbs in Serpentar's lair...Slagbag navigated him through the gap in the counter before Snash and Glargle took the lead. When they reached the thorns, Slagbag poked the man with the topspike of his axe, and the wizard came out with a spell. Once the thorns retracted into their vines, the gate slid sideways, revealing a corridor. At the end was another thorn-gate, and Snash could see, between *those* barbs and vines...

Another redrobe.

Snash swore under his breath. He didn't have the slightest idea of what to do. They couldn't stop and hash things out, and once they got to the gate, their prisoner would surely try to alert his comrade. The man on the other side came up close to the gate and looked out, asking:

"What's all the fuss, Ghoramghul?"

Slagbag jabbed the prisoner with the topspike again. But Ghoramghul said nothing.

"Why are you making those faces?" the other redrobe asked.

Standing in front of Ghoramghul, Snash couldn't see what sort of faces he was making, but knew just what the redrobe was up to.

All going to end here, Snash thought.

But he hadn't reckoned on Glargle.

The creature slipped back between Slagbag and Ghoramghul; as Snash turned to watch, and the redrobe behind the thorns cried, "Here now!" Glargle, who had snatched Slagbag's dagger and scuttled right up him, got to the bull's shoulder, perched there for an instant, then flung himself towards the thorn-gate. Snash was certain he was going to be impaled, but Glargle simply put his arms straight out and shot into a space between two vines, the barrier not hindering him in the slightest; he didn't even seem to slow down.

"Here now!" the redrobe behind the thorns cried again, but Snash saw Glargle, a greenish blur, flying towards him...the man grunted, and they both went down. Then Glargle came scampering back towards the thorns. Looking through, Snash saw the redrobe lying motionless, the knife sticking out of his head.

Slagbag gave Ghoramghul yet another poke. "Open the gate."

The wizard complied, then opened another, on the left, and they went that way...there was yet another gate at the top of a flight of steps, but after that they found themselves in a passage with numbers inscribed on the walls on either side...Ghoramghul paused before one of the inscriptions, saying:

"Here we are."

Snash almost handed him the spell-book and told him to get to it, then paused and looked up Luvliel's number---it didn't match the one on the wall, and all at once he knew that something terrible was on the other side. The Nail was, after all, a *Tenebrian* prison...there was no reason whatsoever to think that *all* of its inmates were White Committee members...

Snash glanced at Slagbag, who boxed Ghoramghul sharply on the ear....Ghoramghul put his hands up and led them farther down the hall. Snash consulted the book again, and this time the numbers matched.

Snash gave Ghoramghul the book, and the southerling read...a rectangular area of the wall began to give off a golden light, and all at once the stone simply melted away. A soft breeze sighed through the opening, laden with a sweet scent.

"Who's there?" a lilting voice asked.

Snash stuck his head in, hoping he hadn't caught the princess at a bad time. Suffused in her own radiance, she was across the room, sitting on a kind of bed...it was made of stone blocks with a thick green mat apparently rooted in it--- the green stuff was *grass*, or so Snash thought. He'd seen it used as packing material, but it had always been brown and dead---it was much nicer alive. There was more on the floor, and also, on leafy stalks, strange colored nodding things, red and blue and yellow and purple---the word *flowers* came to mind, also *blossoms*, and *blooms*, although he'd never thought of those words before. Between the smells and the colors, it was just about more than he could take in, even without the golden vision of the fay princess on her bed, gown flowing down to the floor...

"Aren't you that little fellow who helped me?" she asked.

"Yes," he said.

"And you're here to help me again?"

He nodded.

She rose, straightening her gown, and asked: "Who are your friends?"

"That's my mate Slagbag," Snash said, pointing.

"Slagbag," said Luvliel, the name sounding almost charming on her lips, even though Snash got rather the feeling she didn't think it was all that charming herself, and had really made an effort.

"That's Glargle," said Snash, indicating the gremlin.

"Glargle?" she asked, apparently rather surprised.

"*Ja*," said Glargle.

"The one who's been after the Gauntlet of Dominion for a thousand years?"

He nodded. "Almost got it yesterday, too."

"Imagine that," said Luvliel, then eyed Ghoramgul. "A prisoner, I assume?"

"Needed him to use the book," said Snash, proffering it to her.

She said, "You don't anymore," and took it.

Grinning, Slagbag raised his axe and made as if to chop the wizard.

But Luvliel said: "No."

"Why not?" Slagbag asked.

"We're the *nice* ones."

"Since when?" asked Slagbag.

"Since you joined *me*," she said.

"I'm a yark," he replied.

"And I'll overlook it," she replied. "There, see? No *need* to kill him."

Ghoramghul had knelt down, and was picking flowers and sniffing them, the silliest, sappiest expression Snash had ever seen spread across his face.

"Why didn't that happen to us?" Snash asked.

"You think I can't control my own *flowers*?" Luvliel asked, and laughed musically.

Snash looked about. "Is this cell *always* full of them?"

"Only about half the time," Luvliel replied. "The warden's always trying new tricks, but he hasn't sterilized the place yet....What's all that racket below, by the way?"

Snash hestitated, wondering what to tell her about

Slippriman…but then, the detonations and the sounds of magical combat just *ceased*, and she went to the door and looked out, Snash going too and looking round her.

"You haven't answered my question," she said.

"It's Slippriman," he said.

"Slippriman?" she asked. "What's he doing here?"

"Fighting Gage Ghouls. One was the Shark Lord himself---"

"The Shark Lord?"

"So I think this silence right now---"

"Means Slippriman's been beaten?"

"Yes."

"We're still in a very bad situation, aren't we?"

"Yes."

"Hmm," she said. "But what if I were to take the book, and go through the tower, and let everyone out?"

"Not everyone in the tower is nice," Snash pointed out.

"Everyone I *like*," she replied, and went out into the hall.

Snash beckoned to Slagbag and Glargle. Leaving Ghoramghul with the flowers that had neturalized him, they followed. Luvliel consulted the book, then ran off down the corridor with them at her heels.

But the quartet hadn't gone far when they began to hear the crunchy stamp-and-crackle of myriad hobnailed boots.

"What do we do?" Snash asked.

"Let's just see how *many* there are," said Luvliel.

They waited as the tramping grew thunderous.…around the bend boiled a flood of eastrons and yarks, blades glinting in the torchlight. Snash heard Slagbag snarl, and the beefy bull stepped up beside Snash, hefting his axe, breathing in through his big nostrils.

But Luvliel seemed barely put out. Sleeve fluttering, she raised her arm, said:

"Blossoms, blossoms, *blossoms!*"

And stamped, gown flouncing.

Between her and the onrushing enemy, flowering flora *burst* from the floor, shooting up right out of the bare stone; the yarks and eastrons got about halfway into it before they got smiles rather like Ghoramghul's on their faces, and started to stagger, and drop down into the midst of the color-splashed green, and begin to pluck flowers by the dozens, by the scores, more flowers bursting up to replace them. Everyone seemed to be having such a good time that Snash almost wished it would happen to him...

"There," said Luvliel. "We're in a drum tower, we'll just go round the other way---"

She started to turn, but a shrill dead voice, fleshless and piercing, swept down the corridor, uttering words Snash didn't know but flinched at anyway; still gawking at the flower-pickers, the runt saw the vegetation suddenly wither and shrivel, petals and leaves falling...round the bend, towering over the kneeling yarks, came the Shark Lord, eyes flaming beneath his crowned helm, a great spiked hammer clenched in his gauntletted hand...and if all that weren't bad enough, there were another two Gage-Ghouls to back him up. But the sight of all those yarks and eastrons picking blossoms seemed to take him aback, and he paused, crying:

"I believeth not mine eyes! What ponces are here? Away with thee, away, away!" With that, he started forward again, swinging that great hammer, smashing a half-dozen yarks or men into the walls on either side with every sweep, though all of the corpses were still smiling, as far as Snash could tell...

"Back to my cell!" cried Luvliel, and Snash and his buddies sped after her, and got to the chamber while the Shark Lord---by the sound of it--- was still bashing away. Ghoramghul was lying on the bed and singing softly, dropping flowers onto his face; ignoring him, using the book, Luvliel sealed the wall up...then she faced the opposite wall, and magicked an egress in it. Outside, there was only leaden sky.

There came a tremendous impact. Looking where the first door had been, Snash saw that four of the stone blocks, about six feet up, had been driven in towards him, as though a great hammer had caught them right where their four corners met...

"He'll be through in a moment," said Luvliel, sounding *nowhere* near as agitated as Snash thought she should. Raising her hand, she cried: "A small yet sturdy tree!" and stamped, and up sprang a little but doughty-looking one. Snash had no idea what she wanted with it, but as if sensing his puzzlement, she told him: "We'll go down my hair," and started unbinding it.

That comforted him briefly, though he didn't know why, and he looked to Slagbag, then Glargle, both of them displaying this *Go down my hair?* sort of look.

She answered: "Your skepticism is misplaced," then tied her hair to the tree, just as another hammerstroke crashed into the wall.

"Snash, Glargle, cling to me," she cried. "Slagbag, you climb down last---"

Snash heard wings thumping, and something huge and dark appeared outside the door Luviel had opened...even though he couldn't see much past her, he knew there must be a sharkrider out there---

The fay princess began to dodge aside; at the same time, Snash heard another crash from behind, followed immediately by rustly thuds, as though a whole bunch of blocks were landing on thick flowery grass...Snash spun round.

There was a hole in the wall now, big enough for the Lord of the Gage-Ghouls to stride on through, which he did, holding his hammer straight out with one hand, a tiny bead of eye-watering blue light appearing at the tip of its spiked stave. The bead flared, and there was a blinding glare, off on Snash's left, as a bolt screamed by; he had no sense of anything passing the other way, but as the light faded, he saw that the ghoul-chieftain had disappeared from the doorway.

Snash looked at the window. The sharkrider outside was gone...

Blasted each other, he told himself.

"*Down my hair!*" cried Luvliel, and lowered herself partway out the opening she'd opened; Glargle skittered over her and down her back, and when Snash started to climb out, he saw the creature hanging from her slender white fay ankle...lifting his chin, Snash gaped at Tenebria spread out before him, blackened with yarks...then he clung to her neck and swung his legs down. Kicking both feet against the wall, she swung out and began to drop. She still had some of her hair curled up on top of her head, and even though it played out awfully quick, it still seemed to take longer than Snash would've thought...finally though, the coils were gone, and there was only the unbound strands, growing out of her scalp at tremendous speed, braiding as they passed between her thumb and fingers...she started to spin, and Snash was subjected to a series of swift sickening glimpses of tower, then sky, then tower, then sky...looking up, he saw Slagbag, already distant, coming down in a series of jerks, legs outstretched towards the wall, kicking much as Luvliel had done at first. Snash hoped he wasn't burning his hands too bad, but he could easily imagine that Luvliel's hair might be a most unpunishing rope.

Amid all his dizziness and nausea, he remembered the sharkrider who'd been outside the window...he thought he caught a glimpse of him, spiralling away and trailing black smoke. Snash hoped the shark hadn't been hurt too much.

Already Luvliel was approaching the base of the tower, where it rose from the pinnacle it had been built upon, and she soon descended into a slot between two piers of stone. Down and down they plunged, but soon the Princess stopped growing her hair out so quickly; as they approached a wide shelf protruding from the side of the crag, she slowed to a halt the instant her feet touched the stone---Snash felt hardly a jolt. Glargle had climbed partway up her skirt as she neared the shelf, and he let go immediately, scrambling off a few yards and trembling and whispering to himself in his weird language.

Snash looked up along the hair...the chimney above was quite dark, but the rope was shimmering blondly if faintly...after a time, he made Slagbag out. He had the hair between his feet now, and was lowering himself hand over hand, very swiftly. When he landed, Snash asked:

"How're your palms?"

"They're not burned, if that's what you're wondering," said Slagbag. "Sliding down felt downright *good*." He looked at Luvliel. "Do all fays have hair like yours?"

"Actually, yes," she said.

"Can you suck it back into your head?"

"Want to see?" she replied.

"Sure."

"Then we'd all better step back. Have to let it pile up before I pull it in."

They retreated from the chimney; then she gave the hanging hair-rope a tug, and instantly it went slack...out in front of them on the stone, between those stone piers, loop after loop of glimmering blond fay-cable began to accumulate.

But presently Snash began to hear screams, long steady ones...down into the hair fell a yark, then an eastron, then two yarks, then three eastrons, then three southerlings just for good measure...soft as the golden coils were, they weren't enough to cushion a very sudden stop from a mile up, and once the hair was completely covered in bodies, that jolt got even more dramatic. Snash wasn't counting, but if someone had told him that two hundred yarks and eastrons and southerlings had gone smash in front of him, he wouldn't have been surprised.

Luvliel sighed. "You know, I *thought* I felt something crawling around up there."

"Couldn't you see?" Snash asked. "Fays can see very far, can't they?"

"Yes, but we have to shift the lenses in our eyes--- rather a nuisance."

"Why didn't they just untie your hair?"

"They want me alive. Glargle?"

"*Ja?*" he asked.

"Would you give me that knife?"

He handed her the one he'd killed that redrobe with...Sighing again, she severed the hair-rope about a yard from her head.

"I thought you were going to suck it back in," said Slagbag.

"I don't want it anymore," she replied sadly.

Chapter 15: Bowels of Adamant

They went to the brink of the shelf and looked down. Perhaps two hundred feet below, there was a great flat roof, of flagstones perhaps, that abutted the cliff; Luvliel summoned another small but sturdy tree, grew some more hair, and down everyone went...when they alighted on the roof, she tugged once more, and her hair dropped, and Slagbag actually got to see it going back in this time.

"Is your skull full of hair, then?" he asked her.

"Of course not, silly," she replied, with a laugh.

"Where does it all go to?" he asked. "And where does it come *from*?"

Luvliel began: "Far away, across the sea, in the West That Went Elsewhere, lived the Lady Tressia. Even though she was an angel, she'd taken on flesh---"

"What's an angel?"

"A servant of the All-Father."

"Who's he?"

"The Creator of everything."

"What's that got to do with your hair?"

"I'm getting to that."

"Sorry."

"You're forgiven."

Slagbag grunted.

"Say thank you," she said.

"Thank you," he replied. "But what about this lady out west?"

"She'd been sent by the All-Father---"

"The Creator?"

"Him. He wanted her to teach the first fays the basics of hair-care. Before the sun was made, under the light of the moon, she lived among the fay-children, and came to love them, and decided they'd take better care of their hair if they had the best available, save for the All-Father's; so she plucked strands from her own head, one for each fay-child, and planted them in the children's scalps; and from that time forward, fays have been able to achieve the most remarkable effects with their follicles."

"Is that *true*?" Slagbag asked.

"Haven't you just climbed down a mile---and more---of my own shining locks?"

"Well yes," he said. "But all that stuff about angels and planting strands...I don't know, it seems..."

"Implausible?"

"Yes."

"What if I just told you I had magic hair?" she asked.

"I'd be more inclined to believe it."

"Consider it said."

He seemed satisfied with that.

Bordering the roof on three sides was a low wall, and they went to that and looked over. There were a number of windows in the sheer stonework below. Luvliel summoned yet another tree and hitched her hair to it, but before they could pull the same stunt with it, a Gage Ghoul screeched somewhere above them, and Snash looked to see a shark, wings extended, plummeting down the face of the pinnacle, almost as though it were simply falling...for a moment it was lost behind the jutting stone ledge, but then it swooped back out into view, and dived once more...

"Get on!" cried Luvliel, and Snash clambered onto her again... luckily, the window was a scant fifteen yards down, and unbarred...pushing off with her feet, she swung out, and back in, sailing through the casement onto an extremely dusty floor in an empty room. Snash and Glargle dropped off her...Snash turned to see Slagbag swing himself in. The big yark staggered, nearly fell, then pivotted and flattened himself beside the casement, pulling his axe from his belt.

Suddenly Luvliel screamed and was yanked backwards towards the window, precisely as though someone with preternatural strength had unfastened the hair from the Small but Sturdy and was jerking it up. She immediately started growing it out, but was almost tugged back into the casement before she was up to speed, and able to give herself some slack...Slagbag hewed at the hair with his axe, but that wasn't the tool for such a job, and he didn't accomplish much of anything. Luvliel, though, still had that knife, and even as she ran in circles, throwing off loops of hair, she reached back and severed the strands, which parted with a pop, then whipped out through the window. The Gage-Ghoul shrieked again. Then came a terrible impact from above, and dust fell from the ceiling, and little bits of stone flaked off and fell...

"*Raus! Raus!*" cried Glargle, who was over by the door, which was wide open...beckoning frantically, he added: "*Schnell!*"

Out they all went, him first...racing along a narrow passageway, Snash heard a second impact, which sounded as though it had blown clear through the ceiling back there...things were crashing and clattering.

Galloping on all fours, a bad sight from behind even if he did have a loincloth, Glargle was still out in front; Snash wanted to pass him just to change the view, but try as he might, only succeeded in getting a closer one. Off on Snash's left, Luvliel, chugging along, was evidently having the same problem, looking very like a fay princess who wished she could run with her eyes closed.

Glargle was mercifully out of sight for a moment after he zipped into another corridor...Snash was tempted not to take the turn, but did so, coming out onto a covered walkway, perhaps a bridge, lined with arches...to the right, there were outcroppings and towers, all rising against a steep dark cliff; to the left, there was sky, and the Tenebrian plain...

And something massive and smoking, dropping down into view.

Snash thought it must be the sharkrider who'd been blasted, the one who he'd seen fly off; but as the shape halted in the air, hovering, he realized he was looking at a hellrog, its smouldering demonic body held aloft not by fins, but tremendous pinions. Its fist gripped the truncheon of a mighty morning star, the weapon's redhot spiked head suspended by a chain emitting *the* most diabolic clinking Snash had ever heard, even in chain-rich Mount Adamant.

"Princess," he cried.

"I see him," she replied, sprinting along.

He kept glancing towards the left...another dark huge shape appeared. In fact, every time he passed an arch, there seemed to be another hellrog hovering outside it, and *all* their mace-chains were clinking.

As though acting upon some agreed-upon signal, the hellrogs all roared at once; Snash was buffetted sidewards by a hot wind, but somehow kept his feet. Afraid to look to the left now, he just kept going.

At the end of the arcade was an open door, which had been closed a few moments earlier; Snash guessed Luvliel had managed that. Just as he got through, he felt---right up through the soles of his feet---a jolt that told him that the walkway behind had simply been smashed out of existence.

Don't want you *alive*, he thought.

He continued into a lofty hall with tall pointed windows....two rows of columns marched down the center. He sensed movement behind him, felt a rush of air, then a boom, as of a huge door being closed magically by a fay-princess; then came a clack like a lock locking, and Snash, quite reasonably, figured she'd done that too.

They were going along an aisle between objects that he would've taken the time to really look at if he hadn't been running for his life; he got a clearer idea of them before he got close and they blurred...even under the circumstances, he was reminded of what he'd seen of the Spike and the surrounding towers and turrets and bartizans from outside. Down in engineering, there'd been things called *models*, which the engineers made before they made much bigger versions...were all these little fortresses the original models of Mount Adamant? He felt like a giant as he ran between them.

He began to notice shadowy devil-shapes in his peripheral vision, hovering outside those tall windows...the contents of the room ceased to interest him. Up ahead, Luvliel was approaching another door, and slowing---for whatever reason, it wasn't co-operating with her.

Snash halted with Slagbag and Glargle.

"Can't you open the door?" Slagbag asked Luvliel.

"Be quiet," she said, and Slagbag clammed up. She chanted things under her breath, but the barrier didn't budge...Snash hadn't the slightest idea what the problem was, although there was no reason why he should expect to...Glargle was whimpering...Snash looked back the other way. He could see a half-dozen hellrogs outside the windows, three hovering on either side---

Suddenly a seventh came crashing straight down through the ceiling in a storm of dust and broken masonry, and even as that one was still plunging, the arch at the far end, shut door and all, simply burst apart; the hellrog that had done the damage was just emerging from the billowing debris-cloud when the one who'd come through the roof landed in front of him. One crashed through the wall on the right, not even bothering to turn sideways to get through the casement; another blasted through on the left, neither of them stopping until they had butted their way through a couple of columns. A second one came through the roof...the rest exploded through the walls, leaving very little of them standing....grinning huge flaming grins, they lifted their morningstars and advanced in a troop, disdaining the aisle, toppling models and crushing them underfoot. Though their mace-heads always seemed about to clip the tops of their wings, they never did quite, ripping instead through one column after another to right and left; both collonnades had been completely destroyed by the time the foremost hellrog halted in front of the fugitives, laughing down at them, each *HO!* gusting forth in a blast of flame, the other hellrogs gathering behind him.

Staring up at the hellish titans, Snash was vaguely aware of Luvliel's voice behind him---she was still chanting, although he didn't think she was going to do much good at this point.

But luckily for him and her (and Slagbag and Glargle), she didn't have to; Snash heard a grating noise, as of big stones shifting, then a rumbling from above and off to the sides, and the hellrogs all lost their grins and looked up, realizing perhaps that maybe, just maybe, they shouldn't have taken out those load-bearing members. Streamers of dust, scores of them, fell from the ceiling, and the places where the walls were still up began to crumble; the ceiling held together a little while longer, but that just meant it was largely intact when it came down on the hellrogs.

A thick gust of dust billowed across the floor towards Snash. He coughed and rolled his eyes, feeling all gritty. When the miasma cleared, he saw a great field of rubble, open to the sky, in front of him, and as you can probably surmise, he hoped that was that for the hellrogs.

But then the rubble started moving.

Stones heaved up, tipped, slid down, rattling...shaking debris from their heads and shoulders, making blubbery noises, the demons thrust themselves up out of the detritus, their faces evincing a weird mixture of embarrassment and furious anger, their wings hanging at odd angles from their backs, as though they'd been broken by the falling ceiling.

But even as they lifted their maces and began to advance once more, Snash heard the floor groaning beneath them, undoubtedly from the weight of all the rock that had landed upon it, and all at once the surface just caved, about to Snash's feet---down the hellrogs all went, looking more embarrassed than ever as they vanished into the depths, Snash retreating as far as he could over the remnant of floor.

"There," said Luvliel.

He looked round.

She'd gotten the door open, and they all went through...then stopped.

They were in a part of the fortress where neither Snash nor Glargle had ever been, and were at a loss for which way to go. Behind and below them, the hellrogs soon began thrashing, and bellowing curses, and that was enough to get the fugitives moving...they simply had to get out of the immediate vicinity of the demons, preferably into passages where a hellrog couldn't fit. But even though Glargle hadn't been in this particular section, he'd been in ones *like* it, and he'd had, of course, lots of practice finding sneak-routes.

"*Alte* section," he said as he all-foured along. "*Alte* shtorerooms, for shtuff no vun vant. Forgotten. No vun come in hundreds of years, maybe. But zere must've been *bewacher*. Guards. Ve look fur *wachlokal*. Guards big shneaks. Dig holes so zey can get out and shteal, get between walls, no vun see. Zey find most of the shneak-routes, or make zem."

They went down a long winding stair that Snash thought couldn't possibly accommodate hellrogs, even if the demons had been taking squeeze-lessons from sharks. Luvliel sprung an ancient padlock on a door at the bottom, and they found themselves in a storeroom similar to the one where the models had been collected, although the windows were only along one side, and higher up.

The contents were---to judge by the dust and rust and verdigris---very old, great jars and crates, statues of dragons and devils in stone and bronze, thrones, armored wagons, boats, and three portcullises of different designs, leaning against a wall; there were models of fortresses that didn't appear to be Mount Adamant, torture devices, seige engines, lots of stuffed monsters, some mounted as though they were fighting each other, along with loads of braziers, basins and bathtubs of sinister design, and altars, and sacrificial paraphernalia, and obelisks inscribed with Serpentar's laws in different languages, and monoliths with slogans that Snash had never encountered, including, "It's Sundown in Tenebria," "Ask Not," and "Change."

"Chust look at all ziss crap," said Glargle. "I sink half ze fortress is full of crap like ziss. Serpentar shteals, he doesn't vant anymore, it goes in shtoreroom. Serpentar says, make catapults, get zem, sinks he can get better vuns, old vuns go in shtoreroom. Gets hundred new sree-legged things that hold fire..."

"They're called tripots," said Luvliel.

Glargle acknowledged with a nod, then continued: "He decides zey suck, zey go in shtoreroom. Ziss Adamant is shtupid place. No *vasser*, no place to catch fish. Everyvun mad all ze time. Everyone shpying, playing nassty chokes. If Glargle had ze *liebchen*, and could do anysing mit it, Glargle vould do better."

"*Liebchen*?" Luvliel asked.

"Gauntlet."

"It would destroy you," said Luvliel.

"*Nein*," Glargle replied. "It vould chust sit zere, on Glargle's hand...alzough, zat's good enough for Glargle. Snash said he'd let Glargle keep."

"Oh did you?" Luvliel asked the runt.

"Actually," said Snash, "no I didn't."

"You have no authority to give it to him," Luvliel said.

"Vhat, iss *liebchen* yours?" Glargle asked.

"No," she replied.

"Serpentar's, *ja?*"

"*Ja*, I mean, yes."

"Kill Serpentar, vill it vurk at all?"

"You know what, that's a very good question…"

"Don't vorry. Glargle take it away and marry it, du never see it again. Alzo…"

"What?"

"*Du* not ze leiter."

"*Leiter?*"

"Ze Boss. Zat's Snash."

"I never claimed to be the Boss," Snash told Luvliel.

"Who let *who* out?" Glargle asked the fay princess.

"Well," Luvliel said, "Snash may have, but…"

"Snash ze boss."

"Can he do magic?"

"He never vound up shtuck in cell. Princess vass tricked. Came here like silly person. Snash *shmart.*"

"Will you please shut up?" Snash asked.

Glargle stood up and saluted. "Snash ze boss."

He stayed shut up until they emerged from the great chamber, when he pointed and said:

"*Wachlokal.*"

The arch, with the words "Guard Room" above it, was across the hall; the door was still on its hinges, but when Slagbag tried the handle, the door just dropped backwards, and went to fragments and dust when it hit the floor…they went inside. Piles of rotten wood looked as though they might've been chairs and cots; off the main chamber was a room that Snash thought had probably been a small armory. There were no other doors or hatches, or cracks, at least none that Snash could see; but then Glargle started sniffing, and his nose led him to a wall, at which he commenced to scrabble…with Slagbag's help, he began dislodging stones.

"*Do* you want to be the boss?" asked Luvliel beside Snash.

"No," the runt replied.

"What *do* you want for yourself, then?"

"Something better than Mount Adamant." Snash paused. "What are *you* going to do with us?"

"What do you mean?"

"If you win. What will you do with us yarks?"

"I really don't know," she said. "In the Committee, I always argued that creatures made from fays---however twisted---couldn't be entirely evil. Certainly, there'd be the occasional report...but mostly, our experiences were...unencouraging."

By then Slagbag and Glargle had opened quite a hole, and the bull had risen back to his full height, and was staring at the fay princess.

"Unencouraging?" he asked, sounding pretty surly.

She shrugged. "Encourage me."

"We rescued you," he said. "Isn't that enough?"

"Keep *on* encouraging me."

"But what will you *do* with us?" Snash pressed. "Once Serpentar's gone?"

"We don't make war without a reason," she replied. "Don't give us one."

"I wouldn't," said Snash. "But I can't speak for all the other yarks...if one of us *did* start speaking for all the others, I think it would just be Serpentar all over again. Then again, I also think a lot of us might be just plain bad..."

"Then we'll do what we must," said Luvliel. "But...certain assumptions will have to go. You're living proof of that."

"So," said Slagbag, "yarks really *were* made from fays?"

"Yes they were."

"So you and me---we're *related?*"

"We are."

He rubbed his bald black pate. "I wish I had magical hair."

"I wish you did too," she replied.

Into the hole they went, finding themselves in the place where the guards had stored a lot of their own loot...there was a tunnel delved through solid rock, with plunder lined up against one wall, smallish examples of the sort of things that were stored in the big hall; Snash guessed they'd been taken because they'd be easier to carry and hide. There was a veritable menagerie of little stuffed monsters, quite a few tripots, and even a (very) small portcullis. Snash wondered what the guards had been trading for such stuff, or if, indeed, they had simply lusted after the items. He had never been an enthusiast of tripots himself; if he were going to steal something from the big storeroom, it would've been one of the models. He liked those. He thought he might be able to sit and stare at one for hours...

The tunnel went on quite some ways, the plunder thinning out...they came to a place where the passage had once been blocked with a stone barrier, but that had crumbled, and they started along a narrow path, sloping gently downward, with walls riddled with small caves and no apparent ceiling. After a time, the sides widened out, and the four found themselves descending switchbacks beside an immense chasm. Far below, a river of lava snaked; above rose tremendous heights, with great outcroppings and crags rising against formations yet more distant, dim light from archways and fissures above delineating the massive shapes.

"So where are we going, anyway?" asked Slagbag.

"Someplace where I can rest awhile," said Luvliel. "I lost a lot of hair back there."

"But once you've rested," Slagbag said, "where do we go then?"

"Back to the Nail," she said. "To free my friends."

"What if I don't *want* to go?" he asked.

"Suit yourself," she replied airily.

"Where *would* you go?" Snash asked Slagbag.

"Out of Mount Adamant. Off on my own somewhere."

"They'd spot you once you were in the open," Snash said.

"Well, what are *you* going to do?"

"Go with the princess."

"You'll never get back into the Nail," Slagbag said. "If it wasn't for Slippriman drawing everyone off, we wouldn't have got in the first time."

"Yes," said Snash. "But now they'd have to deal with the Princess."

"You know," said Slagbag, "When it comes to growing flowers and hair, and lowering everyone from way up high, she's the best thing ever. But I didn't see her face down any hellrogs or Gage Ghouls, meaning no disrespect, of course."

"I'm not a warrior," Luvliel conceded. "At least, I haven't been so far. But I think I might be able to get back inside anyway. And once I started letting everyone out, they could do the fighting. Greydolf is mightier than any of Serpentar's servants."

"Who's Greydolf?" Snash asked.

"A wizard. An incarnate angel, actually…"

"Like Tressia?"

"He's her brother…the All-Father imagined them as siblings. That's why Greydolf's hair and beard are so striking, even though haircare isn't his mission…he was created to oppose Serpentar, along with the other wizards."

"Like Slippriman?"

"Yes. And Arboghast the Aquamarine, Palomino the Golden, and Rhustamir the Rhuddy."

"What about Tim Bimbottom?"

"Is he here?"

"Yes."

"Who told you?"

"Slippriman….is Bimbottom a wizard?"

"No," said Luvliel.

"Some other kind of angel?"

"I don't know, although…he is ancient, powerful, and very, very strange. Even the wise and the good are nonplussed by him, for he dances and sings in ways that they wouldn't. But the wicked…to them he is a scourge. They'd sooner leap into rushing torrents, or off cliffs onto sharp rocks, than abide his antics."

"Slippriman thought Bimbottom might beat Serpentar."

"I don't know about that," said Luvliel. "Of all the angels that have descended from the All-Father's halls,

Serpentar is the mightiest."

"*Serpentar* was an angel?"

"In charge of snakes. They were rather more important then, and he felt that *everything* should be made of them...but when the All-Father insisted that the world should contain a number of things, Serpentar would have none of it, and rebelled, as is told in the lay, *The Downfall of Serpentar*, or, *Snakes Diminish'd.*"

"I should like to hear that," said Snash.

"Well," she said, "if we live through this, I shall sing it for you myself. I have quite a nice voice, you know."

"I believe it," he replied.

They came to a place where the switchbacks ended, on their side, at least; there was, however, a bridge of ropes and slats, and they crossed the chasm on that. About then, Luvliel decided at last she really couldn't go much further, and they took themselves aside into the first suitable slot, which as luck would have it, had some water trickling down one wall...they took turns catching it in cupped hands and drinking it. Yark that he was, Snash wouldn't have minded the oily aftertaste even if he hadn't been parched...Luvliel clearly thought it was pretty disgusting, but had two double handfuls anyway. Afterwards they shared the dried fish and the caviar...dipping into the fish-eggs with two fingers, Luvliel somehow managed to look good while eating them...she pronounced them "first-class."

Afterwards, since Slagbag had gotten a bit of rest in the compost, he got first watch; Snash closed his eyes and was out almost immediately...

When he came to, Glargle appeared to be asleep, but Slagbag was still awake, looking out through the mouth of the slot...Luvliel was sitting against the wall, her light subdued at the moment. Her eyes were open, and she appeared to be awake, though Snash wasn't sure---she was quite motionless. He found it somewhat alarming; cocking an ear, he leaned forward to see if he could hear her breathing, whereupon she asked:

"What didn't you want to tell me about Slippriman?"

Snash jumped.

"I really need to know, I think," she said.

Seeing no point in keeping it back now, Snash replied: "He's a traitor."

She regarded him steadily, made him most uncomfortable, in fact. "And what makes you say that?"

"He was working for Serpentar," he answered. "I saw it myself."

"He switched sides after he was captured?"

"No. Before that, while he was the head of your Committee. Wasn't he saying you should take those fake gauntlets and bring them to Tenebria?"

"He was," she said. She was silent for a while. "You know, I never *did* like him….he was always asking if he might paint little pictures of me…They were good likenesses, but I don't know, it was…Uggh, creepy." She shivered. "And he was *so* concerned about neatness. *Fays* weren't neat enough for him. He stayed in my palatial treehouse, the Luvliloft, one time…every time I turned around, he was running his fingers over things, checking for dust…also, the first time we found one of those gauntlets, he argued that we should use it ourselves, or rather, let him use it…then he changed his tune, of course."

"Who came here first?"

"Greydolf," she said. "He thought it was a bad idea, but bowed to our decision. Then it was my kinsman Rondlefrond, the Lord of Reftdingle. After him it was Dwimli the Dwelf-King, then Tharathorn the Thwift, the Thoon-to-Be-Rethtored…When Tharathorn didn't come back, we sent *four* Ling-lings…"

"Ling-lings?" Snash asked.

"Pandas, from Merriador. After them, we tapped Oakenchin the Oakenguy…"

"What's an oakenguy?"

"An…oak puncher."

"What?"

"A cowboy of the oaks. He was reluctant at first,

argued he'd stick right out, since there aren't any trees in Tenebria...but Slippriman talked him into it, saying that the oakenwives had been spotted around here somewhere."

"Oakenwives?"

"The oakenguys' spouses. They disappeared a *long* time ago...I suppose Slippriman was simply lying."

"Who came next?"

"Me. Got turned into a *conch*....I certainly hope Arboghast, Palomino, and Rhustamir stayed put."

"Slippriman never mentioned them," Snash said. "But he's been here a couple of years at least. He was tied into a lot of things..." He paused. "What if they took him alive?"

"What if they did?"

"Suppose he's up in the Nail now...that's where they'd take him, if they caught him right outside. Are you going to let him out? Tell everyone else what I told you? He tried to convince me that he hadn't really turned---"

"That he was just trying to trick Serpentar?"

"Right," Snash said. "You do believe me, don't you?"

"I think I do," she replied. "Although...I *can* be lied to. Hence the fact that I'm in this situation now. But Slippriman always did give me the creeps. And you never have."

"I'm really quite a sneak," he admitted, just to be honest. "I've had to be."

"But would you come to my treehouse and check for dust behind my back?"

"No," said Snash. "I'd very much like to go there sometime."

"You have a standing invitation. I'll sing you the Fall of Serpentar, if I haven't already."

"I expect I'd want to hear it again," he said.

Finally Slagbag said he'd like to catch a nap, and Snash took watch, placing himself at the opening. He could hear the lava way below, distant hissings, rumblings, and chuggings; looking across the chasm, he could see the cliff there painted faintly from beneath with the molten stone's red light, deep shadows being cast by overhangs and ledges. Looking up, he strained his eyes, couldn't see anyone on the switchbacks, took some real comfort in that; it had been some time since they escaped from the hellrogs, and no one seemed to have picked up their trail since then. He couldn't quite think why, though...

Dust was pretty deep, he told himself. *Must've left some very clear tracks...*

As if to lend weight to this particular conclusion, a dim drumming reached his drooping ears, which he lifted straight up; the sound was coming from above, getting louder with each passing moment....already traced out in orange, arches and crevices glowed brighter, and little twinkling spots of fire---

torches, Snash thought---

appeared, streams of them that came flowing down ledges and zigzags, merging to form larger steady streams, almost as though lava were trickling from the openings to join the great river at the bottom.

"Look at 'em all," said Slagbag, coming up. "Listen to those drums..."

Luvliel joined them, glowing rather brighter now that she was rested. "We must've left some very nice tracks in that dust," she said.

"Any chance you could shut that light of yours off?" Slagbag asked.

"No, sorry," she said. "It's a manifestation of my inner goodness. It would only go out if I stopped being nice."

"Actually," Slagbag said, "it kind of reminds me of the light from those big spiders. And they're *not* nice."

"But they're luminous because Glolob's their mother. And she sucked the light from the Larch of Effulgence, which was a very nice larch indeed....she didn't come by it honestly."

"Serpentar's shnakes glow," said Glargle.

"Oh, they're just *hot*, that's all...what point are you trying to make, exactly?"

Neither Glargle nor Slagbag had an answer for that.

"We'd better do something about that bridge we crossed over," the princess said.

They went back up a ways, and while Slagbag started in on the ropes with his axe, Luvliel began a spell. But before she could achieve anything with it, Snash, who was looking back up at the little fires hundreds of yards above, saw huge numbers of them suddenly flying downwards---he guessed that the fellows up there must've jumped. Then, long about the time when the horn-blast that seemed to have precipitated this process finally reached his ears, he realized that *no one* had jumped---they were all archers up there, and they'd just released a storm of fire-arrows, literally thousands. Luvliel had seen it too, and broke off with her spell; along with Snash, Slagbag and Glargle, she flinched back against the wall of the cliff, began a different incantation. As the arrows sped down, each trailing a thread of firelit smoke, Snash was sure she'd never finish the second formula, but then the missiles---in front of him and his friends, at any rate---started striking something invisible and bouncing off, some of them leaving tar-soaked flaming wads stuck to the unseen shield. Outside the barrier, which seemed to curve, arrows were raining and rattling against the cliff-face, the switchback, the bridge...several hundred lodged in the span, in fact, and the ropes began to go up almost at once.

"The orders regarding me," said Luvliel, "seem to have changed."

"We won't have to cut the bridge, at least," said Slagbag.

She banished the shield with a wave of her hand; the flaming wads dropped away. Glargle out in front, the fugitives raced away down the trail. Snash kept glancing over his shoulder; another blast of fire-arrows descended. But this time there was no need for the barrier; the crevice they'd rested in was just ahead, and Glargle, apparently hearing the arrows shrieking down, just ducked into it without any prompting, followed by the others. They went some distance up it before Snash turned....outside, a sheet of arrows blazed past, although some struck the lefthand wall and bounced far inside, breaking apart, the pieces burning.

Slagbag ran further up the crevice. "Dead end," he cried.

"Can't stay in here," said Luvliel. "They'll just keep bouncing arrows in till they burn us alive."

"Vhat you vaitingk fur?" cried Glargle, and was back outside like a shot...they followed, stepping between the

284

burning tar-lumps....Another flight of shafts was already on the way, but the ledge took a left turn ahead...as Snash rounded the bend, he saw, off on the fringe of sight, the flaming hail slant down. But almost as soon as that swarm whooshed by, another volley descended, at a very different angle, some arrows clipping the ledge on the right, and Snash realized there were archers above him, on his side of the chasm...before they could loose another barrage, Glargle, again without being told, dashed into a tunnel on the left, and the others followed....presently, after many twists and turns, he announced:

"Know vhere ve are!"

They paused.

"And where are we?" Snash asked.

"Hard to deshcribe. But Glargle hass been here. Could get to mail room from here, he sinks."

"Do we *want* to get to the mail room?" Luvliel asked.

"No," said Snash. "But there are some stairs near it. They go way down, towards the big wheels, the ones that draw vapor from the volcano... there are tunnels to let the vapors out, and they open beyond the foot of the mountain."

"And what about the Nail?"

"We're not going to get anywhere near it---at least not for a while."

"Have you been down by those tunnels?"

"No," Snash said. "But I've seen maps. And I was always asking about things---"

"We can't get out that way," said Slagbag. "Those passages are all full of vapor. That's the whole point of them. And then there are the *wheels*. How could we get past them?"

"There's one wheel that was shut down a while ago," said Snash. "It was the smallest and oldest of the lot, and they still aren't sure if they want to fix it. If we could get near the mail room, I think I could find my way to that tunnel."

"Glargle head fur mail room, zen?" Glargle asked.

"Right," said Snash.

"Snash ze boss."

Off they went.

"Those wheels," said Luvliel to Snash.

"What about them?"

"Are they the ones he gets his diamonds from?"

"Yes."

"Greydolf told me about them, once. He knew a great deal about this place...was always reminding us about Serpentar's riches, and how he tried to buy anyone he hadn't beaten."

"That's why he owns the east," said Snash.

"The *far* east. The parts his army can't reach. But he's also tried it north, west, and south. Used to send *me* gifts, gold necklaces, bracelets, rings with diamonds like pigeon's eggs...I got letters, too, asking how I was doing, telling me how things were going in Tenebria, trying to start up a correspondence. They were signed, *Your devoted admirer, S.*, although I don't think he actually wrote any of them. I never answered, and always sent everything back. He gave up about five hundred years ago..."

She paused. As they'd progressed, the drumming had grown steadily fainter, but all of a sudden there was a whole lot more of it, from somewhere ahead of them, in different rhythm, as though someone had thrown open a huge door.

"Not try fur mail room now, I sink," said Glargle.

Snash asked; "Do you know anything about those stairs I mentioned?"

"*Ja.* Could take longer vay to zose."

"Go on then," said Snash.

"Snash ze boss."

Glargle led them as far as he could via shneak-routes, and the drumming got much less threatening, but then he told them: "Musst take bit of rissk," and led them out into passages that, in spite of the fact that they were nasty and damp and constricted, were, according to Glargle, "not-shneak," which is to say, authorized. Even though Snash didn't recognize them at first, since Luvliel literally put things in a new light, he soon realized where he was---heading towards the steps that would take him down to the monster cells, and Glolob's lair.

"Hold it," he told Glargle. "We don't want to go this

way. There's a prison for monsters down there, and we'll set them off. They'll all start roaring."

"*Nein*," said Glargle. "Not go past Seventeen. Head uzzer vay."

"Can we?"

"Ve *must*. Only vun guard down zere, anyvay. Drunk most of time."

"All right then," said Snash, and they started on down. But once more, the drumming got much louder, as if that damn door had opened again, although, obviously, it couldn't be the same one; there were also footbeats, and yells, and all that soon got louder than the drumming, almost as if the fellows out in front really thought they were on the scent, and were speeding up, and leaving the poor drummers way behind.

Speeding up themselves, Snash and his companions came out in the monster block, and turned the way Glargle wanted to turn, but all of a sudden, way up ahead, the passage filled with torches.

"Can't go back up the stairs," said Snash to Luvliel.

"No," she answered.

"But...I think we might be able to get into that room at the end of the corridor."

"What's in it?" she asked.

"Glolob," he said.

"The *Great*?"

"Yes."

"Why would we want to go in *there*?"

"There are holes in the floor," he said, turning, and heading the other way. "For her young to escape through, so she doesn't eat them."

"But how are we going to deal with her---"

They passed Number Seventeen; immediately the monster began to bellow, setting off all the rest behind their doors....down at the end, a fat guard looking an awful lot like Sluglik (*and* his successor, the guard that had gotten bit) was sitting against Glolob's door, chin indenting a second much thicker chin that was bulging against his chest. He was gripping the neck of a slack drinking bag with one hand, the sack lying flattened on his belly...Snash thought he was out completely.

The guard began to stir though, and got sluggishly to his feet, the booze-bag swinging at the end of his arm....even though he looked quite thoroughly sloshed, Snash assumed he *had* to know that someone had set Seventeen off, but...the guard's baggy eyes were closed, and he sure didn't *appear* to have any idea that anyone was heading his way...it seemed he was simply reacting to the cacophony.

But he'd stuck the monster-whistle in his belt instead of hanging it around his neck, and when he tried to put it to his lips, he fumbled and dropped it.

All the while, the monsters had kept up their clamor, loud and strong...Snash couldn't hear the pursuers any longer. Most unsteady, the guard had opened his eys and was looking down at the whistle now... bending over, he picked it up, but started blowing on the wrong end.

"Take his keys?" Slagbag asked Snash.

"No time to find the right one," shouted Snash.

Apparently oblivious to this exchange, the guard blew on the wrong end again...they all got right in front of him to keep him from seeing the approaching torches, and noticing his visitors at last, he cried:

"You set the monsters off, damn you!"

"They go off very easily," Snash replied.

The guard squinted at Luvliel. "You're all lit up." He blinked and blinked again, cocked his head and said: "You're a ... a *fay*!"

He proceeded no farther than that bald declaration, though; if he'd known about the *jailbreak*, Snash would've expected him to say something about that, but...nothing. Snash thought he might've drunken himself into his stupor before the news spread...or that he'd gotten the news but didn't remember...it *was* also possible that he was uninformed because no one ever told him anything.

"*Fay turncoat,*" said Snash. "Very important. She asked us to show her around. She's particularly interested in seeing the mail room."

"Well, you're in the---" the guard paused, then got a wicked look on his drunken mug as that deep-seated yarkish impulse to pull a mean one on his brethren bubbled up

288

through his inebriation. "*Right* place."

Slapping the drinking-bag up under his armpit, he unhooked the keyring from his belt, held it right up to his face, then a little farther out, biting his lower lip...was he seeing double? Could he still pick out the right key? He closed one eye, moved the keyring nearer to his open one...Snash couldn't stand watching him and turned, looking at the torches.

They'd been farther away than he'd thought at first, but even taking that into account, the arrows would be starting soon, assuming, of course, that there were archers up there...

He heard the guard say something.

"What?" Slagbag cried.

"There you go," shouted the guard.

Snash turned.

The postern was open, a rectangle of spider-light, which Snash didn't think looked much like Luvliel's, no matter what Slagbag said. Expression as stupid as it was malicious, the guard was standing off to the side, but not for long; an arrow--not burning---shot by Slagbag on the left, caught the drunk in the side of the head, and down he went, even as Slagbag dropped to a crouch.

"Oh!" said Luvliel. She sounded as though she'd pricked her finger; but when she went past Snash, he saw an arrow in the back of her shoulder. Snash and Glargle raced after her, and Slagbag came in last---Snash heard him slam the postern. As the sound of the roaring prisoners was shut off from outside, dozens of arrows struck the door, the clangs muted by the metal.

Snash looked up at Luvliel. She'd turned; the arrow-head, a flangeless bodkin-point, had come out the front of her shoulder on a few inches of shaft, but she didn't seem upset at all; reaching up, she snapped it off, then showed her back to Slagbag and said:

"Get the fletching."

"Pull it out?"

"Break it off."

He did just that...Snash guessed it *had* to have hurt her, and pretty bad too, but if it did, she betrayed no hint of it, telling Slagbag casually:

"Thank you very much."

Slagbag dropped the fletching to the floor...then Snash led farther into Glolob's lair.

"Vhy ve come in here, again?" Glargle asked. As Snash surveyed the hanging webs and the (relatively) small spiders clambering in it, he began to wonder himself. The skeins were all full of light, although there was one big patch high up that was much brighter...Snash guessed Glolob was back in there...

"You said there were holes?" Luvliel asked him.

Snash pointed. "There...and there."

"And they lead?"

"Down to the breeding-pits. You can lower us all on your hair---"

Snash broke off as Glolob the Great descended into view like a setting moon. Landing on the floor, the spider queen asked:

"What's this?"

"I escaped from the Nail," said Luvliel. "Just thought I'd drop in, see how you were doing."

"Really?" asked Glolob.

"Really."

"Are we *friends*? When last we met---"

"Back in Murksylvania?"

Legs creaking, Glolob advanced, passing over a couple of those holes in the floor. "You kept me talking while your cousin Rondlefrond sneaked up and stuck a spear in my belly--
-"

She crouched amid her legs and leaned back as if she were about to spring.

At that, though, the postern opened behind them---or so Snash guessed---because suddenly all he could hear was yarks shrieking, and the roars of the inmates up the hall; but since the postern wasn't very wide, the archers couldn't all come in in a great rush---or so Snash also guessed---and there were only a few arrows flying, and they weren't well aimed, although now that Snash thought of it, he wasn't sure who they were aimed at, since all of them wound up in Glolob. She started, and squealed---a most horrible sound---and reared up on her hind legs, forelegs beating, even as Snash and Glargle ran round her to the left, and Slagbag and Luvliel went to the right, the fay princess halting to conjure a Small but Sturdy and tie a hitch to it...then Snash and Glargle raced over to her, and she bent a bit to let them clamber up, then seized her hair with her good hand and jumped feet-first into one of those holes...clinging to her neck, the last thing Snash saw of Glolob was the spider still rearing, being pincushioned by more and more yark-archers, who, even if they were coming single-file, were doing it quickly...then his view was cut off. Glancing up, he saw Glargle shooting down after him, hand over hand...above Glargle was a much slower, dark mass, almost filling the tube, Slagbag.

"So you met her before," cried Snash to Luvliel.

"Good thing Rondlefrond didn't kill her," Luvliel replied.

"Do you know just about everyone?"

"No, not at all. Only met *you* recently."

It seemed to Snash that they went several hundred yards before they emerged through the ceiling of the cavern below, dropping past a suspended spider, who seemed very surprised to seem them...looking down, Snash could see a vast field of pits stretched out below. The holes were all full of compost, but most of them didn't have anyone working them; the only teams he saw were way off on the right, and they had wagons, and were loading the pits there---Snash guessed the holes closer to hand must've been "refreshed" lately.

At any rate, those fellows rightward were so far off that he guessed they might not've noticed Luvliel's descent at all, or maybe mistook her luminous self for a spider---and events bore him out. She landed, Snash and Glargle climbed off, and Slagbag down; then she retracted her hair, and they headed in the opposite direction from those work-gangs, straight down the main walkway.

But Snash and Luvliel grew uncomfortable with being so exposed, even though he thought they might get out of the cave and the next one over without meeting anyone. There were, however, heaps of slabs and boulders at the foot of the walls; whenever rocks fell from the walls or the ceiling, they were dragged to the sides, and Snash suggested it might be better to go and shneak among the debris.

Doing exactly that, they passed into the next cavern, which was deserted, except for a few spiders on the ceiling; the pits were all empty. Again, the runt and his friends stuck to the rocks, and got through the next door. Glargle announced he knew "chust vhere ve are," and said there was a "vay into vall," and sure enough he led them to one.

"Been here, been here," he said. "Shtart headingk back down soon...get onto shtairs below mail room."

After a level stretch, they began to descend, just as he said, but before long, things went wrong...the passage had been blocked up, and a new one (looking very recent indeed) had been carved...this happened several more times, and Glargle declared they'd better not go on.

"Ziss *verdammt neu* schtuff, can't tell vhere it leads," he said. "Not mein fault. Don't sink *scheisskopfs* who do ziss know vhere zey were diggingk to. Happens all ze time. Ve musst turn round."

And with that, he started to lead them back.

But Snash felt the stone quiver beneath his soles; small cracks opened in the walls, and a stretch of floor dropped away. Once the tremor passed (Snash had a distinct sense of it speeding elsewhere, and it was still making noise in the distance) Glargle ran to where the floor ended now, and leaned out so far that Snash was sure he was going to fall in...then the creature hocked up a big loogie and released it into the depths, putting one of his (proportionately) big hands to his ear.

"Don't vant to chump in zere, *nein, nein!*" he declared presently, then turned. "Glargle could go along vall, but he don't sink any of *du* could...Musst go uzzer vay."

Trudging along, Snash kept expecting there to be side-passages, but there weren't any, and the incline only got steeper...there came a sudden demarcation where it stopped looking as though it had been hacked out by tools, although it kept going anyhow...down and down (and yes, down) they went in a tight corkscrew. As they continued to hang that seemingly perpetual louie, the passage kept narrowing, until Slagbag, with his broad shoulders, had some difficulty getting through, and all the while, the air was getting hotter, and fouler. Steam leaked from crevices, and there were sulphur crystals clumped on the walls---brushing them, Slagbag's shoulders and arms were soon smudged yellow.

"Ve are truly in bowels," Glargle declared.

Snash thought that they'd gone at least two miles by the time they came to a huge tunnel with what appeared to be great threads in the walls, ceiling and floor, as though it had been reamed out by a titanic screw...there was a lot of rumbling in the distance, although it was sustained and regular and didn't sound like any quake Snash had ever heard.

"Is this one of those tunnels you mentioned?" Luvliel asked Snash. "With the big wheels?"

"I don't think so," said Snash. "We're way below those."

"Did Serpentar make this?"

"I don't know," he replied.

"Would've taken some screw," said Slagbag.

"And something *amazing* to drive it....look, there are other holes up that way."

Stepping from thread to thread, they proceeded towards the openings, but only until the rumbling got much louder, and the tunnel began to tremble...to Snash it sounded and felt as though some tremendous machine were approaching, although it was hard to tell from which direction---

At least until the lefthand wall collapsed up ahead.

A mound of debris was swiftly churned aside as a tremendous spinning something---Snash had an impression of a grotesque black profile, mostly mouth, chewing as it turned---came out of the wall. A round rolling eye turned sideways...but Snash's attention was drawn to the thing's emerging body, an enormous metallic screw-like arrangement, complete with threads.

"Hoo boy," said Glargle, "Glargle unsettled, *ja, ja.*"

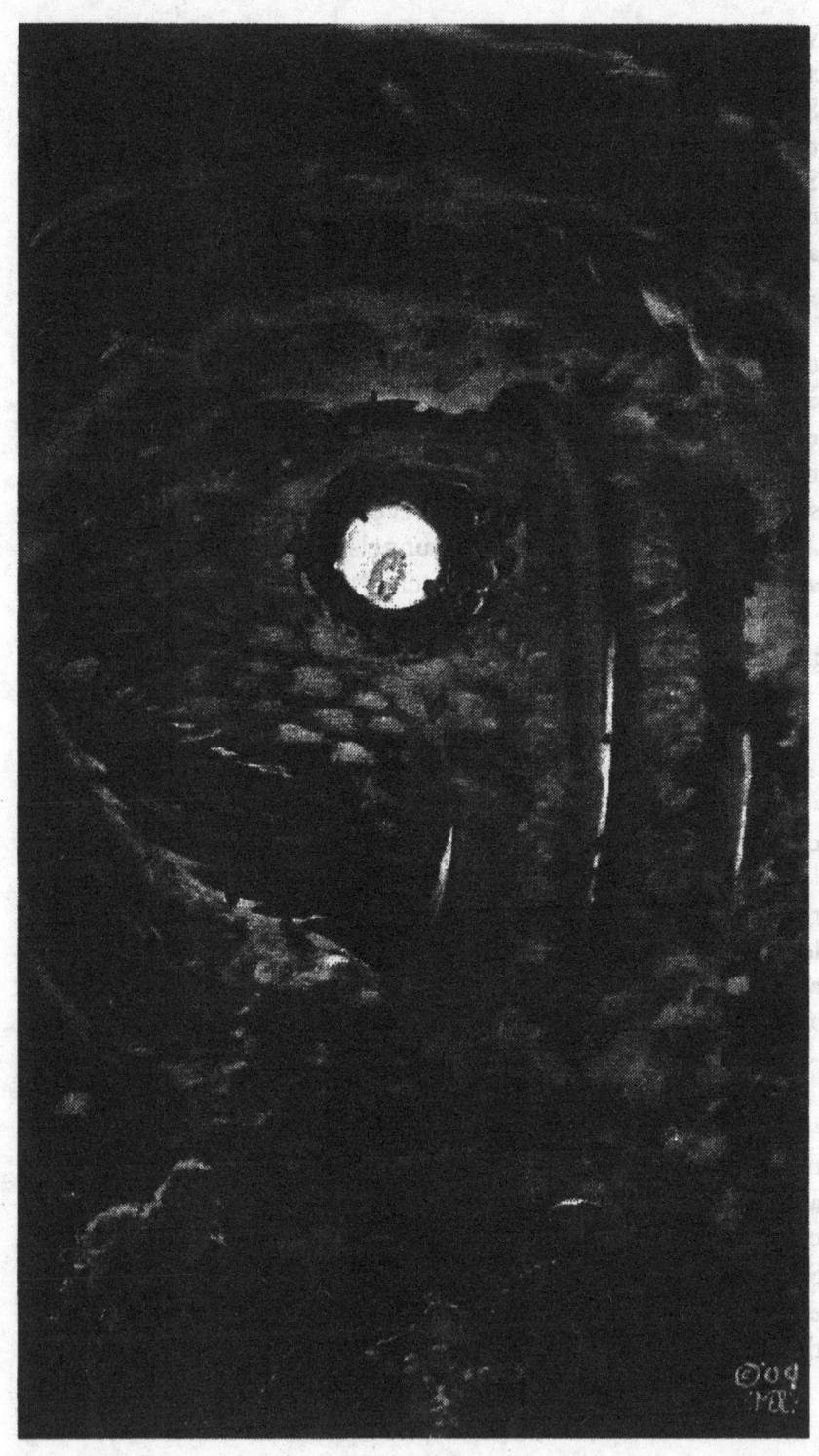

By then, the face had reached the far wall, and began literally chewing into it with a horrifying crunching noise...Snash could only imagine how hard those teeth must be. But within moments the face had gnawed from view, hidden inside the tunnel of its own making. A good two hundred yards of screw followed...Snash thought he could hear things grinding away inside the big damn bolt, like a collection of wheels. When the tail appeared, it was venting black powder, pulverized stone, Snash thought, laying a trail of it between the holes...then the tail, too, was gone.

Luvliel declared: "That was a nameless thing, if ever I've seen one."

"And I, for one, don't want to see another," said Slagbag.

But whatever powers that were weren't listening; even as the din of that immense reaming faded, something else started up behind them, far less grating and fraught with friction, but a whole lot faster; they turned to see another vast spinning metal face, chewing even though it had no stones to chew upon, rising into view from a tunnel sloping up from beneath, as all upward sloping tunnels must do....with nothing to obstruct it, this particular nameless thing was screwing along at much greater speed. Round and round the periphery of the face the boggly eyes rolled, while the huge jaws champed in the center...Snash thought the creature probably wasn't after him and his friends, but it sure didn't look like it planned to stop either, and he didn't fancy the idea of greasing the threads on that massive living bolt...

The others didn't fancy it either, evidently, and were already leaping, two threads at a time, towards the place where that first nameless thing had emerged. But Snash just couldn't keep up...the frog, the bull, and the long-shanked princess (skirt hiked) were all much better jumpers than him...even though he was one helluva runner, he was still equipped, like all runts, with runt legs, which is to say, short ones, and if he'd tried to go two threads at once, he knew he'd come down hard on the second with his teeth. Hearing the screw coming up hard upon him, he was about to resign himself to being reduced to lube when---

Slagbag, who'd already reached the tunnel, thrust out a long arm and yanked him in...flying sideways over the floor, Snash looked back towards the tunnel mouth to see the immense chawing face spin on past, followed by the threads, which all looked pretty sharp, their edges gleaming...then Slagbag jerked him up and deposited him on one of the threads he was standing on.

"*Hate* ziss! *Hate* ziss!" Glargle was saying. "Glargle hates so much, he vish he never even saw ze *Liebchen*, zat's how much he hates! *Ach! Ach!* Ssssss! *Scheiss! Verdammt!*"

"There there," said Luvliel, and went to him, balancing effortlessly on a stone ridge and petting his single-haired scalp.

But Glargle was insufficiently soothed. "Pet Glargle on head? Vhat goot is zat? Shcrews shtill out zere, shcrewing, shcrewing."

"What if I compose a verse, to comfort you?" she asked, and delivered herself of one, right then and there:

> *La-livrithil*
> *Dil silvrimil.*
> *A plenneth*
> *Reth, na-rethrangil."*

"Vhat does zat mean?" Glargle asked.

"Don't worry about screws," she replied.

He drew a deep breath that made his scrawny ribcage creak. "*Du bist* very goot lady," he said.

She petted his head again. "I know."

After a brief deliberation, they concluded that they really didn't have a better option than to continue along the tunnel, and hope to find an intersecting passage that would take them back up. Had another big screw come down the tunnel, that would've been that, but...

Their luck held.

A little screw, a mere twenty-footer, *did* pass through sideways; it came boring out of one wall about ten feet up, and dropped between two threads, demonstrating a limited flexibility as it landed...after the manner of a click-beetle, it began to buck violently, impelling itself ass-over-head out of the trough and forward, towards the other wall...it had to bounce against the barrier several times before its snapping jaws caught in the stone, but once it gained purchase, it began to spin, and rapidly drilled itself in, butt spewing powdered rock.

"With those things chewing everything up down here," Snash said, "you'd think Mount Adamant would just fall in after a while."

Even as he said this, a thin stream of lava started to flow from a crack off to the side; it travelled down between two threads and began to pool on the bottom of the floor; there wasn't very much, but the heat hurt Snash's feet as he stepped over.

"Maybe it's the lava," said Luvliel. "I'd wager it fills these tunnels back up---"

"And the screws just come and gnaw it out again?"

"Unless they go somewhere else. Maybe they're everywhere. Underground, at least."

"Don't say zat," said Glargle. "Make Glargle never vant to go in cave again."

"Have you ever gone this deep before?" she asked.

"*Nein.*"

"Don't go this deep," she replied.

Further along, they found a large opening on the left, unsuitable for leaving the tunnel, but providing a remarkable view; about two yards long, and one in height, roughly squarish in shape, it looked down like a window on a vast chamber with a lake of molten lava at the bottom, great rafts of black material floating on the surface of the liquid stone.

A number of screws were cruising about in the lake, rotating, threads pulling them through the liquid, making trails in the floating black stuff; some came bursting up out of the depths, spun in the air, then splashed back down; others, curving their bodies, were going in circles...Snash saw one heading directly at another's face, only to release a stream of lava it had been holding in its mouth, and dip its head downward, diving just before the spat-on screw spewed the lava in *its* mouth.

Another one was drawing itself up a kind of threaded chute along one wall; at the top, the chute curved out over the lava on a long stony projection; the screw went out onto that, paused when it came to the end, then vented a thunderous "wowr!" and continued over the edge, turning end over end twice before it aimed its nose straight down and plunged into the lava, raising a bright orange splash of same that shot up hundreds of yards.

Snash looked off to the right...several small screws were following a much bigger one...when it pulled itself up onto a slanting ledge, they came up behind, and started bucking, flipping themselves up onto the titan's back, where they settled, apparently none the worse for having landed right on the threads.

"Why are they doing that?" Slagbag asked.

"I think," said Luvliel, "that the big one is their mother."

"They actually want to *be* with her?" Snash asked.

"They're her babies," said Luvliel.

"Glolob eats hers."

"She's not a very good mother."

"Are *you* a mother?" Slagbag asked.

"I have a daughter and a son, " Luvliel said, "Ellethreth and Teleporno."

"Teleporno?" Snash asked, disliking the name for some reason, although he tried not to show it.

"Yes. And I would never, ever eat him."

"What do mothers *do*?" asked Slagbag.

Luvliel replied: "They give birth to their children, and make them good food, and tell them to stand up straight, and persuade them---wisely and gently---to make the proper choices. That's if they're not giant cannibal spiders."

Slagbag eyed her a few minutes more, then looked down at the floor.

"What's the matter?" she asked.

"The closest thing I ever had to a mother was a big nasty fruit in a pit full of corpses."

"Not your fault."

"I wish I had a mother," he said, sobbing.

She just tilted her head slightly to one side, as though she really didn't know what to say. But before she could pet him on the head, or compose a verse to comfort him, Glargle broke in:

"Glargle had muzzer."

"And what was she like?" Luvliel asked.

He pointed to his single follicle. "Had *zwei* hairs on *kopf*."

"Really."

"*Ja*."

"Did she love you?"

Glargle nodded. "She called Glargle *meine kleine Glargyglar*."

"How sweet," said Luvliel, then glanced at Slagbag. But he just growled and turned, and continued up the tunnel.

Chapter 16: Flying with Sharks

Snash was getting right tired of balancing on the threads when he spotted a passage, blessedly devoid of them, off on the right, which slanted upwards, led them to another, bigger tunnel that did likewise, and soon brought them to a corkscrew rather like the one they'd descended in the first place. It was a hard slog, but at last they arrived at the top, of that spiral at least, and Glargle, faced with three openings, sniffed out one that he liked best; they continued up an easy grade until they saw a crack up ahead admitting the leaden light of Tenebrian day.

Out they came into a narrow canyon, its sides about sixty feet tall and composed of ledges, the layers divided by spaces of varying height...down at the bottom, there was about ten feet of headroom below the overhangs. The canyon floor was studded with rocks that ranged in size from pebbles to small boulders.

"I think," said Luvliel, "that I'd better deal with the arrow."

It had troubled her so little, apparently, that Snash had almost forgotten she'd been hit, indeed, pierced quite through....sitting down, she examined the place where she'd snapped off the arrow-point...a bit of stump was still sticking out. There wasn't much of a stain...Snash guessed the arrow-shaft had bottled most of her blood up. She widened the hole in the cloth with the tips of her fingernails so she could see where it was coming out of her flesh.

"One of you will have to help me," she said. "Slagbag, I think, since he's the strongest."

"What do you want me to do?" Slagbag asked.

"Kneel down behind me, and put the point of your claw right into the stump back there. When I say *push*, shove it farther in, so I can take the stump on the other side and pull it all the way out."

"You *sure*?" Slagbag asked.

"Yes," she replied.

"Won't you start bleeding?" Snash asked.

"Yes. But I'll sing a spell. I'll be all right."

Slagbag knelt behind her, stuck out a talon-tip.

"Ready?" she asked.

"Push."

Showing his fangs, muscles working in his arm, he thrust...Snash leaned back to see the arrow-stump, all stained, emerge from her shoulder...when about two inches came out, Luvliel seized it between two of her own nails and plucked it forth, a squirt of blood following it. Pressing a palm to the wound, she sang:

> *Tha-wenethar*
> *Si naeron.*
> *A thorangel*
> *Ongreathon.*"

"What does that mean?" Snash asked.

"Dry up right now," said Luvliel, and he saw that her blood had already complied.

"Ah," she said, working her shoulder, wincing. "Better."

But even though the arrow had been removed, and her blood was all nicely contained, she said it might be best if she rested a while. Then Snash, intensely curious---he had, after all, never been beyond the confines of Mount Adamant---went a ways down the canyon.

As he proceeded, it widened and deepened, and got more twisty and turny, and the overhangs towards the bottom got farther from the floor; numbers of little armored things scuttled out of his way and ran for cover in the shadows....one of them was moving somewhat slower than the rest, and he squatted down to take a look and see if he might want to crack it open for a meal...he hadn't eaten for some while. But---

Stopping, extending two nippers from under its shell and pointing upwards at Snash repeatedly with one of them, the creature, voice very small and tinny, launched into something that sounded like a tirade---an eloquent one---and even though Snash was irritated and almost grabbed a rock, he realized he was no longer willing to deprive the thing of its life, hungry as he was.

"Sorry," he said, and continued on his way. He found some scummy water in a hole, brushed the green stuff to one side, and drank. Then he got back up and looked back.

He could see the volcano looming up over the canyon-rims, and the fortress looming up out of the volcano, with the Spike surrounded by (but dwarfing) all its attendant towers, which seemed to lean inwards, as though they---and it---were all weapons, aiming at the same heavenly target.

Far up, between the summit of the Nail and the top of the Spike, he descried four circling specks, darker than the fume-ceiling above.

Gage ghouls, he thought. *They'll spot us when we leave this canyon*...

But then he reminded himself that the canyon might offer cover for a long distance...when taking his little respites with Slagbag, he'd looked out from windows or balconies and studied the landscape with great attention, and knew that there were slots and canyons, indeed gorges, that cut deep and far through the Tenebrian landscape...many bridges, some collossal, had been thrown across them to allow the passage of Serpentar's armies.

He looked up at the Gage Ghouls again, wondered if they'd be able to spot Luvliel's light from so high up...since she hadn't been hiding under one of the overhangs, he thought he might do well to go back and warn her that she might be spotted from above.

It was then that he realized he could see only two sharkriders now. Probably, it meant nothing, but it made him uneasy; he started back at a jog, but before long he was running, feeling more and more apprehensive. He came to a stretch of rocky floor where he had to look where he was stepping, and when he glanced back up---

None of them were visible any more. Were they coming down on the right, or the left, or both?

Might not be coming down at all, he told himself. *Maybe they're back inside. You don't know they saw anything*...

But whether or not he knew that seemed unimportant; the significant fact was that they could---if they *had* seen something---get very close without betraying their nearness, diving down behind the fortress before going wide and coming in...the canyon walls cut off so much of the sky.

Something *swooshed* heavily, high up and behind him.

He whirled. Whatever the swoosher was, he saw no trace of it, although, given that sound, which was very suggestive of speed, that was no surprise.

He continued up the passage, feeling right panicky...there was more swooshing, but this time the shark who was making it went right over him, looking way too massive to fly, weaving as though it were following the meanderings of the canyon, tail moving lazily back and forth...Snash felt as though he were underwater, indeed, as though the whole world had been flooded.

The shark swung off to the right, showing his side before the rim blocked Snash's view of him...a crackling blast echoed down the canyon. Running round the bend, Snash saw Luvliel, Slagbag, and Glargle huddling under one of the overhangs...the opening at the end of the canyon had been buried under rubble. Right at the moment, he could see no sign of the great aerial fish, but guessed he was circling back. Running in under the ledge, Snash joined his friends.

"Sharkrider," said Luvliel.

"I know," he said. "And I think there's another one about, too."

"Are you *sure* you can't shut off your glow?" Slagbag asked the Princess.

"Quite sure," she replied.

"A shark can crawl in here, can't it?" Slagbag asked Snash.

Snash nodded. "They can get into the damnedest places. Fold their fins---"

"So one could just come right over the side any second now?"

"Yes---"

There was a thud, as though something huge had just landed on a cliff-top...more debris clattered, and stones dropped down in front of them.

"He's on this side," said Slagbag.

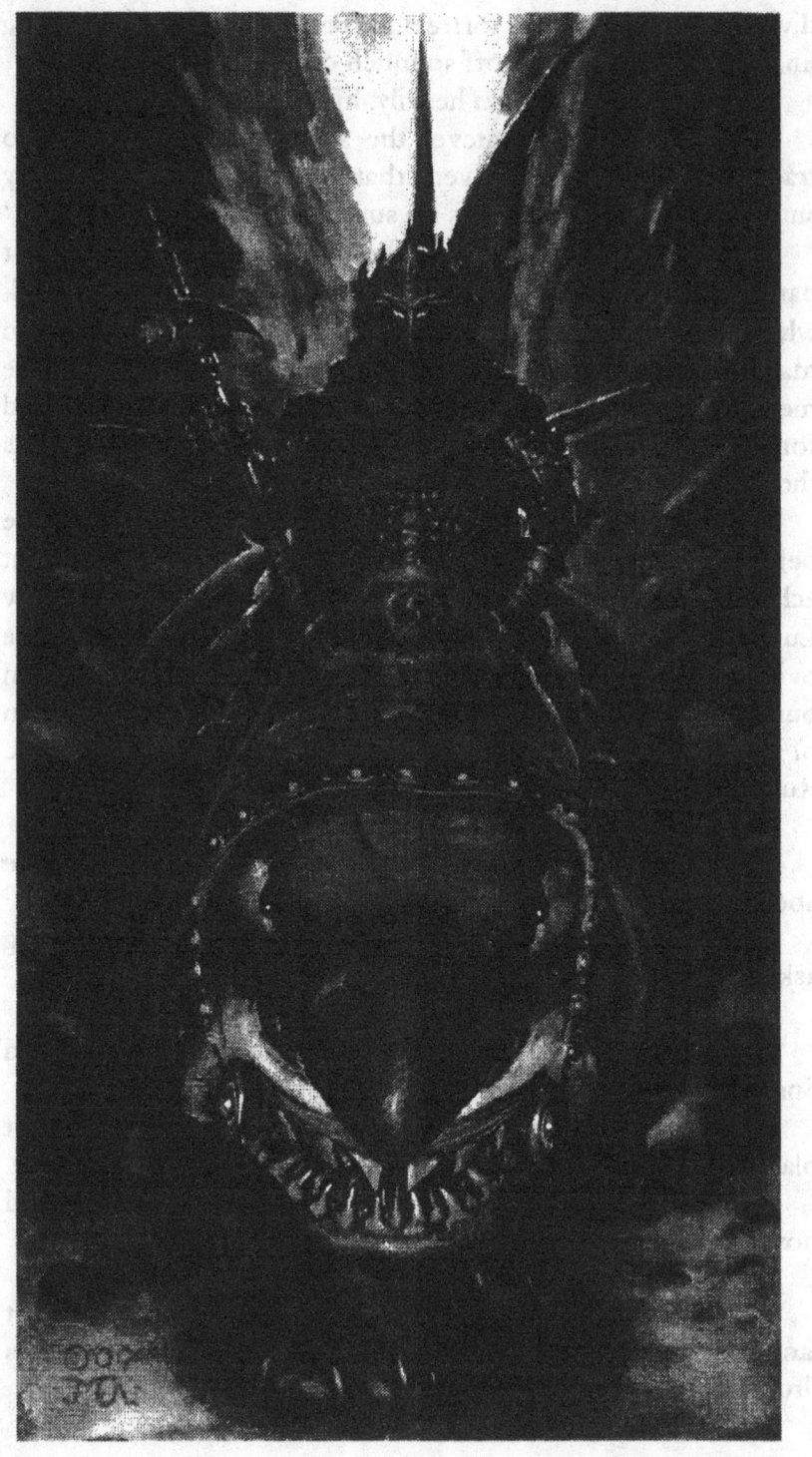

"There's another ledge up there, above this one---" Snash pointed at the overhang. "If you could get up there and hide, you might be able to surprise him."

"Get his *gauntlet*," said Glargle.

"He'd lose control of his shark," said Snash.

"And then what?" Luvliel asked. "Would it turn on him?"

"Yes," said Snash. "The whole lot would rebel if they could."

"How do you know?"

"I've spoken to them."

"*Spoken* to them?"

"We discussed natural law. It's the way things actually work."

She laughed. "I'm familiar with the concept---"

"Don't see anything yet," Slagbag said, out from under the overhang...jumping up on a rock, he thrust his long arms straight upwards, and jumped again. Evidently his mitts connected with a good solid clawhold, because, using only his arms, he hauled himself some distance up before swinging a leg up on the side...then, with a last grunt, he was gone.

Snash heard all sorts of activity from Glargle, and turned to see the gremlin clinging to the underside of the overhang...as Glargle practically galloped, upside down, towards the front, Snash saw him go from a ghostly figure against solid black to a gangly silhouette against the light before he too went up and over.

More rocks rattled down. Snash didn't know if Slagbag or Glargle had dislodged them, or the shark. Several moments passed. Then Luvliel stood and made as if to go out, but Snash tugged her long sleeve.

"I'll draw his attention," she said. "He'll be less likely to notice our friends."

Deeply moved to hear her call them friends, Snash nodded, let her sleeve go...and went out hand in hand with her.

Yet more fragments were tumbling, and he looked to see a shark crawling over the edge of the cliff, head down, wings folded, dorsal and tail fins as well, its rider seemingly not the least bit discomfitted by the angle of descent, sitting in his saddle quite perpendicular to the fish, and the cliff, for that matter. Snash could clearly see the ghoul's burning eyes, and the points of his crown; clenched in the ghoul's metal-sheathed right hand was the great hammer that the runt remembered so vividly from the cell, back in the Needle.

Luvliel began to retreat, down the canyon, still hand in hand with Snash...he glanced up and to the left. There were at least five feet between the overhang and the ledge above, and the space was very dark...he could see no sign of Slagbag or Glargle, although that was just as well.

Reaching the floor of the canyon, Carcharias twisted round, following...between the way he moved his tonnage and the glimmer of his myriad teeth, the spectacle was absolutely terrifying. With all that, even though Snash wasn't sure he could read the shark's expression, he thought he read a terrible unhappiness there; the shark's eyes were flat dead black, but his brow was furrowed, and he seemed to grimace as the Shark Lord jabbed him with his spurs, driving him forward.

"Luvliel," said the ghoul chieftain. "What *shalt* thou do? How many steps backward wilt thou take? Retreat will not avail thee, for here I am, more than thy match, following upon my giant shark. And there thou art, abett'd by a single runt, without even a minion of mine to blast me by mistake---"

Luvliel started a spell, the one she'd conjured the invisible barrier with, or so Snash thought, but the Shark Lord just extended his hammer, aiming the topspike at the ground before her feet, that little blaze of blue-white light having reappeared on the tip, fiercer and more vehement than Snash had remembered it...Luvliel was about halfway through her spell when the ghoul sent a bolt of lightning into the floor, which heaved up in a shower of excrutiatingly hard and sharp bits, and between those fragments and the sheer shock, Snash and Luvliel were pummelled onto their backs, bleeding in scores of places.

But to Snash's amazement, the princess stood up, staggering, and cried:

"Minion yourself!"

"Aye," said the ghoul. "I glory in my servitude. For my will is My *Lord's,* and none is stronger."

"Toy with me all you like---"

"As though I needst thy permission, Lady," the ghoul answered, and launched a bolt into the overhang on her left. Fragments peppering her from above this time, she fell with a shriek, and Snash flung his hands over his eyes, feeling a second later as if every spot on his body that hadn't caught a rock the last time caught one now. He yelped and curled up....Voice dim in Snash's ringing ears, the ghoul was saying:

"Ah, Lady. So sweet to see you bleed. My Lord will savor this memory of mine."

Snash lowered his hands, saw her rising again. Clenching her fists, she cried: "You're *nothing*!"

The sharkrider laughed. Snash looked towards him...huge dark form shuddering with mirth, the ghoul was sitting high in his saddle, hammer over one shoulder, Carcharias appearing very despondent beneath him, his grin completely gone, quite an accomplishment for a mouth so full of fangs...

"I think," said the Shark Lord at last, lowering his hammer, pointing the spike directly at Luvliel this time, "that I have indulged my cruelty as much as I safely might...'tis high time I sent thee on thy way."

That bead of blue light appeared on the tip yet again.

But---

Before the Shark Lord's power could burst forth, Slagbag leaped up, atop the overhang, as though he had been crawling along the ledge, and bounded onto Carcharias's back, beside the ghoul.

"Huh?" said the sharkrider, and twisted in his saddle, just in time for Slagbag to pluck the ghoul's eyes out from under his crown. Raising a horrifying scream, the Shark Lord cast aside his hammer, reached with both hands into his now-empty hood.

But Slagbag was screaming too, whipping his arms around, as though the burning eyeballs had stuck to his skin; finally one came flying from his palm, and struck a wall with a flaming splat, then went out; the other he managed to fling to the ground beside Carcharias, where it seemed to flatten a bit, but still remained intact...blowing on his hands, Slagbag turned to face the Shark Lord.

The ghoul was still fishing around inside his hood, as though he might yet find his missing glazzies, but suddenly the futility of the thing seemed to strike him, and he just began to lash out, smashing Slagbag sideways from Carcharias's back, knocking him against the overhang. Still, dropping between Carcharias and the ledge, Slagbag came straight down, on his feet, and whether it was chance or no, his hobnailed sole landed on that second eye, and squished it out in a gush of flames.

"Carcharias!" the ghoul cried, stretched his arms out to right and left, fingers extended; the shark's face assumed an unmistakable frown, then split wide open as his mouth yawned, and he went stumping directly for Luvliel on his short legs.

We're dead for sure, Snash thought, *but at least Slagbag pulled the bastard's eyes out---*

But he never had to settle for that last little bit of comfort.

Along the ledge Glargle came hopping most froglike, diving towards the sharkrider's outstretched gauntlet, yanking it right the hell off him as he sailed by. Bouncing into the side of Carcharias's snout, he dropped to the floor of the canyon.

"Huh?" said the Gage Ghoul, yet again, and the eyeless hood turned towards his gauntletless invisible hand.

Carcharias stopped dead.

Glargle bounded up in front of him, waving the gage.

"Somesing has changed, *ja?*" the gremlin cried.

"Carcharias!" screeched the sharkrider from his saddle. "Be not a fool! A chance thou hast not! The Inevitable is---"

With a tremendous violent thrust of all four legs, the shark propelled himself yards off the floor of the canyon; as the fish dropped back down, the Shark Lord rose high out of his saddle, seemed just about ready to go flying off, then was pulled back down by his stirrups. Carcharias shoved himself up once more; this time the stirrup-straps snapped, and the Shark Lord somersaulted upwards, detached.

Backing up, Carcharias opened his mouth, and down the ghoul went into it, headfirst, going about to the waist before the shark clamped his jaws on him. Snash thought he was about to see the Shark Lord bitten clean in half, but Carcharias didn't want to eat any of him, apparently, and whipped his head to one side, flinging him against the overhang.

As the ghoul dropped, looking partially deflated, Carcharias came forward, snapped him up again, thrust up with his forelegs, and flipped the ghoul way back, towards his tail; then as the shark's foreparts sank down, and the ghoul was just sailing by his freshly unfolded tailfin, Carcharias, twisting sideways and glancing back, smashed the ghoul into the righthand wall with his hinder end, and then, as he bounced off, struck him again.

And again.

And again.

With each impact, the ghoul looked limper and flatter, until finally his robes slapped against a wall and hung there for a moment before peeling off, obviously thoroughly vacated of their former tenant. Panting, Carcharias laughed, then looked round at Snash, and grinned for what must've been all he was worth---it was just about blinding.

"Snash," he laughed.

"Carcharias," Snash said.

"You little rodent. What *does* it take to put a stop to you?"

"Since it hasn't happened yet, I just don't know." Snash indicated the empty robes. "Speaking of someone who's been stopped...is *he* dead, do you think?"

"He can't die. But he's *gone*."

"Is there another rider up there?"

"No," Carcharias said. "He's here in the canyon, two bends down...Number One told him to stay put, even if he heard something---didn't want to get blasted by one of his own boys again..."

"Will you go down there?"

"Sure. But someone should put the Shark Lord's robes on."

"Why?" asked Luvliel.

"So I'll look like I still have a rider," Carcharias said.

"That way I can take that other ghoul by surprise."

Luvliel pondered this. "I *am* the tallest..."

"And it would cover up your glow," called Slagbag.

Luvliel limped over to the garments and put them on, pulling the hood down far over her face to conceal as much of her light as possible, then resting the crown on top of that. Coming back, she asked Carcharias:

"How do I look?"

"Different."

"You're sure you can take the rider by surprise?"

"No," said the shark. "But the idea appeals to me. Whacking His Lordship just now really whetted my appetite."

Glargle came up to Luvliel and proffered her the gauntlet. "Don't forget ziss," he said. "Part of se coshtume."

"You're willing to give it up?"

"Iss not ze *liebchen*," he sniffed. "Not even close."

She put it on, then hauled herself up onto the shark with a chain-ladder that depended from the saddle...the saddle had a very high pommel and cantle, and she took hold of the former with her left hand, resting the gauntleted one in her lap.

"I don't have that hammer," she said.

"Don't worry about it," said Carcharias. "Buckle yourself in."

There were straps attached to the cantle, and she fastened them as he continued: "My former master said straps were for mortals, and he never bothered with them, but the latest saddles all came equipped---"

"All set," said Luvliel.

Snash, Slagbag and Glargle moved aside, then followed at a distance as the shark headed off down the canyon. Even though he had those little legs, he seemed to *flow* more than anything else; going up and over boulders that Snash would've skirted, the fish's great rubbery bulk rapidly became something Snash never would've recognized if he hadn't known what it was...the dark mass dipped and rose, then slid from sight beyond a rocky pier.

When Snash and his companions didn't hear anything,

they rounded the buttress themselves, just in time to see his folded-down tail slipping behind the next bend...they were about two-thirds of the way to that when Snash heard soft raspings in back of him, and looked over his shoulder to see the second shark sneaking along a wall, having obviously come up and over, and down from the rim...

Disobeyed his orders, Snash thought, guessing the Shark Lord really wouldn't have minded, given the circumstances, if he'd still been a going concern...the fish flung himself down, landing on the canyon floor with a great plop....a cloud of dust and grit rolled over Snash and company...Snash blinked and rubbed his eyes as Glargle coughed and spluttered.

"What *have* we here?" asked the rider.

"We've come for your shark," Snash said.

"So be a good fellow and dismount," said Slagbag.

"*Ja*," said Glargle.

The ghoul stood, booted feet planted on either side of his saddle, and cried over their heads:

"My Lord!"

When, for reasons we've already discussed, there was no answer from up the canyon, he cried it again...presently Snash heard the sound of a huge fish-body dragging over boulders, and back came Carcharias, tail first, Luvliel looking maybe too thin but still fairly convincing in her ghoul get-up, at least from behind...the sharkrider let Carcharias get very close, Snash and his buddies bunching up between shark-snout and shark-butt.

"My Lord!" cried the ghoul a third time. "The runt have we, and the sneak, and the bull whose name we know not, but where is Luvliel?"

He was, of course, looking right at her, although he had no way of knowing that; she said nothing, ditto her mount.

"Why stay thou silent, lord?" said the sharkrider. "Why the turn'd back, and a tailfirst approach?"

But his questions never to be answer'd were; Carcharias sprang towards the wall on the left, clambered halfway up in a tight quarter circle and turned his head round, the maneuver accomplished with such speed that Snash was left even more in awe of the fish than he already was. Too late, the ghoul realized his peril, and went for his hammer, which was in a boot beside his saddle; but Carcharias was already hurtling down at him, and got his jaws down over the rider's shoulders before he could bring the weapon into play...backing back up the cliff, the shark swung his victim side to side until the ghoul dropped his hammer and his gauntlet flew off. Then Carcharias let the ghoul drop to the canyon floor in front of the other shark, Snash, Slagbag, and Glargle barely scrambling out of the way.

"All yours, Carcharadon," said Carcharias.

To which his comrade replied: "Why, thank you, Carcharias," and advanced upon the Gage Ghoul, who was even then trying to rise...bashing him back down with his snout, Carcharadon switched to stamping on him with a forefoot, which wasn't very large in proportion to the rest of him, but big enough to flatten a Gage Ghoul, particularly with so much fishy weight being brought to bear...pop-*pop*! went the ghoul's eyes, flying out his hood after the second stamp...when they landed, Slagbag jumped on *them*.

"Scheissy day fur eyeballs," Glargle chortled.

When Carcharadon was *quite* finished, he asked Carcharias: "Who's that on your back?"

"Princess Luvliel," Carcharias said.

She took off the Shark Lord's crown, pulled the hood back, and waved.

"Pleased to meet you," said Carcharadon. "I assume the skanky amphibian is Glargle?"

"I'm chust as Gott made me," Glargle answered.

"And the bull---?"

"Slagbag," the bull replied.

"All right then," said Carcharadon. "What now?"

"We get Slagbag into those robes," said Snash, pointing to the ones the second rider had vacated.

Carcharias nodded. "Pull the same trick again. See if we can't free another one of *us*."

"But who'll we put on him?" Carcharadon asked. "Snash and Glargle are too small to pass as sharkriders---"

Glargle just clicked his tongue. "Shnash shtraps in, Glargle climbs on shoulders, Shnash holds onto *mein* thighs."

Unenthused at the idea of holding those thighs, let alone the thought of the back of his neck being a crotchrest for the gremlin, Snash suggested a different tactic:

"A riderless shark could pretend he's being chased, by you two." He indicated Carcharias and Carcharadon. "Fly towards the other riders. Carcharias and Carcharadon come up on his flanks, then go after the others."

"They'd never know what hit 'em," said Carcharias.

"Actually," said Luvliel, "that all sounds very good to me, but I'm kind of hanging up here, perpendicular to the saddle with the pommel in my stomach, and I really would appreciate it if you'd climb down."

Carcharias complied, but as he did, he warned:

"When it comes to blows topside, you're going to have to put up with a whole lot worse."

"I shall steel myself," she said. "But it seemed to me there was no need for perpendicularity just then."

"Perhaps," he conceded.

There were two large leather bags attached to Carcharias's saddle, and he told Snash and Glargle to ride in those. Opening one, Snash found a number of items secured by straps: scrolls, a couple of folded telescopes, fat sacks of coins, a small box marked "Gage Repair," tins of shark-liniment (they smelled pretty strong even with the lids on), bags of something called "Shark Treat" (which smelled even stronger in a different way), and a large casket emblazoned with the words "Shark Aid" and a picture, red against dark wood, of a shark in bandages. After getting rid of the coin-sacks (it was a struggle, since they were *heavy*) Snash had more than enough space for himself, and climbed in between telescopes and Shark-Treat, holding onto a couple of straps.

"You fellows ready?" Carcharias asked.

"*Ja!*" answered Glargle, over on the other side of Luvliel from Snash.

"Ready!" cried Snash, hunching down, hanging on tight, tilting first against the scrolls on the saddle's side, then back against the pungent Treat bags as Carcharias climbed back

313

up the canyon wall, Carcharadon beside him---looking over at Snash, Carcharadon laughed and shook his head. Snash could very well imagine the sight of his little head sticking out of the saddlebag was pretty amusing.

Little as it was, his noggin felt heavy, and he leaned it back, eyes fixed forward, which is to say, upward...at first there was mostly cliff, and above that, a mere strip of leaden sky, although the sky widened out as Carcharias got closer to the top.

A sharkrider went over, not too high up, although Snash didn't see him again until Carcharias and Carchardon cleared the rim...then the rider, about two hundred yards away, swung into view around Luvliel. She was tilting her head back and shielding her face with one hand, perhaps to cover what could be seen of her glow.

The rider veered in towards them; Carcharias and Carcharadon leaped up from the stone, a powerful shudder passing through Carcharias(and Snash too) as his wings began to beat. The rider didn't appear to notice anything amiss at first, then halted his mount, shark hovering.

"My lord?" he cried, but---

Unlike that last Gage Ghoul, this one needed only to have one "My Lord" unanswered before he was on full alert, and reaching for his hammer, and aiming its glowing spike, at Carcharias, or so it seemed to Snash.

Yet however good the weapon was for brutalizing fay-princesses, it was way too clumsy to take out speeding sky-sharks; even before the lightning blazed out, Carcharias and Carcharadon peeled off to right and left, and when the bolt missed them utterly, they swerved round behind him.

He was diving, trying to gain speed, and since the land sloped away, he had enough room, so long as he hugged the earth. But his two pursuers had already built up way too much momentum, and closed swiftly, even as he accelerated, and Carcharadon called to Carcharias:

"Shall I?"

Carcharias answered: "By all means."

Carcharadon closed in for the kill.

Snash saw the Gage Ghoul trying desperately to twist

in the saddle, and point his hammer backwards, but his next bolt was so far off that it nearly hit Carcharias instead...then Carcharadon was upon the ghoul, and past him, having clipped him in the back of the hood with the blade on his wing, slicing the hood off his shoulders, head and all, apparently. Snash saw it come rolling back over the wing, still looking like it contained something.

Carcharias and Carcharadon swung back once more...the ghoul's mount was rolling and bucking in midair, and finally the decapitated rider dropped from the saddle, clothes deflating as they fell. Turning, the latest freedshark, who seemed to have an unsually wide maw, cried:

"Carcharias! Carcharadon!"

To which they answered: "Bigmouth!"

"There are two more," he said.

"Where?" asked Carcharias.

"In the canyon. Got suspicious, went to take a look..."

He turned, the other sharks coming up on either side of him...they swerved over towards the canyon, which was quite wide by that point, and followed it uphill, along the lefthand bank. Some distance ahead, it curved to the left, and Snash saw two sharks just beginning to emerge from the depths, clawing over the edge. Their riders seemed to know that something had gone terribly wrong, because they spurred their mounts into the air the instant they came out of the canyon, and wheeled them round towards Mount Adamant.

But even though Carcharias, Bigmouth, and Carcharadon were all climbing, momentum was once more decisive---they were already hauling pretty hard, while their still-enslaved brethren were just getting started. As the ghouls' lead dwindled, one twisted and discharged a bolt; it seared the tip of Bigmouth's nose off and he bellowed a word unknown to Snash that the runt figured nonetheless was probably a big sharky "DAMMIT!" Then Bigmouth avenged his schnozz-point by giving the Gage Ghoul his starboard wing-blade, right in the back of the neck.

As for that other rider, he'd evaded Carcharadon's first pass, banking aside; but all four of the liberated sharks were above him now, and he had no chance whatsoever of climbing through or by them to the fortress, so he headed away to the east, diving, trying to use the nap of the earth to accelerate.

But even though he had a good lead, Carcharias, who now lit out after him, was evidently the much faster beast, if the way he closed was any indication; Snash was pressed progressively harder against the uncomfortable junk behind him, wind screaming over his face, his lips flipping, his long ears flapping, his eyes tearing up.

Continuing to gain, Carcharias followed the ghoul into a slot that cut through the middle of a black plateau; they ripped in and out of narrow turns for a while, until a pillar of rock hove into view, standing up in the middle of the canyon, with very little leeway on either side...tilting his mount up on its side, the sharkrider tried to thread the gap on the right, but succeeded only in smashing his head and shoulders against the pillar, wrenching himself out of the saddle, and clipping off the upper thirds of his mount's dorsal and tail-fins...Gasping at the sight of that terrific impact, Snash leaned way over in his saddlebag as Carcharias banked leftwards, up and out of the canyon to the left, then circled round, back towards the pillar. The latest freedshark was coming slowly his way, doing something that could only be characterized as an aerial limp, blood streaming from the tops of his fins.

"Sorry, Sawtooth," said Carcharias, hovering.

"Not your fault. Couldn't believe the bastard tried to slip through..."

"On the other fin, he's gone now," Carcharias pointed out.

"On the *other* fin," said Sawtooth, "I wouldn't mind having my fintips back."

"Would you say you're incapacitated?" Bigmouth asked, approaching with Carcharadon and that other shark, whose name hadn't come up.

"Let me at 'em," Sawtooth said. "Although...what exactly is the plan? And who's on Carcharias?"

"Princess Luvliel," said Carcharias.

"And who's that on Carcharadon?"

"Slagbag," said Carcharadon.

"A *yark*?"

Slagbag doffed his hood. "What's it look like?"

"But..." said Sawtooth, "what's the plan?"

"You escort me to the Nail," said Luvliel.

"And?"

"I free the White Committee." She held up the book. "With *this*. It's full of spells. I'll open the cells with them."

"We could land on the top," said Carcharadon. "You could take the stairs down."

"Any other riders left up there?" asked Luvliel.

"No," said Carcharias. "There are five on long patrol, and three with the army---"

A horn blared, from within the fortress, Snash thought...others answered, also from the stronghold, but soon the runt heard more distant notes, off to the west, where Serpentar's host, like a black fog upon the ground, was already funnelling into a shadowy pass between two crags.

"But," Carcharias continued, "someone's seen something, and the lot will be coming back, the last three first, I expect..."

"Then there's the matter of the hellrogs," said Bigmouth.

Luvliel replied: "Half of them got their wings spindled by a falling ceiling."

"Had they just cut all the load-bearing members?" Carcharias asked.

"They had."

All the sharks burst out laughing.

"Hellrogs," said Carcharadon.

"Still leaves ten, though," Carcharadon said. "They'll be out soon..." He looked up towards the Spike. "But they won't really know what's going on yet...Might be best if we dealt with them before we drop you off."

"*Can* you deal with them?" Luvliel asked. "You're outnumbered two to one..."

"But we're smarter. And *much* faster. They have wings, but they're just to get them from place to place. Hellrogs weren't made for fighting in the air. They're really vulnerable from above, because they're blinded by their wings and their smoke...We could spiral back, around the tower, up into the fumes...wait for them to come out of the Hellrog Porte..."

"Best get about it then, hey?" said Sawtooth.

Bigmouth lifted a fin. "For Freedom, the Fellowship, and Replaceable Fangs!"

Carcharias nodded, crying: "Up Sharks! Down Serpentar!"

His brethren seconded that with a shout, and then, humming a scary but stirring tune that Snash had never heard before, the lot turned back towards the fortress, climbing, wings pounding the air...all at once, as though the humming had just been an introduction, they broke into lyrics as scary and stirring as the tune:

> *"Our jaws are strong,*
> *Our teeth are knives.*
> *And those who face us*
> *Lose their lives.*
> *Our fins behead,*
> *Our tails do crush*
> *Our opposition*
> *Turns to mush.*
> *We are the Lords*
> *Of wind and cloud,*
> *We see our foes,*
> *And laugh out loud!*
> *So now beware,*
> *For now we fly,*
> *To make you die!*
> *To make you DIE!"*

At DIE! They just started over, and midway along, Snash found he was singing with them, and he thought he could hear Glargle singing along too, quite hideously, over on the other side of Luvliel. Undoubtedly out of niceness, she never did take up the words, but once they embarked on a third run-through, Snash saw her tapping her fingers on her leg, and nodding her head in time, although he thought she must be doing it unconsciously.

319

As they drew nearer the Spike, though, the sharks canned the anthem, though Snash thought it a pity and didn't see the point, since they'd already been spotted. But as the sharks swept south, then east and up, they left the watchers in those western casements with no fish to see, and as for the windows the sharks were shooting by at the moment, nobody much seemed to be looking out from them, probably because all the horns had been going off on the other side of the tower---the fish weren't tripping any alarums now, at any rate. Climbing past their own aeries on the top of the Spike, and into the fumes, they swung round towards the west once more before they halted and hovered....Luvliel fanned a hand before her face.

"Oh, how unpleasant," she said, although Snash was rather surprised to discover that the fumes, condensed as they were by the outer air, were rather less noxious than what he'd grown used to in running the Spike.

Still, they were pretty thick, and looking down (the saddle was strapped onto Carcharias just in front of his wings) Snash couldn't see through them. He thought it might be different for the sharks, however, and that soon proved to be the case, because Carcharias, cried: "Now!" as though he'd just seen exactly what he wanted to see, and all five sharks swung to starboard and slanted downwards.

As they dropped out of the clouds, Snash saw seven hellrogs, wings beating, waiting in front of an archway opening in the side of the Spike, up near the top--- he guessed it was the Hellrog Porte, and that the other demons were just about to come out too. None seemed to have heard Carcharias's cry, or indeed, to have the slightest awareness that five huge flying sharks were diving at them; Snash thought those hellrog wings (which *did* look very fearsome even *if* they reflected poor design-choices) must've cut off a lot of sky, just like their smoke, as Carcharias had said.

Carcharias tilted. Flattened against the side of his saddle bag, heart in his throat, Snash saw a hellrog, all smoke and flapping pinions getting bigger and bigger as the distance closed. Not afraid of the smoke, Snash made the mistake of inhaling once he was in...he just had time for one agonizing

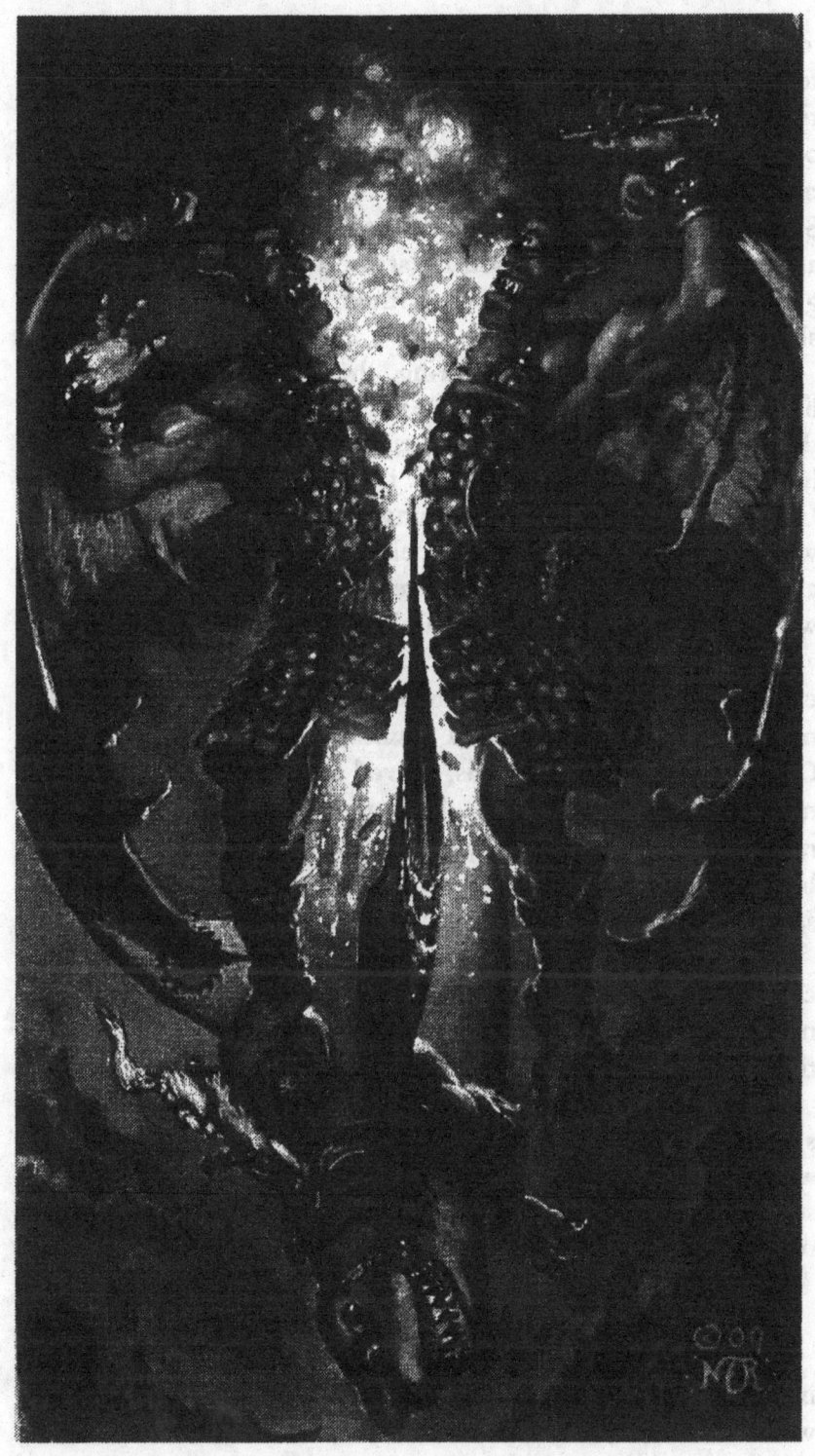

cough before he heard a fierce snapping, shearing sound, and felt a tremendous jolt through Carcharias's body. The shark righted himself as he cleared the black miasma, and Snash's butt bounced against the bottom of the saddle bag; then the big fish began to climb, pressing Snash yet again against the Shark-Treat, which was lumpy, but luckily yielding. Coughing again, he found himself staring at the fume-ceiling, Carcharias going, apparently, straight up…then, to Snash's horror, the shark tipped backwards.

Coughing and sputtering, the runt hung on for dear life, upside down. He simply closed his eyes, until he could feel that he was merely hanging at a right angle…there was another hellrog directly below him, flying straight up towards Carcharias, whirling his morningstar, somehow missing his wings the way hellrogs did; below the demon, five others, already hit by other sharks, were spinning out smoke as they whirled down towards towers and turrets and crags.

"Come on!" bellowed the one who was still in business, evidently unaware that his backup was so sorely reduced, his mace-head going round and round. Maintaining his descent, Carcharias turned on his axis, moved a bit to the side at the last moment…the blade on his wing shore through the morningstar's chain, then passed down between the hellrog's horns, splitting him crown to crotch in a burst of flames. Snash saw fifty percent shoot upwards on the fringe of sight.

Wing burning, Carcharias pulled out of his dive, climbed once more, up towards the ceiling…Snash saw three more demons taking the big plunge, along with the halves of the hellrog who'd been bisected.

Before Carcharias reached the fumes, he levelled off, still burning. Only three other sharks converged…the fish whose name Snash had never learned was nowhere to be seen….Carcharadon and Bigmouth hovered in close, and beat out the fire on Carcharias's wing.

"What happened to Shredder?" Carcharias asked.

"Gogmagog got him," cried Sawtooth, farther off.

Carcharias, Carcharadon, and Bigmouth bowed their heads, and Snash found himself doing the same. But Sawtooth went on:

"Right before I got Gogmagog."

Out of sight behind Luvliel, Glargle cried: "Effingk A! *Gott mitt uns!*"

"Shouldn't there have been a tenth hellrog?" Carcharias asked.

"I saw him," said Bigmouth. "He was watching from the Porte---I thought maybe he'd come out to play, but no such luck."

"Can you drop me at the Nail now?" Luvliel asked.

Carcharias turned westward...to Snash, it was beginning to look as though some of the dark formations on the ground were heading back east. He also thought he made out three flying black specks...

"Sawtooth," said Carcharias, "station yourself between the Porte and the top of the Spike...that last 'rog might try to come out through the top. Bigmouth, Carcharadon, you come with me...once I set the princess down, we're going to go off and settle those ghouls over there."

"What about the ones on long patrol?" Carcharadon asked.

"No sign of 'em yet. It's going to be a while." Carcharias glanced about as far back at his rider as a shark might be expected to glance. "Here you go, Princess. Next stop, the Nail."

Chapter 17: Ding-Dong!

Bigmouth, Carcharadon and Carcharias all swooped down towards the Nail, where there was enough space at the top to land a shark, surrounded by a low wall without crenelations or loopholes. Snash could see a bunch of tiny figures...most were scurrying about in a panic, though a couple were hacking away at a hatch in the roof, as though someone had locked them out. There were also some archers, although Snash didn't spot them until Carcharias got an arrow in the snout, and another missile lodged in the saddle not far from Snash's bag. The sharks circled once, then slanted down, tipping up on their sides to rip their wing-blades through those blokes on the roof.

But the blokes---all of them eastrons---hurled themselves flat, and the walls were just high enough to shield them from shark-fins; the fish skimmed over without doing any damage at all.

While his brethren stood off, Bigmouth flew back on in, and Snash saw him twitch and jerk as though he'd taken a couple of shafts...then the shark took up position over the roof, lowered his tail, and started whipping it back and forth as he turned in a slow circle. Swept off the flagstones, helmets and weapons and pieces of armor flying, bodies struck the wall, some jolting to a halt against it, others flipping up and over, taking the long plunge...once the roof was fully pacified, Bigmouth got out of the way so that Carcharias could touch down.

Luvliel dismounted, and as Snash climbed out of his saddlebag, Glargle came scrambling out from under Carcharias's chin. Snash looked up at Carcharadon, who was off on the left, waiting to land...a big grin on his face, Slagbag waved from the saddle.

"Looks like he enjoyed his shark ride," said Carcharias.

"Does," said Snash, although he hadn't had much fun himself.

Carcharias continued: "But once he's down, we're off."

"Don't you want to keep him?" Luvliel asked, removing her helmet and pushing back her hood.

"By now they'll be expecting a trick," said Carcharias.

"Besides, you could do with a big bull to back you up."

With that, he climbed over the side so Carcharadon could land, and once he did, Slagbag got off.

"See you in Hell," said Carcharadon to Luvliel.

"Oh, you will not," she replied.

He laughed and vanished over the low wall, reappearing, airborne, a few seconds later, flapping off and joining his buddies...all three wheeled towards those black specks which, while still specklike, were rather less so.

Slagbag was taking off his Gage Ghoul duds. Luvliel was already mostly out of hers, and had already dropped the gauntlet. Glargle, removing a sack from one of the dead eastrons, emptied it out, put the gage in it, and slung it over his back.

"I thought you didn't want it," Luvliel said.

"Vell," said Glargle, and shrugged, "if you're not viss ze vun *du liebe, liebe* ze vun you're viss."

Luvliel got a look on her face as though she wished she hadn't heard that, and as if to change the subject, said:

"We'll need to arm my colleagues."

"Lot of dead eastrons to pick over," Slagbag answered.

Luvliel glanced at the bodies, looked as if maybe she wasn't glad she'd changed the subject after all, but got down to business anyway. Finding a black double-recurved bow and a quiver, she set about gathering arrows, which were strewn all over the flags. Slagbag buckled on swordbelts and shouldered baldrics. Not particularly suited to lugging a lot of weapons for someone else, Snash concentrated on finding one for himself, locating a sheathed sword that was a bit too big for him, although it had probably been a mere backup for the eastron he took it from. Glargle got an additional knife and thrust it into his loincloth, but Snash had no idea where it went...exactly.

Along with the weapons, they'd also gotten some jerky and water from the eastrons...Luvliel drank some, but didn't partake of the jerky, even though Snash thought it rather good...the eastrons had this dark salty sauce that they used as a marinade, and he'd been acquainted with it at Overflowing Fist...he didn't know what sort of creature *this* jerky was from, but he didn't really care.

Anyway, it was all snarfed as quickly as tough eastron mystery meat could be snarfed, and they went over to the hatch. It showed many bladestrokes, and looked like it was just about stove in, although there was still a padlock attached, with what appeared to be a snapped-off key in the lock; Slagbag caved the trapdoor with five heavy two-handed axe-blows, then led the way onto the stairs beneath, Luvliel right behind him, an arrow nocked on that black bow. Following them, Snash heard her start in on her flower-spell, but then a voice cried:

"No, Lady, hold!"

And hold she did.

Snash looked past her. One of those red-robed fellows was standing at the bottom with a small crowd of yarks.

"I was watching from a window, down below," said the redrobe. "Saw what happened to the hellrogs...."

"And?" Luvliel cried.

"We'd like to throw in with you," the sorcerer replied.

Slagbag began: "My Lady, you can't trust---"

"I trusted *you*," she replied.

"What if he's lying?" Slagbag asked.

"Trusting him would be the nice thing to do."

Slagbag slumped, shaking his head as though she had him.

"You there, red fellow," she said, lowering her bow. "Come up here."

He mounted the steps.

"Say, don't I know you?" she asked.

He nodded. "I did some work on your cell. As a matter of fact..." He paused, blushing.

"Yes?"

"I fell in love with you the moment I laid eyes on you."

You bastard! Snash thought; even though neither of them had a chance with her, the guy *was* competition of a sort...at the very least, he was hogging her attention, although Snash knew just how he felt, of course.

As for Luvliel, she seemed to take the man's adoration completely in stride, and turning to Slagbag, said:

"See, this is all going to work out."

Letting her bowstring go slack, she put the arrow back in its quiver, slung the bow over her shoulder, then brought out the book and showed it to the redrobe, saying:

"I want to free all the White Committee members."

"Might I kiss your feet?" he asked, irritating Snash profoundly.

"First things first," Luvliel said.

"Does that mean I get to later?" the redrobe said.

She laughed. "Heavens no! But, if you *truly* love me, you still have to do what I say."

His shoulders slumped much the same way Slagbag's had. "Oh, all right."

He led the way, and tried to get the fellows down below to open a lane, but the yarks wouldn't budge.

"You're *him*, aren't you?" a runt asked Snash.

"Who?"

"The one who started it all...who beat Serpentar."

Snash had no idea the word had spread so quickly.

"Are you---Hrag Urshathur?" a bull asked.

"Ask me again if we win," Snash replied.

"You mean we might not?"

"Well, if I'm *not* Hrag Urshathur..."

"The redrobe told us *nine* Hellrogs went down." .

"The sharks did that," Snash replied.

"But you got the riders off the sharks, didn't you?"

"Mostly it was the sharks themselves..."

A brain asked excitedly: "Can we kiss your feet?"

"No!" he said. "Why would you want to do *that*?"

"It seems like the thing to do," the brain said, the others nodding.

Beginning to actively hope he *wasn't* Hrag Urshathur, Snash answered: "You can't kiss my feet!"

They looked at each other, saying: "Can't kiss his feet."

He tried not to let his disgust show. *Oh*, he thought, *if we only had some females...*

They all went down a level, and that wretched redrobe raised a thorn-gate, undoubtedly thinking he'd impress Luvliel thereby...Snash could just *tell*. According to the damnable pest, there were three Committee members on the floor, Rondlefrond Lord of Reftdingle, Dwimli the Dwelf-Earl, and Tharathorn the Thwift; Luvliel could've looked up the numbers in the book, of course, but the redrobe knew exactly where to go, and led them straight to Rondlefrond's cell, or rather, the spot on the wall with his cell-number on it. With the book already cracked open to the relevant page, she read the spell out, and the stones dissolved in front of her---out came a light rather like hers, a trifle less golden, perhaps.

"Luvliel?" cried a voice from inside.

"Beloved kinsman!" she replied, beckoning.

Bearing a strong facial resemblence to her although looking a *wee* bit more butch, a tall fay man appeared, clad in spotless white. He was somewhat taller than his kinswoman, slightly bigger across the shoulders, but very narrow at the hips; his yellow hair would've been as wonderful as hers if it had been as long. Without another word, the fays embraced. Then----

Rondlefrond spotted the yarks.

Gasping, leaping back, he pointed frantically, shaking his finger.

"They're on our side," Luvliel said.

"Are you cracked?" he demanded.

"No worse than usual," she replied, with a laugh.

"They're servants of the enemy!"

"No," said Snash. "We've turned."

"That's Snash," said Luvliel. "He started the uprising."

"Uprising?" Rondlefrond asked.

"Me freed, five flying sharks turned, nine hellrogs destroyed, and the whole White Committee about to be let loose."

Rondlefrond just shook his head, sputtering: "But...but... those are *yarks!*"

"Yes," said Luvliel patiently.

"Our mother was *killed* by yarks!"

"But she was also very nice," said Luvliel.

"So?"

"She'd want us to do the nice thing now....Really, cuz, I've learned a few things since Snash freed me. This situation calls for a certain broad-mindedness."

Rondlefrond pointed. "*Yarks!*"

"They're *on our side*," she said. "Now, we're wasting time...Do you want to get back in your cell, or help us overthrow Serpentar?"

He slapped the back of his long Fayish neck, looking most unhappy...Glargle went up to him, tugged on his sleeve, and said:

"Ach, sss, don't be azzhole."

As though he was smelling the gremlin's crotchrag, (and he might well have been), Rondlefrond asked: "Who *is* this?"

Luvliel ignored the question, thrusting the bow towards her kinsman.

"Brought this for you," she said, and unslung the quiver...after a few more moments, he accepted them both, although he was plainly reserving some deep reservations.

"*Sehr gut*," said Glargle, patted him on the tiny white-tighted butt (Rondlefrond straightened, looking most affronted) and went back with Snash.

Luvliel turned to the redrobe. "Dwimli," she said.

"Follow me, My Lady," he replied. "My name is Mnildor, by the way."

"I'll do my best to remember it." Coming from anyone else, this might have seemed something of an insult, but Snash sensed she truly intended to put herself out.

As they went along, there were a number of vehement whispery exchanges between Luvliel and Rondlefrond that Snash couldn't quite catch...Glargle was going along at Snash's side, clucking laughter.

"Chust look at zose leotards," he said.

Snash was unfamiliar with the term. "Leotards?"

"Tight vite pants. Glargle vouldn't be caught dead. Better off viss *gut* honest loincloth."

Snash agreed with him about the leotards, although he wouldn't have wanted to suffer Glargle's groinwrap either.

"*Sehen, sehen!*" Glargle cried. "Little funny buttocks, vun up, uzzer up, repeat…looks like somevun juggling oranges in his pants…"

With that, Rondlefrond turned and said:

"Listen."

"All ears," Glargle replied, cupping his tympani with his big webbed hands.

"If we're going to be allies against Serpentar," Rondlefrond went on, "you'd better stop making fun of my behind."

Glargle just scratched his all-but bald pate.

Rondlefrond asked: "How would you like it if I made fun of that stupid single hair of yours?"

Glargle pulled it down and inspected it, crossing his huge eyes. "Vhat's wrong mit it?" he asked, sounding genuinely puzzled and hurt.

Rondlefrond huffed and continued up the hall with Luvliel.

"Vhat's wrong mit *mein* hair?" Glargle asked Snash as they started forward again.

Snash *did* think he'd look better without it, but didn't have the heart to say so. "Nothing," he replied.

"Not as zo Glargle had choice," Glargle said. "Besides, look shtupid in vig. Glargle tried vun vunce. Vass blown off by hurricane vind…"

Hurricane meant about as much to Snash as *leotard* had, but before he could ask about it, Mnildor halted, saying:

"Dwimli."

Luvliel opened the cell.

"My lady!" cried its inmate.

"Most chivalrous dwelf!" she replied.

Out rushed a stocky fellow, taller than Snash but still pretty short, with a long red plaited beard. He was wearing a rough tunic, belted at the waist, and baggy trews; on his feet were stout boots, the soles very thick, perhaps to boost his height. He knelt before Luvliel, who asked:

"Do you still have that lock of hair I gave you?"

"I do, my lady," he said, rising. "Although I'd hate to tell you where I hid it---"

Suddenly he looked off to the side and hopped three feet in the air, his beard flying up over his face as he came down, booted feet banging the floor.

"*Yarks!*" he cried.

"They're with me," she said.

"How---?"

"Don't worry about it. I already explained *everything* to Rondlefrond...we still have a number of Committee members to free, and I don't intend to keep explaining everything to everyone. Slagbag, please give Dwimli an axe."

Slagbag stepped forward and pulled out one of the ones he'd slipped into his belt.

"Tharathorn," said Luvliel to Mnildor.

They proceeded along the corridor and did the needful for the Thoon to Be Rethtored...the first that Snash saw of Tharathorn was a very very long booted leg, stepping out into the hall...the process actually looked kind of leisurely to Snash, indeed, not very thwift at all, until he realized what a big stride he'd just seen...so tall that he almost clipped his head on the top of the opening, handsome in a ruddy, craggy way, if a bit horse-faced, Tharathorn stepped up before Luvliel, and bowed.

"Tharathorn," she said.

"Yeth, tith I."

"Shpeaks mit a lisp," said Glargle to Snash.

"Thith ith not a lithp," said Tharathorn, in the tones of one most familiar with this accusation and *extremely* tired of it. "I thpeak an ancient dialect of the Common Thpeech, in which thth had not yet become thth. Wordth change over time. Thounth become other thounth."

"Was Slippriman once known as Thlippriman?" Snash asked.

Tharathorn nodded. "And Therpentar wath called Therpentar."

"You haven't asked about the yarks," said Luvliel.

"I figured there wath no need. Theeing Rondlefrond

and Dwimli---" here Tharathorn waved, "I athumed you had already explained, and allayed their fearth, tho..." He paused. "Are you going to free all the other Committee memberth?"

"Yes," she said.

"Might I make a thuggethtion?"

"You might."

"I think I should take the Dwelf-Earl and the Lord of Reftdingle on ahead, which ith to thay, down, to hold off anyone who might be coming up."

"Good idea," she said.

"Take us too," said one of the bulls, nodding towards his comrades. "We'll help."

Tharathorn didn't appear to fancy the idea, but Rondlefrond said:

"I have given the matter of these yarks a bit of thought, which is all that time allowed, I'm afraid; and I've concluded that they would've tried something already if they were playing us false."

"Very well then," said Tharathorn, and accepted a long straight sword from Slagbag....leading the way with very long strides, Rondlefrond, Dwimli and the yarks practically running to keep up, he headed off.

"Ling-lings," said Luvliel to Mnildor.

They had to descend a number of floors, but Mnildor, on the way up, had already opened all the thorn-gates that might've inconvienced them. They heard fighting down below, and passed scattered bodies, yarks and eastrons, who'd apparently met up with Tharathorn's troop; it sure seemed to Snash that Tharathorn couldn't be meeting any genuinely organized opposition. There was, moreover, the possibility that there'd been even more defections...Mnildor couldn't have been the only person in the tower to have seen that battle between the sharkriders and the hellrogs.

"Ziss goingk surprisingly vell," Glargle declared. "Glargle cautiously optimistic, *ja, ja*..."

When they reached the ling-lings' floor and Luvliel opened the cell, four extremely chubby black and white bears rolled out into the hall, almost as though they'd been stacked up on each other, leaning against the wall. But they immediately righted themselves, and bowed to the fay princess, each making a fist with one paw and putting it knuckle-first against the palm of the other.

"My Lady," they all said at once.

"We're freeing everyone of interest," Luvliel said.

"*Hau*," they all said simultaneously, nodding.

"Pandas?" Glargle asked Luvliel.

She answered: "There is a prophecy, to whit:

'*Seek for the feet that are hairy*
On black and white butterball bears.
The Gauntlet will fall in the lava,
And up will go all of our shares.'"

"You sent zem because of *zat*?" Glargle asked.

"We did. Also because of their prowess in fighting in vertical array."

At that, with amazing speed, they climbed onto each others' shoulders, making a four-panda pillar. Snash was extremely dubious about the utility of this; he also thought they were lucky the ceilings were so high.

"That's Mr. Ru on top," said Luvliel. "Next one down is Sai Yuk, and under him is Fei Hung, then Hei Kwan."

"Where can we be of most use?" asked Mr. Ru.

"Go down the steps," said Luvliel. "Follow the bodies…Tharathorn is clearing the way for us, with Rondlefrond, Dwimli, and a bunch of yark defectors."

Again the pandas put fist to palm, then left, once more at remarkable speed, still stacked, wobbling hardly at all.

"Anyone else on this floor?" Luvliel asked Mnildor.

"No," he replied.

"Greydolf," she said.

Again they descended…Glargle told Snash some things about Greydolf.

"Chased Glargle around for vhile. Followed him right into Dark Land. Caught him sitting in sump. He say, 'Glargle, vant to know about ze *liebchen*.' Glargle say, 'Glargle doesn't have, vant to sit in sump some more. Not many sumps in Dark Land, *nein, nein*.' But he take Glargle avay and find him much better sump, outside mountains. Such goot sump, almost vant to marry it, forget about *liebchen*. Greydolf say, 'be goot, Glargle, marry ze mud, don't look for bad sing any more.' Glargle almost listen. But vhen Greydolf go avay, I hear ze *liebchen* calling, all ze vay from back here. 'Glargle, come and be my husband,' *liebchen* say. So Glargle realizes his heart's shtill mit *liebchen*, and he leaves sump, goot as it vass---"

He broke off, as Luvliel was getting down to business again, the result being the dramatic egress of an old fellow in dun robes; he looked something like Slippriman, although he was shorter and not as thin, and his beard was silvery rather than white and much fuller and longer----of all the beards Snash had seen, he thought Greydolf's hands down the best. Apparently taking everyone in at a glance, the incarnate angel said:

"A whole host of things must've led up to this, I think."

Luvliel smiled, as though she thought that was very well put. "You have said it." She indicated Snash. "This is the cause of Serpentar's problems."

Greydolf eyed him. "Your name wouldn't be Snash, would it?"

Snash nodded.

"A very interesting variety of runt," Greydolf told Luvliel. "They've had trouble with them...if you'll recall, I always argued that we might run across throwbacks..."

"You should stop talking about him as though he's not here," said Slagbag. "While *you* were locked up in your cell, he--"

"Say no more," said Greydolf. "You're quite right. I've been rude."

"That's Slagbag," said Luvliel, nodding towards the big yark. "He's chosen to be nice too."

"More and more interesting," Greydolf said, and asked him: "Might I have one of those swords your belt's stuffed with?"

"Curved or straight?" Slagbag asked.

"Straight."

Slagbag gave him one very much like the one he'd given Tharathorn.

"Who else have you freed?" Greydolf asked Luvliel.

"Rondlefrond, Dwimli, Tharathorn, and the Linglings," she replied. "They're downstairs, making trouble..."

"Perhaps I should join them," Greydolf said.

"What about the other one?" Mnildor asked.

"Other one?" Luvliel asked. "What do you mean?"

"The other incarnate angel."

"Slippriman?" Luvliel asked.

"He's here?" asked Greydolf.

"Three cells down."

"Don't let him out!" Snash broke in.

Greydolf eyed him from under grey bushy brows.

"He's a traitor," said Snash. "He was working for Serpentar."

Greydolf looked as though this didn't come entirely as a surprise. "How do you know?"

"I was his orderly," Snash said. "He set all of you up."

Greydolf looked to Luvliel. "What do *you* know about this?"

"Only what Snash told me," she answered.

"And what's your opinion?"

"I don't know what to think," she said.

"He *was* working for Serpentar," Mnildor said. "Practically his right hand for a while..."

Snash said: "He told me he was only trying to fool him, because he'd been captured, but..."

"These are grave charges," Greydolf said. "Slippriman is the head of my order...Under the circumstances, there isn't enough time for me to sort all this out. While we're out of our cells, we're not out of Mount Adamant, let alone Tenebria, and Serpentar is, in all likelihood, taking steps. We need Slippriman's power...badly."

Persuaded, apparently, for the time being at least, Luvliel nodded.

Snash cried: "But----"

"Slippriman was my brother in the mind of the All-Father," Greydolf said.

Snash replied: "He's gone real rotten in the meanwhile."

"There's no help for it. We'd better free him."

The spell to unlock Slippriman's cell wasn't in the book of course, since he'd been captured after it was written, but Greydolf, Luvliel and Mnildor all put their heads together, operating on the assumption that the spell must be similar to the one for the last lock, given Slippriman's similarity to his brother; Greydolf provided Slippriman's true name, Mnildor wedded it to a numerical progression, Luvliel cast the whole thing into verse, and they got it right on the first try. Great rips in his scorched bloody garments, Slippriman came out, his beardless face looking less gaunt than it had, but only because it was all swelled up with bruises...his nose had gone crooked, and one of his eyes was nearly shut. Ignoring Snash, he smiled when he saw Greydolf; three of his upper front teeth had been knocked out.

"Greydolf," he cried. "This is indeed beyond all hope!"

Greydolf regarded him thoughtfully.

"What's wrong?" Slippriman asked.

Greydolf was silent a moment more, then said: "We have work to do."

"Yes?"

"Downstairs," said Greydolf. "While Luvliel frees everyone else."

Slippriman glanced at Slagbag, then told Greydolf: "Tell the yark to give me a sword."

"Curved or straight?" Slagbag asked.

"Curved," said Slippriman.

Slagbag tossed one to the floor in front of him.

Slippriman said: "Pick it up and hand it to me, hilt-first...*yark*."

When Slagbag didn't move, Slippriman turned to Greydolf, who held his stare, cocking his head slightly to one side...apparently realizing that he was achieving nothing,

Slippriman shrugged and quickly picked up the sword, smiling first at Slagbag, then Snash, the expression quite subtle, but all the more murderous for it...Snash felt as though he'd been whipped across the face.

"Come then, brother," Slippriman told Greydolf. "To war."

Next on Luvliel's list was Oakenchin...he was incarcerated on a floor whose ceilings were *remarkably* high, and once the oakenguy emerged, Snash saw why---he had boughs sprouting from his head and shoulders, and if you counted all of that, and why not, he was about fifteen feet tall. The doorway had barely accomodated him, and even his leafy branches had rustled mightily against the lintel and sides. His chin was indeed pronounced, and had had all the bark rubbed off it; down the sides of his long face ran two mossy sideburns, and he had a great droopy green moustache....seeing Luvliel, he bowed, creaking. Astounded by the oakenguy's flexibility, Snash flinched to see him swing his foliage down to within an inch of Luvliel's head, but it didn't seem to bother her...an oak-leaf landed across the bridge of her nose, and for a moment she almost looked as though she would leave it there, before she took it away, between two fingers, by the stem.

"Good to see you again," she said.

He straightened. "So they caught you too, eh?"

"Don't we feel silly?"

"And it's high time we redeemed ourselves...is there a gigantic fight in the offing?"

"There is."

He rubbed his gnarly long-fingered hands together. "Ha! I'll teach them not to turn oakenguys into snails..."

"What sort did you become?" Luvliel asked.

"A tree-snail, as you might expect," he replied. "You didn't stumble across Greydolf, did you?"

"Yes. He's downstairs, fighting alongside Slippriman, Tharathorn, Dwimli, Rondlefrond, and the Ling-lings."

"Perhaps I'd better join them," Oakenchin said. "Will there be fire, do you think? Hellrogs?"

"In all likelihood."

"Ah," he said, and sucked in a deep breath, his leaves vanishing back into his branches and twigs. "Makes me a good deal less flammable."

"Will you have enough room?" Luvliel asked. "To negotiate the passages? Most of the ceilings aren't this high..."

He just snorted a powerful oaken snort and got down on all fours, with his huge mass of boughs extending way out in front; he crawled forward a bit, then back, scouring floor, walls and ceiling with his branch-tips; the sound alone made Snash want to run like hell, and that was before Oakenchin set all his branches to writhing...even though the oak-puncher was clearly a good guy, Snash thought the squirming wooden limbs were one of the most intimidating things he'd ever seen, even compared to Serpentar's thorns.

"Like something from a very bad dream, yes?" Oakenchin asked, getting back to his big rooty feet.

"I never have bad dreams," said Luvliel.

"Of course you don't." Catching Snash staring at him, he said: "You should see it when I spin."

"Worse than Shcrews, maybe," whispered Glargle in Snash's ear.

"Good thing he's on our side," Snash whispered back.

"Good thing you're on *my* side," said Oakenchin, and started to start off.

"Wait!" cried Mnildor.

Oakenchin turned.

"What about *them*?" Mnildor asked.

"Them?"

"The rest of you."

Oakenchin seemed quite puzzled.

"The others of your kind," said Mnildor.

Oakenchin glanced at Luvliel, who still had her finger bookmarking Oakenchin's page; she turned it, and her eyes widened a bit, and her lips parted slightly---it was the closest thing to an expression of shock that Snash had ever seen on her. She began to flip forward, her fingers moving with the manual dexterity of which only fays are capable...

"What is it?" Oakenchin demanded.

She looked at him.

"Dare I hope?"

She nodded. "They're *here*."

He clapped a hand over his mouth, great green eyes suddenly welling with tears, and after drawing a breath that made his trunk quake, he said:

"Well...let them out."

Luvliel went down to the next cell-number, recited the spell---as she pronounced what Snash guessed was the true name, he heard Oakenchin draw another enormous breath, then release it in a long rapturous sigh as the cell's occupant stepped forth, little shorter than the oak-puncher himself but a whole lot curvier, eyes lined with dark twigs like long lashes...

Snash guessed at once that she was one of the oakenwives.

"Lissomleg," said Oakenchin.

"Oakenchin," the tree-woman replied.

For a few moments more they stood staring at each other, tears streaming down their cheeks of bark...then they rushed into each other's arms, lips knocking together, branches intermingling and squirming.

"*Ach*, whoa!" cried Glargle. "Go find isolated shpot in forest, don't subject poor Glargle to ziss..."

But locked, indeed, *interlocked* in their ecstatic embrace, all their branches rubbing and rattling, oakenwife and oakenguy seemed not to hear. Luvliel's mouth dropped all the way open, and her cheeks grew red...Snash found the arboreal clinch strangely.... *moving* in a very disturbing way.

"Oh," said Slagbag, who was plainly having a similar reaction. "That's...that's..."

All of a sudden, myriad acorns were budding on Lissomleg's limbs and dropping to the floor in a rattling hail.

"Come, come," said Luvliel at last. "Really, we have quite a few oakenwives to go, and..."

"You go on ahead," said Oakenchin. "We'll catch up to you."

"Really," said Luvliel, "you're dropping acorns all over the floor, and---"

"I'll scoop 'em up and put 'em in my pouch," said

Lissomleg, out of the side of her mouth, which was still pressed against Oakenchin's.

"Fine, fine, whatever," said Luvliel, and went by, tip-toeing between the young 'uns, Snash, Slagbag and Glargle teetering after her, somehow managing to keep themselves from mashing any of them, but just barely. Once the acorns thinned out and going got easier, Snash heard some oakendoings that sounded weird even by recent standards and glanced back, didn't quite know what he was looking at...Glargle had paused too.

"Glargle sinks he's seen it all, now," he said, "and he's not happy, *nein, nein.*"

Luvliel opened cell after cell, springing oakenwife upon oakenwife, with names like Lithebough, Suppleback, Slendershoot and Toothesometrunk; Snash was counting, and all told, there were sixty tree-women. Getting wind of the fact that Oakenchin was just down the hall, they hastened in his direction.

"I wonder how Lissomleg is going to feel about that?" said Snash.

"What?" asked Mnildor.

"All the competition," Snash said, thinking of his own jealousy regarding the redrobe; it still bothered him, even though Luvliel plainly didn't care for the man at all.

"I can just imagine," Mnildor said. "Although, I can also imagine that Oakenchin might not mind."

"What's he going to do with sixty oakenwives?" Snash asked.

"I don't know," said Mnildor. "What would *you* do with sixty female yarks?"

"I'm not sure, exactly..."

"Would you like to find out?"

"If there *were* any female yarks."

Mnildor laughed.

Snash and Slagbag both gave him sharp glances; Luvliel drew nearer to the redrobe, asking:

"What are you hinting at?"

Mnildor laughed again.

With Luvliel leaving a trail of magical footprints for the oakenfolks to follow (the floor itself actually went sparkly where she planted her dainties, making the prints impervious to the scuffles of succeeding feet), the redrobe led two floors down...the ceiling was much lower there. Stopping in front of 701, he told Luvliel:

"Look in the book under YS."

She cracked it open just about at the back, flipped a couple of pages.

"Well," she said, "if there was any possibility that I'd be damned, which I'm happy to say there isn't, I'm afraid I would be."

With that, she uttered the spell...stone vanished.

"Come on," she said, beckoning. "It's all right."

Wearing a coarse shift that didn't quite conceal a shape that Snash had never seen on a yark (but which he nonetheless liked a lot), a runt about his size came out, very black, but with blue eyes and long blonde hair.

"Snash*etta*?" Luvliel asked...Snash had already caught the name during the spell.

The curvy blond runt nodded. Aside from her basic runtiness, Snash noticed a peculiar familiarity about her features...

"There you go," said Mnildor, patting Snash on the back. "A yarkette."

"*Runtette*, to be precise," said Snashetta.

"But," Snash said, "*I* was grown in a pit. We all were."

Mnildor answered: "Best way to maintain a certain...uniformity of product. And, if truth be told, to insulate you from softening influences...make you just plain meaner. But Serpentar's always maintained a small population of females. As a hedge against Fruit-blight and Yark-blight, so he can restart the population if he has to."

Snashetta approached Snash, and said: "What's your name?"

He told her.

"You don't have any hair," she said.

"No I don't," he said.

"Do you like mine?"

"Sure," said Snash. "Looks rather like *hers*---"

He turned towards Luvliel.

And realized why Snashetta reminded him of someone.

"Are you all right?" Snashetta asked, sounding very concerned.

"How many more yarkettes are there?" Snash asked.

"Nine," said Mnildor.

"I thought you said there were sixty."

"No, I asked what you'd *do* with sixty---"

"We've got to get them out of Mount Adamant," said Luvliel. "Before the Gauntlet goes into the lava, if it ever does..."

"Why?" asked Slagbag.

"Because this fortress was made with it," she answered. "And if the Gauntlet goes, the Spike's going to come crashing down---"

Just then Snash began to hear the unmistakable sound of an oakenguys' bare boughs scraping against the sides of a stone passage.

"Well," said Oakenchin, getting to his knees after he came crawling into view, "what now?"

"Where are the oakenwives?" Luvliel asked.

"They'll be along in a bit...they're just back there scooping up all the acorns---" He paused, squinting at Snashetta, looking rather baffled.

"You'll have to get them out of Mount Adamant," Luvliel said.

"Eh?"

"The oakenwives and the acorns. If we destroy the Gauntlet, everything will crumble, and if you want to revive your race---"

"We want to *fight*," Oakenchin said.

"There'll be plenty of that," Luvliel replied. "Just getting out of *this* tower. And if we make it to the Spike, *you'll* have to go down the main stairs, and Serpentar's troops will be coming up... ...And if you make it through them and get outside, there's a huge army between here and the mountains."

"Oh good," Oakenchin said, rubbing his hands, the sound quite abrasive.

"I like your attitude," Snashetta said.

He eyed her again. "Excuse me, but...are you a *female* yark?"

"I am."

"A *blonde* one," said Luvliel.

"Stranger and stranger," Oakenchin answered. "Mercy me, I thought it was a wig." He glanced at Luvliel. "You know, though, now that I'm better informed, she looks rather like you, no offense."

"None taken," said Luvliel. "To tell you the truth, it's a family resemblance---"

"Yes, now that I think of it, I suppose it would be."

Luvliel continued: "And it's my considered opinion---as a fay, and thus an ultimate earthly arbiter of taste---that she's actually on the cute side."

"Thank you," said Snashetta, and did a little thing where she bent her knees with one foot in front of the other...Snash had no idea he'd just seen a curtsy, although he rather wished she'd do it again.

"Hadn't we better free the rest?" asked Mnildor.

"Absolutely," said Luvliel.

As they freed the other nine yarkettes, it became apparent that there were, in addition to runtettes, brainettes and bullettes...one of the latter made straight for Slagbag.

He rubbed his head, laughed, and said: "Uhh."

Pointing a clawed thumb at her ample bosom, which was heaving beneath the rough cloth of her shift, she said:

"I'm *Nudzu.*"

He looked down at the floor and replied: "Duh."

"Is *that* all you can say?"

"Maybe---"

Suddenly she cried: "I want to *do* something with you!"

"What?"

"I don't know!"

"*Und* Glargle hopes nobody shows you," Glargle broke in disgustedly.

By then, all the oakenwives had come up.

Oakenchin asked Luvliel: "Who remains to be sprung?"

"Bimbottom," the Princess replied.

"Oh my," Oakenchin said. "I think me and the

oakenwives will just head on down to the fighting."

"Can't say I blame you," Luvliel replied. "Go, go."

Her contingent didn't even try to keep up with them...Mnildor led Bimbottomwards...Nudzu and Snashetta worked their way forward and bracketted Luvliel on the stairs...the three blondies were quite a picture.

"Snashetta says *you* say yarks and fays are related," Nudzu said.

"I do," Luvliel replied, "because we are."

"And you're a princess?"

"Yes."

"I don't believe in aristocracy," said Nudzu.

"Won't be getting any curtsies from *her*," Snashetta told Luvliel. "I have a rather more balanced view, however...my preference would be a constitutional monarchy."

Right behind them, Snash said: "You sound like a shark."

"Oh?" asked Snashetta and Nudzu together---there was, of course, no reason why that observation should've made any sense to them.

"Constitutional monarchy?" Luvliel asked. "How did you discuss all this?"

"In correspondence," said Snashetta.

"You were passing messages?"

"All the time."

"*I* never figured out how to pass messages," said Luvliel.

"It's easier than you might think---"

But before Snashetta could reveal the secret, Mnildor said: "This is the floor," sounding most unhappy to have reached it...gulping a bunch and looking unsteady, he took awhile to get them the rest of the way. Even as the stones began to dissolve under Luvliel's spell, a deep voice, resonant and *extremely* fruity, rolled out into the hall:

> *"Tim, Tim, Bottom-bim,*
> *Singing while in storage.*
> *Purplish-pink his trousers is*

And his boots is orange..."

"Tim!" Luvliel called...the cell stood quite open now. But the unseen singer just kept on as if he'd heard absolutely nothing:

> *"Tim, Tim, loony him*
> *Laughing for no reason.*
> *Bouncing like a crazy ball*
> *In a rubb'ry season!"*

Snash grew aware of a distinct slapping noise, as though something large and buoyant were going back and forth between floor and ceiling, or even wall and wall...he *almost* looked around the corner, but decided against it.

"Tim!" cried Luvliel, rather more loudly.

The singing and bouncing stopped.

"Come on," said Luvliel. "You can put your finger up against the side of your shiny red nose all you like..."

The bouncing started again, and so did the big voice:

> *"Oh well, what the Hell,*
> *Jello-bell, my darling.*
> *Fleet flies the withy-wisp*
> *And the feckled farling!"*

"*Tim!*" Luvliel cried.

But he continued:

> *"All yell 'turtle-smell!'"*
> *Mind the peevish starling!*
> *Dawn pinkens dingly dell*
> *Where the roots are gnarling!"*

"Tim, a bit of this---"

But he only switched to another song:

> *"Ding-dong, bing-bong*
> *Ringy-ringy ring-rong*
> *That's old Tim's song;*

Sense it maketh not.

He's a weird one.
Some would say a queer one.

Tim, Tim, Bim, Bim
Bottom Bottom Bot!"

"Tim," cried Luvliel, "We really have something of a situation here---"

Suddenly he came leaping out, as vivid an apparition as one would never wish to see, accoutered in orange boots, purplish-pink trews, and a cerulean blue jacket; he was very round through the belly, and had an alarming round and red face, with a bulbous scarlet nose and great bright-blue eyes...on his head was a hat of a green so loud that Snash was *sure* he heard it....in Tim's hatband jiggled a plume about five feet long. One toe way out, he sailed to the floor, flattened and bulged noticeably when he struck, and kept quivering even as he gathered himself up.

"Now then," Luvliel began, but he immediately launched into another verse:

> *"Old Tim, bold Tim,*
> *Prison couldn't hold him*
> *He's at large now,*
> *Acting awful odd.*
> *You can't catch him.*
> *You will never match him.*
> *Tim, Tim, Bim Bim*
> *Bottom Bottom Bot!"*

Snash was about to point out that prison had been holding him quite well until Luvliel showed up, when old Tim put both hands to his copious belly and started laughing uproariously, his whole body shaking....as everyone looked on aghast, he began skipping round and round them, as though he expected by this to free all their captive mirth, although Snash thought Bimbottom was doing quite enough laughing for the rest of them, indeed the whole rest of the world, perhaps....

Luvliel put her hand to her head as though she were getting a nasty headache...all at once Tim stopped, blinking. Then, accompanied by a noise that sounded to Snash kind of like "eeee-*yooop!*" Bimbottom crossed the space between him and Luvliel, seized one of her glowing hands, raised it to his shiny red lips, and gave it a passionate kiss. As she snatched it away, he said:

> *"Don't mind poor Tim.*
> *Shouldn't really blame him.*
> *He's just this way.*
> *And you know it well.*
> *Still he'll help you*
> *Wait and see what he'll do.*
> *Tim will give them*
> *Bottom-bimmish hell."*

"Oh," said Luvliel, massaging her temples with her fingertips now, "I don't doubt it in the slightest."

And neither, if it came to that, did Snash....Bimbottom looked his way, saying:

> *"You there! Little yark!*
> *Stop with all your scowling!*
> *Tim's the man when times are dark.*
> *Bad things run off howling."*

"*Ja*," said Glargle. "But Glargle vould like to run off too."

Snash was expecting more verse in response, but old Tim just slapped his fat knee with a big pudgy hand, and launched into another round of bombastic laughter, during which he began bouncing between floor and ceiling, the overall effect rivaling Serpentar's blazing rage for making Snash feel like he was going completely out of his mind...the thought of Serpentar and Bimbottom going head to head left Snash shuddering.

"Timothy T. *BIMBOTTOM!*" Luvliel cried, as though she were nearing the end of her rope.

Tim stopped, bulged and wobbled a bit before subsiding into mere quivering...then he took her hand again, kissed it, and skipped away.

"Coming?" he called over his shoulder.

Chapter 18: The Bridge and the Bimbottom

Now while everyone was being freed upstairs, Tharathorn, Rondlefrond, Dwimli and the defectors had swept down level after level, meeting mixed squads of eastrons and yarks on the steps, none of whom wanted to tango---fleeing back down, the cravens found themselves pinned against a thorn-gate. But the redrobe on the other side hadn't really grasped the situation, and raised the barrier, whereupon Tharathorn and co. drove down through the fellows who were in the process of trying to get under it, and managed to snag that redrobe before he could close the gate again. From then on the gates were no longer a problem, and Tharathorn's troop kept pushing everyone down before them.

But a company of guards, having thought things through, stayed off the stairs; waiting till Tharathorn's boys went through, they came down behind *them*.

That availed them little, however, because the linglings, rushing to join Tharathorn, came down behind *them*. And when, *farther* down, another group of guards had the same brainstorm, Greydolf and Slippriman came down upon *them*.

Afterwards, the wizards (who were the mightiest fellows and made the very best vanguard) went to the front and everyone else hung back, and whenever any more guards tried the same trick, they were caught between the hammer and the anvil. Thus it was that the erstwhile prisoners and their yark erstwhile jailers, having strewn the stairs with corpses (and created many interesting puddles where the red blood of eastrons was marbled with the black blood of yarks) came relatively unscathed to the floor where the bridge crossed to the Spike.

There, things got even worse for the home team, even though huge numbers of guards had been waiting in barracks and store-rooms, and on the next floor down; even as they counter-attacked from several directions, the oakenfolks arrived from the stairs, and got down on their hands and knees and reamed, some content to crawl with their leafless writhing branches out in front, others (Oakenchin among them) spinning as they advanced. Their branches got all full of bodies and body-parts, and a lot of boughs got snapped off, but...no

351

one who tried to buck those scouring onslaughts survived.

Seeing that the oakenfolks had everything in hand, Greydolf, Slippriman and the rest went out to the portcullis, looking through the bars...out on the bridge, five hellrogs were flailing away mightily with their morningstars, gouging chunk after chunk from the middle.

"Trying to cut us off," said Slippriman to Greydolf.

Dwimli and Tharathorn were at the wheel that controlled the portcullis; Greydolf gave them a nod, and they unlocked the device and began to turn it. Off to one side, a counterweight dropped; up rose the spiked gate.

"Stay here," Greydolf told the others....the hellrogs were a job for wizards. He and Slippriman marched out onto the bridge.

Up ahead, lined abreast, the hellrogs saw them coming, stopped in mid-flail, all five getting clonked on the noggins by their own mace-heads a moment later. They staggered, but recovered swiftly, and started banging away again in no time, sparks and black stone-bits flying each time their weapons smote the span.

"What did that little yark tell you?" Slippriman asked Greydolf.

"That you were working for Serpentar," Greydolf replied.

"It was a ruse," Slippriman replied. "I was undermining him."

"There's no time for this now," said Greydolf.

"You believe that runt, don't you?" asked Slippriman.

"I'm reserving judgement."

"I see---"

Once again, the hellrogs had halted their efforts, although this time on the downswing, leaving their mace-heads sitting on the pitted span.

"Slippriman, you traitor!" one bellowed.

But with that, Slippriman drew his sword and leaped behind Greydolf, poking him in the back with it and crying:

"Traitor to *who?*"

At this, the hellrogs all put their heads together and started conferring furiously.

Over his shoulder, Greydolf said: "You truly awful---"

Slippriman whispered back: "Think outside the box. We attack while they're conferring, yes?"

Immediately seeing the wisdom of this, Greydolf drew his sword, and he and Slippriman charged them before the hellrogs could stop conferring and whip their morningstars back up. Slashing at legs, bellies, hips, the mages blew clear through.

"What do you say?" Slippriman asked Greydolf. "Back at them?"

"What do you think?" Greydolf cried, and charged again, not realizing until he was in amongst them that Slippriman had stayed behind...

Upon reaching the bridge-level, Luvliel's band met Oakenchin and about half the oakenwives in the great circular chamber at the bottom of the staircase that led down from the main checkpoint.

"Where are the rest of the oakenwives?" Luvliel asked.

"Making sure no one comes at us from underneath," Oakenchin said. "Once we head out across the bridge, I'll signal, and they'll be our rearguard."

"Your branches are very messy," she said, even as an eastron's arm slipped from one and plopped upon the floor.

"I've been very busy," he replied. His eyes shifted to Bimbottom.

"Tim," the oak-puncher said, "you're just as orange, pinkish-purple and blue as ever."

But Bimbottom only pointed to his chartreuse chapeau and said:

> *Don't forget the hat now*
> *Cat now,*
> Sprat *now!*
> *Garish green it is now*
> *Diddle all the day!"*

"Don't quite know how to respond to that," said Oakenchin.

To which Bimbottom replied:

"Don't care if you do now
Boo now,
Hoo now!
Unfortunate for you now
Piddle on the hay!"

"Piddle on the hay?" Oakenchin asked.

"Piddle on the HAY!" Bimbottom cried, and seemed just about to burst into another riot of laughter when Luvliel took him by the hand and led him off towards the bridge. Following, Snash heard Lissomleg tell Oakenchin:

"Hadn't seen him in two thousand years, and it wasn't long enough."

"There, there," Oakenchin began, although Snash didn't catch the rest of it. Great pounding sounds had been coming up the corridor from the bridge, but now they'd ceased, replaced by hellrog-roars, and the kinds of detonations and cracklings that Snash'd heard when Slippriman had been brought to bay over in the Spike; Tharathorn's company was gathered on the threshold, on and off being silhouetted by flashes of light. As Luvliel approached with Bimbottom, Dwimli looked back...the small crowd parted, and Snash came up at Luvliel's side as she stood eyeing the combat in the center of the bridge...

"He ordered uth to thtay back," Tharathorn informed the princess. "Already thent two of them over the thide..."

Snash knew *he* meant Greydolf, since the dun mage seemed to be all alone out there, slashing with his sword, flinging out bolts of force or fire with his free hand, dodging in and out, cape streaming and billowing, among three spindle-winged hellrogs who were constantly getting in each other's way and beaning each other with their maces as they tried to bash him. Streams of blazing blood were crawling down all over them, pooling and smoking on the bridge.

"Where's Slippriman?"Luvliel demanded."I don't see---"

She broke off, wincing as two of the devils caught each other with simultaneous skull-scattering licks; both went flying over opposite sides of the bridge, trailing burning brains through the air, leaving the last hellrog to cope with Greydolf, who was driving him towards the Nail. Flinging fire and slashing away, the wizard was off on the demon's right sometimes, sometimes on the left; sometimes Snash caught a glimpse of him between the titantic legs. The wizard seemed to be having it all his own way, and the hellrog kept retreating, but---

All of a sudden the devil swung his mace, and since he didn't have any other hellrogs to hit, the blow connected, just after Greydolf cried out something about, "You shall not..." Robes whirling, the mage went cartwheeling out into space, and arced downwards, out of sight.

"Greydolf!" Luvliel cried.

"Dun wanderer!" cried Tharathorn and Rondlefrond, and Dwimli sobbed with grief and ripped out two huge hanks of his beard and threw it in his own face.

But as the demon turned and staggered towards the gate, hell-juice sluicing from his wounds, his mace swinging round and round above his head, Bimbottom started towards him, dancing and bouncing in a most squashy and stretchy sort of way as he sang:

> "Hellrog, smellrog,
> Thinks he is so fell rog.
> Tim's unfazed now,
> Frightened he is not.
> Rog won't mash him,
> He will never smash him,
> Tim Tim Bim Bim
> Bottom Bottom Bot!"

And with that, he switched to another song in another language, and even though Snash didn't understand any of it, it seemed that it must be infinitely sillier than anything Bimbottom had inflicted on his allies; this was accompanied by a frightful intensification in the sheer wierdness of Bimbottom's movements, as he struck one pose after another that Snash could never have imagined *anyone* striking. The runt was glad Bimbottom was turned the other way, sure that if he'd actually seen Tim's fat blubbery blue-eyed red-nosed red-cheeked face as all of this was going on, he would've fled shrieking with a gushing nosebleed.

Indeed, not even the hellspawn vanquisher of Greydolf the Dun could tolerate it, although maybe it was the fact that the poor demon had already been through a lot and was crisscrossed with scores of flaming wounds; but Bimbottom's mere approach was enough to stop the devil in his tracks, and as Tim got closer still, the hellrog, an expression of diabolic despair on his face, dropped his morning-star and began to totter...when Tim bounced up and kissed him between the burning nostrils, that was the end. Venting an immense groan, the hellrog stumbled to the side of the bridge and chucked himself over the brink...Snash went to the edge himself and watched him falling, tumbling end over end. The demon crashed through the roof of one of the lesser towers down there, and apparently went through floor after floor after floor, right to the bottom, because the spire completely collapsed in a cloud of dust.

"You know vhat Glargle sinks?" asked the gremlin, who had joined Snash to watch.

"What?" Snash asked.

"I sink good iss just as scary as bad sometimes."

Inclined to agree, Snash looked back at Bimbottom, who seemed to have withdrawn most of himself behind the veil again, as it were...at any rate, when Tim turned and came back, Snash didn't feel compelled to run away or commit suicide, not decisively at least, although some of the yarks and eastrons that had come down with Tharathorn ran back into the Spike, rushing by the oakenfolks, who were on the way up the corridor.

"Look!" cried Rondlefrond. "Across the bridge!"

Snash turned.

Ten files wide, a column of ogres was advancing onto the span, holding huge war-hammers across their chests with both hands, great boots stamping in unison, armor-flaps flapping, the spikes on their helmets swaying back and forth as they marched. For all the brutes in front, Snash couldn't see far into the formation, but he didn't doubt that it stretched well back into the Spike, comprised of hundreds, perhaps thousands of the beasts.

"Tim?" Luvliel asked.

He pirouetted to face the enemy, then started to laugh...the sound rolled over the creatures, halted them in their tracks, struck the Spike and rolled back, so loud that Snash had to cower and put his hands over his ears. He could see the ogres wobbling, swaying, some letting their weapons fall. Then Tim went jouncing towards them, mostly on tiptoe, belting out another song in that horrifyingly silly language. Before he got anywhere *near* the ogres, they were turning tail, and when the rout backed up on itself, flinging themselves off the bridge just as the hellrog had. As the song parted the column like a cleaver, Snash saw that there had indeed been thousands of the beasts, just on the bridge alone. But by the time Bimbottom reached the center of it, they had, in their despair, completely emptied the span of themselves.

Once again toning himself down, he came back towards the Spike, singing:

> *"Couldn't take merry Tim,*
> *Didn't dare to smite him.*
> *Threw themselves off the bridge*
> *Rather than abide him.*
> *Cools Tim his Timness now,*
> *Doesn't want to sear you.*
> *Mutes Tim his queerness now*
> *Cause he's coming near you!"*

As Bimbottom came up, Rondlefrond asked: "Can you take Serpentar, do you think?"

The question seemed to cool Bimbottom's Timness even further. Indeed, his answer was disconcerting in a wholly uncharacteristic way:

> *"He's a fierce one.*
> *Fellest of the fell one.*
> *He's all snakes and*
> *Awful charring heat.*
> *Tim's no liar*
> *Future still looks dire.*
> *Like as not we're*
> *Headed for defeat."*

"*Ach*, sss," said Glargle. "Not vhat Glargle needs to hear."

Bimbottom turned those great discomfitting blue eyes upon the gremlin.

"Evitable iss exorable," said Glargle.

"*Gott mit uns*," said Snash beside him.

Whereupon old Tim smiled, took off his bright green hat, bowed, and swept the pavement with his plume.

They waited till their oakenfolk rearguard came up, then started across. Arrows came sleeting down from the Spike, but Bimbottom deflected them; he was leading the way, of course, and had a song for projectiles:

> *"Swerve now! Curve now!*
> *Lose your freaking nerve now!*
> *Tim has come to creep you*
> *Off your course!*
> *You can't stick him!*
> *You will never prick him!*
> *You're no match for*
> *Timness at its source---"*

Coming to the pockmarked center of the bridge, he stopped suddenly, looking down to the right, near the edge...Snash saw an arrow stick in Tim's hat-brim, and another catch in his sleeve up by the shoulder. Nearer to hand, Glargle jumped as a dart landed near him, striking fire from the pavement, and another sliced Snash's thigh.

But Bimbottom got back to his antics right pronto, and

the arrows started veering away once more…Tim pointed to what he'd seen, then went on a little way.

The others came up. Some of the gouges the hellrogs had made were quite deep; at the bottom of one, looking smudgier and bloodier than ever, Slippriman was sprawled. Snash guessed that a whirling mace had clipped him, or that Greydolf, in all his runnings and blastings-about, had accidentally knocked him in.

At any rate, Slippriman was stirring now, and Dwimli and Tharathorn went down to help him up. Slippriman was acting woozy as they climbed out of the hole, but when he reached the top, he shot Snash a glance that was shocking in the crystal clarity of its malice; putting his back to the runt--- Snash was between him and the edge of the bridge--- he reeled and stumbled backwards, tipping the little yark.

Luckily, Slagbag was close enough to shoot out a claw, and pulled Snash back. Settling on his feet, Snash eyed Luvliel, wondering what she'd made of all that…she sure looked mighty suspicious, but before she could say anything, Slippriman, still staggering a bit for appearance sake, pre-empted her, shouting to be heard over Bimbottom:

"Where's Greydolf, by the way?"

It was an excellent ploy, quite enough to put her off her stride. She drew a deep breath, said: "The last hellrog---"

Her voice trailed away.

"I see," said Slippriman, with the most awful expression of phony sadness…Snash wanted to hurl himself at the wizard, but Slippriman, as though sensing his thoughts, looked at him as though he'd like nothing better, and Snash held himself in check.

"Well," the mage went on, "Old Tim will more than take up the slack….shouldn't we be leaving?"

Luvliel nodded, wiping her eyes.

There was a gate on the Spike side, and after the ogres had all taken their headers off the bridge, the valves had been closed, but they weren't equal to Bimbottom, who posed and sang and sillied at them till they slumped and softened, tearing free of their hinges, sagging inwards like limp rags; when he led his friends over them, their feet *squished* in the mushified steel.

Swiftly the company passed along the corridor, and everyone who made the mistake of getting in their way got swept up the passage by Old Tim and ended by jumping into the Spike's throat; when he emerged onto the landing, it was quite clear, and the stairs were too, at least for some distance, both ways...Looking down from the platform, Snash could see Tim's victims, hundreds of tiny dark figures, against the lava-glow, falling and falling *and* falling, getting tinier all the time. About a half-mile down there was a long winding column of troops, which appeared to reach all the way into the volcano, but it seemed to have stopped dead...Snash could just guess what they thought of that rain of bodies dropping past them.

Tharathorn, Rondlefrond, and Luvliel were all looking down too; presently Snash heard sounds very like those of oaken-feet coming up behind him, and lifted his chin to see Oakenchin leaning over him, taking a brief peek into the depths before he leaned back.

"Here's where we must part," said Luvliel to the tree-honcho. He sighed a deep hollow sigh, and said: "Really would like to head on up with you, but...We *do* need to plant all those acorns, so---"

He beckoned the oakenwives. As they came up, Luvliel said:

"Ladies, do you think you could accomodate the yarkettes in your pouches?"

"Why would we want to?" Lissomleg asked.

"Because there are only ten in the whole world, and if yarks could make *babies*, everything would be a whole lot nicer."

Lissomleg said: "Our main pouches are pretty full of acorns right now, but..."

"But?"

"There are always our auxiliary pouches---"

"Hey!" Snashetta cried.

"Yes?" Luvliel asked.

"Did it ever occur to you to ask *us*?"

"It's for your own good," said Luvliel.

"I want to go with Snash and *fight*."

But Nudzu said: "I hate to side with the aristocrat, but getting us out of here sounds like a good idea."

"Snash?" Luvliel asked.

He glanced at Snashetta, who shot him a really vehement look...while he was moved that she wanted to fight beside him, and didn't want her stuffed into a pouch against her will, he *really* didn't want to bring her on a no-doubt one-way trip up to tangle with Serpentar...

"Luvliel's right," he said.

Snashetta stamped her foot, fuming, though the other yarkettes were tucked in without any fuss...Lissomleg pocketted Snashetta.

But a moment later, a little black arm hooked over the top of the pouch, and up popped Snashetta's head; blowing blonde hair out of her mouth, she burned Snash that look again. Then Lissomleg pushed her back down, just before Oakenchin led his troop down the steps.

They didn't keep to the stairs long, however; to Snash's astonishment, they began to move from the steps to the curving wall, their rootlike toes digging into the cracks between stones; soon the whole lot of them were spiralling down at right angles to the wall, about eight feet above the steps, branches swaying, arms chugging at their sides; all of them had powerful voices, and they began rooting and tooting and booming an extremely martial-sounding song that Snash much preferred to Bimbottom's material, and the words, when they started, went like this:

> *"Although we are trees*
> *We can go where we please,*
> *And march along walls*
> *With the greatest of ease!*
> *Our wrath is white hot*
> *And our cause is most just*
> *From this horrible place*
> *We will bust out or bust!"*

"Farewell!" cried Luvliel, waving a diaphanous fay-hanky. "And may you find an ideal spot for each and every

362

acorn, sufficiently watered and well lit---"

"Are you *quite* done?" Slippriman asked.

"They're my beloved friends," said Luvliel.

"But are you *done?*"

"Somevun kill him," said Glargle.

"Would you like to try?" Slippriman sneered.

"Not right ziss moment," Glargle answered.

"What about you, Princess?" Slippriman asked.

"You haven't had due process," she replied. "And in truth, we need you..."

"He's going to stab us in the back," said Slagbag. "He let Greydolf take on those hellrogs all alone, what do you bet---"

But at that, Bimbottom, who'd been striking a series of impatient poses all during this exchange---it occurred to Snash that no one had explained anything about Slippriman to him---cleared his throat, and Snash cringed, expecting yet another musical interlude.

But Slippriman merely answered: "Quite right, Tim," and Bimbottom held off, for the moment at least, to Snash's very great relief.

"Up we go," said Rondlefrond.

Chapter 19: Dancing with Serpentar

Way down in the shaft, the bodies had stopped raining past the ogres, eastrons and southerlings in the column that had halted; I and E officers were haranguing the regular officers to get everyone moving again.

But more movement was not to be, at least not upward...something mystifyingly and intimidatingly musical was approaching from above, along the wall of the chimney, just above the stairs, and it occasioned much discussion. The closest thing to a concensus was that the prodigy was hard to make sense of...the notion that it was some sort of giant furry caterpillar, which enjoyed a very brief vogue, was advanced by certain eastrons. By the time the phenomenon got close enough for the guys in front to realize that it was a file of grinning, rooting-tooting tree-people walking at right angles to the walls, fists pumping furiously at their sides, it was already too late, not that comprehension would've provided any protection...Showers of arrows weren't much help either, and as for axes and swords and spears, well...

Swinging his long arms, enjoying himself royally, Oakenchin whisked the full first fifth of the enemy column off the steps before he decided to catch a breather and head to the back of the oakenfolk line....taking his place, Lissomleg did terrible execution as well, followed by Toothesometrunk and a few of the rest, but the stairs were cleared before everyone could get in on the action.

The tree-people did, however, come to a great adjoining corridor which gave every sign of being a main route to the outside, and once they proceeded along that, more opposition did materialize, and there were enemies to spare, men and ogres again. But getting through them on the flat was a slog, not at all like chugging down the side of the shaft and brushing foes away like they were gnats.

"What if," panted Lissomleg during a respite, "we look outside and see Serpentar's army coming for us?"

"We head straight at them," Oakenchin said.

"There might be too many."

"Then we better hope the Gauntlet goes into the fire. If the tower falls, that army will scatter."

"I don't know," she replied. "Even though fighting our way out is plainly the thing to do, I fear we might never mingle our branches again---" She looked at him longingly.

"We'll just have to wait and see," he replied.

"No," she said, coming towards him. "Here we are, in the middle of this nice respite..."

He fended her back. "What if they come at us again, when we're scooping up all the acorns?"

"You're right," she said. "Please forgive me---" Suddenly something seemed to occur to her, and she opened her auxiliary pouch and looked down into it.

"What's wrong?" Oakenchin asked.

"That little yarkette, she's gone---"

"Oh my. When was the last time you noticed her in there?"

"Just before we started down---"

Lissomleg broke off; somewhere up the hall, an eastron yak-horn had sounded, and armored figures swarmed into the corridor from two sides...

As yet unstopped, the Bimbottom express continued up the steps, but as they neared Serpentar's landing, a mass of inspirational exhorters burst out of an arch below and came up at them shouting things like, "No You Won't!" and "Yes We Will!" but not doing too well on the steps because they were wasting their breath and wearing long leather coats; they were armed for the most part with shortswords and knives, and weren't very good fighters---Tharathorn, Dwimli and the yark defectors from the Spike killed them practically at will.

But there sure were a lot of the fanatics, and fresh ones kept tossing the wounded and the dead over the side and rushing to be killed, and to Snash, who was watching from above, it began to seem as though all of I and E must've been waiting in ambush---when Tharathorn's yarks began to go down, and it started to look as if the Thoon-to-be-Rethtored and the Dwelf-Lord might be got by and backstabbed, Slagbag tapped Snash and cried: "Let's kill some of those arseholes!" and down the two of them went.

It was all confusion and jolting and jostling and noise after that...Snash lost track of Slagbag, and found himself on Dwimli's right...stabbing underhand with his sword, he kept low, and Dwimli's axe kept sucking through the air, back and forth over his head, showering him with black I and E blood...the arseholes seemed to be concentrating entirely on Dwimli, and so Snash actually got to stab quite a few of them, and while in general he didn't much care for the idea of yarks slaughtering yarks, he really hated the slogan-spitters, and felt like he was truly accomplishing something.

One finally took notice of him, and slashed him across the cheek and the nose before one of Dwimli's strokes ripped into the brain's brain; Snash's eyes filled up with tears, and something struck him, and he fell backwards, blacking out for a moment.

When he came to, a sloganeer was sidestepping along the wall next to him. Seeing Snash looking at him, the fatskull started to bring a falchion down, screaming:

"Yes We Will!"

Then someone, a yark about Snash's size, answered: "No You Won't!" in a high-pitched voice and rushed down and chopped off the brain's forearm with a falchion of his own. The inspirational one howled and clutched at his stump, and right after that, Dwimli shut him up with a shot to the mouth, then returned to matters elsewhere...after a few more moments, the exhorters finally had enough, and faded back down the stairs.

Snash rose, looking at the runt who'd saved him. The fellow was unarmored save for a light leather helmet with eyeguards...in fact, he was clad in a coarse shift rather like Snashetta's, and seemed to have breasts...Snash tried to tilt the mask up, but the helmet was strapped on, and the other runt slapped his hand away, then uncinched the buckle and took the helmet off. Sweaty but still unmistakably blonde, Snashetta's locks were plastered to her scalp.

"What are you doing here?" Snash cried.

"Couldn't stand that pouch," Snashetta said. "I caught up with you fellows a while ago. One of the other runts leant me the helmet and the sword---"

"How come I didn't spot you?" he asked.

"You weren't looking the right way," she said.

He considered this...all the action *had* been upfront with Bimbottom, and Snash *had* been trying to keep an eye on Slippriman...indeed he'd been looking uphill almost the whole way.

"You should've stayed in your pouch," he said. "If this tower collapses, we're all going to die."

"I don't care," she said. "I've spent my whole life locked up and doing calisthenics---"

"What?"

"Exercises. And I want to vent my frustrations, and die with you."

"You don't even know me---"

"Yeah, but I really like what I see---"

"*Kommt, kommt,* you two qveers," cried Glargle from above. "Leavingk, leavingk."

Snash reached out and squeezed Snashetta's claw. Then they followed Glargle up the steps.

When Bimbottom reached Serpentar's landing, the ogres who stood in front of the great thorn-gate impaled themselves on the spines after a brief dose of his medicine---Snash didn't actually see them do it, but Bimbottom didn't sing for long, and when the runt came up onto the platform, they were hanging limply.

Old Tim wasted no time in dealing with the gate itself after that, and he sang and pranced until the thorns drooped, and the ogres slipped off, and the snakes inside slid halfway out onto the floor, then stopped...at last, the whole barrier just dropped away from whatever was holding it up, collapsing into a low soggy rampart across the threshold, like a wall of limp noodles---Snash was familiar with noodles, having had them several times during his sojourn at Overflowing Fist.

Ahead lay the corridor with the thorn-walls and even more snakes, but Bimbottom just bounded across the deflated gate and went dancing along; steel snakes struck at him from the sides, but he kept singing, arms going everywhere at once, so much so that it began to seem to Snash that he had a lot more than two. Each time a snake-head darted near, Tim flicked it with a finger, the serpent dropped, and not a one managed to hamper his progress, the corridor echoing with his song:

> *"Beptiles! Feptiles!*
> *Wicked metal reptiles!*
> *Tim just flicks them*
> *Smartly on the nose.*
> *Snakes now! Sakes now!*
> *Doing what it takes now!*
> *Tim will teach them*
> *Being bad just blows!"*

And while all this was going on, the thorns to right and left were slumping, sagging to the floor, splaying out, once again like overcooked pasta, over the fallen snakes. Standing beside Luvliel with Snashetta, Snash watched from the threshold, thinking:

We're going to win…

He regretted the thought almost instantly however, because what happened next followed so hard upon it that he couldn't help but think he had jinxed himself, and everyone else for that matter….Glargle went: *"Scheiss!"* and Tharathorn cried: "There!" and Rondlefrond shouted: "Ware, hellrogs!" and Snash looked to see Serpentar's last five, wingless now, coming down from the sharkrider aerie, armed with swords that looked a whole lot more functional than those morning-stars they'd been swinging when they'd destroyed those load-bearing members.

Snash glanced back at Bimbottom, but Tim seemed unaware that anything was happening…the next thing Snash knew, Luvliel was racing towards the stairs, gesturing and chanting for all she was worth. The steps exploded with color, dozens of flowers, but not little ones like Snash had seen so far---these were *huge*, wide and yellow on thick dark stalks, and the hellrogs *really* had to work to send the nodding blossoms flying, roaring out curses that were sulphurous (even by the standards of Mount Adamant) as they chopped two-handed.

In spite of all that sound and fury, Snash's attention was drawn to something flying down into the chimney, wings beating as it descended...his first thought was that it was some kind of giant vulture, but then he decided it didn't look exactly like a buzzard...as it dropped lower and lower, he decided the word *eagle*, which he'd never had cause to apply to anything before, had best be applied now.

But when he saw who the bird's rider was, the whole nomenclature question was driven from his mind. Sitting on the avian's back, steadily if problematically, was none other than---

Greydolf!

And all in white too!

"There he ith, unlooked for!" cried Tharathorn.

"And on an eagle!" cried Rondlefrond.

"Yippee!" cried Dwimli, and ripped some more hair out of his beard, this time for joy, apparently.

Greydolf waved, then swung the eagle towards the hellrogs, who were still trying to hack their way through the flowers; extending his sword, he began to blast the demons in all sorts of ways. Snash cheered as one hellrog fell into the shaft missing an arm, then cheered again as another rocked against the wall of the stairwell with its head half knocked off.

But the runt's exultation suddenly turned to dread when the last three, in their desperation, hacked through the remaining flowers and came plowing down onto the landing, Greydolf pummelling them from above and behind.

Luvliel flung herself to one side, dodging the stroke of a giant sword; Rondlefrond wasn't so lucky, and was sheared in two from shoulder to hip. The ling-lings went into the chimney all in one stack, and Mnildor got tacked down right in front of Snash, who managed to slip between a hellrog's legs...everyone was running all over the platform, trying to avoid being creamed. Greydolf blasted a hellrog down, and Slagbag ran up to the devil and hacked him in the head where he lay, splitting his skull open before retreating with a yell as he was splattered with burning drops.

Two of the hellrogs managed to reach the arch, and there they turned at bay. Tharathorn rushed in close and chopped one in the ankle, and it began to hop on one foot; Greydolf's eagle flew in over the landing, and the wizard began discharging burst after burst of blue force into the other devil.

Snash looked about wildly for Snashetta...she was running towards him. But suddenly she stopped, glancing off to the side---

Slippriman stepped in front of her.

Grinning hideously at Snash, the wizard raised a bony hand and seemed to be getting set to do some discharging of his own. Wincing in anticipation of the shock, Snash put a hand up over his face---

Then saw, between his fingers, Snashetta run round from behind and sink her fangs in Slippriman's thigh.

Slippriman lowered his arm and looked down at her as though he couldn't believe what he was seeing; then, snarling, he aimed his palm at her, and her features went grey-blue as his hand began to glow.

Snash howled and sprang at him, tried to stab him in the chest. Slippriman brushed him aside with a sweep of his arm, and Snash landed hard, but he was up in a moment...Snashetta had let go of Slippriman's leg and was back behind him now, the wizard twisting to try and see where she'd gone...Snash still had the sword and went for him again, this time slashing his leg, then his arm, before he suddenly found himself with Slippriman's hand glowing point-blank in his face.

"Slippriman!" came Greydolf's voice.

Slippriman put his hand behind his back and toed the floor.

"He was going to blast Snash!" Snashetta cried.

Greydolf's eagle landed...Snash glanced over at the gate, saw that the hellrogs had been most decisively put down. Coming out from behind Slippriman, Snashetta took Snash's hand.

Greydolf dismounted, asking: "*Why* were you going to

371

blast Snash, Slippriman?"

"What's one runt between angels?" Slippriman replied.

"Somevun *kill* him!" Glargle shouted.

Slippriman whipped his hand out from behind his back, snapped off a blast. But Glargle had already leaped into the air, and the impact struck the floor.

"Stop it, brother," Greydolf said.

"Why?" Slippriman demanded. "What *will* you do?"

Greydolf said nothing.

"Face it," said Slippriman. "I'm with you for the long haul. You need me---"

Snash heard a thud.

Slippriman went up on his toes and gasped...there was another thud and he coughed out a bolt of blood, then fell on his face, two great dark stains merging in the filthy cloth on his back.

The topspike of his axe dripping, Slagbag was standing over him.

"That wasn't nice!" cried Luvliel.

"Sorry, My Lady," Slagbag said. "But I'm just a yark, so forgive me. Had to be done."

Greydolf told Luvliel: "When I was fighting the hellrogs on the bridge, Slippriman just stood back."

Snash went over to them. "I told you. He was a traitor."

Luvliel nodded.

"Didn't you *die?*" Snash asked Greydolf.

"Fell two thousand feet and landed on a *very* sharp tower-top," Greydolf replied. "But I'm back now."

"Why?"

"My mission wasn't finished. So the All-Father pried me up off that point, restored my life, dressed me in white, sent me an eagle while I was hovering *above* the point, and, well...here I am. Are you complaining?"

"No, not at all," said Snash.

"I'm called Whitedolf now, by the way. Whitedolf the--
_"

"White?"

"Yes."

372

"Hadn't we better catch up to Tim?" asked Dwimli.

"Good thinking," said Whitedolf.

They mushed through the limp thorns across the threshold, and between the ones in the corridor; Snash could see Bimbottom up ahead in the chief of staff's chamber, up on one boot-tip but leaning over parallel to the floor with both hands under his chin, going serenely round and round, as though he were being turned by an invisible hand.

"Where's Serpentar's sanctum?" Whitedolf asked Snash.

"I'm not sure what you mean," Snash replied.

"The place we're likely to find him."

"Well, there's a big snake-head that opens its mouth, and if you go through that---"

He broke off as Whitedolf's eagle, whom they'd left behind on the landing, began squawking furiously...everyone turned. Tharathorn, Dwimli, and Tharathorn's yarks were between Snash and the eagle, but the bird was hopping way up into view, pointing with a wing and carrying on. Whitedolf translated breathlessly:

"He says watch out, he's not in there, he's out here."

"He who?" Tharathorn asked. "Ith he referring to himthelf?"

The eagle gave one last *aaawwk!* and flapped up out of sight; but then the darkness beyond the arch went suddenly orange, and Snash saw the bird, or what he *guessed* was the bird, drop back down, charred black and trailing smoke.

That orange glare was still illuminating the landing, coming from off to the left, and getting brighter all the time. Tharathorn's yarks came running past Snash, Tharathorn himself and Dwimli held their ground.

"*Auf wiedersehen!*"cried Glargle,somewhere behind Snash---the runt heard palms and flat feet slapping away into the distance.

"I guess we'll find out now," said Slagbag beside Snash.

"What?" Snash asked.

"If you really are Hrag Urshathur."

Snash sure didn't feel like it at the moment---he seemed to be pure terror, through and through. Under his breath he began:

"*Gott mit---*"

Then faltered as Serpentar, absolutely incandescent, came round the corner, up off the floor, eye blazing white, Dwimli and Tharathorn going black against his light. On either side, the deflated thorns and snakes withered utterly,shrivelled by his heat---Snash could already feel it.

"Really," said Whitedolf, "I was expecting him to wait in his sanctum."

Dwimli and Tharathorn were backing up; why they didn't just flee, Snash surely didn't know---perhaps they hadn't realized how fast Serpentar was coming. But when finally they did indeed turn, Dwimli's beard was burning, and so was Tharathorn's hair; they took a couple of steps, their backs going up in flames, and almost as though they'd decided they were going to be consumed and there was no point in running, they stopped once more and turned again, a human torch and a dwelfish one; Snash heard them howling as they struck out with sword and axe, but Serpentar made no effort to avoid the blows, the blades melting as they struck him...as he passed between the two heroes, they simply collapsed into embers.

It occurred to Snash that Tharathorn would not be rethtored anytime thoon.

What are you waiting for? the runt asked himself; he noticed that even Whitedolf had decamped, and was racing after the others, into the Chief of Staff's chamber.

But one figure was bouncing and tiptoeing the other way, Old Tim, no surprise; feeling as though a wall of heat was thrusting him up the hall, Snash raced by Bimbottom, joining Snashetta in the chamber, Luvliel and Whitedolf nearby, all of them watching as Tim went to meet Serpentar, singing:

"*You should desist*
Dad above is so pissed.
Brother mine,
You're very very bad.
Gott's *not* mit *you.*

Sent me here to hit you.
You have made Him
Very very sad."

"Brother mine?" Snash asked Whitedolf.

"Yes," the wizard replied. "The Bimbottom Brothers. Fraternal twins in the mind of the All-Father."

"Serpentar *Bimbottom*?" Snash asked.

To his amazement, the Yark Lord and Master of Tenebria blazed hotter and *responded*, bellowing: "Tis a lie!".

Tim halted, but still he sang:

"Don't deny it!
Shouldn't even try it!
That's your name and
We both know it's true. .
Might be goofy
Maybe even poofy
But tough luck
Bimbottom *goes with You!"*

Snash still didn't buy it, not that it mattered. Serpentar had him feeling like a brick in a kiln; heat rippling his image from head to foot, Bimbottom began to caper most maniacally, making him seem even more hallucinatory than ever.

As for the Yark Lord, he'd stopped, a mere inch or two off the floor, very close to Tim, as though he was inviting his sibling to do his worst. Tim danced round and round him, getting stranger by the moment, but Serpentar only said:

"Think thou to cow me with thy antics, clown? I wot them well. Like them I did never. But frighten me they did not."

And with that he began to turn slowly, following his brother's movements, staying face to face with him, or rather, eye to face, the serpents that comprised his head retracting from the eye-cavity and forming that terrible hood behind the hovering white hot orb with its squirming pupil…lengthening, they swayed and struck, driving into Tim in spurts of flame; Serpentar began to wave his arms in a right snaky way as well, and fire burst from his gauntlet and his naked hand (rather less from the latter), the flames shooting into his sib's ears from either side.

But Tim kept dancing, and started singing once more, in the most absurd-sounding tongue yet; his arms were going everywhere again, and seemed to multiply, and suddenly Snash realized that he was *indeed* looking at literally dozens of actual limbs, all whipping and being right snaky themselves. Watching Tim and Serpentar having it out, Snash was finally convinced that they were brothers, embodiments of a terrible liberty, freedom gone bad and freedom gone, if not good, then sideways. Even though he was still singing, somehow, Tim was also playing a flute now, and a trumpet, and banging away with cymbals, and plucking away madly on several stringed instruments, never flinching or pausing as his brother's snakes, writhing and striking in time to the music, darted into his flesh again and again. Tim seemed to be getting bigger, and Snash couldn't see any wounds or burns; more heartening still, Serpentar's light was definitely fading, and even though Snash continued to think of himself as a brick in a kiln, the comparison was seeming less apt.

Tim's doing it, he told himself. *He's going to drain every last bit of heat from---*

Tim fell silent and stopped.

Jinxed 'im, Snash told himself.

All of Tim's arms but the original two disappeared. He stood tottering, still face to eye with Serpentar. Admittedly, the Yark Lord seemed a good two-thirds less fiery, and was unsteady too.

But Tim's silence and stillness just didn't bode well...

"I think," said Serpentar, "that I've more left than thee."

And with that, he thrust his arm out, gauntlet driving into Tim's chest with a dull *pulk!* that was most evocative of something penetrating something called Bimbottom.

A big smile still on his shiny red mug, Tim started another verse:

> *"Oh well, truth to tell,*
> *Tim's not feelin' swell now---"*

But that was as far as he got before his body swelled and burst, the flaps and straps and shreds flying out from under his head, which dropped out from under his hat, which hung in air for a moment or two before dropping back onto his head, which had landed upright. Wiping a bit of Tim from his still-stinging cheek, Snash thought:

We're cooked.

Most unexpectedly, Serpentar began to dance, mimicking his brother's movements with awful accuracy and doing the most precise imitation of Tim's voice as he sang:

"Yark Lord's popped him.
Seems to have stopped him.
Tim's fat head is lying on the floor.
Got no gut now.
Chest or legs or butt now.
Yark Lord's gloating
Couldn't ask for more!"

He lit just long enough to kick Tim's head way off to Snash's right, then levitated again and asked Whitedolf:

"And what shall be left of *thee?* Most flammable thou look, with thy wondrous hair and beard, and flowing robes and cape---"

With that, he discharged a great blast of fire---

At Luvliel.

She raised another of her invisible shields, but a lot of the flame, striking the curving unseen surface, splashed off to the sides, burned two of the yark defectors right down to the bones. There weren't many of those blokes left.

But to Snash's amazement, they *all* rushed towards Serpentar, even the burning ones, as though they'd already agreed on one last vainglorious gesture. Snash shouted and almost joined them---

Before he saw what happened, which was *damn* gruesome.

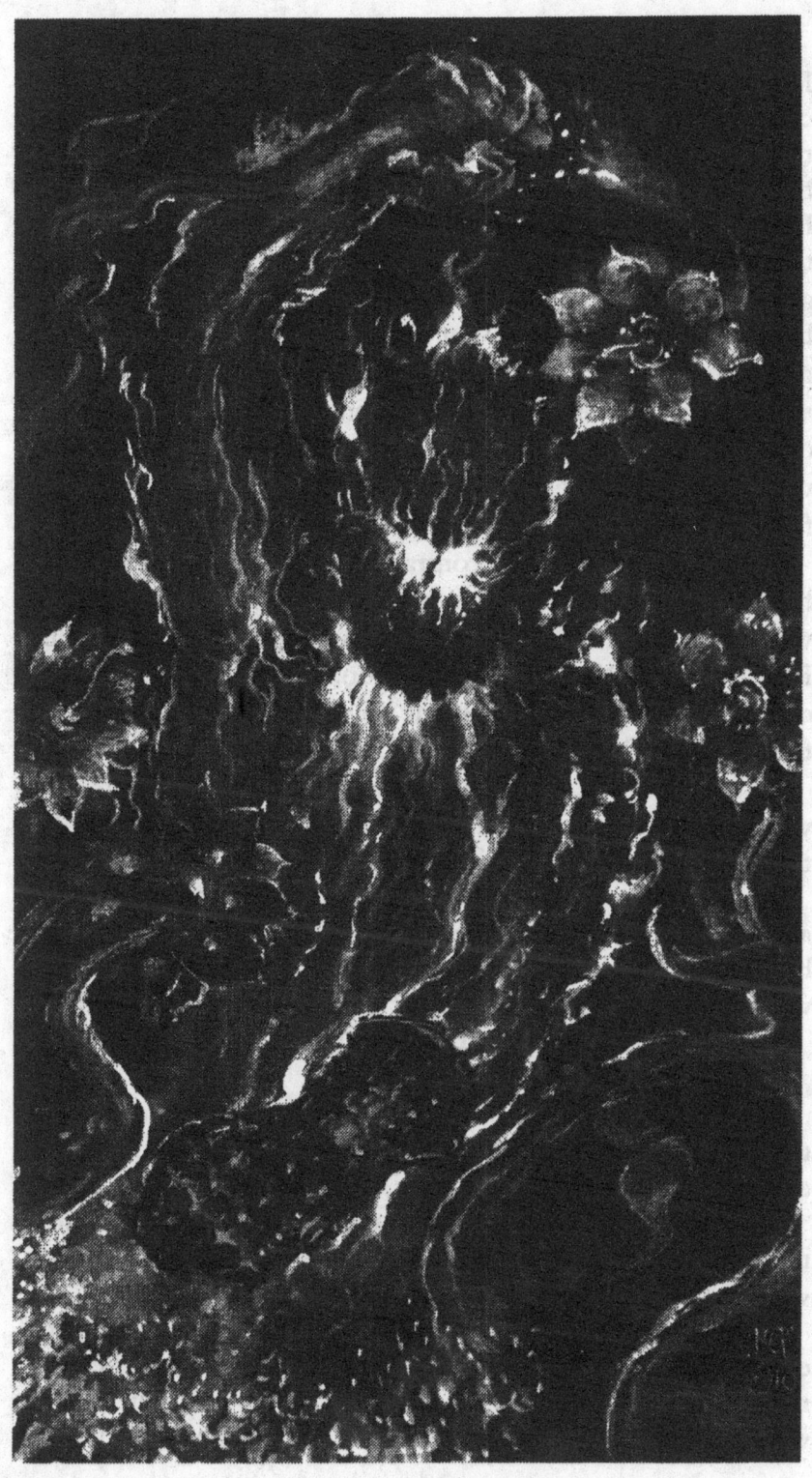

Still, they'd bought some time for Whitedolf and Luvliel, who'd gone over onto the offensive; down from the ceiling screamed a white whirlwind, which swept round and round Serpentar; Snash guessed that was Whitedolf's work, because the other bit, involving flowers as it did, had to be Luvliel's---up from the floor the blossoms grew, trying to twine themselves around Serpentar's legs, white icy flowers on thick gelid stems. Despite the cold wind, Serpentar melted them before they got too high; but more sprang out of the floor all the time, and even through the white vapor, Snash could see that Serpentar's red was fading even farther. Heat was flying out of him; with his hood opened, the interior of the furnace was exposed...suddenly the hood-snakes darted for cover, re-forming his head.

As the radiant fan contracted, Snash glimpsed someone beyond Serpentar, and when he realized it was Slippriman, he was startled, considering those holes Slagbag had put in him. But if Whitedolf was any indication, wizards just didn't stay down, and right at that moment it was a good thing, maybe, if the erstwhile Dun Wanderer and Luvliel had some help...

Slippriman's mouth was going, and one of his arms went up as he---apparently---added his magic to Whitedolf's, the cold wind getting manifestly whiter and faster.

Serpentar's arms and snakes drooped, and he drew his arms in...the flowers seemed to be getting some purchase on him. Beyond all hope, Snash began to wonder if Luvliel and the wizards were about to finish what Tim had started---

Then caught himself...

Will you never learn?

With a great *crack*! Serpentar snapped his fists back out, the flowers all broke off, and he sent two orange bolts flying, one from his eye and one from his gauntlet

The first smashed into Luvliel's shield, not penetrating it, but driving her, shield and all, way back across the floor, where she slammed into the wall and crumpled.

Yet the bolt from the gage, aimed at Whitedolf, was even more potent. He had a shield too, but the strike went right through that, and if he didn't fly so far as Luvliel---there was something about the way he took the impact that made him seem much *heavier*--- he still fell blackened and smoking onto his back, a great rent blown open in his chest.

It sure looked to Snash as if Whitedolf was badly in need of another resurrection.

The Prying Eye turned towards the runt, but only for an instant; behind Serpentar, Slippriman had begun blasting away, and the Yark Lord, visibly much cooled, but with no apparent urgency, turned.

Immediately Slagbag hurled himself at the Yark Lord and drove his axe well into his back, the blade slipping between snakes and sticking, but just for a moment, because there was still enough heat left in Serpentar to melt the head right off the weapon; Serpentar twisted, caught him with an iron elbow; Snash heard a sizzling thud, and Slagbag went spinning aside, clutching his shoulder, steam rising from between his fingers. Serpentar returned his attention to Slippriman.

The wizard was hammering him with frozen blasts now, but Serpentar seemed willing to take them for a few moments...he began to draw his arms in again, and Snash knew more bolts were in the offing. Slippriman managed to shield himself before they came, but even though they were plainly *much* weaker and much less orange than that last brace, they still put him down--- he wasn't opened up like Whitedolf, but Snash thought he might be dead at last.

Serpentar wasn't taking chances, however. He raised his gauntlet, and Slippriman lifted limply from the floor, limbs hanging. When the Yark Lord flung his hand back down, dashing the limp form against the shiny black stone, Slippriman seemed absolutely inert.

Still that wasn't good enough for the Master of Tenebria; he raised Slippriman to a greater height, dashed him down again---

Just as Glargle, carrying a pair of tongs which he'd gotten from *Gott* knew vhere, rushed in from the side and, easy as you please, plucked the Gauntlet off him.

Serpentar clanged to the floor.

"*Liebchen*!" Glargle cried. "*Ach, mein liebchen*!"

And with that, he ran off cackling, backwards, towards the hall, with the gauntlet trailing on the floor, still clutched in his tongs.

Serpentar hunched his head and shoulders, shook his head incredulously, and then, feet clanking, cooled snakes grating harshly against each other, lit off after him, passing Slippriman's motionless form.

But the ostensible corpse had only been biding his time; he got back up and lit out too, still pretty fast despite the abuse he'd taken, after Serpentar.

Snash looked for Snashetta, and when he didn't spot her immediately, he thought maybe she'd joined those other yarks in that mad charge, and had been burned up...admittedly, he hadn't *seen* her do it, but...

"Snash," she said.

He whirled.

She'd simply been behind him. Relief rushed through him.

Slagbag was picking up a scimitar that one of the dead yarks had dropped. Luvliel was stirring...Snash wanted to run to her side, but...he'd already wasted too much time being frantic over Snashetta. He couldn't let Serpentar get the gauntlet back; before he even realized it, he was running along the hall, Snashetta and Slagbag hard behind.

He almost caught up with Slippriman before the wizard reached the landing. Then both of them stopped dead. Looking past the wizard, Snash could see Glargle at the edge of the platform, holding the gauntlet out over the shaft with his tongs, Serpentar perhaps three yards away, watching.

"Vun shtep closer," said Glargle, "And ze *Liebchen* goes bye-bye."

"Thou wouldst not," answered Serpentar.

"*Nein?*"

"I see it in thine eyes."

"Ach, bull*scheiss*, how can du see anysing *mit* zat hole in your face---"

"I'll make thee another gage."

"Vant *ziss* vun!" Glargle insisted.

"Yet thou wouldst destroy it?" Serpentar edged nearer, cooled metal squealing.

But Glargle only thrust the gauntlet out farther, saying:

"Glargle vill die *mit* his *Liebchen*."

Serpentar remained where he was.

All the while this had been playing out, Slippriman had been creeping closer to Serpentar....Snash hadn't a clue how Slippriman planned to get the gauntlet, although it was pretty plain the wizard was refraining from magic because he didn't want to knock Serpentar into Glargle and thus send the gage into the fire...Snash had already considered trying to push Slippriman into Serpentar himself, and had dismissed the idea for the same reason.

But, he thought suddenly to himself, *what if Glargle ducked out of the way?*

Snash leaned out from behind Slippriman, caught Glargle's attention, waved sideways until Glargle started to move; then the runt rushed forward, slamming his shoulder into Slippriman's behind, which probably wouldn't have been enough---

If Slagbag hadn't rushed up at the same time and given the wizard a big shove between the shoulders.

Slippriman jolted forward onto Serpentar, who didn't budge at all, but Slippriman's arms whipped round the Yark Lord at the impact, and there was a frightful sizzling sound, and Slippriman howled in agony, steam jetting out from between him and Serpentar wherever he wasn't pressed flush. Stumbling sidewards, Snash saw that Slippriman's cheek was stuck against Serpentar's head, which in spite of everything remained pretty effing hot...Slippriman's eyes bugged and rolled wildly, and his mouth, lips writhing, was way open, pouring out more of that howl...As much as he hated the venomous old horror, Snash had to look away.

Gauntlet still tonged, Glargle was scampering up the steps towards the sharkriders' aerie, and Slagbag was hard behind...Snashetta seized Snash's wrist, dragging him towards the stairs. When they reached the foot of the stair, he pulled free and looked back.

Still stuck to Serpentar, Slippriman, shrieking and struggling, was completely alight...the Yark Lord had managed to pry the wizard's arms away from his sides, although now...they were stuck to his hands.

"Snash!" Snashetta cried---she was already well up the steps, and he raced after her.

When he got to the top, he saw Slagbag chasing Glargle around...still holding the gauntlet by the tongs, the gremlin kept giving the bull the slip, as Slagbag cried repeatedly, "You have to throw it in!" and Glargle answered, "Snash ze Boss! Say Glargle keep ze *Liebchen!*"

Snash and Snashetta ran up, got Glargle between themselves and Slagbag.

"We have to destroy it!" Snash cried.

"*Ve?*" Glargle cried. "*Ve* don't have it! *Glargle* does! And Glargle's keeping it."

Snash looked back towards the stairs.

Oily black smoke was billowing up.

"Glargle's *not* going to keep it!" Slagbag cried.

"*Vill!*" Glargle cried.

"Wait, wait!" Snash said. "What about that *other* gauntlet?"

"Uzzer?" Glargle asked. "Oh, *ja!*"

It was still hanging from his back in a sack.

"You vant?" he asked.

Snash started forward, but Glargle unslung the bag and hurled it; Snash caught it in midair.

"What are you going to do with that?" Slagbag asked.

"Watch," said Snash, then told Glargle: "Give me the tongs."

Glargle opened them, let Serpentar's gage drop, then scooted them to Snash...grabbing the spare gage with them (to make it look like he had the hot one) Snash ran off towards the Spike's gaping maw.

But he soon discovered that keeping the gauntlet locked between the pincers while he was running was no easy matter... had to appreciate Glargle's mastery of the technique, especially once the gauntlet slipped free, and Snash found himself kicking it across the stones...pausing, he almost picked it up with his right claw, then realized he might have an audience---

Which he did.

Off to the right, Serpentar was rising into view above the stairhead, framed by the blaze from Slippriman's body, which was *still* stuck to him; as he came over the top, Snash saw flaming fluid streaming down between the Yark Lord and the wizard, Slippriman's rendered fat. Feet clanging like hammers on an anvil, metal rubbing and screeching, Serpentar strode along beside the chimney-mouth, moving to cut Snash off as the runt snatched up the gauntlet with the tongs and raced forward once more...

Almost immediately, the gage slipped loose again, and again Snash kicked it. Spinning round and round, it got almost to the chimney-mouth before it halted. Dropping the tongs, Snash spurted forward as fast as he was able, glanced aside at Serpentar, saw him coming, stiffly but swiftly, marching towards the prize, drawing a black curtain of smoke around the rim of the yawning shaft, a trail of fallen-away Slippriman-pieces leading off beneath the smoke towards the stairs.

Don't look at him, you idiot, Snash told himself, locked his gaze back on the Gauntlet---

And halted, because Serpentar had already gotten where they were both going. Bending forward, the Yark Lord reached out for the gauntlet. But---

It seemed as though he'd forgotten that he had Slippriman's wrist stuck to his palm, and he pawed the Gauntlet with Slippriman's burning hand before he appeared to realize his predicament...furiously he began scraping wizard-stuff off on his other arm.

Snash readied himself for a spring, thought he'd try to hurl himself forward onto his belly, shoot under Serpentar's hand through all the burning Slippriman-bits that were falling to the flags, and try to knock the gauntlet over the edge.

But almost as though Serpentar were aware of his thoughts, the Prying Eye turned Snash's way, and the runt hesitated, even stepped back a pace...Serpentar kept staring at him, even as he continued scraping Slippriman off.

Something drew Snash's attention, off on the fringe of sight, big and Slagbaglike, speeding towards the Yark Lord and not being too quiet about it. Serpentar's wiggling serpent-pupil shifted farther to the side---

"*Bimbottom!*" Snash cried.

The Eye contracted; the pupil shifted back and got shorter.

"You *are* a Bimbottom, aren't you?" Snash asked.

"I am a thing unto myself," Serpentar said, working away madly. "I have no brother, as I had no father. I am uncreated. The Inevitable Inexorable---"

"Well," said Snash, as Slagbag closed in, "I'm Hrag Urshathur---"

Lashing out with his scimitar, Slagbag sliced through Slippriman's neck, sending his burning skull flying before the edge clanged into the back of Serpentar's head and bounced off.

The Yark Lord straightened...seeing his chance, Snash spurted forward, and kicked the gauntlet over the edge, crying:

"Ha!"

Roaring, Serpentar hurled himself out into space, Slippriman's beheaded remains still throwing out flames and greasy smoke on his back...Sailing through the air, he snatched the gage about eight feet out and jammed it on his right hand immediately, clearly in the expectation that it would restore his powers of flight.

And to Snash's profound horror, it seemed to.

Serpentar's descent halted immediately...his body swung upwards...he was facing away from Snash, but turned slowly round, the Slippriman-smoke going straight upwards now.

Snash was just about beside himself.

What is this? he thought. *The ghouls couldn't fly. They needed sharks to fly...*

He wondered desperately...would Serpentar stay up if he knew he'd been tricked?

"That's not your gauntlet," Snash cried.

Serpentar paused in midair, lifted the gage. The snake pupil fixed upon it. Then he let his hand drop, and glared at Snash.

"*Exorable!*" the runt cried.

And down the Yark Lord went, and down and down, Slippriman going mostly to bits now, burning fragments and blackened bones spinning free...striking a bridge, Serpentar took a good part of the middle out of it, then went through another one farther below....

Snash realized Slagbag was standing next to him.

"Hrag Urshathur?" Slagbag said.

"Just said it to rattle him," said Snash.

Snashetta came up on his other side, asking:

"Where's Serpentar?"

"Can't see him any more," said Snash.

"If he lands in the lava," Snashetta said, "will it kill him? He's some kind of fire-devil, isn't he?"

"I suppose," said Snash, "But that lava's a lot hotter than he is, I think..."

He looked over at Glargle, who was capering around the Gauntlet of Dominion, reaching out to touch it every once and again, then snatching his hands back, as though it was still too hot.

"He's a happy fellow," said Slagbag.

"For a little while."

"The whole tower's going to come down, isn't it?" Snashetta asked.

"That's what I've heard," said Snash.

"We're going to die, right?"

He just had time for one nod before she flung herself against him and wrapped her arms round...feeling pretty awkward, not at all sure that returning the embrace was the right thing to do, he did so anyway, and enjoyed the clinch so much that he only remembered it wasn't going to last forever when the stone started trembling beneath his feet.

"Think he hit the soup," said Slagbag.

Suddenly Snash remembered Luvliel, detached himself from Snashetta, and ran towards the stairs, even though he guessed he couldn't accomplish anything...he was too small to carry her anyplace, and there was no place to carry her to; if indeed the Spike was about to collapse (and the tremors were worsening by the second) she was going to die just like everyone else in it.

He did, however, feel a tremendous surge of completely irrational relief when he saw her come running up onto the stairhead, holding Tim Bimbottom's head by the hair.

"My Lady!" Snash cried.

"What happened with Serpentar?" she asked.

"I tricked him," said Snash. "With the Shark Lord's gauntlet. I threw it into the shaft, and he jumped in after it---" His eyes strayed to Bimbottom's face, and damn if it didn't look like old Tim was conscious!

"I don't believe it," said Slagbag, somewhere behind Snash.

But Tim only replied:

"Wet me! Get me
In a pail of water
Bod will grow back
In a little bit.
I'll regain my
Kidneys and my bladder
And my butt so
I can take a..."

Snash missed whatever rhymed with *it*...a tremendous boom echoed out of the chimney and a great blossom of flame and smoke mushroomed up...fragments of masonry, chunks of bridge, perhaps, arced overhead, smashing down into the Gage Ghoul towers.

"I think," said Slagbag, "that we're not going to get the chance to water anyone's head---"

There were more explosions...dust puffed up between paving stones, some of which were beginning to tilt or fall in...vast dark billows boiled up to the east and west.

Snash welcomed Snashetta back into his arms.

Glargle crouched next to the *liebchen*, and looking at it rapturously said: "At least Glargle dies *mit* vun he luffs."

But Luvliel replied: "Maybe not."

And pointed.

Down came Whitedolf the White, on another eagle, unless that first one had been resurrected too...and hardly had the great bird landed when Carcharias and Carcharadon landed behind him, Bigmouth and four other sharks, many of them

sporting big bloody bandages (much the same way C and C were) circling overhead. Nobody had to tell anybody to get aboard; Luvliel climbed up behind Whitedolf, and Slagbag clambered up into Carcharadon's saddle; Snashetta went up Carcharias's chain like a shot, Snash following. Opening his saddle-bag, he uncinched buckles and hurled out a bunch of stuff to make room for the yarkette.

Just before he climbed in with her, though, he remembered Glargle, and saw the Gremlin down at the bottom of the chain, a most miserable expression on his face, his steaming hands stuck to Serpentar's gauntlet...there was no way he was going to get up a ladder.

Seemingly unaware of the problem, Carcharias bounded aloft.

"Glargle's still down there!" Snash shouted...by then there was so much rumbling that he really wasn't expecting Carcharias to hear, but the big shark circled swiftly round...Snash had a brief glimpse down the side of the tower, enough to see that the Spike had begun to sink into the crater, all the lesser encircling towers crumbling about its disintegrating base...

As the shark swung back in over the summit, Snash, hanging onto a strap and leaning far out from the saddlebag, saw Glargle hunched forlornly amid dozens of dust-spurts, paving-stones dropping out all around him...At Carcharias's approach, the gremlin turned and glanced up; Snash saw his mouth open. Then Carcharias passed over, and Snash's view was cut off, although he was pretty sure the shark must've grabbed Glargle with one of his foreclaws.

Carcharias climbed up towards the fume-ceiling and halted just below it among the other sharks, who were hovering; he turned. With most of the dust blowing off to the southeast, Snash could see that the crater-rim on which the fortress had been built had developed a great circular crack, and was sinking steadily...even though what was left of the tower still retained its shape, a net of fine fissures, most numerous towards the bottom, had spread up through the black stonework, all of them puffing out dust. Some of the outlying towers still remained intact, but that didn't last long;

the slope was obviously shaking so hard beneath them that they began to sink down as well, looking almost as though they were falling into holes of their own until the bits of them went rushing down the mountain-side in great smoking avalanches. Dust was shooting up everywhere, drifting southward on the wind; still keeping its outline, particularly towards the top, the spike was halfway down into the crater now, a vast shadow descending amid the clouds. Just at the end, it began to tilt eastward, losing all its form as the fragments of it crashed down onto the mountain's slope, below the new and wider rim…the dust reddened, and out of the volcano, up through the miasma, burst a titanic fountain of lava.

As for Serpentar's army, it had only closed about half the distance to the tower, and as far as Snash could tell, it had stopped; there were many columns and formations, and some appeared to be scattering, particularly those at the front, little dark specks fleeing north and south…

Whitedolf's eagle flapped up beside Carcharias and floated on the wind.

"Might as well head on down, yes?" Whitedolf cried.

Carcharias nodded, and down they all glided…Spotting an incongruous something that looked like a small patch of forest some ways from the foot of the mountains, Snash guessed it must be the Oakenfolks, and that turned out to be exactly the case, the eagle and sharks putting down directly in front of them….freed from the oakenwives' pouches, nine yarkettes stepped out from under the woody eaves, Nudzu in the lead. As Slagbag leaped down from Carcharadon, she opened her arms wide, he ran right in between, and Snash thought he did a pretty fair imitation of his own clinch with Snashetta up on top of the Spike…The runt and *his* squeeze clambered to the ground.

Glargle was squatting under Carcharias's wing, hands still glued to the Gauntlet, although there was much less steam; Snash guessed the gage must've been cooled quite a bit by the air passing under the shark.

"Dropped Glargle!" Glargle said. "Dropped him he

did, at the last moment, ach, sss, *scheiss!*"

Carcharias backed up a bit, and turned his head. "Maybe I *should've* landed on you, at that."

"*Nein, nein*," said Glargle. "Chust in pain, zat's all....deep down, Glargle is content. Has ze *Liebchen*, alzough he'd like it better if his hands veren't shtuck to it..."

Snash and Snashetta wandered over to Whitedolf and Luvliel, who'd just gotten down from the eagle.

"Why were you sent back this time?" Snash asked the wizard.

"I'm not quite sure," said Whitedolf. "To reassure everyone, Maybe? Dispense advice?"

"Did you speak with Rondlefrond and Tharathorn---"

"And Dwimli and the Ling-lings? Yes, briefly. They said to say hello."

"Is that the same eagle?" Snash asked.

"Yes," said Whitedolf. "His name's Thorondolf, which, roughly translated, means, 'Dolf-delivering eagle.' I've worked with him quite a bit..." He stroked the eagle's feathery leg. "Yes I have, haven't I boy?"

Thorondolf cawed.

"So then," said Whitedolf to Snash. "What went into the fire? The Gauntlet? Serpentar? Or both?"

"Serpentar," said Snash.

"And you made it happen?"

"I did."

Whitedolf smiled. "You just about make up for all the other yarks who ever lived."

Obviously, he meant it kindly, but Snash was stung. "It wasn't our fault."

"Excuse me," said Whitedolf, "truly, there were extenuating circumstances---"

He paused as a particularly hard tremor passed through the stony ground...the earth had been shaking on and off ever since everyone landed, but that last jolt was the first to feel genuinely threatening to Snash, and he looked past Whitedolf, up at the mountain.

The lava-fountain had subsided, but the great smokes boiling out now remained bloody. A brighter red appeared in

the midst of them, and Snash thought the fountain was shooting up again, before he detected a definite shape, almost like the top of a head; that collapsed, but another rose up again, getting higher before it too fell back in...each time it rose up or re-formed itself, the "head" got a bit higher, and began to manifest a blazing eyelike spot, about halfway up the "face."

"He's not dead, is he?" Snash asked Whitedolf. "That's *him*, isn't it?"

Whitedolf replied: "I must say, I wasn't expecting him back so soon."

"You came back real quick. Twice."

"I have a friend in a very high place---"

A thing like an immense orange hand had clamped over the rim of the crater, and another appeared to its left. Shoulders rose---or formed---beneath the head, which appeared to have achieved some kind of stability. Pushing down with its hands, a glowing lava-Serpentar thrust itself up from the depths, and Snash thought it must've been about as tall as the Spike had been, indeed much taller, given that it was standing-waist deep in the crater...distinct streams of brighter-colored liquid were crawling snakelike up towards the head, and down over the crown, vanishing into the eye...

"What can we do?" asked Snash.

"Get on our eagles and sharks and go," said Whitedolf, "Pretty damn quick, I should say..."

"What about the Oakenfolks?" asked Luvliel.

"I'm thinking," Whitedolf replied.

As for Serpentar's latest incarnation, it lifted a leg and put it over the side of the volcano, almost as though it were stepping out of a bath...Snash felt a wall of heat roll over him.

"It's going to take him about three strides to get here!" Snashetta cried.

But as soon as the giant's pedal extremity came down beside the mountain's foot, things started to go wrong for the molten prodigy; its leg began to wobble, the instability spreading up into the body...the glowing form began to develop great migrating bulges, and the head nodded forward, onto the chest...one arm lengthened, parted, slopped down onto the slope. The head lifted once more, rocking side to side…the giant pulled its leg back into the crater, but left its foot on the ground…the head slumped down on a shoulder and flattened into it, only to fight its way back up for a brief span before tipping backwards and apparently flowing down behind. The arm-stump and the other arm, which had been getting steadily longer, dropped off the trunk, which seemed to be both shrinking *and* sinking. The mass that had once been the giant almost dipped below the rim, then struggled back up, succeeded in forming a figure once more, even though it was smaller and less distinct than the last; but that almost-body lost its shape even quicker than the first figure had, and a third upthrusting didn't get much farther than forming a hump…plainly, for all his power, Serpentar didn't have nearly enough to impose his will on the stone he'd suffused. When the hump went down, that seemed to be last of it, although no one wanted to make the call. Finally Glargle cried from somewhere:

"*Und* shtay down!"

Everyone else raised their fists and cheered…Snash spotted the gremlin waving the gauntlet above his head, two-handed, of course. Snash wondered how exactly he was going to get unstuck…

"Whose gauntlet is that?" Whitedolf asked.

"Serpentar's," Luvliel replied.

"Oh?"

"I told him he could keep it," Snash said, even though that wasn't quite true.

"Are you the boss?" Whitedolf asked.

Snash almost said *yes*, but checked himself. "Let's just say I'm someone to be reckoned with."

"Can't argue with that," said Luvliel.

"I suppose not," Whitedolf replied, then asked her: "What *are* you going to do with Tim's head there?"

"Put it in water."

Whitedolf looked closer at the head. "Might be a while before we find any, old boy."

But Bimbottom replied:

"*Tim will wait then.*

He will estevate then.
He'll get shuteye
Drop off for a time.
Please don't rouse him
Until you can douse him,
He's so weary
Can't think of a rhyme!"

Whereupon he closed his eyes and began to saw logs
most exuberantly, lips blubbering.

"I wish I had somewhere to put him," said Luvliel, just
as a shaft of yellow light beamed through the fume-ceiling,
which had been breaking up all along; the fay-princess went all
golden against the dark maroonish background and she looked
heavenwards, chin tilted up, Tim's sleepy-head depending from
her hand.

Snash and Slagbag squinted and shaded their eyes.

"Is there going to be a lot of light from now on?"
Slagbag asked.

"Probably," Luvliel answered.

"We'll need sunglasses," Snash said.

"We could always stay out of the sun," said Slagbag.

"We've done enough of that," Snash replied.

Chapter 20: Care and Feeding

As it turned out, a not inconsiderable number of yarks, eastrons and southerlings had escaped the fall of the Spike; most had seen the way things were going, and had bugged out before the grand demolition. They began approaching Snash and company in small groups, and he went to treat with them accompanied by Whitedolf and Slagbag, Carcharias and his remaining brethren circling overhead; most of Serpentar's erstwhile servants had already heard of Snash, and were quick to bend the knee to him, even though he didn't require it...reminded of Bimbottom's situation by Luvliel, he asked the newcomers for some water, which went into a pockmark in the ground...Luvliel set Tim's head upright in the little pool, the water halfway up his chin...he continued to snooze.

The army, meanwhile, had regrouped, and closed in from the west, but it halted before getting too near...in all likelihood, the sharks were the reason. But soon an eastron rode up with a message from Colonel Gragragh, the highest-ranking yark in Serpentar's forces.

"Tell him to come ahead," said Whitedolf, the rider rode back, and presently an armored coach drawn by fell beasts arrived. Out came the huge yark-colonel, jaw angular and jutting, his eyes hidden by sunglasses; he was helmetless, but wearing a byrny of black-lacquered scales. Two smaller bulls followed him, lugging sacks full of lumpy things...the bags looked like they must be pretty heavy, given the way they made the bulls' arms knot. The bulls deposited them in front of Snash and Whitedolf; then Gragragh prostrated himself, and they did likewise.

"Get up," Whitedolf said.

They rose.

"What's in those bags?" Whitedolf asked the colonel.

"Show him," said Gragragh to his underlings, who untied the drawstrings and started to dump the contents....out bounced a bunch of brain-heads.

"Enough!" cried Whitedolf.

The underlings tipped the bags back up.

"Who were they?" Whitedolf asked.

The colonel said: "Burning Curiosity boys, slogan-spitters from I and E. We've got about forty more sacks back there..." He jerked a thumb over his shoulder toward the army. "After we saw those sharks take out those sharkriders, right overhead, things started heating up. And when the tower came down, everybody still loyal to Serpentar got the axe...thought you might like to see some of the heads...You're Greydolf, right?"

The wizard had given the rider his original name, seeing how no one would've heard of the new one...he nodded.

"How'd you get out of the Nail?" Gragragh said. "Did someone get hold of that spell-book that went missing?"

"I did," said Snash.

"And you are---"

"My name is Snash."

"The one who beat Serpentar in Yarks and Spiders?"

Snash would never have guessed that the news had reached the army before they left Mount Adamant, but...evidently it had travelled fast.

"In short," said Whitedolf, "Someone to be reckoned with."

"Someone to be reckoned with," Gragragh repeated. "Am I supposed to bend the knee to a *runt*?"

"You don't have to," said Snash.

"Well hurray for *me*...Everything's going to be just the way we want now, eh?"

"I doubt it," said Snash.

"Some wouldn't," said Gragragh. "There's been a lot of wild talk. *Unrealistic.* But I don't believe in prophecies, and I don't think things'll get better just because Serpentar is gone, and everyone's jawing about Hrag Urshathur. What are you going to *do* with us?"

Familiar as he was with that exact question, Snash wasn't ready for it, was indeed amazed to have it directed at him; why would that army, which numbered in the millions, allow *him* to decide its fate? Admittedly, he had Whitedolf on his side, and Luvliel, and the oakenfolks, and the sharks, and those fellows who'd escaped Mount Adamant. But still, he didn't think that was enough for him to truly assert himself, unless he *really* pushed the line that he was Hrag Urshathur---

and he didn't want to do that.

"I'm not exactly sure,"he said."But as far as I'm concerned---for what it's worth---you're all free."

"What does that mean?" asked Gragragh.

Snash looked at Whitedolf hoping for some help, but the wizard just prompted him with a nod, as though he thought Snash was doing just fine.

"What does it *mean*?" asked Gragragh again.

"That you shouldn't be whipped or killed---"

"*Ever?*"

"Unless you've really got it coming. And that you shouldn't have to work unless you get something out of it."

"We'd actually get *paid*?"

"Right."

"No investing in the future?"

"Not unless you want to."

"And our bosses wouldn't take our vacations for us?"

"No. And you could *quit*."

"Quit?"

"You wouldn't have to be a cog in someone else's machine, unless you had some say."

Gragragh was silent. "But how would all that *work*?" he asked at last.

"Not everyplace is like Tenebria," said Snash. "In some places, no one's a slave, and things work anyway."

"I might be willing to stay on for a bit," said Whitedolf. "Bring in some people. We'd have to get rid of the plunder economy of course...Divert some water in here, get some agriculture going...the oakenwives would be right handy for that. Even with the Spike gone, there are still hundreds of ironworks and smelts left...we could begin exporting steel, metal goods. There are diamonds and gold...I could arrange meetings outside, see if I couldn't get some investment in here..."

"Snash said we wouldn't have to invest," said Gragragh.

"I'm not talking about *you* investing. I'm talking about other people investing."

"Will there be a Five Thousand Year Plan?"

"I would argue against it," said Whitedolf.

"If you're so smart," said Gragragh, "how did Serpentar catch you?"

"I came because I was outvoted by my colleagues. If I had it to do over, I'd resign."

"Well, you have to learn from your mistakes," said Gragragh. "Tell you what. Come back with me, and let the army look you over. But Snash should do most of the talking." He looked at the runt. "You can tell everyone how you beat Serpentar."

Snash and Whitedolf drew off a bit.

"What do you think?" Snash asked.

"We should go," said Whitedolf. "I think your story will make quite an impression."

And so they went, meeting with the chieftains first, human and yark, in a huge tent...they were greeted with suspicion to say the least, and a lot of ugly sentiments were expressed, and Gragragh had to knock a few heads, but finally things calmed down sufficiently for Snash to begin his tale, and before long, everyone was simply rapt...by the time Snash finished, the chieftains, even the humans, were all trying to touch him and asking if they could kiss his feet.

While all that was going on, the whole army had closed in round the tent; there was a rocky outcropping nearby, and Snash went up to speak from that. He didn't have a very loud voice, and there were way too many blokes for everyone to get close enough to hear, but somehow, as he repeated his story, the salient points made their way back to the back, and by the time he was done, the whole host, millions strong, was acclaiming him the prophecy fulfilled.

They held a great feast that night, with genuinely good stuff, which the BC and IE boys had had quite a bit of; the oakenfolks came over, and the sharks, and Snashetta and Slagbag, and Glargle and all the rest, Luvliel included, carrying Bimbottom's head plunked in an upside down helmet full of water---Tim was already regrowing his body, but as yet, it was much too tiny for him to be ambulatory.

It all went on till morning; Snashetta fell asleep with her head in Snash's lap. As the sun rose into Tenebria's first clear sky in five thousand years, Snash put on one of the hundreds of pairs of sunglasses he'd been given, and Luvliel sat down beside him and said:

"You and Snashetta seem to be getting on just fine."

"Oh, we are," Snash replied, adjusting his shades. "But..."

"But what?" Luvliel asked.

"What do I *do* with her?"

"What do you mean?"

"What does a yark do with a yarkette? I mean, I know about hugging her, and that's very good, but I don't think we're actually accomplishing anything---"

Looking uncomfortable, Luvliel said: "Perhaps you should ask Whitedolf."

"Or maybe he could ask me," said Slagbag, sitting down on the other side of him with a big smile on his face---he was wearing sunglasses with downward curving horns at the hinges.

"Why *you?*" Snash inquired.

"Because I spoke to this southerling, see? And he gave me some tips---"

"Where's Nudzu?"

Slagbag nodded towards a nearby tent.

"Well," said Luvliel, putting her hands on her knees and standing up. "I'll see you fellows later."

Once she was gone, Snash asked: "How was it?"

"Not bad at all," said Slagbag, sounding as if it had actually been a good deal better than that.

"So what do you do?"

"Well," said Slagbag, "she's got to be in a pretty good mood first---"

Later on that afternoon, once they'd gotten some shuteye, Whitedolf and Luvliel, having appropriated a bunch of Burning Curiosity writing gear, began drafting letters, to go out by eagle and shark; they were just taking a break outside the tent when Oakenchin arrived.

"Think I'll take the girls and head east," the oakenguy said. "Heard there's some rivers out there...we'll do some digging and heavy lifting, see if we can't get some water into this basin."

"Excellent," said Whitedolf.

"What are you up to?" Oakenchin asked.

"Writing some letters...would you like me to send for the other oakenguys?"

"Tell you the truth," Oakenchin said, "I wouldn't mind being the only oak-puncher this side of the mountains for a while. I'm having the time of my life."

"I can imagine," said Whitedolf.

"I presume," said Oakenchin to Luvliel, "that you're putting in Lissomleg's orders for those seeds."

"Just put the seal on the scroll," said Luvliel. "The dispatch should reach the Luvliloft by tomorrow morning,"

"Very good," said Oakenchin.

"You *are* going to send for the other oakenguys at some point, aren't you?" Whitedolf asked.

"Oh, I don't know," said Oakenchin. "Once the ladies figure out I haven't, they'll get around to it themselves, I shouldn't wonder. But in the meantime---"

"How many acorns have you stockpiled already, do you think?"

"Lots and lots and lots."

Oakenchin turned back towards the oakenwife grove...five or six of the tree-women noticed him looking, and began waving energetically.

"Think I'll, ah...go *pack*," he said.

By that time, Bimbottom's body was almost completely back, and he announced his intention to leave.

"Where's he from?" Snash asked Luvliel, while Tim was dancing around Whitedolf and irritating him quite a bit if Snash was any judge.

"The Bottomlands of Merriador," she replied.

"You know," said Snash, "he sure did come in handy, but...I'm not really put out that he's leaving."

"I know what you mean," said Luvliel. "These circumstances---nation-building, and all---don't really call for such a...such an...*eccentric*, even anarchic presence."

But hardly were the words out of her mouth when Tim left off on Whitedolf and came bounding over, singing:

> *"You're quite right now*
> *I can be a fright now.*
> *Little bit 'o Tim*
> *Goes quite a longish way.*
> *He don't mind*
> *He knows his limitations.*
> *He'll go home and*
> *Diddle all the day!"*

He swept off his hat and bowed to them, then went bouncing away towards the west.

"The Bottomlands, eh?" Snash asked.

"Yes," said Luvliel.

"Ever been there?"

"I don't think I could take it."

The sharks and eagles returned with responses that were mostly skeptical; the sharks in particular had had a great deal of trouble in getting anyone to treat with them at all, although they were able to point out (convincingly) that they no longer had gage-ghouls riding them, and that had gotten their feet---or fins---in the door.

Still, no one quite trusted them, and it fell mainly to Thorondolf (who'd always been associated with Greydolf) to make the rounds again and again, and convince everyone that the letters were genuine. Even after that, it took a lot more letters from Luvliel and Whitedolf to get any co-operation, and they had to fly out via eagle a couple of times and make the rounds of all the notable citadels before they were promised any help. But at length it became plain to Serpentar's foes that they had everthing to gain from a free and prosperous

Tenebria, and quite a bit to lose if the yarks inhabiting it went on being their bad old selves, even if they didn't have Serpentar riding herd on them. Groups of advisers and potential investors soon came to take a look, and most of them concluded there was something to the plan and decided to give it a shot.

The army remained bivouacked for a while; Snash and Whitedolf and Luvliel et al. had moved their operations to a fortress called Ironrock, which stood on a stony prominence in the midst of the host. Things didn't always run smoothly; the yarks remained quarrelsome creatures, and there was a lot of practical joking and fighting, and Snash was called again and again to calm things down...his stock remained high with everyone, and the officer corps, led by Gragragh, seemed to be solidly behind him.

Luckily, although not surprisingly, there were plenty of provisions---the army had been supplied for a very extensive campaign. Moreover, there were great stocks of food all over the country, and more came in regularly from farms in southern Tenebria, and the subject lands beyond; when it became clear that the new regime was actually going to pay rather than merely take delivery---the army had had a mobile treasury, and great troves of gold and jewels had been discovered at fortresses in the mountains---the flow of food into the country actually increased, and Whitedolf concluded that they had enough wealth on hand to maintain this state of affairs for five or six years, more than enough time for the oakenfolks to get the agriculture going.

As for the water, the tree-people had indeed located two rivers, and diverted them back into their old courses, which is to say, right into the Tenebrian basin, from which Serpentar, apparently because he didn't much care for wetness, had diverted them long ago. Using the seeds they'd gotten from the fays, the oakenwives began gardening furiously, and got great numbers of yarks to co-operate with them, by offering very good wages, courtesy of those treasure-troves; investors, more all the time, moved in, and began to cater to the workers, and employed a lot of yarks and even men, themselves. They also began spreading the cash around up in the mountains, and put those mines and smelts on a paying basis, and it wasn't long before Tenebria (the name hadn't been changed yet, although there was much discussion about what it should be changed *to*) was exporting large quantities of ore and metalwork.

Even though much of the army was absorbed by the new economy, it remained very strong, with most of the troops posted at the borders. Many old mountain fortresses were repaired and heavily garrisoned---with huge hosts in the field, north, east, and south, Serpentar hadn't needed the strongholds, but those same armies were a potential threat to new Tenebria. Fortunately (but not surprisingly) the three hordes had fallen to fighting one another---their chieftains contacted Snash with some regularity, trying to bring him in on their side, but needless to say, he remained aloof.

One day, as Snash and Snashetta (who was now very pregnant) were standing on the top of Ironrock's tallest tower (it wasn't much compared to the Spike, but oh well), Carcharias came and set down; there wasn't room right on the roof, but there *was* a steel perch whose stand ran right down the center of the tower; unlike an eagle, who would've landed across the crossbar, the shark landed along it, clinging with his underclaws, wings drooping on either side, almost to the roof.

"I must say," he said, "things seem to be working out here. I never would've guessed it. The Fellowship is impressed."

"But you were always talking revolution," said Snash.

"True," said Carcharias. "And how to go about constructing a new society. But that was always for ourselves. Us sharks. Never meant to apply any of it to you. We wanted to escape somehow, get some females, go set up in some mountains, far from here. But, I think, we're going to establish ourselves in those peaks right over there---"

He nodded towards the great wall off eastward.

"Well," said Snash, "it will be good to have you."

"You should come to address us yarkwives," said Snashetta. "Snash tells me your Fellowship was rather like our

Sisterhood."

"He told me your Sisterhood was rather like our Fellowship," said the shark.

"Have you lined up any sharkwives yet?" she asked.

"I've stopped in a few places, in the course of my courier duties...I have some prospects. Carcharadon and Bigmouth are rather further along, but...no point in rushing things."

"I should think you'd want to, after all that time you lost as a prisoner."

"It wasn't as bad as you might think. They brought in some females every once in a while. Conjugal visits. Sharks get pretty cranky, you know, even if they do have magic metal control-rods buried in their brains."

"Does yours give you any trouble?" Snash asked.

"Headaches. Sometimes. At least, I think they're from the rods, but..." He looked at Snash thoughtfully. "Glad we didn't eat you."

"I'm glad too," said Snash.

Rather to Snash's surprise, Glargle stuck around for quite some time; with Luvliel's help, he'd gotten his hand removed from the Gauntlet, and had found himself a little cave, with a trickle of water running through it, out behind the fortress, and there he'd settled in, "Exshtended Honeymoon, *ja, ja*," is how he put it. Whenever anyone saw him, he made many references to "Married bliss," and "Being a newlywed," and though no one ever really followed up on any of that, he was generally treated with considerable honor, something he'd never experienced before, which accounts, perhaps for why he stuck around as long as he did.

Still, he was a solitary creature by nature, and one day, declaring he needed to bring the *liebchen* back to his *alte Vaterland*, where they'd enjoyed their first "moment of joy," he came to Snash to take his leave.

"Vill you miss Glargle?" Glargle asked.

"Oddly enough," said Snash.

"Vell, Glargle vill miss *you*. If he effer gets tired of

honeymoon, maybe he vill drop in unexpected, vhat do you sink?"

"You have a standing invitation."

"Can Glargle haff hug?"

Snash let him, although he wasn't too happy to get in a clinch with the skank. Glargle was sniffling by the time he stepped back, and he wiped away a tear.

"Come on now," said Snash. "You've got the *liebchen*."

Glargle nodded. "And ze *liebchen* has Glargle. Glargle iss comforted! *Auf wiedersehen!*"

About five months after getting pregnant, Snashetta delivered herself of no less than ten little yarks, all of them black and squirmy and about five inches long; Snash would've been kind of shocked if he hadn't already seen Nudzu's babies, which she'd delivered about a week before---Slagbag had sired about fifteen. In both cases, the broods, or litters or whatever, were mostly female (and the females were already kind of Luvliel blonde), but that was just as well, given the acute yarkette shortage. The babies looked small and frail, but they all had healthy appetites, and were born with full sets of teeth, and much preferred fell beast to nursing, which was also just as well, since their moms had just so much in the way of milk. The young 'uns also grew at a tremendous rate, doubling in size before their parents could even come up with names for all of them.

At any rate, when it came time to bestow those monikers, Whitedolf and Luvliel decided it might be a good thing to hold a ceremony; Slagbag and Nudzu's kids all got regular yarkish names like Slagbag and Nudzu, and yes, Snash and Snashetta, while Snash and Snashetta named their boys Whitedolf, Tharathorn, and Dwimli, and the girls, Snashetta, Luvliel, Blondiel, Fei-Hungiel, Hung-Kwaniel, Mister Ru-iel, and Sai-Yukiel. All the notables of the New Tenebria gathered round and had a blast, and even though every citizen was invited, far too many of them were solidly employed by that point to show up.

The next day, Luvliel told Snash she'd better get back

to the Luvliloft.

"I am, after all, the sovereign of my own land," she said. "And I've had word via Thorondolf that my people are pining for me."

"I can see how they might," said Snash. "I'll pine for you too."

"But you have Snashetta, and all those little yarks."

"I know," he said. "And they have me. I'm comforted---" He stopped, suddenly realizing he sounded just like Glargle.

"What's wrong?" she asked.

"Nothing."

"Is Whitedolf going to stay a while longer?" Snash asked.

"He told me he's planning to. Now that Serpentar's out of the way, he has nothing else to do than 'meddle here,' as he put it."

"Could you give me a lock of your hair?" Snash asked.

"Certainly," she replied. "Just don't..."

"What?"

"Even if times are *very* dark, ever hide it..." She broke off, shuddering.

"Yes?"

"Forget it."

"Can I have a hug?"

She knelt down, and he embraced her and started sobbing.

"Don't be *sad*," she said. "Once you have everything nailed down here, you should come to visit me in the Luvliloft. Bring the whole family. I'd like to show you off."

"Oh," said Snash, "we surely will."

Getting things thoroughly nailed down took five more years, by which time Tenebria---they still hadn't changed the name---had had its first (mostly) fair elections, and a thriving economy, even exporting food to its neighbors; most of the oakenfolks (a number of oakenguys had arrived soon after the baby-naming party) actually decided to stay on, and the whole Tenebrian basin had gone green, except for a few areas reserved for industrial activity, which were generally pretty smelly, and characterized by labor unrest. Some yarks actually decided they liked the old days better, and struck out on their own, and there was some banditry; but on the whole, most folks seemed to think the new Tenebria a vast improvement on the old one.

Snash served for a while as Boss, with Whitedolf as his chief adviser and Gragragh and Slagbag running the army; but after some particularly difficult negotiations with the legislative branch, Snash decided not to seek re-election after his second term, and turned things over to the opposition, who, in spite of everything, didn't look as though they were going to destroy all his good work. Then he and Whitedolf decided to take a holiday, and Snash brought Snashetta and half the kids; the brood was fully grown now, and some of them had lives of their own, and couldn't or didn't want to come---Snash and Tharathorn, who'd never liked his name, didn't get along. But everyone who went on the Grand Tour had a fabulous time; all the Free Peoples were tremendously excited to see the yark who'd destroyed Serpentar, and Snash never got tired of telling his story. Having gone first to the Luvliloft, he wound up back there after making a great circle, and he spent several months with Luvliel in those wondrous sylvan surroundings before he and his whole crowd went back home.

After all that fun, though, things were rather disquieting upon his return; his replacements had made a muddle of some things, and labor trouble had gotten widespread---the oakenfolks were having some trouble with their workers. Moreover, a resolution had been rammed through the Assembly to the effect that Snash wasn't Hrag Urshathur.

But Oakenchin, upon hearing that Snash was back, asked him to mediate the problems, and, trading on his still-enormous popularity, Snash did just that, laying the groundwork for his triumphant return to Ironrock and the position of Boss several years later.

Late one afternoon, as he was standing once more

upon Ironrock's crown, looking at the volcano, which had gone most dormant (the lava had drained right down the shaft to wherever lava went) he heard a rushing sound, and looked to see Carcharias gliding towards him, followed by another, smaller shark; swinging his tail forward, Carcharias lit upon the side of the tower and hooked his chin over the top, conceding the perch to the other shark.

"Lord Boss!" he said. "Congratulations on your return to power! And say hello to the wife! Carcharadonna, Snash, Snash, Carcharadonna."

"Carcharadonna?"

"Yep. His sister."

"Pleased to meet you, Snash," she said.

"When did you get married?" Snash asked.

"Last week," said Carcharias. "A modest service. I don't like fuss and bother."

"I understand," Snash replied. Aside from naming ceremonies---they'd just had another, for Snashetta's third brood--- he hadn't much use for fuss either. "Sure took you long enough."

"Had to find the right sharkette," said Carcharias. "Carcharadon had been hiding her."

Just at that moment, Snashetta came up, and was introduced to Carcharias's bride.

"What a lovely surprise!" she said. "Would you care to stay for dinner?"

"Do you have enough?" Carcharias asked.

"Plenty of fell beast, and some actual beef---you could land in the courtyard."

"What do you think?" Carcharias asked Carcharadonna.

"Sounds good," she said.

"See you below," the sharks said, and headed down--- just as Slagbag came up with Nudzu.

"Hey, were there just a couple of sharks up here?" Slagbag asked.

"Carcharias and his new wife---"

"New wife?"

"They'll be joining us for dinner." Snash laughed. "Have you forgiven Carcharias for smacking you with his tail that time?"

"Sure," said Slagbag. "It's actually kind of a fond memory. Something to tell the kids."

They stood for a while, looking out over the vast basin with its two great rivers and many oxbowed streams and myriad patches of green. Even though the sun was close to setting behind the mountains, the light was still abundant and gorgeous. Snash had acquired a taste for sunsets, so long as they were properly filtered through shades.

"We really do need to stop calling this place Tenebria," Slagbag said.

"We can discuss it over supper, with Whitedolf and the sharks," said Snash, and they went on down the steps.

A small but sturdy tree.

Born in 1952, author-illustrator Mark E. Rogers is best known for the Samurai Cat books: *The Adventures of Samurai Cat, More Adventures of Samurai Cat, Samurai Cat in the Real World, The Sword of Samurai Cat,* and *Samurai Cat Goes to the Movies.* The sixth and final installment in the series, *Samurai Cat Goes to Hell,* was published by TOR.

His other books include Yark, *The Dead, Zorachus, The Nightmare of God, The Expected One, The Devouring Void,* and *The Riddled Man.* One of his novellas, *The Runestone,* was made into a movie; and *The Dead* is presently under development as a feature film---with a screenplay by Mark---at KNB-EFX.

Mark's work has been adapted by Marvel comics, and has appeared on the cover of <u>Cricket Magazine</u>; he's published three art portfolios, and a collection of his pin-up paintings, *Nothing But A Smile,* is available from Xenophile Books.

Mark lives in Newark, Delaware, with his wife Kate---a philosophy professor at the U of D---and their four lovely kids, Sophie, Jeannie, Patrick, and Nick.

www.ingramcontent.com/pod-product-compliance
Lightning Source LLC
Chambersburg PA
CBHW011737010726
47496CB00010B/2980